Visions of Recurrence

By Paul Turelli

Visions of Recurrence
Copywrite by Paul Turelli
April 2022

Many thanks to:

Barbara Grant, Cover Design
 StraddleTheTurtle.com

Michael Boulden for his continued insights

Tina R. Sorensen
Online Marketing Consultant
Tru Solutions
 Trusolutions.com

Sophia Myers
Web, Graphic & Online Designer
The House of Designs
 thehouseofdesigns.com

Books by Paul Turelli

Series of Dreams:
All novels within the *Series of Dreams* are entirely
fictional.

Awake Again
Asleep for the First Time
Dreaming Gaia
Visions of Recurrence

Testimony: A Prelude

Poetry:

Windy Morning Innocence

Non-Fiction:

Denver Water Supply: From City Ditch to Two Forks
(Denver Public Library and University of Colorado,
Western History Collection)

For Rosemary

CHAPTER ONE

Stephanie Tomasetti

I can't believe I'm in trouble already. We've only been in school for about a week. My freshman year, first year in high school. Me and two of my friends, Keith and Jenna, were smoking at lunch, back by the dumpsters. The day after my fourteenth birthday. Stupid. Almost immediately they got sent to the assistant principal and of course I got diverted to my dad, who happens to be the principal.   Lucky me. They got detention. I got suspended. Not fair, I know, but I had it coming. I was in trouble several times last year as an 8th grader and I promised a new start. Especially to my dad who was hoping not to have a 'conflict of interest.' I get it.
The conversation went something like this:

Tell me what happened.

I hadn't seen Keith and Jenna most of the summer and we decided to have a cigarette. I know, same thing happened last year.

Are you smoking all the time? You told me and your mom you weren't.

No. I don't really like it that much.

What I didn't say is that the three of us smoked pot the three times we were together over the summer.

So why now, especially after our conversation, not so long ago?

I don't know what to say.

It's not peer pressure. No one pressures you into anything, Stephanie.

No. You're right.

And like we talked about, I'm not just your dad here. I'm the principal.

I know. I'm sorry.

Sorry?

Well, that I broke my promise. Or intention. You know.

And for smoking?

Honestly, not really. No big deal.

It is a big deal. You're fourteen. You don't want to get hooked. Oh, you know all that.

I know.

What should be your consequence? Just curious what you think.

Whatever you give the others, I guess. Detention. I don't know.

It's a Friday. I'm suspending you the rest of today and Monday. Put you to work on something.

I get it. Not fair though. I doubt that Keith and Jenna will be suspended.

No, they're not. But I'm taking into consideration our talks. Last year and all that happened.
Before we started this year and what you agreed to.

Makes sense. I deserve it.

We've been round and round on this Stephanie. You get straight A's. Never had a B in your life. Ever. You never got into trouble in 7th grade or before that. I just want to understand. So does your mom.

Bored, maybe. I had that opportunity to go to L.A. and maybe do some acting with Sharon. A bit part. Tim was all for it. Phil agreed to represent me. Disappointed probably

     – there I go, putting the blame on parents not letting me get my way -

But we've been over this. We're all for you acting. It wasn't a good time.

I know.

Look, we promised you that we'd support your desire to go to L.A. and see what happens. But you promised to stay out of trouble and get into our theater department here at the school right away. Start there. We'd evaluate after the first play.

I know. I know.

Anyway. I am suspended. By the way, Tim is THE Tim Prescott the famous actor. Still the number one box office draw after all these years – or so I'm told. He's a friend of our family and he lives close by. At least when he's not on location or traveling. And Phil is Sharon's agent, and my mom's agent, too – even though Mom quit acting not long after she won an Academy Award. Oh, and Sharon is like my aunt. I call her Aunt Sharon all the time. She grew up with Mom and Dad and is famous, too. She gets in trouble a lot and my parents aren't sure if she's a good influence. Sharon was busted for breaking the law during protests for Native rights, and Women's rights and the environment, all kinds of stuff. She's radical. A lot of people hate her because she's so outspoken. But I love her. She's a great actress. I watch all the movies I can over at Tim's private screening room at his house. I've been doing it since I was probably five. Sharon, Tim, other people in the business will sit with me and talk and talk about the movies. I love it.

Mom was a great actress too. I love her movies, especially *Hull House*. She does not like talking about it much. She's entirely into her art now. Painting. The Gallery. More of a businesswoman, I guess. Don't get me wrong, I love her movies, too. Just Sharon really loves to talk about the art of it, the challenge, the joy she gets out of it. Her husband Vinny is that way too. He does comedy, stand-up mostly, but he's been in some films. I want to be in movies too. Mom and Dad know it.

Dad took me over to the gallery where mom works. He dropped me off.

Jennifer

Danny showed up with Stephanie a little after lunch. I knew something was wrong by their body language. Danny explained everything calmly and quickly and then he had to get back to school.

I situated Stephanie in my studio, attached to the larger gallery, and we talked for a long time. She loves

Madonna, so when we had finished talking, I put on one of her records, *Like a Prayer*, that Stephanie had brought over a long time ago.

Stephanie likes the early Madonna. Scruffy jeans, midriffs, retro look. The hero worship thing was very junior high, and I can see she will fade out of that phase soon.

Like me, she's an avid skier and loves the outdoors. She rides horses a lot over at the pueblo with many of her native friends that she grew up with. God, I know she's smart. Brilliant to a fault. Drives me and Danny crazy when she does something silly like this.

Stephanie looks a lot like Danny. Her hair is not as dark as mine, more brownish like her father's. She has an athleticism or physical nature about her. She is an even better skier than I was at that age, but she's full force into snowboarding now.

All winter she goes to Santa Fe Resort, or Angel Fire, or up to Taos to ski.

She is also a reader. A closet bookworm. As wild as she can be, she will get lost somewhere in our house with an author and read every book. Mostly crime thriller stuff. One book right after the other. She does her homework religiously, and quickly. She makes it look easy.

Stephanie's friends are a long list. She has her native group over at the pueblo who she mostly rides with. This has been ongoing since second grade. She also has a skiing group in the winter, mostly older than her. There are various cliques she goes back and forth with but doesn't want to be with the most popular ones for very long.

Keith and Jenna, who she got in trouble with today, are mostly hippie types. I know they smoke pot and have tough home lives. I like them a lot and encourage them to come over whenever they want. Keith is a cute kid. I only wish that he'd at least try a bit harder at life. Nothing seems to motivate him. I think our daughter likes him because he's good looking as well as easy going. He places no expectations on her.

I'm not at all upset about what happened today. I'm sure it was hard on Danny. He dreaded and probably knew this was going to happen eventually. I was firm with Steph, telling her she couldn't go riding this weekend. That she needed to help with cleaning around the house.

She was fine with it all. We ended up laughing. She wants to make it up to her dad and doesn't know how. I encouraged her to at least try talking with him about it without him bringing it up.

Take responsibility.

The whole Hollywood thing, and movies and fame, are always on her mind. I love Sharon, I really do. She's a sister to me. My best friend. A great actress and rapidly becoming a legend, if not a controversial one. Stephanie's desire to go be with Sharon and be a child actor or live in L.A. is our toughest issue. Danny gets angry occasionally. Mostly at Sharon for being so influential and outspoken. Steph idolizes her, even more than Madonna. When Sharon told her that she could arrange a meeting with Madonna, that about broke our back.

I hate to see Steph get so into the acting scene, but I get it. I loved it once, too.

Stephanie is also a twin. Her brother, Julian, is a little over two hours older than her. Julian usually shows up here at the gallery on Friday afternoons around 4:00. He is strictly into music. Has been ever since he was four. He plays the piano and guitar and bass. Religiously. Bass might be his best when push comes to shove, Jaco Pastorius and Ray Brown being others on a long list of his heroes. Lessons twice a week – sometimes three - from Cindy, who is the wife of Billy the new head basketball coach. We have known Billy and Cindy my entire life. We built a small music room attached to my own private studio. We liked the idea of designing a small, simple studio for him and his buddies who play all the time.

Soundproof.

And there he was. I could hear him unlock the door next to us. He is a quiet sort. To himself mostly. Julian was unpacking gear, turning on the stereo. One of his new band favorites, The Cars, I think. Steph looked at me wondering if we were going to talk with Julian or leave him be.   Usually, I leave Julian to himself. He would never continue to work on his music over here if I were the doting mother. This time he knocked on my private studio entryway. He never, or hardly ever, came over. When I let him in he said *hi*, only to confirm that his sister was in trouble. He knew she'd be over here with me. They smiled nervously at each other, but nothing really said.   That is until Julian asked her if he could bum a cigarette. That broke the tension.

A few of his friends were coming over to play.   They were all older than him.   Two boys, Stuart and Frankie were juniors and a girl, Melanie, was a senior.   Julian was only a freshman, but he has known these kids for ages. Playing together in the playground and now with musical instruments.   Melanie played an acoustic guitar and was the co-lead singer, at least when Julian wasn't singing.   I liked her voice a great deal. Stu was the bass player, and he was superb.   Julian liked bass but it wasn't his first choice.   Frankie mostly played an electric lead guitar.   He needed the most work because Julian loved playing lead. Julian would slide over and play piano as a first preference. What they needed was a drummer. A few kids had come and gone but no one stuck around. Stephanie asked me if she could sit in with them and Julian shrugged, he didn't care.   He liked his sister and they usually stayed out of each other's way.

Even though I always kept my distance from what was becoming a band, I wanted in the worst way to offer my suggestions and direction. Melanie and Julian were strong willed, and they were very much the leaders. I was proud of our son. He reminded me of Danny in his take charge ways and confidence. A leader from the get-go. Age never seemed to be an issue.   Melanie was stubborn about who sang what part but didn't really care about who played what instrument.   Julian was such a passionate musician and far ahead of everyone else, no one argued with him about song selection.

Danny was currently an Elvis Costello wanna be. He wore those black frames with longer hair than Elvis. They called themselves *retro* this and *retro* that. If they ever become a real band, they want the word *retro* in the name. The Beatles, The Stones, a steady diet of Bob Dylan lyrics mixed in. They resisted punk but liked the drive of new wave. For only being in high school they were well versed in my era of sound. Danny and I had fed them a steady diet since birth and instead of rebelling from those classic rock and roll sounds, Julian embraced it all.

They turned off The Cars album and started in on playing "While My Guitar Gently Weeps." I could easily shut their door and then my own door and seal myself off in relative silence. But I liked to listen in. Eavesdrop. Julian was banging away at the Hammond electric keyboard that he treasured even more than his Fender guitar. He copied Ray Manzarek so the song was already sounding more like the Doors than the Beatles. Frankie was no Eric Clapton, nor a George Harrison, but his style was along the lines of wanting to get there. Aspirational. He played clean and slow. They were creating an eerie sound, but they were in sync. Stu' s bass lines were surprising. He was doing his best to mimic McCartney's unusual underlying tempo. Melanie was hammering away at her acoustic just like John Lennon had done. Powerfully, driving Julian into an improvisation on the keyboards. Melanie would sing with an ache in her voice that made me want to cry. They stopped and started over after a discussion I could not hear. It sounded like Stephanie had said something too. I smiled at the banter and the fun they were having.

They started again. The tempo was quicker. Julian was singing lead this time with a more desperate tone. There were two electric guitars in power drive, with no keyboard. Melanie's acoustic and backup vocal was even more emphatic. The song became faster, nothing like the original, and Julian was taking the Costello approach of hyping the sound from the blues to freneticism. When they were done everyone was laughing. Stephanie was the loudest and clapping the hardest.

I then shut the doors and returned to my studio. I was working on a difficult piece for a show I was planning in Paris over Christmas break. I had this one last work to complete. My weariness was catching up with me. I was attempting an entirely new style. It was angry, I realized. The colors and format were not necessarily appealing or inspirational. Raw emotion. Much of this was because of our Women's League and much of the frustration underlying the liberation movement. We were stronger, our voice louder, but not necessarily making inroads on the political and policy levels. I was making a statement.

We had been through a lot of loss over the past two years as well.

First, George died. He had been close to us going back to when we first relocated to Santa Fe. He was way overweight and smoked too much, but it was still a surprise and a sudden passing. We sold his and Louise's house and we had her move into our guest bedroom.

She has a bathroom and small living area with a television, keeping busy and to herself. It was going to be temporary, but she works hard keeping our place clean, helping with cooking and shopping. Most of all, she gets along with the kids and with Danny. She's very much a surrogate mom for me.

Then James's wife died after a few years of declining dementia. James is 85 now and has removed himself from the gallery in a steady fashion. We sold their house and built a cottage on our fifteen acres. He lives by a stream and in the trees, away from the desert brush, and is as happy as can be. He goes over to the pueblo with Stephanie a lot and sometimes stays over there for days on end. He's a member of our family as well, but he normally only joins us for dinner on Sundays. He and Julian have a wonderful relationship, which started at the gallery, building the studio, talking about native music and instrumentation of the surrounding tribes.

I'm very much the owner and manager of Rio Blanco Gallery now. I have a staff of seven full time employees and a part-time accountant. Our tourist business alone keeps us in the black. All the rest is a largesse of amazing, never-ending growth. My paintings have evolved in their style over the years. Since I quit acting and concentrated on my art, I was getting more requests from benefactors and commission work. Rio Blanco is now worldwide in its sphere.

Walking away from show business was not a tough decision with two young ones and the bizarre hours and demands of film. As I watched Sharon's career explode on the scene, and her relationship with Stephanie grow, a part of me missed it. At least I was feeling like an outsider in my own home. Like I was *only* a painter or *only* a mom, for god's sake. But that's what I was and that's okay.

With this show in Paris coming up, a business trip mostly, Danny and I agreed to take the kids and make it into a family vacation.   Everyone is excited about it.

But why this gnawing sense of grieving?   Of loss? When Danny became principal two years ago, his hours were varied, and he was on the go. The kids were more and more independent. I sit here right now staring at the canvas, not nearly finished, and not with any direction as to where it should go.   The anger had worn thin, slipping into sadness and acceptance, even stylistically. What I need to do is finish it and move on.

Deep inside I am tempted to take on an acting job with Stephanie. I don't want to mention it. Or maybe flip the switches to help Julian form a real band. They are good enough already and could play small clubs around the southwest.   Maybe I will start with asking about a drummer.   Ease into it.   Julian will resent any overt influence I may play.   He's that head strong. And talented.

Mostly I want for Danny and I to move beyond these years of child rearing. His professional development, and mine as well, have been all we could ever hope for. He is just now finding his stride as an administrator and I'm happy for that.   We have been taking care of others for a good long while and I'd like for us to rekindle a fire of purpose together.   It feels like a new age is dawning and we need to be on the same page.

Danny

When I got home it was quiet. No one around. Of
course, it was early for me, around 5:00. Louise was
making something that smelled scrumptious. Initially
when we decided to move Louise and James over to our
place, I was weary and not so sure. It's worked out well,
though. I looked through the mail. Not much but a
formal letter from the New Mexico Archdiocese caught
my attention. I'd read it later. I grabbed a beer and a
warmer jacket and sat outside on the back veranda.
Our property spread out to the dessert in colorful
splendor, craggy mountains along the horizon. It was
even chillier than I thought, so I went back inside,
changed out of my suit and into comfortable warm
clothes, and returned outside. The cottage we had built
especially for James was in the distance. I could see the
chimney smoke emerge above the pinon tree line. He
loved making his own fires. I knew that he mostly read
art and spiritual books and took long walks.   He seemed
happy. Tim and Shelly's place was in the far distance.
They were married now. No children. I've come to
really appreciate them both. Very good people. Kind
and caring. I hardly even think of Tim as a movie star or
someone famous. Doesn't dawn on me.
I was second guessing my decision to suspend Steph.
What a way to start her high school years. I love that girl
so much. She's ready to burst out on her own and we
can hardly contain her. She has a rugged prettiness
about her. A toughness, maybe arrogance sometimes.

She's not all that into teen stuff, except her skiing. And Madonna. And she loves her horseback riding friends over at the pueblo, many of whom don't go to school, and they live simply, very rudimentary lives. She knows her movies and is ready to give acting a try even though she's never been trained or even been in a high school play. Jennifer and I are aware and are attempting to figure out the timing of it all.

Jennifer walked in and I could see her through the sliding glass door. She grabbed a beer and spotted me outside. We smiled. She had on a new floral dress, designed for the fall. She was given to scarves lately, the Paris preparation I guessed. She grabbed a full-length layered coat.

"So, you had to suspend Stephanie?" she was prodding me good naturedly, taking a seat.

"Yeah, she's the reincarnation of Sharon; just like her."

"I suppose. We weren't exactly saints in high school." It dawned on me that we were making love at fifteen and the kids were only one year away of that moment in time. More memories of what both Jennifer and I had done rushed in. I shuddered.

We sipped our beers. I reached over and held Jennifer's hand for a moment, to make connection. She rubbed my knuckles.

"You know, Danny, I feel like you do, exhausted lately, and we need to talk. Maybe about the next year or two. We have a lot going on and this high school thing with the twins ..." she tailed off.

"I get it. Really, I know where you're headed. We have the Europe trip over Christmas, but it would be nice if you and I could do something."

"Exactly. We've been so busy with moving James and Louise – which is fine. And Bill's funeral was just this past summer."

"I know, I miss Bill a lot." Bill was a spiritual guide to us both. A wonderful friend. He had been the officiant at our wedding. "You're right, we've been through a lot."

"And the kids junior high non-stop, run, run, run."

"When was the last time we did something? Just you and me; I think we're needing the same thing."

"I can't remember. Just you and I."

"What about spring break? I'm sure we can leave the kids with Louise for the week."

"Where? I mean what exactly?" she said hopefully.

"I have no idea. We will have been to Europe. Let me think on that. Surprise you."

"I like that idea; you can surprise me."

We sat in the rapidly descending sunlight, absorbing the cold. We loved the scent of the land, never tiring of it. I broke the quiet, "We should talk more about Stephanie. I was thinking about making a timeline, a defined idea for her. She's dead set about acting and we might as well move forward."

"Well, I agree." She hesitated. "But honestly, I had this idea that maybe I jump back into acting. Maybe have her do something with just me. Or with Sharon again. Or all three of us."

"Oh, lord. Here we go." I was trying rapidly to process the suggestion. Honestly, it was nice not having Jennifer in the acting world again. She was thriving, and happy with her first passion of painting.

"Don't worry, Danny. I'm just thinking about it. You and I will decide on anything for Steph. It scares me a bit."

I sat silently. Best to let Jennifer mull it over. I was preparing for the inevitable.

She changed the subject, "I have an idea about Julian, too. They sound great, Danny. You haven't heard them in a while. I know they're young, but I think they could make a go of it. You know dances, small clubs. They look older than high school kids, except maybe Julian. He's so funky, it doesn't matter. The girls will love him."

"Now, that I'm all for. I was thinking of getting Billy and Cindy with him, with the band. You know how they've been so instrumental, supportive. Make a plan. Mostly to find a drummer."

"Perfect. I know Julian will listen more closely to them than to either of us."

We could hear the kids walk in. Loud, excited. I turned and saw that Julian's singer friend Melanie was with them.

We got up and went back inside. Julian asked if he could have a beer in his jokester way. All three of them grabbed 7-ups. It was assumed that Melanie would be eating with us. She may even stay the weekend. We never knew with any of their friends. Any and all were welcome as long as they communicated with their parents. It's like we were a revolving door of kids. Jennifer went with them into the large den where the TV was turned on to *The Simpsons*. I could hear them say that Sharon's 1996 movie, *Purple Flowers*, was going to be on TV at 8:00. Grounding Stephanie, the suspension itself, was not affecting her at all. I was half tempted to make her clean the bathrooms or something instead of watching the movie, but let it go with a smile. I loved that movie. It was my favorite of Sharon's. She had won an Oscar for *Rio Norte*, way back in the day, and another for *Solitude*, but this was my favorite of hers.

I stood there next to Louise, helping get dinner ready, and she turned and smiled, looking so much older these days. She knew it would turn into another movie night. She loved every bit of it. So did I.

CHAPTER TWO

I am Ihy, spirit of the Dendra temple, God of music. Child of Horus and Isis. I ride the falcon and sing of love. I am the source of fertility, birthed from Earth herself. I hold

*the sistrum, adorned with menat necklaces and adorned
with a red and white Pshent crown.*

Julian Tomasetti

It was a Saturday morning. My bedroom faces east, and
the sunrise was my clock. I didn't mind waking with the
sun, even on days following late nights. We were up
well past 1:00 am, watching movies. Mom and Dad, and
Louise, slipped out after Sharon's movie. Melanie and
Steph go way back, knowing each other from
elementary school. Melanie is much older than both of
us, but she hangs out with Stephanie even as much as
with me and the band. Or what I want to make into a
band. It's all that's on my mind anymore. We sound
good. We've been at it for three or four years, at least
us four who are in Cindy's music program.
Melanie and I will head back over to the studio later
today. Just she and I will work through some set lists
we really like and what we think are the best. Maybe
we can make a tape or something later next week.
I'm back into Bob Dylan again. I know he he's a favorite
of dad's, which is fine by me. I don't mind the
generational bullshit. Dylan's amazing no matter what
anyone says about his voice. In fact, I wish I could sing
like that. I copy everyone's voice; Lennon, Costello,
Morrison, Ocasek, Petty, even Chrissie Hynde. I put on
Desire and was playing "Isis" over and over with my
headphones on loud. I wanted to match Dylan's piano
syncopation with the vocal, just like he did. Maybe

seven or eight times, just listening. I kept telling myself
that none of today's crappy sounds compared to this.
And the lyrics. Damn. I had been trying to write my
own music, my own lyrics, but it wasn't quite flowing.
Melanie was good at it, and we were starting to find a
sound of our own. I could come up with a melody or riff
and she always had words that fit the mood.
I was really into Melanie. She is a bit intimidating
physically, maybe *all a man can handle* is what they'd
say, but I find her really hot, alluring. Especially when
she wears those black and white funky clothes and lots
of jewelry. Too much makeup. Colorful arrays of lipstick.
We've been friends for so long, I've watched her go
through boyfriends and phases. She always dumps them.
She can be mean, no doubt about it. I've been
wondering if I should try something more than the
friend thing. We are always so close. Physically close
when we sing. Our words rhyme. We laugh.
I don't really have any other friends. Adults, mostly.
Cindy, my music teacher knows me better than anyone.
Her husband, Billy, is close to Dad, and knows Mom and
Dad since they moved to Santa Fe. Maybe even further
back. Maybe even in Colorado. Billy has every album in
the world, and we talk for hours about rock bands. Their
basement is loaded with music posters and memorabilia
and autographs. I love hanging out down there after
Cindy and I finish a lesson. He was a hippie in his day.
He doesn't bother to hide it much even though he's now
a teacher and coach. He tells me stories about seeing
bands and great people like Jimi Hendrix. I get so
wound up. Tim and Shelly are cool too. Their stereo is

top of the line. We have friends of the family, a gay couple, Sam and Karen, who are so awesome. They know everything about cutting edge music. Not the disco stuff or radio stuff. More along the lines from England or in Europe. James, of course, is like my grandpa. I grew up with him, visiting the pueblos, going to Indian ceremonies. I love the sounds, the mantra-like over and over drumbeats. I'm glad he lives with us. I'll go down to his cottage and just sit by the fire and hear him tell stories. He has a look about him that I want to put on an album cover. Like he sees shit that no one else sees. He looks right into me like he knows all about me. It makes me feel special. He makes me feel special. I get along with Frank and Stu. They're cool. Frankie is getting better and better on guitar, and we've learned to trade licks. He was with Melanie for a while but I'm not sure what happened between them. They hardly talk, but they like being in the band together. Weird tension sometimes. He stays over here at our house all the time while we work on graphic drawings for stories he made up. Stu is just right on bass. I feel bad for him with all his acne, and he just seems so alone. Mom raves about Stu on bass, doing all she can to help with his self-confidence.

I can hear mom getting breakfast ready. She always makes a big batch of pancakes on Saturdays. Enough for everyone that spends the night. We've had as many as fifteen over, all kids from here or there. There are so many sleeping bags and blankets and couches. No problem.

Then there's a knock on my door. I can barely hear it through the headphones.
It's Melanie and Stephanie. They look out of sorts, hair all messed up. Stephanie is going to clean all day, especially the basement. Then mom and dad have her working on the storage unit for the Gallery all day Monday. Steph doesn't seem to mind at all. Melanie is ready to go over to the studio already. Let's eat first.

Jennifer

I love making pancakes on Saturday mornings. I love our home, this kitchen. The expanse of our views and the living room. It's warm. Our kitchen table is big and wooden, like the one back in Georgia O'Keefe's house. Room to eat and socialize. Far from a TV.
Danny is sleeping in. I insisted. Louise has already eaten and is headed out to a meeting with some people at her church.
Melanie is up and asks me about Sharon and the movie we watched, *Purple Flowers.* I told her that most of it was filmed in Laguna Beach even though it was set in Hawaii. Sharon's husband Vinny was the tough guy in most of the scenes. Julian and Steph knew all this already and I was glad we didn't talk about any of it last night and interrupt the movie. I also told her that it was Tim's first movie as a director. I told her that it was my favorite, Danny's favorite too; Sharon's best movie of her career thus far. Probably the range of emotion and sheer beauty of the film. It was a remake of a 1930's, depression era movie called *Bouquet* with Barbara

Stanwyck. Melanie had met Tim on occasion and was always curious about everything about him, like every other fan in the world.   Steph knew all about Barbara Stanwyck and went into the actress's life story.   Julian tuned her out, which he always did when Stephanie went on a movie jag, and Melanie was mesmerized that Steph even cared about the old legend.

Mel and Julian dashed out to the studio on their bikes. I told them I might go over to the gallery, which did not register with them at all.   Stephanie asked me nicely about cleaning the basement and I showed her where the supplies were. She put on her Walkman and disappeared downstairs.

I cleaned up and then ventured back into the bedroom. Danny was still asleep with the drapes shut tight. It was pitch black. I took off my clothes and slid in.   My caress was slow, easy, drifting over his lower body.   That did the trick. We rocked the bed gently then ferociously. It was a nice way to start a Saturday.

Stephanie

I had my headphones on high to Destiny's Child.   The basement was a mess. I needed to pick up clothes and towels.   Take up dishes and glasses.   I even dusted like dad told me to.   The bathroom down there was the worst, so I used rubber gloves.   Most of it didn't really bother me.   I thought a lot about the movie we watched.   Well, the movies, but Sharon was always on my mind when it came to acting.   I had seen the movie when it came out, with Sharon as a matter of fact, but seeing it on TV was fun. I hated the commercials, but we hung in there. I found myself mimicking each and every facet of Sharon's facial features, her walk, her body language, her *delivery*, as mom and she and Tim would say. I took off my headphones, looked in the mirror and presto, I was Sharon. Exactly like her character. I could see myself saying and doing the same things. There was a scene at a beach, at a bar or some outdoor restaurant, neon lights of liquor and night on the ocean. Sharon was the sexiest damn woman on the planet, and she played it all so subtle. It was in her eyes. Mom rarely spoke about acting, but when she did she told me it was in the eyes, the unspoken message. Film will capture it, she would say. Sharon had it down like it was the easiest thing in the world. Sharon had told me that it was in the *restraint*, she used that word when we watched movies. Don't give it away, make the audience want more. I never really knew what Sharon was talking about until last night as I watched her take a scene to a point and then it was like she vanished. Sharon was almost like a ghost the way she could disappear into the character and into the story and then exit. The other actors seemed as though they were not expecting it. Sharon improvised a lot, I knew that much, and I had no idea how to practice that. It never felt like she was acting. Not like acting in television sitcoms. Or made-for-TV movies or anything else I'd watch. It's weird, mom's old movies were the same way. I'd look at mom around the house and then watch one of her movies and I secretly wished I could talk with that woman up on the screen. Tell me how you do that, I wanted to scream. I want to do the same thing. It's in me, mom. One time I was at Tim's house, and we were messing around on his pool table. Tim and Shelly would tell me about mom's career, how amazing they thought she was. Especially on stage, Tim would emphasize. I wanted mom to tell me all about it like how they did. But mom never would. Someday, she'd assure me. I was starting to resent that she wasn't listening to me. mom's listening to me, though. I know she is. Even last night I could tell. I'd look over at her during one of Sharon's scenes, and I just knew. Like I KNEW she'd want to act again.   I was hoping she'd do it with me. I vacuumed everything, even using the attachments. I had never used them before. It was fun in a strange way.

So, why did I smoke with Keith and Jenna? It was a question I couldn't really answer. I saw them in the hallway. They asked me to have a smoke at lunch. We'd done it a lot in junior high. I just did it. I'm tired of them and their whole scene, or non-scene. Whatever they are is always the same and I fit right in and then leave. They are a couple sometimes or they're not together. Even when they're not, they smoke and get high and barely pass their classes. I started hanging out with them off and on since sixth grade and it doesn't make sense anymore.   Dad tried getting them involved in stuff and they never even tried.

I won't be able to go riding today, or tomorrow.   That's sad. I love it over at the pueblo. Riding with my friends is one of the freest things I've ever done in my life.   I love horses and the entire relationship with the dirt and trail and pinon pine.   Even there, though, I'm starting to wonder about, well, what's next?

I need to join the drama department. Start at the beginning like mom and Sharon did. Dad's right. I gotta start somewhere. It's like I want to get from point A to stardom without all the in between. And mom is right. Even Sharon says this over and over, it's not about being a star, it's about art. Maybe I need to figure that out.

I mean I look at my brother and he's almost 24/7 figuring out his art. That's all he cares about. His music. He never talks about being big or anything. It's in him. Acting is in me too. I know it. I KNOW it. It's like mom, when we talk about the gallery, her paintings, or other paintings in a museum, she knows the art, the creation. Intimately, she can spot it. When I watch movies, when I watch the great actors, the actresses I admire, it's like I can spot something inside of myself. It's who I am.

I look at the ski posters down here on the walls, framed and beautiful.   My skis and boots. My gear. It's another one of those things that I do with all my heart. Just like mom did when she was growing up and when we go skiing together. Or Sharon goes with me once in a while. It's another way to do my thing. I see that. And, secretly, I look at dad, and see his golf photos and trophies. His basketball coaching awards and how they won the state championship two years in a row. He is a great teacher, too. Everyone I know that was in his speech and debate classes became successful and bragged about my dad. He does it all so quietly. He is so patient with me. I get all these A's and his response is only to encourage me to always be honest with myself and pursue my dreams.

Then we butt heads because it comes to acting again. I'm back in front of the mirror, spraying the glass cleaner. I really look at myself. I can see that dad KNOWS, too. I think I'll go talk with him.

I went upstairs and found Dad in his study. He was reading a letter with some quiet music on the stereo. He listened to a lot of jazz.

He invited me in, and I sat on the couch. I told him that I finished the basement and asked what else I could do today. He said he was proud of me and that we should eat lunch. I asked him about the letter in his hand because it looked important, with the kind of lettering and a seal of some kind.

He said it was from Bishop Sheehan of the New Mexico Archdiocese. It had to do with some work Dad was doing with the native population and the Catholic Church. Dad oversaw what he called a 'reconciliation process.' An *outreach*. Dad still went to church about twice a month. I've gone with him, but he never makes us go. Mom doesn't go and neither does Julian. Louise goes every Sunday. The letter, whatever it said, caught my attention. From nowhere I said I'd like to go to church tomorrow if he was going. He made a joke that it wasn't part of my suspension. I laughed and even cried a bit and told him I was sorry for breaking my promise. We hugged for a long time. I still wanted to go to church with him.

We ate tuna sandwiches and talked for about an hour. Mostly about acting. About the movie we watched last night. Dad had a great attitude about it all. He was never in awe of any of the glitter. He was proud of Mom and was blunt that he was glad she gave it up for her painting. She was a true painter at heart. Even though she had won an Oscar, her paintings were an even greater achievement he thought. He talked about Sharon, and their high school days together at Columbine. I had heard some of it before. About Mom and Sharon's first play, *Helen Keller*, and wanted to hear all about it again. Dad was straight forward - If I promised to come in first thing Monday and register with the drama department, he'd introduce me to the teacher, Mrs. Kanoska. He'd lift the suspension. I still had to help clean the storage facility for the gallery. Maybe after school. I agreed right away.

Mom had gone over to her private studio to paint. I didn't want to bother her. Dad was going to run errands over at the church. I was still grounded, wondering what to do. I had read every John Grisham novel, about eleven of them, just finishing *The Testament*. I didn't have homework.

I took a long shower and put on winter clothes. It was that cold out. I took the long path down to James's cottage. There was smoke coming out of the chimney and that gold glow of light from the picture window beckoned me. My heart raced to see him. I hadn't seen him in a few weeks.

He answered the door, dressed in a big sheep skin, woolen sweater. He was smoking a pipe, a habit he started about the time he moved in. Or maybe he always smoked, and I never noticed. James always wore native jewelry and colorful shirts, highlighting his flowing white hair. We hugged without saying a word.

He situated me by the fire and disappeared into his small kitchen. He put hot water on the stove. I knew he was making hot chocolate for me. He came out with slices of homemade banana bread he had made yesterday.

James looked at me like he always did. Right through my soul, beyond my eyes. It's like he had a channel to my birth, into my heart, and he went right there to the beginning. He knew I was there for a reason.

I told him that I got suspended for smoking a cigarette on school grounds, but mostly for breaking a promise to my parents. He smiled and offered his pipe to me. He urged me to take a puff. I did. It was sweet tasting and smelled wonderfully. He brought out the cocoa and after a sip, he had me take another puff on the pipe.

"This is better than cigarettes, Stephanie," he said matter of fact.

"I agree. I don't really like cigarettes anyway."

"I know. I know. If you ever want to smoke again, just come down here and we will smoke from the pipe. It's better for you."

I laughed inside. Mom and dad wouldn't be surprised. It was James. I took another drag and he loaded up his pipe again with a granular substance of treated tobacco from the pueblo. It's what the older people, men and women, smoked over there.

I ate a piece of delicious banana bread and sipped my hot chocolate. We didn't talk much. We never did. It was like we were communicating without words. Ever since I can remember, as a little girl, James would sit with me and play a game or with a toy and he'd be studying me with great interest. Just like now.

"Did your dad get you in much trouble?" he asked.

"No not really. We had a good talk this morning."

James contemplated that and puffed some more. He got up and stirred the fire, putting in another log.

"It's about your acting isn't it?" he asked me.

Of course, he was right. He was always right. "Yeah. It's the only thing that we seem to fight about. But I need to get into drama classes, like Mom started out doing. Learn more about it first. It's what I want to do though. You know that James."

He nodded and closed his eyes for a long time. He was chanting or something under the silence. He did that a lot, too. Then he reached over and took my hands and looked me in the eyes. His hands were bony, old, wrinkled, strong.

"It is time for you, Steph.   Not long now."

"You mean to act?"

"Yes. It's in you. I've told you that."

"I know. You've always supported me. Believed in whatever I was doing. Even skiing. Especially riding over at the pueblo. You were always over there cheering me on."

"Listen, Steph." He let go of my hands and leaned back in his chair. He took a deep breath. "There is a saying about the sun and the moon, the earth and stars, their rotation and paths they follow. The light they emit and reflect and send our way.   I have seen this in your parents, very early on. And in Sharon, too. You and your brother inherited the same gift."

"Acting?"

"No, not acting exactly. Creating. As the earth creates. As God creates. As you are a creation from the same source."

I was listening closely because over the years I've learned that James talks like this. Like a code or something. It's real though. That much is true.

"And Stephanie, you and your brother have reached the time of telling. I won't be here to see it or hear of it."

"What do you mean? Leaving? You're talking about dying, aren't you? You're doing great, James. Don't say that."

"Yes, I'm doing well, dear. Don't worry. All I'm saying is that it's time. The time is soon. This will be hard for you to understand, but I will be here to see you bring forth your fruit, from the vine. I used to call it the Holy Grail, but your parents told me that doesn't make any sense as an analogy. Just drink it in, Stephanie."

He wasn't done. He sipped his cocoa. He lit the bowl again and took a deep inhalation and offered it to me. I took hold of the pipe and smoked deeply. It was filling my lungs, my bloodstream.

"What I am saying is that I will be gone when you begin to see. To see things. I won't be here to help you or guide you. You will need to lean on your father for that. Your mom will be busy with your brother. Don't get me wrong, your mom is with you on the acting, but I am talking about the seeing."

"The seeing? I don't get it."

"I know dear. I know. Smoke some more. Relax and take it in. You will be there soon enough."

We sat there for two hours. James spoke of Native American reconciliation with the Catholic Church and my dad's efforts in the community and the region to bridge the gap in the long history of European exploitation. James looked heavy hearted, like it was an impossible task. I told him about the letter my dad had from the bishop. James did not even react.

"I love your dad, Stephanie," that's all he could say on the subject as he changed it to my brother. "Julian is a wonderful young man. Tell him I need to talk with him sometime. He's busy now. Just like you are. The two of you speak the same language, you know."

I laughed. I didn't know exactly what he meant.

"It's like your mom and dad. They speak the same language. It's a Native American way of saying that wherever you travel, whatever your journey takes you, you can speak the same language."

I laughed, thinking of my brother that way.

"For now, you listen to Sharon, don't you?"

"Yes, I do. You say the word *listen*, and I think I get it."

He laughed in that ancient tone. "Well, pretty soon your mom will be speaking with you. She and her friend, her sister, Sharon, will be speaking in unison. Like the sun and the moon."

James would fall asleep in his big comfortable chair. I put another log on the fire and quietly left. I kissed him on the forehead.

I wandered around our property. There are small deer trails here and there. I went over to Tim's land and noticed the house was shut down and silent. They were gone. It was windy and I began to shiver, not wanting to go home. There is a stream I like to sit by. I call it my rock. No one probably knows about my little secret place. The mountain range in the distance had snow on it. Not a lot. A dusting. Early in the year for that, I thought. A kind of frost in the air and on the land. Growing up here I learned to see and listen like the Native American community I was so close to. Their awareness of the land, of animals, of weather, all of it had rubbed off on me. It's like the stream was talking, like the wind. That same language James was talking about. I don't know how to speak in the tongue of some of my friends at the pueblos but there is a rhythm like what I'm getting at. Especially when they sing. I try to sing like that when I sit here, let the echo of the gurgling water provide the words. The wind moved me along. I got up early the next day. Even set my alarm. I had picked out a light blue dress, long sleeves, and a white sweater. I hadn't worn this stuff, maybe once before. I grabbed a long coat I hadn't worn in a long time as well. I made my way into the kitchen. Dad was making coffee. He was glad to see me. I could tell he wasn't sure if I was going to make it or not. He likes to go to early mass, Louise, too. The 8:00 am service. Louise was already gone. She often does altar duty or gets things ready for the days' Sunday services. Dad doesn't eat on Sundays, or not until dinner. He offered me cereal which I declined. I poured a glass of orange juice. He was wearing glasses more and more and his temples were showing gray. He was always in great shape, but even now I noticed he was getting heavier. Julian and I had given him an expensive sweater for his birthday, and he had it on. A rich, deep brown, with heavy buttons. I really liked it. It looked good on him.

The sun was already colliding with our large, scenic picture window. Mom was asleep. Julian, too. Dad collected his coffee mug and we headed over to church. I hadn't been in so long, it all seemed new to me again. The smells, the aromas are always what hits me first. Like hickory smoke and wine and oil and sins lingering in prayer. The old statues and murals. Dad liked to kneel and light a candle. He said it was for me this morning. I'd say only ten or fifteen people made it to early mass. I know the later services are more crowded. I'm not sure why dad keeps going to church. He rarely talks about it. He never, ever, expects mom or any of us to go, although we all know we are welcome. Often he doesn't even like the Catholic church. So much of it bothers him. There's a lot of baggage there, I can tell. There's a relationship to God, with Jesus, his faith, that is real. Important to him. He loves the tiny community as well. Along with Louise, and George when he was alive, they'd be involved in all kinds of events. We'd go sometimes, but not very often. I look at mom and dad's wedding picture and there's a priest, I don't know who, and Bill, who was an Indian holy man and good friend of our family who died recently, doing the ceremony together. It looks odd somehow. It's also who we are as a family.

I went to communion. It's part of the ritual, the ceremony, that is most important. Honestly, I get something out of it. It's mysterious. Maybe even superstitious. It's probably the only time I pray. At least in a formal kind of way. I pray by the stream and in the wilderness all the time. But this is different. There is a kind of cleansing feeling that takes place. Hard to describe.

The priest, Louise, a few of the other older people, hugged me after the service. There is a kindness. A humility that attracts to me this place. I can see that part of it that keeps my dad returning.

As we drove out of the near empty parking lot, Dad said he wanted to go over and check on Tim and Shelly's place for them. They were in Canada; did I mind going with him? I love their place. It's so gorgeous yet simple inside. They have amazing taste in everything. Artwork, photography, décor. Their playroom, or pool table room, is the most fun place to hang out. He did a quick walk- through. I always notice a handbill, or poster they have framed of Mom and Tim in a play, *Bob, Carol, Ted and Alice*. There's not a lot of posters or Hollywood stuff in the house, but this one is prominently displayed. Which is odd. It's not what I'd think of with Tim and all his fame and the millions and millions of fans and money he's made in action movies. I wish I knew more about it that play. No one likes to talk about the play very much, and that doesn't make sense to me.

When we got home, Mom was reading the paper. She was wearing glasses more often too. She got up, still in her pajamas and robe, and hugged us both. She offered to make breakfast, but I made it easy, fixing my own bowl of cereal. Dad bragged to mom about how nice I looked, and everyone took notice of me at church. She smiled, looking me over, complimenting me.

I ate quickly and went to my room and changed into more comfortable clothes. I wanted to talk with them about taking drama, about acting, before Julian got up. Sunday was one of the few days he slept late.

They had moved to the kitchen table and were talking. "We were just talking about you, honey." Mom said.

"How proud we are of you," Dad added.

I smiled.

"Do you know, we were saying, that you have never had anything but straight A's since kindergarten. And we never push you or anything. You do it on your own. And even when you get in trouble, over this past year, you seem to rebound and take responsibility for it." Mom was pouring it on.

I sat down and didn't know where to start. "Dad and I agreed that I'd go in first thing tomorrow and sign up for Drama. I want to get in the class, and I want to be in whatever play they're doing. I'll do set design like mom did. I want to get going on this. It's what I want to do, and I don't want to be demanding about it or try to jump into Hollywood and all that. I realize that I have a lot to learn. Just like Mom did. Like Sharon had to do."

They smiled. Mom looked like she wanted to talk then double checked with a glance to dad.

"Look, Steph. It's been a tough year. A lot has been going on. But we hear you. I'm proud of your desire to act. I get it. I've never liked talking about acting because it's a tough business. It's brutal. It's not all fame and fortune, and I never wanted that anyway. I loved to act. It's like my paintings."

I knew this much. She was leading to something.

"Your Dad and I have talked this over, and I think I'd like to get back into it. I will give Phil a call and see what's up. It's been so many years, but I'm still technically under contract with him."

I started to squirm in my chair. Anticipation.

"Oh, Stephanie," she started, stretching her arms up high – probably out of frustration, "I don't know. You must understand that there's no guarantees in any of this. It's so tough."

I shook my head in agreement. Then she went on, "Sharon has had an amazing career. And I had a wonderfully lucky time at it. Even though it's hard work, there's a lot of luck in it. We both have been successful. Sharon especially. Ninety-nine percent of actors never make it this far. You know that."

I didn't even shake my head. I knew this absolutely. Then Dad took over, "Your Mom had a good idea. Phil can pretty much get his hand on any script. Maybe he can find one that you and Mom can work on around here. She and Sharon used to do it all the time. Walk around the house and rehearse. Learn the lines. See if it's a fit. You've never had a class. Never trained. Never been in a play. Even in junior high, you only pulled the curtain or helped with make-up. You stayed away from it like it was beneath you."

I chimed in, "I know. That was a big mistake. Maybe I was afraid to find out I wasn't any good. But I want to try now. At the high school. Get involved. First thing tomorrow." I turned my attention to Mom, "Mom, I get angry at you sometimes because, well, you are one of the greats. Right here in my house. My mother, and an Oscar right here, or locked up over at the gallery. And I never get to hear about it or even see it. I've been getting most of it from Sharon."

"I know. I'm sorry. It's time, though. I want to share it with you. I just get afraid. For you. But I'm proud of you. I want to make it fun. We can read lines. I can help you with whatever you take on at the school. Even Sharon may want to jump in at some point. I know it. Let's see what Phil can stir up."

I could feel my joy turning to tears. I tried to keep it calm but hugged her hard and with a gasp. Then I got up and hugged Dad.

Julian

I had slept in longer than usual. I blame it on Melanie. We had spent most of the night over at the studio. We worked on our music, lyrics, set lists, things we wanted to tape at some point. We needed a drummer. Desperately.

Then I kissed her. Impulse. Her dark lipstick was inviting me. Or her eyes. Or her boobs. Or her jeans. I'm not sure. I thought she'd push me away, being so much older than me. She pulled me closer. We stood up and moved over to the couch. We stayed on the couch for a long time. I had never felt a girl's breasts. Her's seemed so big, her nipples erect. It was a new sensation. I sucked on them. I hadn't kissed like that, either. Our tongues and wetness. I was taller than her, but she seemed physically in control of the entire episode. Melanie has reddish blonde hair with transparent blue eyes. I had never been so lost as I was in her blue eyes and her hair falling over me.

I couldn't drive yet. Mel's mom had a small Dodge Colt which the band was allowed to borrow on rare occasions when we needed to get around. We drove away from the gallery to take me home, then diverted to Tim's place and just parked in their isolated driveway. I came in my pants with the intensity of making out. A mixture of embarrassment and ecstasy. Then she dropped me off at home. I'm not even sure what time it was.

I needed to shower but dropped into bed immediately. As I walked into the kitchen the following morning, Stephanie was hugging dad. It looked like they were serious about something. Mom was getting up out of her chair and asked me if I wanted breakfast. I shook my head no and grabbed the cereal box and a bowl. She pulled out the milk and a spoon for me.

It probably had to do with her getting in trouble.

"How'd you and Mel get along?" Mom asked me.

I adjusted my glasses. I realized that I may have bent them in the physicality of last night. "Fine."

She wanted more. "We have a set list we'd like to record soon. Maybe make a tape. We need a drummer."

"Full steam ahead with the band, then? You have a name?"

"Not yet. *The Retro Sky*, or something like that."

"I like it. You guys sound good when I get to hear once in a while." She paused. I took a big slobbering spoonful of Honey Nut Cheerios. "Do you mind if I help you a bit? Maybe with finding a drummer. Or just sit in some time. I don't want to get in the way."

I considered this carefully. Mom, and Dad too, could certainly help a lot. But I liked that we were doing this on our own. Besides things had changed, literally overnight. Melanie and I were a thing. I was thinking about that for now.

"Well, Julian, let me know."

"Sure, Mom, I appreciate it. You know. I would like you to sit in on a few songs we're doing." I wanted to keep her engaged. It seemed like a good idea.

"I'd love that. Just say the word."

She leaned in close and whispered, "You have lipstick on your mouth and face."

I reacted. Rubbing my lips with the back of my hand. Sure enough. She took a napkin and wiped my cheek, even my neck. I was embarrassed but smiled.

Mom was grinning, "Glad you two could figure out what direction to take the band." She got up and went to the refrigerator and poured me a glass of orange juice. Neither Dad nor Steph caught any of that. I was relieved.

As I sat there finishing the milk at the bottom of the bowl, my mind drew a blank as to how to find a drummer. I drew the question out, loud enough for all three to hear, "So, we've been through three drummers. All of them came through Cindy's music classes. They were all bad. And none of them knew how to work at it.

Any suggestions?" I almost hated to bring everyone into this as soon as the question popped out.

Mom was about to say something when Dad jumped in, "The music department would have the best avenue for someone your age. Newspaper advertisements I don't think would work as well for you. I could ask down there for you, but Julian you may do better if you went directly there yourself. With Mel or the band. Tell Mr. Vaitaitis what you're looking for. Ask him about it. That way it won't seem like the principal is involved."

Then Steph added, "I've thought about that too. Dad's right. They have a nice band ensemble. I saw them play once. And don't forget about the marching band, they have plenty of drummers."

Mom didn't add anything. She was raising her eyebrows at me with a funny *caught you* look.

"I like that idea." And I meant it.

"What are you up to today?" Mom asked.

"I thought I'd go riding," I said in a bland, humorless tone. I rarely rode horses, but I was making a dig at Steph.

"Ha, ha," and she reached over and hit me on the shoulder.

"I don't know. I have some Math homework."

"You want to go see *Sixth Sense*? There's an early show. I think it's at 3:00."

"Isn't Steph grounded? I mean, yeah, that would be nice."

"*Isn't Steph grounded*," Steph mocked.

"I think we can make an exception," Dad added.

We had already watched a lot of movies on Friday, but I wanted to see this one. Bruce Willis looked pretty cool in the advertisements.

"We haven't been to a movie theater together in ages," Mom said as she cleaned up around the kitchen.

I went back to the bathroom and examined my face. A very slight trace of purple remained on my neck. An almost hard to see redness, not quite a hickey, was underneath. I remembered the details now. I had been lost entirely at the time. Should I call her? Were we boyfriend-girlfriend? I had no idea. I didn't have a mobile phone yet. Some of the kids did. Not many. I didn't see the point. Neither did Melanie, so it didn't matter. I called her from the den. Neither of us said much that helped with defining what was happening with us. She, however, said something like, *let's do that again*, with a giggle. I was all for it. Then I told her about asking the band teacher about a drummer. That my Mom and Dad were trying to help us. She paused. A long time. She asked me to hold on. More empty air. She changed phones or something, telling me that this was our deal, our band. I assured her that we would make the decision, she and I, the band. My parents were just trying to be helpful. They weren't trying to control anything. She eventually agreed. She knows them. The thing was, both Melanie and I were starting to get impatient, wanting to make a leap into playing live somewhere. We'd been rehearsing, working on at least twenty songs, over several years. And we liked the chemistry with Stuart and Frankie. They were good guys. Good players.

Right before we hung up, I told her that my mom saw the lipstick. She knew about whatever happened. Melanie laughed.

"What did happen, Julian?" she asked mischievously.

I stammered. "Whatever it was, I liked it a lot."

"Me, too." Then she said she had to go.

Danny

I don't know when I have felt happier about us being together. We went down to an out of the way deli that had recently opened. After sandwiches we walked around town, bundled up. Julian and I cracking jokes about the Allman Brothers. The long jam sessions. He was very much wanting to sound like Greg Allman, both vocally and on keyboard. He was more enamored with the psychedelic sounds of the era but was more and more into the blues riffs Greg produced. We dropped into my favorite bookstore for about twenty minutes. All of us were engaged in books. Steph, of course was looking for another mystery. Jennifer always drifted to the art section. This time both were looking at a novel they had heard about. The Harry Potter series was the rage, and they were looking over the latest release. Julian loved biographies. He read everything on rock musicians, the 1960's stuff mostly. He loved a book he had read on Buddy Holly and was asking me about him for weeks on end. He was thumbing through John Densmore's *Riders on the Storm*, on the Doors, Jim Morrison and Densmore's relationship in the band, and as friends.

I just took it all in. Watching them interact. I thought about how Jennifer and I had been here hundreds of times over the years, since way before we got married. She remained the most beautiful woman I know. She has poise in motherhood. As she looks to reenter the acting world I am confident of her direction. Of Stephanie, too. Veering over to Julian, his keen savant-like ear and intellect, I have no doubts with him either. I was a lucky man.

The theater had a nice crowd on a Sunday afternoon. I sat in the dark pondering over a dark cloud that I had been struggling with. As I grew deeply involved with the Native American community, starting out with educational outreach with James, with Bill and the northern tribes, all of it expanded into the southwest region. Being a Catholic at heart, I realized more and more the terrible history the Church had played in settlement colonialism, specifically with the traditions in which I now lived. I started outreach about two years ago to see what I could do to help bridge that gap in the present day. Most of it was hopeless, but I persisted in at last making connections wherever I could. Our bishop had been in close contact with me, supporting me in sentiment but never really making any efforts on his own part. It seems the Vatican had caught wind of what was going on and wanted to build an inroad in that direction. Pope John Paul was a man I greatly admired. His international impact was remarkable.

Once the lights went down and the previews finished, we settle in to watch a very good film. Jennifer and I sat close and watched from our own perspective. The kids were whispering back and forth, very much attempting to figure out the mystery. I think by the end they knew the secret about Bruce Willis's character. Neither Jennifer nor I guessed it. We were surprised.

Exiting the theater, we were hit by a blast of freezing wind. We walked quickly to a nearby bakery and grabbed a table, eating fresh cookies. We drank hot tea or hot chocolate. Jennifer and I were smiling, listening to the kids go back and forth about plot, the story line, the suspense of it all. Jennifer was not aware of the director M. Night Shyamalan, indicating how long she'd been out of the business. And I was very into cinematography, watching the camera work and lighting whenever I watched a movie. Fujimoto had been on the set of a lot of Jonathan Demme projects, so I was familiar with his style. This was well done.

Steph was particularly excited about the whole evening. She blurted out that she and Mom and Sharon might be working on 'a script,' causing Julian to look questioningly at his mom. Jennifer explained it all, that she might throw her hat back in the ring, so to speak.

"About fucking time," Julian exclaimed. We all sat there in shock. Then we all laughed.

"I suppose so," Jennifer replied.

The kids ran ahead to the car while we strolled in the bitter cold, holding on to each other. I felt like we were on the cover of *Freewheelin' Bob Dylan*, as I was holding on to Suze Rotolo …

I arrived at the office around 6:15. I like to fix the coffee in the front office, look over my agenda. Line things up.

Cheryl, my secretary, gets in around 6:30. We meet right away on Mondays. Upon finishing and reviewing various schedules and meetings, phone calls to make, I asked her to have Billy come down to my office at his planning period during second hour. She asked me about Stephanie, she was concerned, this being my daughter's first year and her first visit to the principal. I thanked her for reminding me. I had her remove Steph's name from the suspension list and changed it to detention. I told her that I was going to have Steph clean out the Gallery's storage unit after school. Cheryl nodded.

At second period Billy knocked on my door and then came in and sat down. He was carrying a small package. I stood up and we embraced as I once again congratulated him on winning the basketball state championship last year as he opened the package and unfurled our third state championship banner in boys' basketball to be hung in the gymnasium before our first game this year. We traded stories, relived the excitement of it all. I was proud of him and the kids.

"I have a favor to ask you, Billy." I changed the subject.

"You got it. What's up?"

"I'm really grateful to Cindy and all that she's done for Julian, and ..."

"He's a great kid," he interrupted, "I'm amazed how far he's come over the past two years especially. Cindy goes on and on how great he is, especially on keyboards, but he's getting very impressive on that Fender."

"Well, yeah, and the band they've got going is sounding good I hear. But what I wanted to ask you is if you can do some sniffing around down in the music department. I've asked Julian to go directly to Director Vaitaitis and ask about a drummer.   It's like the missing piece in the puzzle.   Julian trusts you and likes you a ton, he talks about your knowledge of music, all the memorabilia you have.   I just don't want to intrude as Dad, especially not as principal."

"I already know the perfect kid.   He's from one of the pueblos, I'm not sure which one.   He doesn't try out for band or the ensemble, but I've heard him play down there in the music room.   He was messing around on the big drum set, you know, the big fancy one, and killing it."

"Who is he?"

"His name is Alo.   He's a sophomore.   I've had him as a student.   He struggles in school, has a tough life.   I think his dad was a drunk, died in an accident.   No idea about his mom, or even if he has one. I think he lives with his uncle. But Alo loves his music.   He's big on a lot of stuff. Indian sounds of course, but he knows his rock and roll. He likes Cream, the Who.   Hard edge.   He told me he can play jazz, likes the feel.   Not sure where he hears his music or how he picked up on all this."

I sat and thought about this for quite a while.

Everything in me wanted to call Alo down to my office, meet this kid.   "Look, see what you can find out about his friends, what he's up to.   Ask him more about his music.   Don't say anything to Julian yet about this.   He'll figure out I'm involved right off."

"Can I ask him about the band, how's it going?"

"Yeah, yeah, that's a good idea. He'll probably tell you about needing a drummer. Maybe mention Alo then."

"You got it, buddy. Umm, I mean boss."

We shook hands, embraced again.

I called Cheryl back in. "Will you look up a kid named Alo? I don't know his last name. Probably a sophomore or junior. I want to know his schedule, his grades, any discipline issues. Whatever we got on him."

"Can I ask why?"

"I'm looking for a drummer."

She shook her head and walked out.

Alo Freebird. What a name. Fitting. Fresh from Lynyrd Skynyrd and the Hopi southcentral pueblo. The poorest of the nations. It's a tough location. I've been there with James, and Bill when he was alive, many times. His uncle has parental rights. Uncle honorably discharged, medal of honor, purple heart. Korea. No sign of a mom or dad. I spotted that his vaccines were not up to date. Hospitalized for nearly three months his sixth-grade year for an undisclosed medical reason. He slipped through the cracks of school bureaucracy. English second language classified, qualifying him for special needs assistance and staffing. Alo had terrible grades. Probably should never have been promoted from grade to grade. Reading and writing skills in the second to third grade level range. Received a music student award in eighth grade, best in the state. Received an award for every year in junior high for Good Citizenship. Positive attitude, willing to help his teachers. Those notes caught my eye. Never in trouble in terms of behavior but misses way too many days of school. Repeated fifth grade for long stretches of truancy. He receives government aid for just about everything. I gotta meet this kid.

When sophomore lunch rolled around, I went down to the cafeteria to pretend I was helping with supervision. The kids weren't normally a problem at lunches, but I like to show my face several times during the week. Mr. Vaitaitis, the band instructor, was in line getting his lunch. He caught my attention and waved me over in line.

"Hey, your son, Julian, came to my office this morning. He was asking me questions about a drummer. For his band. Very polite. He introduced himself, shook my hand. I gave him two names, but I must be honest, they are not all that good. I mean they do fine in the marching band, but they aren't fit for a rock and roll band or anything right now. I didn't say that to Julian. I just told him not to get his hopes up for what he's wanting."

I thanked him and shook his hand.

I spotted Alo right away in the back table with several other native students. He was laughing. Expressive. Good looking kid. Didn't look like he had bathed and wasn't eating much. His clothes looked tight and threadbare. Long black hair and could pass for 21 if he had to. He kissed the girl next to him. They looked cute together. I decided to leave it alone for now. I'd let Billy do his thing with Julian. Somehow I was knowing, like I knew things sometimes, were going to work out in a certain direction. This Alo kid looked like he fit whatever was going on in the Universe.

I went through my routine for the day. Not especially difficult. A lot of afternoon meetings with teachers. Next up was my other twin child.

I had Cheryl retrieve Stephanie from her last period class about five minutes before the bell rang. She already expected it. She had her coat and backpack, ready to go. I told Cheryl I'd be gone for about half an hour.

Stephanie was in great spirits as we drove away. She had followed through and signed up for Drama class, got the course change approved with a counselor, and signed up for the fall play tryouts. *Music Man*. God, I thought, does every school in the country, every year, produce *The Music Man*. Most predictable thing in the world.

"Didn't mom get started with *Music Man*?" she asked.

"Sure did. She designed sets, helped with costumes. She practically ran the show. It was her junior year. You have a jump on her."

"I don't really want to do those things. I will if I have to. I put my name down for the lead, the librarian."

Of course you did, I thought and did not say aloud.

"That's great Steph. I'm proud of you. Just rehearse a lot and I bet you get the role. And I'm proud of you for following up with our discussion. It means a lot. In fact, you don't have to clean out the gallery storage unit if you don't want. It would help your mom a lot if you did."

"I want to. I've been thinking about it all day. It will be hard, but I have my Walkman and some tapes. I'll be

fine. I even dressed for it with these old jeans and
sweatshirt."
"Well, I appreciate it. A lot."

Jennifer

Danny drove up and I got in as Stephanie ran inside the
storage facility.   We talked about how much I should
have her do. The storage area is enormous and needed
a lot of sweeping and dusting, organizing. I was going to
hang out, but not do much of the work. This was
Stephanie's opportunity to step up.
I was ecstatic to hear about her signing up for Drama
class and *The Music Man*. Danny and I laughed about
that, talking about the prelude moments to my career.
It was fun. I asked Danny if I should still go ahead and
call Phil, maybe Sharon too. I was having cold feet.   He
gave me a green light. Encouraging me with whatever I
wanted to do. He was with me.
He then told me about this kid named Alo, maybe a
drummer for Julian. From the Hopi pueblo. Poor and
struggling in school.   Billy was going to do a little
reconnaissance for us.
We were being involved parents, with high school kids
who would resent any interference. Just call us
surreptitious, I told myself.
There's a small office in the storage unit. The unit is
heated, and air-conditioned, to protect the artwork, the
valuables everywhere. Security is high. Cameras and
locks, codes, everything.   After I gave Steph directions
and supplies, I retreated to the office and picked up the

phone. First call, Sharon. Sharon had one of those new portable phones, so I tried that first. She picked up right away. She was in a limousine in Miami, headed to dinner to meet Vinny before his show at the Comedy Club. I was one of three people who had ever reached her on her new phone. We exchanged the pleasantries, the updates, the gossip, the love, and more of the love, before I cut to the chase. She was itching to hear. Probably knew already. She knew me that well.

"I'm thinking of calling Phil. I'm wanting to get back into the game."

She was shrieking on the other end.

"Hear me out. Stephanie never forgave us for not letting her do the small part you had lined up for her way back when. It was a bad time and ..."

She cut me off, "I know, I know, I'm so sorry. You know that. There was a quick deadline, quick turnaround, and I opened my big mouth. Aunt Sharon fucked up."

"No problem. Listen, though. Steph's never had an acting lesson. You know that. I think she's barely worked on two plays in her life. In junior high. Costumes, I think. Anyway, she stands in front of her mirror and mimics your movies, mimics every movie every role, thinks she can do it. She signed up for drama, the play – get this, it's *Music Man*, can you believe it?" I was referring to the first time she and I worked in theater at all – a play at our alma matter, Columbine.

"No shit." I could hear her drag on a cigarette. She told she me that she quit last time we talked.

"Oh, and by the way she got in trouble with Danny, the principal, for smoking on school grounds – see I can blame you for that, too."

"Oh, no way." She was laughing hard on the other end. "That girl knows better."

"Yeah, whatever. Oh. We all watched *Purple Flowers* the other night. On TV. I loved it. Danny loves it of course."

"Ahh, Danny ..."

"Stop it ..." A cigarette would be nice right now, I thought. And a glass of wine. "You should see Steph impersonate you in that bar scene. Actually ... I'm serious, she does an amazing job. Not melodramatic or anything. She has it down."

"It's a good scene. I always liked that one."

"Stephanie wants to act. I caved in and told her I'd look for a script. Something she and I can read around the house. A teen role, with a mom or aunt or someone for me to play. A mother-daughter thing."

"And an Aunt Sharon thing?"

"Well, I don't expect that from you at all. But what are you up to? You scheduled out for the next five years?"

"We're meeting you guys in Europe over Christmas. The Rome-Italian thing for Vinny and Danny. I have absolutely nothing else planned. Phil's pissed off, but when is he not pissed off? If you call him, tell him that if he doesn't find something for Steph, I'll never work for him again."

"He's heard that before."

She was laughing some more. "Jesus Christ, Jennifer. This makes me so happy. I miss you so much. It's been a long time. Let's see what we can dig up, in that filthy world of Los Angeles … say, how's Julian doing. His music? He's fucking good, you know that don't you."

"He's amazing. He's trying to put together a band. He's only a freshman and he has all these older kids in the band now. Looking for a drummer. They want to make a demo tape. He'll probably hit you up on that too. Studios in L.A. you know."

"Glad to. It won't be hard to get someone to listen to it. Let's hear what he's got.   I can't get to Santa Fe for a while, probably not at all before our Christmas Trip. Send me whatever they *lay down* – they say lay down, don't they?"

"I guess. No idea. But I will."

We exchanged so much love I was crying I missed her so much.

Next was Phil.   I wanted to get a drink. Instead, I went out and circled the unit. Stephanie was doing a bang-up job. She didn't hear or see me, jamming on her headphones. I let it alone and went back and took a very long deep breath.

Phil answered the phone instead of a receptionist or secretary. I froze. *Weird*, I thought.

"Hi Phil, this is Jennifer, I …"

"Jennifer Who?"

"Braxton. You know, I'm still under contract with you. Look in your discarded files."

"I don't have any Jennifer's here in our stable of actors and actresses begging for work, giving up their lifetime in places like Iowa or Colorado or New Mexico or wherever. How are you? I miss you, Jennifer."

"Oh, Phil. I'm so glad to talk with you. I haven't actually seen you since the play finished in San Francisco, right?"

"How many years ago? I forget."

"Me too. I'm old and fat and have ten kids and need a job. Just like you said."

"Maybe you can play Aunt Bea on the remake of *Mayberry*."

"I'll take it."

"Okay, I know you. What do you want? You're coming back aren't you?"

"I'd like to."

"Well Halleluiah! Hell has frozen over. I'm sure you called Sharon first. Does Tim know?"

"No."

"Saints be praised. You came to me first. You're growing up Jennifer."

"It's from raising twins, two teenagers."

"How are Stephanie and Julian? Danny doing okay?"

"All is well."

"And? I do have to go soon, not being rude or anything. I can set some time for you later, but I have to go in a few minutes."

"I'm just really glad I caught you, Phil. Stephanie is fourteen now. She's never acted. Never had training. Never been in a high school play. Never anything. She wants a movie role with me, or with me and Sharon."

"Just like her mom. I'm spitting up my power drink all over my desk."

"Look, I know you gotta go. We will talk later. Can you have your people look through scripts and send something with a teen role. Doesn't matter how big.

Something I can read with her, rehearse. Help her with?"
"Ah fuck, here we go. The thread is pulling. Jennifer is
back in my life. I will alert the Academy."
I said thanks beyond being audible.
"Sure, I'll send you boxes of shit. Let me know if any of
the scripts are worth a damn."
This time I was audible, and we hung up.
I really needed a drink. I mean really. I called over to
Danny's office. Cheryl patched me through.
"How's it going over there? Stephanie working hard?"
He asked.
"She's doing great. Uhmmm"
"You called Phil, and ..."
"I talked with Sharon first. She sends her love and lust
and all that to you. Anyway,"
He was laughing.
"Anyway, Sharon got me all emotional."
"Of course."
"And then Phil told me he'd send some scripts to read."
"I'm sure he died when he heard."
"It went well, actually."
"Good."
"What're doing? I can call Louise and ask her to feed the
kids. I want to talk with you. Let's go to our favorite
place, sit in the back. Eat high starchy food and get
drunk."
"It's a Monday."
"Oh yeah."
"I'll meet you there in an hour."
"It's closed on Mondays."
"Oh yeah. What about Jimmy's Bar?"

"It's a dive. They have decent pizza though. Thick crust should make us feel fat as hell."
"Okay, we'll meet there."

Francine is Jimmy's wife; she sat us in a large booth. We've known them a long time, before we had kids. They were doing a few takeout orders, but we were the only ones there for some pizza and drinks. I ordered whiskey sour, make it Royal Crown on ice. Danny did the same. A medium deep dish, thick with everything. And I asked Francine if we could smoke, some restaurants did not allow smoking anymore. She looked at me closely. Danny kicked me under the table. No problem. Where can I get a pack? She'd bring a pack, Marlboro, okay? Yes, thanks.
I lit up immediately and coughed.   Danny played with one and finally lit it up. He barely inhaled. We both tackled our drinks.
"Danny, you remember your first year coaching high school basketball?"
"Of course, we almost took state. Didn't expect to win half our games."
"And you won two state titles with that group."
"I was lucky, we had some kids move in from California. Young. Fast. Quickest group I have ever coached." Danny put out his cigarette, ordering another round already.   I lit up my second and was starting to feel the nicotine rush through me. It was gross, but I was having fun.
"And you had three kids win state in Speech. One in Humor, I think, the other two in Exempt?"

"That's right. Great kids. You helped with some of them. Oh, and we had the Rodriguez brothers take state in debate."

"You took them to nationals in Philadelphia."

"Bombed-out, but quite a memory." He grabbed my hand, "What's up Jennifer?"

"You sat in on city council those three years, your work for the Archdiocese, with the Native outreach with James."

"Yea, yea, help me here."

"I'm so happy for you, so proud. When we moved here from college, we had no idea."

"I know, I know. It was scary. You hit the ground running and I tried to keep up. Something else, what is it?"

"You know, Danny, we still have that scary shit in the future, that undercover whatever when we are in our sixties. The QANON thing."

"I never forget. It's those visions. We haven't had those in a very long time. I'm very glad. Relieved. Is that where this is headed? Did you have a vision or dream or something?"

"No." I took a deep drag. Another swallow. The rich taste hit me hard. The pizza arrived. I'd let it cool down first.

I went on, "James and Bill always called it the Holy Grail, which never meant a thing to either of us. Blessings. Drink it in. Acceptance. That kind of thing."

"That's for sure. No doubt about that. Your career. The kids especially."

"And your career. That's what I'm getting at."

"Jennifer. I know that. I'm so happy. I love this place. This community. Our family." He waited and I took a piece of pizza. He did the same.

"And my career. As a painter, I mean. Do you know that I am one of the top five *most in demand* artists in America? My works are through the roof. And the gallery is incredibly successful. The Women's League artists are world famous, some of them. So, even my acting. How could I walk away from it all? After an Oscar, a successful Broadway run?"

He was going to butt in, but I was on a roll.

"You know what?" Pizza was filling my mouth while I tried to talk. I gulped more whiskey to wash it down.

"Slow down. No hurry." Danny patted my hand.

"I'm so happy I had those years with the kids. Going to your games. Getting involved with the school. Time to paint. Always paint, just like Georgia did. Stylistically I grew and grew and evolved into a better artist. The best I could ever hope for. I have this show coming up in Paris and then I want to stop painting. For now, anyway. I really think it's time for me to go back."

"Me too, me too." Danny was grabbing his second large piece. More drinks. I lit a cigarette after my first piece.

"Do you mean that?" I asked.

"Absolutely. I mean, it's a tough world and you know I was glad you were home, to be a mom, to be with me, with us. I love your paintings. Even more than your films, your acting."

"Really? I am asking honestly now. You like my paintings more? I'm a good actress."

"Of course you are. But I've always said that I like your paintings more. Ever since you gave me a pencil sketch, the one in my office, your first self-portrait, for my sixteenth birthday, nothing can replace your art in my soul. Not even your acting."

I went quiet. I was feeling the chemicals of alcohol, smoke, cheese and heavy meats and olives and everything rumbling in my body.

"Jennifer, if you're needing something more from me to move forward, you got it. I have no problem at all. I look forward to seeing what happens. You and Sharon alone are enough to set the world on fire. Wait until the press gets a hold of this. And if we get Steph involved too, it will add another kind of fuel to a raging fire."

I laughed at that one. I realized how afraid I was. I was apprehensive. Not of Danny or the kids or Sharon. Was it something I could do again? I don't think I had ever felt the fear of failure in my life.

We ate, or Danny ate. I drank and smoked. One piece of this gigantic pizza about kills me. I got drunk. Danny was sipping his drinks now. It was a work night for him. Our conversation turned to Julian. We were excited. His talent was through the roof. We wanted to start hearing more of the band. We heard him around the house, his piano, acoustic guitar, electric guitar, bass guitar, never his band. And we noticed he was saying 'his band,' more and more. Even Melanie slipped once and called it Julian's band.

I told Danny about Julian having Mel's lipstick on his lips and neck.

Danny laughed. "I kind of thought something might happen sooner or later. I think Melanie is feeling the clock tick. Not the thirty-year-old pregnancy clock, the graduation from high school clock and Julian is three years younger than her. She's robbing the cradle in high school world."

That was so true. I saw that too.

"What about Steph?" he asked. "She goes through guys that like her like water. They always leave the house looking like they had their heart pulled out of them. Pure rejection."

"I know. She's either oblivious or, I don't know. Some of her friends are big question marks to me. No idea. She is so focused on herself. She reads for days, and I never hear a peep. She skis for weekends and I never hear her talk about it. She rides for weekends and barely mentions any of it. She does her homework religiously and hands us her report card without even opening the envelope. Straight A's over and over and it doesn't faze her. All she talks about are movies. This actress, that actor. Those lines, that set of lights, camera angles – you know, you've taught her a lot about that part of it – and she even reads movie reviews. All the time. I never did that."

"It's engrained her, that's for sure. You, know, Jennifer. She loves you. She admires you. She wants you to pass on who you are as an artist. She doesn't have much interest in drawing; and you know Julian likes to draw a lot with that kid who does those weird comics. She wants to have what her mother has."

"I've thought a lot about that. You know, this is sounding off the wall, but I think Julian wants what you have. You know, you don't play an instrument, but you are, at heart, a musician. You know everything about music, the era he loves. You are a rock star in your own way. I think it's okay if you start taking the initiative. He will be more receptive of his dad than his mom. It's their age right now."

He sat and thought about it for a long time. I went to the bathroom. My eyes looked like shit. Red from smoke. Four whiskeys. I wasn't done. I washed up and went back and asked for one more drink. Danny declined.

When we got home, it was later than I thought. Almost 11:00. Louise had left a nice note. *Both kids drifted to their rooms on their own around 10:00. Quiet night.*

Sex is central in our life together. Ever since we were fifteen. We have had countless adventures, have tried almost everything in books and manuals and in our imaginations. Tonight, I was drunk, and Danny was being sweet. Caring. He was there for me, like always. I had this urge on a cold fall night, to take off all my clothes, all our clothes, and walk outside our master bedroom veranda, out into the garden, covered over now in fall leaves and receded into hibernation. I wanted the cold air to highlight Danny's body. To grasp my own flesh and not let go. The silver stars flooding the night. The moon. That is all I wanted. He agreed.

CHAPTER THREE

Music should never be harmless. Robbie Robertson

Danny

I had an appointment setup with Bishop Sheehan on Thursday morning. We'd have an early breakfast before I went to the school. They served breakfast at the Sunrise Café beginning at 6:00 am. We'd meet there and then.

Sheehan is an interesting man. He had come to office by appointment after a sexual scandal in the church in Albuquerque led to the resignation of the previous bishop. The entire sex scandal issue in the church was paramount. The cover-ups and lies were emerging in a darkness I found reprehensive. They were not only disturbing they were a distraction to my aims of bridging much of the animosity within the Native American community over the Catholic Church's role in settling the West. Essentially stealing their lands and homes and wreaking innumerable harm on their heritage and traditions. Indian rights were volatile now, rightfully so. Just ask Sharon who was jumping into the fire with Native American causes and had been doing so even before her first Academy Award acceptance speech which was ridiculed over and over - and she continued getting an enormous amount of flak for it. The negative press was ferocious.

I liked Sheehan. He was trained in Rome. He was moderate in a very political world. His attempts to work with me were lukewarm but he wasn't ignorant. He knew the reality of the native population in our region, extending beyond New Mexico into California and everywhere there had been missions. He and James were at odds whenever we met, so I met with him alone this time. He was starting to feel pressure from the Pope himself. John Paul was pleased with the divergent, even exploding growth in the Church, especially among Hispanic culture in the Americas. The ever present "Indian question" in the United States was to be no longer swept under the rug. Yet there was no promise of recompense or even a formal recognition of past atrocities and there was little repentance. It was a time to listen and wait. I had the feeling; no, I KNEW that the native community was beyond waiting, but even so there was no consensus on what they wanted from the Catholic church.   There was infighting within their ranks as well.

What I wanted from Sheehan this time around was his direct involvement. To meet and to listen. Himself. Quit sending a priest from Tucson who is in his first year. Or a delegation of nuns, who, for the most part, were vocal and ready to act. That strategy had backfired on Sheehan, and they were not asked to represent him anymore.

I could tell he wanted to turn me down outright. He was not wanting to take this on. Too much scandal already. Why dig up ancient history when the past was already haunting the pews, the newspapers, the courts, and the

Vatican? He was feeling John Paul's pressure. John Paul was a man of conviction who wanted to make things right. Trouble was, even John Paul was overwhelmed behind closed doors. This sexual scandal in the Church was expanding and beyond even his control. It was tearing up the Church.

Sheehan said the Pope wanted to meet me. Was it possible?

I was stunned. Of course, it was possible. I immediately explained our plans to go to Paris over Christmas break and head to Rome and Abruzzi for a family exploration of our heritage. He told me he'd check into those dates. Maybe we can take advantage of the timing.

And, by the way, where in Italy were the Tomasetti's from? I told him in Abruzzi province, a small town called Castiglione Messer Marina on the Adriatic Sea. My grandfather was the youngest of twelve who came through Ellis Island around 1897, via the port of Genoa. He said he'd have the Vatican library investigate it for me.

Sheehan also promised me that he would pray about coming to the next meeting in Taos. Five Indian councils had agreed to meet and discuss the Catholic issue, the history of Missions, and reconciliation. With or without anyone from the Church. I was acting as a *de facto* representative neither sanctioned nor requested. It made Sheehan uneasy, and probably angry, that I was doing this on my own. Or with James, or with James and Bill. Or with Sharon the wild and crazy actress. Or my wife. Or whoever was driving this cause.

I left it there for now. Ecstatic about the possibility of meeting the pontiff himself.

Sheehan said he would pray for me and my family as he made the sign of the cross on my forehead, right there in the restaurant.

Julian

Billy saw me in the hall and asked me to drop by his classroom at my free period, even though he was teaching a class. Why I still call him Billy, when I should call him Coach or Mr. Saxon, I wondered to myself. I've called him Billy since I was a little kid. I better change that now.

Melanie and I were acting like boyfriend and girlfriend in just a day or two. She was a senior with a completely different schedule than we lowly freshmen. We found a way to find each other at our lockers – in different halls – or in passing periods, logistical miracles.

And we'd kiss. Strange places like in the gym when it was empty. She was always wanting to suck on my neck. I was terribly self-conscious about the marks, the hickeys she was leaving. I was a marked man, now.

Her breasts, her boobs, her tits, her nipples were taking over my thoughts. Even so, I was beginning to think about getting into those jeans of hers. It was only a week or so before I, stupidly, asked her if I could. We were at the studio after school rehearsing a few songs. Our vocal arrangements. The rest of the band would arrive any minute. She laughed. *Whenever you want* is all she said. Then she whispered as the guys came in, *if I can get into yours*.

Billy, Coach Saxon, is a tall guy. He is intimidating to those that don't know him. He has a scar below his ear. His hair is longer than most coaches. He still acts like a hippie if you get him to talk even for a minute about music or bands. He knows more than anyone I know. Even Cindy, his wife, my music teacher, can't keep up with him. He and Dad get along great, coaching mostly. When they get together, which is often, they listen to amazing albums, talking endlessly. I have been overhearing it my entire life. Absorbing it. Memorizing most of it. If I ask Billy about, say, Little Richard, he can pull out his entire collection. Play me anything I like on his amazing stereo. Tell me everything about the back-up band. Anything. I had an interest in Neil Young's *Harvest* album early on, and Billy gave me a few months of education on Buffalo Springfield, all of Young's discography, the history of Laurel Canyon in L.A. He had all the albums, certainly, and the books and posters. Amazing. The whole ball of wax. I was singing "Broken Arrow" for months. I learned to play it on guitar and the electric keyboard. I'd get that swirling sound messing with the knobs. It was my first real attempt at singing the lead, just like Neil. *Could you tell that the empty quivered, brown-skinned Indian on the banks, that were crowded and narrow, held a broken arrow?* I love that verse.
Billy motioned me to the back of the room by his desk. The kids were busy.

"Time gets away, Julian. How're you doing? I've been meaning to talk with you for quite a while. High school good to you?"

"Doing great. Love it, really."

"You got a band going, I hear."

I wasn't sure how he knew. No big deal. "Yeah, they're good. I like the sound."

"I'd love to hear you guys sometime." He said.

"Sure. You know we practice over at the Gallery, the studio over there."

"I know. That's so cool. When's a good time?"

Now I was on the spot. An audience. "Fridays usually. Right after school."

"This Friday, then?"

"Sure." I was nervous.

"What are you into these days? Still into Costello? What are you working on?"

"Not sure why but I keep coming back to Greg Allman. His voice. I like the blues of it. His keyboards. They're different, repetitive. I like the jam sound."

"No doubt about it. They are one great band. I have some live stuff of theirs at the house if you want to hear some real jamming. "Whipping Post." At the Filmore. The best live album ever made."

That peaked my interest. "Could you bring it Friday? Cost of admission."

He smiled. "No problem."

"Okay, Julian, are you ready to go live yourself. Your group?"

"Well, no. We need a drummer. Cindy helped me with some guys, but none of them worked out."

"Really?"

I knew something was up. He already knew, I could tell.
"Well, I know a kid. I was talking to him. He's from one
of the pueblos. He's a sophomore. Alo Freebird. No
kidding. Freebird. Can I bring him Friday?"

Not so subtle. I get it. My mind was racing. Was it Mom
or Dad? How'd Billy get involved in this? "Sure. Our
drum set just sits over there. It's a simple 5-piece. Does,
what's his name, Freebird, or Alo, have a drum set?"

"I think so. He lives on the reservation. He must
practice on something. I didn't ask. I'll find out …
maybe he can sit in on a song or two. What about
"Broken Arrow," I know you play that?"

"Tell him to be ready to play 'Beyond Belief.'"

Billy cringed. He knew that was a tough one for
drummers. And it was in my bailiwick. I loved that song.
My Elvis in full tilt. One of the songs I insisted on playing
bass. Melanie loved to sing the light highlights with
ahhs and oohs driving the fast tempo. She was also able
to take the organ sound, changing chords easy enough
with some reverb. One of the times she played
something other than rhythm guitar. The other two
guys played a syncopated, fine-tuned two chord change
until the bridge. I'd love to hear a good drummer with
us.

I left the classroom not sure if I should be pissed off at
my parents, or happy with Billy, or just fucking curious
about this Freebird-Alo guy.

I got the band together first thing after school. I locked
us into the studio, letting them know everything
discussed with Billy and that a kid named Freebird or Alo

would probably be by Friday to try the drums with us. I was also being way out of line, but was going to ask my parents to sit in. Might as well let it happen. Maybe Steph, too. They could ask anyone they wanted to sit in. We were putting the drummer on the spot, but that's the way I wanted it. Everyone wanted to invite a friend or parent or parents. No problem. They wanted to know more about Alo. I didn't know anything else. We then moved and shifted some chairs over by the sofa. Standing room only otherwise.

I then set up all the microphones we had with the amps situated for an audience. We put the drum set together and decided on our location on a stage atmosphere. I was feeling it. I just had a feeling. The group was excited too.

Set list.

"Here Comes the Sun" to start it off. Melanie takes lead vocal. I play the 12-string lead and back-up vocal, with bass and acoustic back-up from the guys. Alo will be able to start easy if he knows anything about drums at all.

Then the kicker. "Beyond Belief." We'd played it a million times. Just stick with my bass and my blistering fast tempo lyric.   Mel has keyboard, the other guys knew their parts. Let's play the bridge a few times, help Alo with the riff before we kick in for real. We'll see how he thinks.

I asked everyone about "I Can Tell," the Bo Diddley song. I always loved the lead guitar on this one. I put a capo on my Fender, stuffed the holes, and imitated the riffs exactly. Melanie and I traded lyrics, joining in together on *you don't love me no more*, over and over. A nice arrangement, maybe tinged with attitude, like the original. They were all good with it.

We'd give "My Guitar Gently Weeps" a try. We were still rough with it, almost like Velvet Undergound. Why not. Let's go with the version with Melanie taking lead vocal. I had to admit she did it much better than I did. She carried the Beatles songs with a purity and cleanness I respected.

I wanted to play Dylan's "Isis." It's long. Hypnotic. I had made it into more of a Doors song with the way I intoned Morrison in some of the lines. I played straight piano, just like I heard from Bob over and over. They weren't too thrilled, but they went along with me. We worked-in Mel's vocals, sounding just like Emmylou Harris, in several locations. I reminded Stu of the dragging tempo on bass – it sounded better slowed down - and Frank to use a rhythm guitar and just get lost in the repetition, chord change after chord change. Like he was high. We laughed. Maybe we should play high. That was good enough. We went through each song a few times and called it a night. We'd see how it went Friday.

At dinner, I waited and waited. Louise left and went to her room-apartment. Our family conversation was dying down. It was my turn to clean up. As I was taking some dishes to the sink, I asked aloud who had been talking to Billy about a drummer for the band. Both Stephanie and I looked hard at Mom and Dad to see which would give it away, even though Stephanie didn't know what I was talking about. Stephanie read me perfectly.

Dad broke. Mom smiled and pointed to Dad. It didn't bother me. I just said, thanks, I hope Alo works out. We're ready. And, oh yes, we're playing for anyone that wants to listen on Friday at the studio. Right after school.

Stephanie said she'd be there. Could she come early? Sure.
Mom said she'd already be there at the Gallery.
Dad pointed out that it might not be that fair to Alo to have so many people there, but he'd get there as soon as he could. Probably closer to 4:00. I said we'd wait. We'd let Alo mess around, get used to the drum set. Look over our set list. He also said he was glad Billy was on board. I agreed wholeheartedly.
I met Alo. I found him at sophomore lunch and ditched the first part of my Chemistry class. I'd figure out an excuse. I went right up to him, and we talked about Billy and about coming over Friday and playing drums. He was excited. I sat down with him and talked music. He knew his shit. He said his uncle, who practically raised him, had a nice turn table at the lodge at the 'res' – reservation – and they played everything. His uncle used most of his government money as a Korean War and disabled veteran on albums and tapes. He never drank like so many did around there. Alo had a makeshift drum set he put together over the years, nine-piece, but he would rather use ours for a try out. He was a big Ginger Baker fan, which sold me right away. I looked Alo over closely. I was worried about one thing – he looked malnourished, and in need of a bath. Maybe a place to sleep. He looked like so many of the poor kids

in school. I invited him over to spend the night after the try-out, even if the drum thing didn't work out.

I then told him the set list. Billy had told him about Elvis Costello and "Beyond Belief." No problem he said. He wanted to know who played bass because it was important on that song. I said that I did. He just shook his head. He seemed fine with the rest of the list. He'd give "Isis" a listen again. It was the only one he wasn't sure of. He was familiar with the *Desire* album, but mostly "Hurricane." I was surprised he knew the Bo Diddley catalogue better than I did. He knew the Beatles backwards and blindfolded. Ringo wasn't too tough. But he did want to give "Rain" a try, if things worked out. He was talking straight at me. I wanted to play bass on that with a good drummer and do my Lennon vocal thing. I was itching already.

I went to Chemistry class and waved a pink piece of paper at my teacher who was at the black-board talking away, as I went to my seat. He didn't even bother to check it. Principal's son written all over his face.

Friday rolled around. Mom was first one to arrive. She helped with set-up, encouraging me. Thanking me for letting her and everyone be there. Stephanie was already in mom's studio and said she'd be right in. Then people I didn't know showed up. A few parents with their band member kid. A grandparent, even. Several friends. Standing room only already. Dad showed up with Billy and Cindy. Still no Alo.

When he finally showed up he looked like a lost puppy. Which he was. He had no idea where the studio was in relation to the Gallery. He wasn't even sure of the gallery itself. And he walked all over the railroad district trying to find it.

We gave him plenty of time to gather his composure. He did a few rounds on the drum set and I didn't really need to hear any more. He was amazing. He had his own sticks and had a wide range of tempo. Even some jazz. He got up and asked for a bathroom.

Then we started. Mom turned on the tape player in case it was good. The sound check was perfect.

Mel was amazing. Her vocals were perfect. Alo watched Stu on bass and found his comfort easily. Ringo would've been proud of Alo. He pulled it off just right. I heightened the tempo with my 12-string and then let Mel take it home. Nice. Everyone applauded. I had never heard applause before, except at recitals. This took me by surprise.

I practiced the bridge on Costello's song and then quickly counted off to four. Perfect intro, Alo hit right on cue. My bass drove it faster and faster. The lyric blistering into the microphone, I sang directly at Melanie, *charged with insults and flattery her body moves with malice, do you have to be so cruel to be callous* ... drum line on cue ... all the while her organ creating that peculiar Wurlitzer affect.

It was me and Alo bringing it home. I'd see if he could keep up. He did. Mel was matching on the chord and on beat, changing nicely. It reached crescendo, Mel reverbed and played with the matching speed, and we hurried into the final verse. I was drenched in sweat in just three minutes of frenetic pace.

Billy came up and hugged me and gave Alo a big handshake.
Cindy was talking with every one of her students, proud as can be. The try-out was over as far as I was concerned.

Mom looked like she was choked-up.
Even Steph was amazed.
Dad was indeed wiping a tear from his face.
The next songs we rattled off with gusto.
My lead on Bo Diddley was my highlight. My time to really shine. I pushed myself even harder. *I can tell, I can tell* and then Mel grabbing my shoulder in harmony *you don't love me no more.* Then we shifted gears again. Crudely. The rhythm guitars wailed and wept with Mel singing just like Harrison pseudo–Velvet Underground. I was falling in love with her watching her sing. We finished with "Isis." It was all me on piano. Dylan-esque with no apology. Voice intonation, the whole thing was Bob channeled via *Desire*. Practically a solo until Mel would sing that haunting accompaniment. Our love was mixing in the mystical child whirl.
We were done. Everyone went nuts. It went so well I was shivering. The band hugged Alo. He was in. More than in. He had a smile bigger than the drum set.
Mom and dad hugged me then congratulated everyone. Time for pizza. Let's go to Jimmy's bar. All of us.

Stephanie

I was impressed. I grew up with my brother playing all the time, his recitals, his expertise, especially his classical training. This was different. This was a band.

Alo would stay the weekend with us at our house. I had never met a kid like him. We stayed late at Jimmy's Bar then Mom made him sleep in a big tee shirt, made him take a shower, and washed his clothes. She was ordering him around, realizing he had no motherly influence.

The next day Billy came over and he and Dad and Danny took Alo to the mall. Dad bought him new clothes, jeans, packets of underwear and tee shirts and socks, even new shoes - nice quality boots. Toiletries, like toothbrush and q-tips and deodorant. Even a carry all bag for everything.   Billy ran Alo over to his uncle's – who didn't have a phone - to let him know where Alo was going to be and how the band played. He invited him over to our house, but he declined.   Billy and Alo's uncle talked music for over an hour, discussing albums, the drum set Alo had learned on since he was four or five.   Music is all he had to raise him with. Not much else. He had played drums in the Army, a small service band, mostly 50's rock. Because of his war wounds he stuck around with bands in the Western United States. He taught Alo all of it and they both grooved into the 60's sound.

It was fun to hear Billy talk about all this. He's an animated guy.   Like my own uncle, or our uncle.

I tried to talk to Alo about books. The authors I like. I realized quickly that he was practically illiterate. He could barely read and write. The only books he had read were in school and he couldn't tell me much about any of them. He didn't like school very much. I talked about movies, about mom, mostly about Sharon, how I wanted to act. He gave me a blank stare. He had only seen a few movies in his lifetime. They didn't have a television. He had never heard of Sharon, or my Mom. Alo is hilarious though. He tells some great stories about growing up on the res. Like me, we could talk horses. He loved to ride. He is full blooded Hopi and other than the drums, he lived for the horses stalled at the central pueblo. English was his second language, so he struggled sometimes. For whatever reason he hung out with me over most of Saturday and Sunday, more than with Julian. Julian seemed good with it; he was busy, in his own world.

James comes up and eats with us every Sunday. James had a long talk with Julian. I had forgotten to mention to Julian that James wanted to talk with him. Julian was laughing a lot, so it all seemed good. James was also delighted to meet Alo and was very familiar with his uncle. They spoke in their native tongue. Lots of laughter. James would translate, how happy Alo was to be here, thankful for the clothes. The opportunity to play in a band, with friends. Mostly the friend's part, I think. James went on and on about the poverty over there, the severe need. He was ecstatic for Alo.

James, Dad, Mom, Louise, love making a huge Mexican food spread on Sundays. It's a long process. Usually there are more people over, but it was just Alo this time. We crank the stereo as part of the proceedings. It was Mom's turn to pick the music and she was into Alanis

Morrissette's "You Oughta Know" which we listened to before open choice. Some stark stuff on that album, but I loved it. Alo asked if we had any Jerry Lee Lewis, which we did on an old cassette tape. When we played it, he was telling Julian that it might fit his piano repertoire. Besides, people could dance to it if the band ever performed. Julian was all over it. Another spark. *We gotta make the music dangerous*, Julian was quoting someone, agreeing with Alo. Playing live, you can make the audience listen, but you want to make them dance. They needed both. Or at least that's how the conversation was going.

While we ate, my Dad asked about Alo's last name, Freebird. Alo had no idea how that was on his birth certificate. He liked the name and but was tired of the comparison to the famous song. He didn't like Skynyrd very much. I could tell that Julian didn't either. Alo preferred being called Freebird sometimes. Or just plain Bird. It didn't matter to him.

Then we started talking about names for the band. Melanie wasn't there, but she and Julian were set on Retro Sky. Alo liked it. All of us liked it. James went on and on how it meant a lot, more than Julian may understand. We had grown to accept James's cryptic comments.

That night I was snug in my bed reading my lit assignment and Alo came in my room without knocking. He startled me. He looked like a little boy hidden in a fully grown man's body. He flat out asked if he could sleep with me.

I lay there stunned. Was he serious? What the hell did he mean?

"No way, Alo. I hardly know you. I mean, I like you, but we are not sleeping together."

"Oh, I know," he was having difficulty finding the words then broke an awkward smile, "I just want to sleep with you. That's all I meant."

I really struggled with what he was saying. There was no come-on or trying to get laid. There was an unintended sexuality about the situation – or was it intended - but I really didn't think he was trying to have sex. I wasn't sure. Was he putting me on?

"No, Alo. Freebird. I understand. But no."

"Can I sleep on your floor?"

I laughed. "Come on, you have a bed. A nice bed." I got up and took him back to the guest bedroom. He got in and I tucked him in, in an uncomfortable sort of way. I even kissed his forehead and told him he was sweet.

I could barely go to sleep. I made sure the door was shut securely. I also smiled. I wouldn't have really minded if he had slept with me. Just held him. Or he held me. I had no idea where this weird situation was taking me. I eventually fell asleep.

We were moving fast in the morning. Mom and Louise had breakfast going. Dad was already heading out the door. Julian and Alo were dressed. Alo looked like a new person. He had showered every day, ate like a fiend, and slept soundly – probably thinking about me. I was taking my time. Mom usually drove us, but I was getting a ride with another friend who had her license. I skied with her sometimes. They'd get to school a lot earlier than me.

I sat in Dad's study for a moment, looking over some of his framed photos. I liked the smell of the dark leather furniture and cherry wood paneling. The sun piercing the window. Happy for Julian. He's amazing. I let Alo go in my mind. Part of me raced to pursue whatever was there between us, then again, it didn't feel right. He was like another brother. I was circling back to acting. I wanted to get my hands on a script. Start into a character. Be the character. Nothing else really mattered.

I heard the honk of the horn, grabbed my backpack and headed out. I loved Dad's office.

Jennifer

I raced the kids to school, making sure Alo had lunch. He was on a free program, so he assured me there was no problem. He thanked me profusely for everything.

Our monthly staff meeting was at 10:00. I swung by and picked up bagels and fruit, plenty of coffee for eight. My conversation with Trudy this past week went well.

Trudy was my first line assistant these past three years. I told her she would be running the ship if I became *distracted*. My words stuck on acting or performing or a script or any of those.

The meeting went well. I was glad Steph had cleaned out the Storage Unit so beautifully because I asked three of our staff to spend a few days over there and do a new catalogue and computer file on everything. We'd cover the shop for them somehow. Trudy would lead that endeavor as well. I also wanted to move forward on a show in December for our good friend Samantha. She was no longer an officer in the Women's League. Her paintings were the rage over the past two years, so it was about time we gave her an exclusive show. It was noteworthy that her work was similar to mine with the dark emotion, change of temperament. Her style was much different, particularly with her use of acrylic. Still, there was change taking place in the liberation movement. Sam was elated when I spoke with her after a several month hiatus. I promised to have her and Karen – who was our realtor – and their adopted boy just now turning seven over to our house soon. James would want to see them. Not to mention Danny. Always a smile there. Sam's show would be large, so we needed to clear out a full wing. It was fine with me to take many of my works down and put them in storage. Most weren't for sale anymore anyway. James still insisted and I honored his wishes even though they were my works.   I put one of our curators' trained salespeople, Sally, in charge of the show. Publicity. All of it. She only had a little over two months to get it going. The positive aspect was that the artwork and the artist herself were right here.   Sally had access to both whenever she needed. I was certain that Samantha and she would get along fine.

I asked them if we should keep my self-portrait on display in the entry. It had been there for ages. Everyone insisted that we keep it in there. It was in our flyers, in art books. It was a landmark for tourists. I acquiesced.

We did a walk-through of the Gallery, noting anything we wanted to change. Pricing. That kind of thing. Most everything remained status quo.

I withdrew to my studio. I did some drawings with pastel pencil, using imagery from the dreams I was having. A lot of it spurred on by our twins. Those two were inspiring me in an entirely different direction. I played the tape we made of 'Retro Sky,' listening carefully to each song. Over and over. There was still a crudeness, a stark garage band sound, retaining a remarkable synchronicity. Everyone was on key. The timing was smooth. Julian was coming through loud and clear. What struck me even more, was Melanie's voice. She was very good. The two Beatles songs were hers. She owned them. Her back-up on "I Can Tell" and "Isis" were notably different. On the first she sounded like a gospel singer, and I could tell she and Julian were on the same microphone. On the second her Emmylou rendition was spot on. That opening line when Julian sings *Isis, oh Isis, you're a mystical child, What's driving me to you is driving me insane*, captured exactly what I felt about Mel. I knew they were becoming a couple, so it made me even more curious. Their age difference didn't bother me. What bothered me was their compatibility. It scared me.

I made a note to talk with the other two boys when I could, Stu and Frankie. I liked what they did. Frankie was obviously the weak one of the group. He struggled on his electric guitar. It sounded a bit plucky. Maybe it was just because Julian could dominate. Frankie was smoother on his acoustic. More comfortable. Stu was impressive on bass. No problem. I guess I was concerned how withdrawn and lost he seemed. He leaned into Julian for security, even though he was older. I wanted to have the whole band over for one of our Sundays and I wondering why we hadn't. Melanie had been over a lot. Now Freebird. It was time to put them all in the same house. Live together for a weekend. All in all, this was a top notch first try. They were not very far from doing working gigs. Polish things up. They didn't need much except a bit more time. And get a good twenty songs down by heart.

I was procrastinating. I was only this far from finishing my final painting for Paris. I looked at it and I was not satisfied. It was good. It just wasn't as good as the others. There was so much emotion in the paint, I was worried that it may be muddy to the viewer. Muddy like my own heart right now. I wanted to clean everything out and get back to work acting. At least I had made up my mind. I was resolute.

I put on Alanis Morrissette's *Infatuation Junkie*, with all of her emotion and anger which matched up with mine, and the message our League was sending out, and mostly with this upcoming exhibit of mine in Paris. I started to see, really see where I had to go to make this painting the best of the bunch. I cried with rage with dark colors, creating counterbalances and breaking a lot of rules. I mixed a blood red magenta and carefully applied streaks, like vaginal flow. Breast milk whites.

The imagery, the symbolism of color was resonating with me.

I stopped to let the oil settle, flow into the canvas, prepare itself for more blending and coaxing. I went inside the gallery and had a sandwich in our tiny breakroom, noticing we were crowded with customers and tourists. I had no idea why. A busload from Japan, Sally told me. They were dropping big bucks. One of them, an elderly woman, awkwardly asked me for my autograph in what I presumed to be in Japanese as I headed back. I obliged her then rushed back to my cave. I called Danny. Impulse. It's his direct line. I told him about my impressions with Julian, Retro Sky's tape. A few more thoughts on Freebird. He told me he was going to do some digging into the kids' backgrounds. Not so much to snoop but see what else he could do to help. Alo had triggered it in him over the weekend. In both of us. He had meetings after school. Go ahead and eat without him. He would be home by 7:00. Love you.

Danny

Cheryl brought in the files I requested during my quick lunch break. I was moving at breakneck speed but wanted to give these a quick look. I set Alo's aside. I already had that one memorized.

Melanie. Born in Las Vegas. Divorced mom moved to Santa Fe when Melanie was only two. Remarried. Divorced again when Melanie was in fifth grade. Mom works at the hospital as a nurse. Single parent, has helped a from time to time on the junior high parent council and high school PTA, abruptly resigning from her commitments. Melanie has good grades. Awards in math. Honor rolls her freshman and sophomore years. Slacked off her junior year. Impressive music grades. Sings in the choir. In fact, has been in choir her entire school life, performing in many recitals. Awarded music student of the year her junior year. No other activities or sports. Suspended once for fighting. Notation says she was defending herself but hurt the boy who then had to be sent to the hospital with a broken jaw. I smiled at that one even though I knew I shouldn't.

Stu. Born in Phoenix. He has lived in Santa Fe for six years. Stable family life, two younger sisters. Mediocre grades. Music awards for Jazz Ensemble and Band. Awarded Good Citizenship Certificate in sixth grade. Played soccer his freshman year. Not much else on Stu. I wondered why he always looked so withdrawn and even sad.

Frankie. Huge file. Moved all over the country until he was four. A military brat, from army base to army base. His dad was African-American, from Oakland. Killed in Iraq. Frank's grades are abysmal. No activities no positive mentions or notes anywhere in a very bulky file. He did win an art contest, however, first place in drawing, his freshman year. Lots of suspensions. Mostly for fighting. Smoking. Police record: shoplifting. Stole a guitar from a music store in San Diego, on a vacation, when he was only eleven. Walked right out with it then ran. Charges dismissed. Shoplifting again, this time in Santa Fe, stealing undisclosed items from a different music store.   Charges dismissed. Possession of marijuana. Santa Fe. Only two months after his shoplifting charge, almost two years ago. Charges dropped with the stipulation of community service. I looked closely. Cindy had signed off as his community sponsor as his music teacher. I smiled again. I thought Billy knows lots of stuff that I don't know about this band. Single child, all indications of his mom acting as a single parent since his father's death. She works at a dental office as a receptionist. But there were photocopies of his graphic designs. I made a note to have them copied and share them with Jennifer. I knew Julian mentioned his drawings but wasn't aware how good he was. Incredible work, I thought.

All these kids took music lessons from Cindy. I wondered how their parents paid for the lessons. Knowing her, she probably charged whatever they could pay. Maybe nothing. The common thread, culminating in Retro Sky. The band was as good as they were, due largely to her influence. Julian excelled under her tutelage – in classical, jazz, gospel, and especially rock and roll. She was a rocker hippie at heart and instilled that in this group.

Yes. I needed to have this rag tag group over to the house for a weekend. Soon. I wondered if Julian had any idea who this group was that he was putting together – their individual histories. He probably never gave it any thought. Just the music. That's all he cared about.

Cheryl buzzed me on the intercom. I had a call from the Indian Council in Taos. The conversation was quick. They confirmed our meeting in a few days to discuss the

Catholic Church and its history in the region. I was all in. Had the bishop confirmed, I asked? They hadn't heard from him. I said goodbye and called over to the bishop's office. He wasn't in his office. I left a message with his secretary reminding him of the meeting in Taos. I'd be happy to drive. Please let me know.

When I returned to my office later in the day, I had a message confirming the bishop would attend. I could pick him up at the rectory at 7:00 am. I was extremely happy for that news.

Stephanie

When I got home from school I noticed the lights on at Tim and Shelly's house. They were back home from a distant trip somewhere. I lost track with them. I thought I'd walk over and say hi to Shelly. We were practically best friends. They didn't have kids and she treated me like her daughter most of the time.

Sure enough, Shelly was there. Tim was in New York. They had a great time in Canada. Tim likes to fish up there and Shelly is an avid hiker with the wives of some people they know. None of the wives are in show business, so I know that Shelly likes that the most.

"Tim told me about your mom. About you! Acting, huh? You sure?"

"Probably heard from Phil, right?"

"Eventually. Sharon got to him first. I have no idea how she reached us up there. She has a way of getting what she wants."

"She sure does."

"Well?"

"I do hope to get a script or something for my mom and I to read. Look over. I've signed up for drama class and the school play. I know it's a long shot. I'm determined to do what I have to do at this point. I don't think there are acting schools around here except at the Community College. Nothing for my age. Mom's the best anyway."

"You got that right. Tim's pulling for you. He's beside himself about your mom wanting back in. He started making calls from our lodge. He gets the ball rolling."

"That's exciting. I know my mom will love to hear it."

"Don't say anything yet. Or at least give Tim a chance to talk with her. Okay?"

"Yeah, yeah. I get it."

"You want to watch a movie. I have these tapes from the studio where Tim was producing a movie. It's a drama and I know you'll be interested in this one."

"Absolutely! Oh, we saw *Sixth Sense*, finally. I liked it a lot."

"Me too. One of the better ones in a long time."

I called over and let Louise know I was next door. I'd be home for dinner.

I love watching dailies and splices and unedited clips. It gives me a realistic view or window into how it all happens. Tim and Shelly have let me watch these my entire life. And Shelly is good at letting me mimic and try scenes on my own. She can stop and start clips from where she sits in their viewing room.

Opening credits and title ran and I reached over and hit Shelly on the shoulder. It was with Haley Joel Osment, the kid we just saw in *Sixth Sense* and who was also in

Forest Gump. The title was *Pay It Forward* with Helen Hunt and Kevin Spacey. It had a strong kid's role, so I had a sneaking suspension, this was not accidental. The stops and starts. The cuts. The mistakes. Even the moments of improvisation. I came away from the afternoon with several thoughts: I can do this. And Helen Hunt is very good. Kevin Spacey is a pro, he makes it look easy. I was into Hunt and her style. I wanted to see more of her movies.

Shelly told me Tim would be back in two days. Come on over, he'd love to see me. We'll all hook up soon. I hugged her, telling her I loved her. I do.

When I got home, everyone was just getting ready to eat. I jumped right in. Everyone wanted to know about Shelly, the movie. About Tim. Mom and Dad started talking about a trip he was taking up to Taos later in the week. He was going with a bishop or someone important. Then Dad hit us with a big question. Mom already seemed in on it. There was a possibility of us going to the Vatican, meeting the Pope when we left Paris and went to Rome to hook up with Sharon and Vinny. We were going to rent cars and drive over to Dad's original heritage somewhere on the east side of the country.

We were all excited. Meeting the Pope. I had to let it sink in. Julian seemed more outwardly enthused than me. Mom looked happy about it. She wondered aloud if Sharon and Vinny could join us. Dad seemed to think so. Vinny was at least baptized, even if he was very much a lapsed Catholic. None of us really understood why Dad would be meeting the Pope. He tried to clarify his outreach with the native communities with the Catholic Church. None of us seemed to sympathize or have any reason to understand the Catholic Church. All of us were hell-bent on how awful history was towards Indians. How do you pay for that? How do you reach forgiveness? None of us shared Dad's sincere attempts for dialogue. What in the hell was there to talk about? He understood our perspective and didn't even argue. He just said it was on his heart and he was doing what he thought was right.

Mom helped me clean up. I told her I loved my drama class. I had tryouts for the librarian role next week. I was going to read from our high school modified script. We would rehearse later tonight. I had to sing. Several songs. She assured me it was no big deal. Have fun with it. I wasn't so sure. I had been in choir all through junior high. Nothing great. A few solos. I also told Mom more about the movie. She opened up, which I was glad for. Telling me about the technical side of dailies and the clips I was watching. What to look for. How to learn from them. I seemed to get it right away. I had seen a lot of those things. Mom was so wonderful. I could see why she was so great on screen. The way she talked about it as an art-form, that I needed to really start thinking about it as an art. I didn't paint or draw, so I needed to find my analogy. A way to draw myself out onto the film, out into the part, the character. Be the character.

I thought about that late into the night. I could not sleep. I knew that this very point was standing in the way. Not being trained was holding me back - although training and experience were essential, more importantly I needed to think of an avenue of expression that I could fall back on. I thought I'd talk to Dad.

After only a few hours of sleep I got up early and caught Dad making coffee. His extremely early routine. Everyone was asleep. He was surprised to see me. I sat at the breakfast table and asked him about this sense of expression in other art forms. Dad thought about it for a long time, eating, sipping his coffee. He agreed with the point. He went on and on about my brilliance, my grades, my horseback riding, my snowboarding. Reading endlessly. Then he said something that I did not expect. He talked about heredity. I was born with this gift, this gene. The only suggestion he had was for me to go back and watch every movie of Mom's. Study them. Project myself into the parts, the characters, instead of being objective or a disengaged viewer. *Be your Mom.* Disappear into the character like she does. *Be your Mom* he said again. *She is in you.* Her chromosomes carry on inside me. Start there, then it will break through and become you. Not your Mom at all. You might try it with Sharon's movies too. *Be Her.* She would be honored and love to have that bond with you. Break out from her mold. Your Mom's mold. Maybe the breakthrough is not in another art form, but in your very genetic structure, *the soul of my very being.*

He kissed me and had to run.

I also thought that I carried his genes inside me and what that meant. Steady, hard work, with a touch of mystery.

CHAPTER FOUR

'Wherever there are people that are suffering make it your task to serve them.' John Paul said that. So did Jesus. So did Buddha. So did just about anyone that has made any positive impact on this good Earth. Suffering is an interesting human phenomenon. It comes in various forms and shapes and disguises. True, physical suffering is usually easily recognized. Other forms of suffering, not so evident. I would like to think, as your creator, that you can see where you are suffering, at this very moment in time, is so very much like the unrecognized pain in the person right next to you in the grocery line. Or at your work. Or lying next to you in a shared bed. I guess all that I'm asking is that you look, be aware, and be a servant for even a brief moment. I promise. I absolutely promise as God of all things, you won't regret it. And you will be the one healed.

Julian

We rehearsed. We were on a daily schedule. Alo was getting us going on Fifties dance tunes to balance out the long grinding songs of the late 1960's that I loved. Costello had a fast pace. So did the new wave in general. Just not all that danceable like the early classics. Our assortment of songs was expanding. Melanie and I were still splitting the vocals and combining them into nice arrangements.

Melanie and I were also now very close to having sex. Her body was driving me crazy. Her blue eyes — sometimes ocean clear - and blond hair — sometimes light reddish hues. Her incredible hips swaying with her voice. Everyone in the band knew it was bound to happen, if it hadn't already. Frankie was jealous for a time, then he found a girlfriend, a junior, so he lost interest in our situation.

I invited the entire band to stay the weekend with us at our house next week. Mom and Dad insisted. We'd have food, games. Plenty of movies. Lots of music. Whatever, it'd be fun. During the day, we'd head off to the mountains up near Taos. Do some camping on Saturday night. Take everyone home on Sunday. Steph would join us, someone other than Mom for Mel to sleep with in the tents.

We were in the studio taking a break and Mom came over, repeatedly apologized for interrupting. I was ready for her to not be so paranoid about interfering. She wanted to help, that's all. I was fine with that now. She asked Frankie and me to come into her own art studio, which was very much off limits. Frankie looked frightened, like we were in trouble. She had us sit down at a long table at the end of the room and she asked both of us about graphic drawings and novels, the kind of thing she sees us do a lot at our house. She knew we both continued these drawings, and she wanted to know if Frankie had any finished product, including original stories. Frankie lit up, talking about a finished book that he had recently completed. It was impressive, I added. These novels were becoming more and more popular, much more serious than comic books. Frankie talked about *Batman* and *Superman* and *Marvel*. His favorite was the Spiegelman *Maus* Series about the Holocaust. His story was autobiographical about surviving as a kid moving around the country. The kid was the ultimate hero, simply titled *Kid*. Mom was fascinated and asked to see the book and any other drawings. She was very curious about the artwork, as well as the story line. Frankie simply stood up, went back in and retrieved his backpack. He pulled out a large manilla envelope, collection of drawings with hand printed script. He handed it to Mom. She then pulled out another large collection of drawings. Mom looked them over carefully. Studied them. She asked if it was okay to share them with the staff here at the Gallery. She patted him on the back and congratulated him; she liked them very much. Frankie was happy as could be. Frankie then looked up at the large canvas on the wall. He told my mom that he liked her work, too. It had a dark tone to it. Not bad for a background to a graphic design with characters layered on top. She was startled and stood up. She looked at her own work more carefully. She grasped what he meant then asked him to explain more.

"It's like I feel the anger. The image of blood flowing. Of mystery. Something about to happen. All it needs is a character with dialogue. Or a bubble of thought."
Frankie said matter of fact.

She laughed. "You know, you're right, Frankie, it does need character and a bubble of thought. It's just the background right now. I can't do what you do, but the story does need to be told more completely. I appreciate it. Say, have you ever been in our gallery?"

"Never. I hear you're famous. Not just as a painter but you won an Oscar. You never talk about any of that when I'm over at your house. This gallery is all yours, right?"

"Well not exactly. Part of it is true. Would you like to see it?"

Frankie looked over at me, knowing we had more to rehearse. I told him to go ahead. Mom put her arm around Frankie and took him through the side door, holding on to his portfolios of drawings and his book. Not many people get a one-on-one tour of the gallery from my mom, I thought to myself. Not unless she has a reason.

Stu and Alo were working hard as a rhythm section. I realized how lucky we were to have such a strong force at such a young age. Stu was classically trained by Cindy and was adept with jazz and formal music. The rock stuff came easy for him, he just needed to loosen up and have fun with it. Alo was already getting him to free up his hands. Alo was having a big impact on me as well, as we pursued a lot of the Fifties and Sixties favorites. The ones that got your feet moving. Some crooning was creeping into our repertoire because of it.

Melanie pulled me over asking where Frankie was. I told everyone that Mom was showing him around the gallery, looking over Frankie's artwork. A hush of impressed thought took over the room. Then Melanie asked me to give the Everly Brother's "All I Have to Do Is Dream" a try. She and I played acoustic while Alo used wire brush strokes along with Stu's toned down, easy bass. When Melanie and I started singing in complete unison, *I need you so, that I could die, I love you so and that is why, Whenever I want you, All I have to do is Dream, dream dream dream dream dream dream dream,* over and over ... we got completely lost in each other's eyes. Stu and Alo played slower and slower, just like on the dance floor. Eventually we quit on the guitars and were singing a Capella. Simply gorgeous. It would become one of our standards, I thought.

When Frank got back, I pulled out The Pretenders *Last of the Independents* album and played the first song, "Night in my Veins," for everyone. I was not letting go of the current era at all. I wanted to take on this song. We went through the chord changes. I quickly had the lead guitar solid. Frankie got the electric backup easy enough. Mel was underscoring the acoustic. Bass and drums, no problem. We had the structure in about an hour. But then Mel and I got into our first argument over lead singer. Since it was a Chrissie Hynde song, and Mel loved her probably even more than I did, she assumed she'd sing the lead. I was dead set on taking it, changing *he* to *she* in the lyrics. I wanted a driving song, upfront, then let my voice take over. It became a very uncomfortable situation. I agreed to have us take turns. She went first. I let her take a more powerful lead, upped her amp, with her acoustic as well. Then it was my turn. I had Stu and Alo pick up the tempo and I blitzed through the song, using that tremolo Chrissie used. Even more than Mel had.

Melanie and I stood and stared at each other. We both smiled. Both versions were incredible. What to do? I stood there trying to figure it out in my head.

Stu spoke up. Which he never did. We froze. "I have an idea. If we ever perform live, that is." We waited. "Why not let Mel open the night with this song. It's a great tone setting song for any night of music and dance, and it will get the place in the mood. We then do our set. What an hour or ninety minutes? Fly through about fifteen songs. Then we have Julian play his version for the encore. Like book ends. His version will make them go wild and it will be a good way to say goodnight."

Inside, my ego was in the way. I did not want the audience to see Mel as the lead upon the first song. This was my band. On the other hand, I sang lead on about two-thirds of the set we thought we'd play. And Mel and I shared lead on at least three songs. And I'd get the encore to myself.

Everyone was waiting on me to hear my thoughts. Even. Especially. Melanie.

My mind was still processing. I was beginning to visualize what we *looked* like as a band, not just sounded like. I got up and went outside and walked around in the cool air. Breathing deep. I'd always wanted to wear my Elvis Costello black framed glasses, black jacket and black pants. A skinny tie. I knew that Stu would wear his dark green vest he liked so much with a beige shirt. He was into that look, with his scraggly hair out from under a Dodgers baseball hat. I had no idea what Alo would look like. He was wearing his new jeans and tee-shirts and sweatshirts and boots all the time. He was glad for his new stuff. He had that long straight black hair. Cool. Frank wore a jean jacket all the time and black tee shirts with various comic book characters on each one. Graphic novel stuff. He was the only one of us with a lot of facial hair and being black and muscular, he looked much older, tougher than all of us. Sometimes he shaved, sometimes he didn't. Then there was Mel. She was fucking gorgeous with her makeup and jewelry, funky blond hair. Who knew what she'd wear? It would change daily. Funky hippie. 1980's multi-colored skirts and blouses. Pink pants. Red pants. Black bra. Purple bra. New age, punk. She did it all. I knew that she'd be the draw. I had to face that fact.

I went back inside.

"Look," I said, "Stu is right. I like his idea a lot. Melanie will grab the audience right away."

Everyone breathed a sigh of relief.

"Say, I was thinking, walking around. What each of you would wear if we were on stage?"

Everyone said pretty much what I thought. Melanie went into greater detail, depending on how she felt that day.

Of course, I thought, *unpredictable*.

Now we needed a good promotional photo in clothes just like that. *RETRO SKY* Live. And a venue.

Somewhere to play where people can hear us.

Jennifer

I asked Matthew, on my staff, to critique these drawings, this book, the graphic novel world in general. Make photocopies and make notes for me for our next staff meeting. I was sensing a new direction. At least a cutting display for our smaller rooms in the gallery. We had reached an eclipse with our Native Art. The true archaeological value was out of nearly everyone's price range, and I refused to cater to tourist demand for cheaper replicas. I was removing a lot of my own work. What I wanted to sell of my own personal collection, had already sold at astronomical prices. Most of my sales went to museums and private benefactors now. I stored the rest. We were giving Samantha a big showing in a few months. Our walls were fairly covered in other Women's League artists. I was also showing other local artists, only to stay on top of the competition. I was wanting something completely new. Looking at this kid's *Kid*, his drawings, walking around with him in our gallery, Frank was pointing out observations I had not heard since I was a student. I realized that I had grown set in my ways. *Kid* was raw. Very raw. His style, and some of Julian's drawings, were making me think of doing something on this genre. Hit it hard with publicity, which we rarely spent money on. We didn't need to. Move forward. I liked the blunt messaging. The underlying battle between good and evil. The allure of youth. Mostly I liked the bold artistic expression and stylism.

I also knew that once I finished this Paris exhibit I needed to start over. Completely. I was famous. I had made my mark. I was proud of my work and reputation.

Deep inside, though, I was aware that I was taking myself for granted. True, my Paris canvasses were different. They were going to create a stir. Frankie, this wayward lost soul, playing his guitar and drawing every day of his life, taught me something. Or reminded me of something. He woke me up. My desire to act again was playing into it as well. That inner muse was stirring. Danny and I were talking out on the porch right before dinner. It was warmer than it had been the past few weeks. He was leaving for Taos early in the morning with Bishop Sheehan. He was nervous or not very hopeful. He was also happy that he was not going alone. Then we were turning around and welcoming Julian's band for the weekend. James was up to going with us on Saturday for the campout. He was arranging some help on that end, all the particulars, just like he had done hundreds of times before. We laughed and insisted on no peyote or ceremonies or anything like that. Just fun for the kids. Bonfire, maybe some native drum music. Good food for grilling. A hike. That's it. We spoke about Julian's band a lot. I thought we should look into them playing over at Jimmy's Bar. I'd give Francine a call and see what she thought. It was a small place. Maybe they could remove a table at one end and let them set up their drums, amps. It only sat about 60 people but maybe for one weekend they could give it a try. They wouldn't have to pay them anything. Danny thought that was a great idea. Maybe contact Sarah Johnson over at the TV station. Have her mention it on the *Today in Santa Fe* morning program. Sarah knew us both, in fact, had interviewed us both, and she'd be willing to at least think about it.

Then there was Stephanie. It was time. I was expecting to get some scripts in the mail. Both Phil and Tim had contacted me again and were green lighting not just my return but to give Stephanie a look. Maybe a reading. See what she looked like on film. Sharon was itching to get in on this. She and Vinny were going to fly into Santa Fe sometime soon. Maybe stay with Tim. Or they could stay with us. It was still up in the air. We wouldn't say anything to Steph, yet.

Steph had brought home an essay she wrote in her advanced placement English class with an *A plus* grade and full page of comments from her teacher. Steph had written it about Emily Dickinson and the 'essence of genius.' Danny had already read it and I sat on the porch reading it carefully. I wanted a cigarette and a drink. Damn, where were those urges coming from? I cry easily sometimes. I know that. But I was so fucking proud of Stephanie. This was amazing writing. Amazing insights. I stood up and shouted inside for her to join us. "Yeah, what's up?" She took a seat in one of the lounge chairs. She looked so cute. Her hair braided like I did with my own hair. She was into turquoise lately. A big sweater. She was looking like a young woman.

Danny started, "We are so proud of you hon. You are always doing such a wonderful job in your classes, with your grades, and we don't tell you that enough. This paper you wrote …"

"Oh that. No big deal. I worked on it for a long time. Dickinson is one of my heroes. It's like I know her. You

know what I mean? Like I KNOW her. It was an easy
paper to write once you spend some time with Emily's
work. With her."

"Well, it's beautiful. You have a great deal of insight into
creativity and the artist impulse. Not sure where you
got those ideas." I added.

"James and I talk. Dad helped me too and he didn't
even realize it. He was talking about you, Mom. How
gifts are inside the person. Not just developed. I believe
that about Emily. About me, too."

I looked over at Danny. We both smiled.

"Hey, I'm excited about this weekend. Will there be
horses?" She asked.

"I don't know. I let James organize it. Most likely. You
know him. He has horses around all the time when we
do anything in the mountains." I affirmed.

"Are you and me and Melanie getting our own tent?"

"That I'm sure of. Dad will have to get along without me.
I think Dad and James will stay together.   The boys will
be on their own."

"I think Julian and Mel are getting serious. He doesn't
say anything, as usual. I just can tell."

"So can we." Danny said with certainty.

"What do you think of Frankie's drawings? With Julian?
Have you seen them?" I asked her.

"Wow. Aren't they great? I heard you took them at the
gallery to look at them. I love that story *Kid*. Frank can
be so in his own world. Distant. I can barely talk with
him. I know his girlfriend. She's cool."

"How 'bout Stu?" Dad asked.

"Oh Stu. I feel sorry for him. He struggles. His acne mostly. He always looks sad. He perks up when we talk. He has some great ideas for the band, but Julian and Melanie can be intimidating. I tell him to say fuck it and let them know his ideas. They're good ideas."

"Good for you. I like him a lot." I said.

"Then there's Freebird. Alo." Dad added.

Steph froze. She looked uncomfortable. "It was weird when he spent the night with us. He wanted to sleep with me."

"What?!" I interrupted. I sat up and wanted to clear this up.

"It's not like he was coming on to me like some guys do. He wasn't flirting. It was like he was a little boy. Of course, maybe I'm just naïve. He even asked if he could sleep on my floor – there in my bedroom." She was laughing hard now.

Danny was concise. "What happened?"

"I took him back to his room and tucked him in and kissed him on the forehead. Motherly. Weird."

Danny and I looked at each other. We had no idea what to make of that story.

"Well, we called you out here because we're proud of you. This paper is amazing. And this little love story with Alo makes me all the prouder. Be careful. He may have a crush on you. Most likely. Who knows?" I added.

"Tell us, Steph? You interested in anyone. Boyfriend?" Dad asked, cutting to the chase.

"No. I just want to read a script. That's all that's on my mind."

"Good. No hurry on that front." Danny went on. I could tell Danny, as I had been, was starting to get concerned with this teenage high school phase as it was dawning. Visions of our own world back at Columbine High School.

Danny

I set my alarm for 3:30 am. I got up and reviewed my preparation and handouts for what I thought would be about 20 elders of what would be six nations. I asked James to stay back. He and Bishop Sheehan clashed, and I wanted to give the bishop to have a fresh start with this relatively new group. James was fine with it. He had all genuine intentions, hoping it went well. He knew he'd get in the way of any progress.
I also prayed. In an old-fashioned kneeling by my couch in my office. It looked so hopeless. The bridge between European-Christian proselytizing, indoctrination, even extermination, and the native world of the Earth and deep tradition was near impossible to build. My heart was merely hoping for dialogue for the children of a shared community. I had no idea of an outcome favorable for both constituencies. Healing was probably too big of an aspiration. I was a teacher and principal, and I loved these kids. There was much that could be done for their benefit. For the future.
Our drive was pleasant. I was glad that Bishop Sheehan wore a simple collar and jacket. Nothing showy. He had a gift of a Letter of Peace and Love from the Archdiocese to the greater Native Community in the Southwest. That was a huge step, I thought. He was

also inviting them to a Christmas mass in Albuquerque. I couldn't be happier with his openness. Small steps. Tiny steps.

I urged him to listen. Simple as that.

We were greeted with wonderful generosity at the grand Pueblo in Taos. There were pastries and coffee. Introductions were made in graciousness. Name tags. A short Agenda handed out. I was to speak third. Two elders would talk. The first one on the histories of Native-Catholic relations in America. The second on the current relations as viewed by the Council. There was a place for Bishop Sheehan to speak if he chose. There would be a break, then the Council would proceed without us.

And there he was. I froze in the introduction. Robbie Robertson. The great guitarist and iconic member of the Band. The Band of Bob Dylan. My youth flashing before me. He was smiling, shaking my hand. Leather coat. Long hair. I barely recognized him. He was visiting, touring the Southwest on behalf of the Mohawk tribe into which he was born. He owned a home between Santa Fe and Taos. I did not know this. He knew who I was. He had heard of me from various pueblos. Word traveled. He knew my wife Jennifer and her art. The Rio Blanco Gallery. He knew James. He knew my association with my high school friend and famous actress Sharon. He seemed to know me well. I was stupid in awe. I never got that way with famous people. I was now. He sat next to me on my right, with the bishop on my left at the large table.

The first speech was delivered by a woman elder from Arizona. She was blistering. I cringed. How else can you tell the story? No other way. I knew that. Bishop Sheehan sat quietly and took some notes. The second speech was not much better. It did give the Catholic Church credit for opening its various outreaches to the poor from any background. Many impoverished natives were benefiting from those food and clothing programs. A handful of Indians were now in parochial schools without the twisted expectation of following Catholic doctrine.

It was my turn. I acknowledged the history and suffering. I hoped that the Church would do the same in a formal way. That would be one of the most effective steps of reconciliation. Admitting sin and wrongdoing. Repentance. I spoke at greater length about my efforts over the years in outreach to native communities and pueblos for education success for all. I thought our school district was doing a better job of welcoming and supporting Indian children with an affirmation of their heritage and history. Teaching them skills for survival in a Western society and attempting to highlight current Indian accomplishment and culture. My goal was to have more regular dialogue with the larger Catholic Church and our most immediate native community in the hope of finding a way for the future. To get past the history and what that would entail.

There was no applause for my talk like the first two speakers. Not a cold reception exactly. They wanted to hear form Bishop Sheehan.

He stood and thanked everyone. I was happy. His

demeanor was slow and deliberate. He did make a joke about me being a basketball coach and our state championships and our leading scorer being from a nearby pueblo. Everyone laughed. Thank God, I said to myself. Bishop Sheehan read from notes. He acknowledged so much wrong in the past. His voice broke. He also explained the current problems of scandal in the Church which was dominating his own internal prayer life and the politics within the Vatican. He did say he had the blessing of the Pope for any further progress we could make. He was grateful for this small step. He said he could not speak officially on the future, but he read the Letter from the Archdiocese, which he had written. It was heartfelt and full of human love. He then handed the Letter to the chief running the meeting. He then spread his arms and invited one and all to a mass he would perform at Christmas time. It would be celebration of the Indian population in the region.

There was mild applause of warmth.

Then he asked if he could pray in their place and in their presence. All shook their head in affirmative. Bishop Sheehan made the sign of the cross. And prayed aloud. Asking God for guidance. For God's blessing on these leaders and their individual nations. He thanked God for this day and for the shaking of hands of each person he met today. He asked for guidance. Amen.

A small murmur of approval and even an Amen or two. Robbie Robertson put his arm around me. I embraced him as well. All of us ate and socialized for about an hour. It was agreed we would meet again, and several leaders said they would come to the mass.

Robbie – that's what he said I should call him – took me outside by himself. He said that the meeting had gone well he thought. There was a great deal of skepticism in the room, but Bishop Sheehan spoke from his heart and truthfully and that went a long way. He appreciated my comments and efforts very much.

He asked about my family some more. I barely mentioned the twins, they were just starting high school. That Julian was trying to form a band.

"Really? How's that going?" Robbie asked.

"Not bad. Julian is talented. He's found some good kids. We're trying to get them to play live soon. They have a tiny studio next to my wife's Gallery. They rehearse, practice all the time. Dedicated."

"No kidding. Listen, I'm in Santa Fe next week. Can I drop by? I've wanted to see Rio Blanco Gallery for a long time. I'm in Santa Fe all the time and I can't seem to get there."

"Absolutely. We would like for you to come to dinner at our house.   When are you in town?"

"Just Tuesday through Thursday. Two nights. That would be very nice of you. I'd love to, and to meet your family."

"Are you with family, friends?"

"No, not this trip. Council business. I have one big commitment on Tuesday night. Can we meet Wednesday. Dinner Wednesday night? Wait, you have school."

"No problem. I can make it work. How about we meet at the Gallery at 2:00. The kids usually practice around 3:30 or 4:00. They'd love to meet you."

"Fabulous. He wrote down where he'd be staying, and I gave him our phone number."

On the drive home Bishop Sheehan dozed off. He was content. I was hopeful. I was trying to think of all the famous people I had met over the years. All of whom were through Jennifer's career as both a painter and actress. Probably five or six had visited our house. Many others at Tim's house.

The busy weekend was ahead, and I was hoping that the kids would let us sleep tonight. I still had to get to school for this afternoon. I was overextended. I was tired. I'd break the news at dinner when rehearsal was over, and everyone showed up for the sleep-over.

When I finally got home around 6:00, Jennifer, Louise and James were at work on a big dinner for everyone. Tacos, burritos, green chili. Lots of chips and guacamole. Jennifer informed me that Samantha and Karen were dropping in with their seven-year-old son Brandon. They wouldn't stay long, but we hadn't seen them in ages. Tim was in town, so he and Shelly may drop by, too. A party was unfolding. Lots of food and drinks already lined up. Julian and the band would be there anytime.

I pulled Jennifer into our bedroom and filled her in on how well things went in Taos, especially considering my underlying uncertainty. Bishop Sheehan was better than I could expect. Then I told her about Robbie Roberson. How he would be over for dinner Wednesday. She was like a teenager with glee. He was going to be at the

Gallery to see Jennifer's work, whatever was exhibited, around 2:00. Her mind was racing. Then the kicker. He wants to sit in on the band – I mean Julian's band – and hear what they got. Jennifer was processing the whole thing. We agreed to make an announcement at dinner. Once everyone was seated at our big table. We might have as many as 15 seated. No problem we had room for about that many. We'd done it before. The kids had met celebrities before, but this seemed different. More directly related to them, to Julian.

Everyone was piling in. Excitement in the air. Rehearsal went well. Everyone was raving about their set list. Even Stephanie, who had sat in again. Louise was enjoying all the youth and kidding around. James was talking away with Alo and Stu about something. Jennifer was chatting with Frank. Karen gave me a big hug and a kiss, flirting as always. Samantha already talking about preliminary discussions about her show at the Gallery. Their little boy, Brandon, was drawing close to Julian who was acting the big brother, showing him around the playroom. Tim and Shelly showed up. The guys in the band were trying not to freak out. They had not met Tim. Melanie had, and she and Shelly were already talking about the band and the name Retro Sky and how Shelly really liked it.

Everyone had their food, digging in. I stood up and got everyone's attention. It became quiet. I made some guidelines for the weekend, going over the time frame for leaving the next day. Sleeping arrangements. Horseback riding and rules around that. Brandon spoke up and said he wanted to go. Karen looked at me

pleading. I nodded my head okay. Then I said that Tim
had brought some scripts for Steph and Mom to look at.
A lot was going to change as show business was calling
once again. Tim stood and took the stage thanking us
for the evening, the weekend for the kids, happy to have
Jennifer back. He challenged Steph to work hard.
Everyone started to eat, and I had to stop them. I had
one more thing.

I met Robbie Robertson from the Band up in Taos at the
conference I attended, and he was going to visit our
house on Wednesday for dinner. Shock filled the room.
I looked around carefully. Everyone knew who I was
talking about. Even Tim was impressed.

Louise said we'd just have to do this all over again and
have a big dinner. I didn't know if Robbie would
appreciate that, but I let it go for now. Then the killer.
Robbie wanted to sit-in on Retro Sky's practice on
Wednesday afternoon. He wanted to hear what they
sounded like.

Julian looked like he was seeing a ghost, hearing from
the land beyond. Melanie started singing "Up on Cripple
Creek." Cheers went up.

I was about to let everyone dive in and eat, celebrate all
the good news.

Julian stood up and it got quiet. He was nervous.

"Look, I don't know if Robbie Robertson would mind, but
I'd love for all of you," he was motioning to the two
couples who had not heard the band play, "to come over
if you can. I'd love for you to be there. It might make us
feel less under the microscope from one of the greats."

"That would be wonderful Sam said. Jennifer, what do you think? All of us in that studio?"

"Shouldn't be a problem."

"Robbie wouldn't care. I mean, I just met him, but he wouldn't care." I added.

"Let's rehearse a Band song before then." Julian was looking at the group.

Melanie spoke up, "What about 'Ophelia'?" I love that one.

Everyone was agreeing. Julian seemed to like it.

The room erupted. Eating, laughing, talking. It was loud and fun. And early. Louise assigned tasks for clean-up. I about choked when she ordered Tim to help a few of the kids clear the table. He laughed and jumped in.

The band group went downstairs to listen to *Northern Lights, Southern Cross*, playing "Ophelia" over and over. Julian was the only with his guitar and he was trying to learn the lead jam, played by Robertson, of course.

I went back upstairs. Karen hugged me again. Asking me about Brandon going up to Taos. She said she'd go with him, Sam might go too, she had to check. No problem, I thought, except Brandon may not be comfortable – or all that welcome – sleeping with the older guys. The girl's tent, maybe? They're huge family size tents. James strolled over and said not to worry about it. He'd make sure Karen and Brandon, Sam too, would have their own family tent.

I quickly found Stephanie, exuberantly looking over the stack of studio-marked scripts. Tim was urging her to read the one with darker cream color paper. He liked that screenwriter the most.

Jennifer grabbed me, yanking me into the bedroom. She kissed me passionately. Not a husband-wife, you doing okay kiss. A want to get laid kiss.

"I'm so happy," she said, "how are you, Danny? So much going on."

"I really wish we could go to bed early. I was up at 3:30. Emotional day. I want to be naked with you. We'll be in tents tomorrow night.   I guess I just want to be with you."

"I'll go out there and socialize. We haven't seen Sam in a long time, and I want to talk with her more about her show.   Karen said she wanted to touch base with me as I pulled you away. Tim's dying to talk with me. Give me an hour or so. The kids will be fine. Mel will sleep with Steph. Julian can handle the guys. You know everyone will stay up way too late. Our biggest problem will be getting everyone going tomorrow. I think James was already headed to bed. You need to get naked. Comfortable. It's secluded back here. Give me an hour."

I went down to my office briefly and made myself a large whiskey and grabbed a cigar from my desk.

I put on my pajamas and a large coat and beanie cap. Grabbed a blanket and found my outdoor couch on the veranda attached on our bedroom. The stars were blazing in the millions. I sat and enjoyed the taste and the cold air. Not uncomfortable at all.   I could see by the layout of our house, that lights were on downstairs. Cars were already starting up. Both cars left. The kids were already in retreat mode to the playroom or watching TV, or both.

I heard Jennifer come into the bedroom. She was in the bathroom.

I put out the cigar and finished off the last swig of whiskey.

She came out with a blanket wrapped around her. I kissed her deeply. Our tongues rediscovering a memory of what was about to happen. She had nothing on under the blanket. I was enjoying her nipples as she unbuttoned my top and did the same with my chest. I grabbed her butt as she slid off my loose bottoms. She grabbed my cock and stroked with a rhythm I found on her clit. Her legs spread. She was wet and inviting. I lay her down on the padded couch. We were naked in the cold air. I entered her hot tightness, wet and engulfing me as I thrust. We fucked for a long time before I knew I was going to cum. She gasped and I hoped no one heard her or me as I let go.

She held on to me for what seemed like an eternity as she came. Her legs powerfully clutching me. I held tight upon her firm tightening ass, feeling her tremble. We giggled. She said she wanted a drink and a cigarette. I had no idea where this cigarette thing was coming from lately, but I knew there was an old pack back in my office drawer. I put on my PJ's and quickly made it back there on reconnaissance. I grabbed the bottle of whiskey and the cigarettes and another cigar.

We bundled up and had our own party on the porch. We stayed up till midnight drinking and smoking. Counting constellations. Absorbing the moonlight. I put the stereo on in our room, tuned to a quiet jazz station.

We talked and talked. One story after another. Both of us excited. About everything.
Once under our covers our blood flowed into each other, molding us into the night.

Stephanie

Melanie and I went with Tim and Shelly to their house. Mom and Dad were locked away in their back room and I was not about to disturb them. Shelly said she'd bring us back. It was walkable, but it was not well lit, and it was pitch black out. I left a note on the refrigerator just in case. Melanie wanted to stick around with the guys and hash out "Ophelia." Instead, when Tim invited her directly, standing right next to me, she didn't hesitate. Tim set up the viewing room, ready to show me plenty of film clips.   Shelly retrieved soda and snacks.
The first was an early screen test of Mom; turns out it was her first. She looked so young. It was hilarious. Mom was so relaxed and funny. Tim said that this is the first time he knew he was sold on Mom's talent. It was her relaxed delivery. And sense of humor. The next two had been spliced together. A handheld camera filming the theater production of *Bob, Carol, Ted and Alice* with Tim and Mom and two actors I didn't know. The laughter from the audience was startling. The sound was not good, yet I could tell that Mom and Tim were delivering very funny material. She looked so professional. Nothing like it was around the house growing up.

"You're dad thought it would be a good idea for you to see these," Tim said.

I figured. Made sense.

Then he showed us a compilation of outtakes, mistakes of Mom's during *Rio Norte* and *Hull House.* The film style was so different in both. The sets, the costumes. The characters. She was intimidating in both films. I had seen them, certainly. Many times. As I watched the outtakes I could tell how serious she took this. She was in character more noticeably in these clips than in the movies themselves. I could see it in her eyes. This was a woman I did not grow up with. If Dad was right, getting me to dig deep into my soul and find Mom inside of me, it scared me. She was that good.

Shelly said, after one of the scenes, "Try it, they're simple lines. Give it a try Steph." It was from *Rio.* A lawyer. Tough as nails. Tim said he'd play Sharon's part. We stood up. Tim had me speak the lines. We went back and forth. Then he had me take a deep breath. I did. Then we started. I tried hard. I tried really hard, but it was terrible. I wanted to cry.

"Steph, I've seen you do this in front of a TV hundreds of times. Have fun with it. Make fun of your mom this time. Exaggerate."

We did it two more times. I was enjoying it. Melanie gave me a thumbs up. By the third try I was feeling it. I was convincing as a fourteen-year-old lawyer.

"That's it. Now one more time and I want you to remember she is angry with Sharon. She's constrained. Restrained. Think for a minute. Have you ever been angry with me?"

"You? No."

"What about your mom?"

"Definitely."

"Okay, this time we're going to pretend I'm your mom. Think of when you were pissed at her."

I thought of 8th grade, when she wouldn't let me go to L.A.

"Let's go again," he said.

This time I was much, much better. Melanie applauded. So did Shelly.

"Not bad. This is what we're going to start working on. Now let's sit down. I really want you to see these."

They were outtakes of Sharon. *Rio*, *Hull House*, about five other movies. One role after another. This went on for about half an hour. It made me terribly nervous. I idolized Sharon and this was painful. I saw a side of her I hated to watch. She was a terror in some of it. She almost seemed psychotic. She'd be in character, sweeping me away, the audience away, killing it, then bam, a mistake. She'd transform. Not like Mom. It was frightening. Whatever the mistake it visibly made Sharon want to take it to another level. A better level. Not to get it 'right,' but to get it perfect. She was a perfectionist. Mom was great. Mom was wonderful. Mom was the highest standard. Sharon was someone, something else. I didn't know what to say when the lights went up.

Shelly came over and sat by me and put her arm around me. She could tell I was shaking. Melanie went to the bathroom. Tim handed me my 7-up and told me to take a drink. Relax.

"Listen, Stephanie," Tim said, "I wanted to show you these even more than your dad wanted me to show you your mom's clips. Your mom is an artist. She's great in her own right. I can't wait to work with her if it all works out. I love working with her more than anyone in my career. You should look to her as an example. Now, I know that Sharon, your *Aunt* Sharon, is your hero. And she should be that to you, but I wanted you to see her artistry. She is on another level. There has never, I mean never, been anyone like her in my lifetime and I don't think in the history of film and theater. She is completely in her own category. I can't touch her. Phil has no idea how to handle her. Your mom is about the only one I know that gets through to her. I've met Vince, and he's a strong, tough street kid. Big. Intimidating in his own way. He is completely lost around her even though they obviously love each other very much."

I was crying. Shelly was holding me tight. Mel came over and held me too.

"You want to be an actress, right?"

I shook my head.

"There are three kinds of actors. The first are the majority. They make a splash. They perform on a range of competence. Maybe make a living and then are gone. The second are successful and may become a legend. They might even be great artists. They may not be. The third are artists and show the rest of us what acting is all about. That's your mom. And then there is Sharon. You will find your way. Don't settle for the first category. It's a waste of your time and you deserve better."

Shelly spoke up. "Tim, I think you may be putting too much pressure on her. She's only fourteen and hasn't even acted once." Then she turned to me, wiped my tears, and continued, "but you need to know the reality as well, Stephanie. I understand you are in drama class, trying out for *Music Man*. When is that?"

"Next Thursday." I blubbered.

"Keep your mom in mind. Look inside and find the librarian inside you, like your mom found a lawyer, and just like she found Jane Addams in every way in her Academy Award."

"I get that. I think I understand." I managed to say.

"Sharon. I never saw that in her. She's been everything to me as far as wanting to act. You don't see what we just witnessed in the movie theater."

"That's because you never, I mean never, see Sharon. She is absolutely and completely the character. You cannot see her." Tim emphasized. "No one can do what she does. Don't get me wrong, but not even your mom, and I say that with complete respect. I am nowhere near your mom's league."

I was staring at Tim for the first time. He was not the famous Tim Prescott. Not The Number One box office draw. He wasn't my next-door neighbor. He wasn't the fun guy I knew as a kid. He was not a famous actor. He was being my director. He was going to help make me transform into an actress.

Melanie and I got home about 11:30. We fell asleep almost immediately.

Breakfast was a major affair. Mom made pancakes by the stacks. Lots of juice. A box of doughnuts. Everyone was fed and ready to go by 10:00.

James had left with Alo and Julian already, heading up to make sure everything was set up. I couldn't believe how much of an early riser Julian could be. The rest of us caravanned in two cars loaded to the hilt. Dad and Stu and Frank in one car. Me and Mom and Mel in the other, stopping briefly to meet up with Karen and Brandon – Samantha was unable to join up - so they could follow us. We talked the whole way about last night. The film clips Tim showed us. Mom asked a lot of questions about how I felt about it. What I learned. I told her that I cried when I watched Sharon. Something about her clips scared me. I didn't think I could be an actress after watching them. I felt good watching her, but Sharon, something else altogether.

Instead of sympathizing or trying to figure out what was bothering me, Mom gave a good hearty laugh.

"Welcome to the world of acting, sweetheart. Sharon is one scary person. Believe me. I remember when we first acted together in *Helen Keller*, Sharon was beyond anything even back then. Our senior year in high school we did a comedy, what was it? … I can't remember. All I remember is that everyone stayed a good distance from her. Especially her boyfriend at the time. His name was Nick. She was out of her mind. She was also incredible. The audience blew up every night. That's who she is. A great artist is not a good description."

"I don't see that. She's sweet Aunt Sharon."

"I know. She loves you. To be honest, I've thought about any possible project we work on, maybe she should stay out of it. I know her. I know how to work with her. I remember Clint Eastwood directed *Rio* and he relied on me in a lot in those scenes. She was in another world. Her own world. And she won an Oscar. Go figure. I don't mean that. I expected it."

"How do you work with her? I mean you?"

"It's tough. She pushed me to be better every time we acted together. You should watch that movie she did with Jackie Gleason. Watch carefully how she pushes every scene with one of the greatest actors in the world. She makes it look easy, huh?"

"I wouldn't say easy. I'd watch the reality of the outtakes and she frightened me. More like realizing that you must become someone else. Like a possession or something not quite human. Schizophrenic."

"That's right. It's losing yourself and becoming yourself at the same time."

Melanie spoke up. "As I watched those clips it reminded me of singing. Nothing like you great actresses. But I get lost in the song, I'm someone else when I sing something, especially when I'm covering someone I really admire."

"Sounds exactly right, Mel." My mom affirmed.

"I've been approaching acting all these years as a kid mimicking people, copying them. It felt safe. Easy. It's not like that, is it?"

"You'd be surprised how many actors are doing that very thing. Almost all of them. Hardly anyone is creating original art. It's too demanding. Too challenging to the soul. Too challenging to your sanity ... It's like when I paint. I know the painting is not very good if I don't feel that same reaction."

"Mom."

"Yeah, Steph. Tell me."

"I want to do what you do. I want to create. To be original. I don't know if I can do what I saw Sharon do."

"No one can. Don't worry about it. Keep looking inside yourself. Once we start reading, I'll help you look in the mirror. That's all Tim was doing. Helping you look in the mirror."

CHAPTER FIVE

There is no place for doubt in someone who serves the goddess Muse. When you, the artist creates, you must become like a magnetized rod that attracts iron filings. The genius is from your Muse. From the Universe. From the Earth itself. From the fragments of matter flying inside your very soul.

Danny

The set up was what I expected, a compound that I was familiar with. There were five Indian friends of James' with fifteen horses in a makeshift corral and all the supplies. And five large tents. Another tent was a mess tent with a firepit. We'd done this before. The kids unloaded their bags and sleeping bags and headed to their assigned tents. One tent for the guys in the band, one tent for me and James, one tent for Karen and Brandon, one tent for the girls, and the largest tent for the helpers. We all ate some tortillas, grabbed a canteen and made sure everyone had on long pants, decent shoes or boots, and a hat. The trail was not difficult, suitable for all the beginners in the group. It was long, however, and might take four hours until we returned. James made Stephanie the team leader. He'd ridden with her multiple times. She took the lead. James and Alo would bring up the rear. He asked one of the helpers to ride in the middle of the pack. The remainder of the helpers would stay back and prepare dinner. A big barbecue was planned. I rode behind Steph so I could talk with her when the trail opened-up for riding abreast. Jennifer was doing the same with Julian. Stu and Frank had never ridden so they were in the rear near James and Alo – who was an experienced rider. Karen was a decent rider and stuck close to her son.

It was a chilly day, in the mid-50's with mountain shade, but the sun was shining bright otherwise. Everyone was dressed appropriately. No one complained.

I had ridden this trail three or four times. It's gorgeous. Fall colors lingered. Pinon pines emitted their fragrance. Landscapes shifted. I rested into my horse and let him do the work. Enjoying every second.

At the turning point, we all dismounted, had a drink and candy bar. We walked along a foot trail. James asked me and Jennifer if he could take Steph and Julian up to the kiva. Just them. We were suspicious but said fine. They were excited to see what he wanted to show them. The three of them disappeared on a different trail.

We waited. The other kids were getting restless after about a half hour. Still no sign.   I decided to take off up the trail and find the three of them.

They were headed down the hill not long after I started climbing.

Steph and Julian looked perplexed. Maybe shaken.

James explained that he had them sit in the kiva and just look up at the sky. I was nervous already. Jennifer and I had done this before and we had asked him to not do this with the kids. It all sounded harmless until Julian explained that he and Steph saw something in the sky. Like planes colliding into towers.   Like skyscrapers or tall buildings.   Two buildings. Exactly alike. It was vivid.

They thought it was real for a moment. Julian repeated that he was sure he saw it. He was not making it up. Steph said the same thing.

I looked at James with anger in my eyes. He told me that he heard birds calling at the same time. He told me it's inherited.

Julian asked what was inherited. Steph was questioning too.

They didn't seem frightened. I sure as hell was.

I hurried us down the hill and told Julian and Steph we'd talk more with Mom. We needed to head back.

I pulled James aside before he mounted his horse and wanted to chew him out. Instead, I asked what happened.

He said that I already knew what happened. He had no idea what the planes meant or the two buildings.

I walked over to Jennifer and asked her to dismount. The caravan headed out without us. I told her what happened. She was pissed off. I told her the vision the kids had, and she shrugged. Disgruntled.

"You know how these things come in bits and pieces. Fuck. We haven't had to deal with this in ages. Did you have a vision or KNOW anything? Did they?" Jennifer asked.

"No, I promise. The kids seemed fine though. They didn't seem frightened. Like they saw a quick something in the sky, vividly, then it was gone."

"Oh, fuck, Danny. Inherited. Here I was thinking about art or sports or music or even golf. Dark hair, brown hair. Brown eyes. Not inheriting this." Jennifer was trying to process all of it.

"Let's let the kids have a good time. We can talk with them later. At home. Or some other time. When you and I can talk some more," I suggested.

Jennifer agreed.

It was a fun night. The food was amazing. Roasted ribs and hamburgers. Plenty of fruit and baked beans and dessert of homemade apple pies. The kids made toasted marshmallows. I sat with Karen and Brandon the whole time. Being the little boy's friend. He felt out of place with the big kids. He was having fun though. Karen was sad Sam couldn't make it. I didn't ask. Something about an art gathering in Albuquerque. I asked her if everything was all right. She said yes, but I didn't believe her. She held my hand for a second. Not her usual flirting or coming on to me. Like I was her friend. Jennifer came over and helped her get Brandon settle in his sleeping bag. He was exhausted. The three of us found a picnic table and James broke out some wine just for us four adults. The kids were chatting away at the bonfire.

Karen told us that she and Sam were fighting more often. Brandon knew something was wrong. Karen honestly did not know what it was, but they were drifting apart. No affairs that she knew of. Money wasn't the issue. Samantha was tired, is all that she would say when she would get home, usually late from one meeting or another. Karen was the one working all the time but did most of the cooking and getting Brandon off to school. Jennifer was blunt. And asked her again about an affair. Was Karen having an affair? No, she insisted. What about Sam? She cried. Maybe. I don't know. James slid over and hugged her. It's like he knew that Samantha was having an affair. James knew the art world better than Jennifer, better than anyone. He knew the gossip. We all retreated to our tents, under a blazing glittering night sky. There was a sliver of a moon hanging above us all. It's like I saw Sharon sitting there, on top of the Universe, leaning down upon us. I had no idea about that either. It was like Sharon was about to descend upon our world. I shook my head in wonder. Something about this mountain. It always happens this way.

One of the great experiences in life is sunrise in the mountains at campsite. The dew and mist and cold. The rising moisture of frost. A range of colors emerging with light. It changes by the minute. I was up early and helped with starting the fire. I felt at peace with what happened with the kids in the kiva. Not sure why I felt that way. It was inevitable I guessed.

Alo was the first up. He drank some coffee with me instead of juice or cocoa. He was used to this setting. Even helpful with breakfast preparation. Quiet kid. Julian was next, another early riser. He found a bench by the fire and stared into the flame. He had a lot going on in his head. Breakfast was a simple affair of oatmeal and slices of fruit. The oatmeal was excellent, flavored with cinnamon.

One last activity, a one-mile hike over to the lake. We made it over in about twenty minutes. Circling the water, seeing fish jumping. It was glistening by mid-morning. A blue heron was perched on a log by the feeding stream. Jennifer got a kick out of it most of all, mostly because Brandon was so excited to see the large bird.   Jennifer was sticking close to Karen, talking, putting her arm around her.

We were on the road in no time, returning everyone to their homes in good order. I got Alo home last, way out to a southern pueblo. His uncle lived in a shack, of sorts. Run down. There was that clunky stereo Alo spoke about. Hundreds of albums and 45's from the 1950's. A Korean war picture and several medals and insignia. The make-shift drum set, worn and well used. Probably by both uncle and adopted son.

I got home exhausted. I had not slept all that well. Jennifer was asleep on the couch in the den. The kids were in their rooms.

Louise had left me a message that Jimmie my old high school friend had called from his home in northern California. I hadn't spoken to him in almost a year. My dad and I made hundreds of thousands of dollars on his tech stocks in Silicon Valley. Jimmie was a mover and shaker, if not a bit eccentric. He was like a brother, literally.

I went to my office and gave him a call. He was all wired and excited, like he always was. We talked about our families, how we were doing. He wanted to bring his wife to Santa Fe for a quick weekend, get away from the kids. Could we meet up? Two weeks from now. I offered for them to stay at our place. He was already booked into a bed and breakfast that Jennifer and I loved. We'd have dinner. I looked forward to it. Something was up. There always was with him.

I gave a call over to the Eagle's Nest Dinner Playhouse, where Jennifer got her acting start. I knew I'd get a recording. It listed show times on the recording. It also listed upcoming plays for the season. I was curious. Sure enough. *Sound of Music*. In mid-March. I had a feeling. Lots of kids' roles. Stephanie as the elder girl. I could see it. I'd mention it later. I wanted to see how her try-outs at the high school went this coming Thursday. She was only a freshman. My mind was racing to previous plays at our school Who were the girls who had performed previously, over the past two or three years? I was drawing a blank as to who would be Steph's competition.

I listened to the other phone messages on the answering machine. Sharon. My heart skipped a beat. Her voice was that way. Assertive and strong, yet full of love. She and Vinny were in town. Now. Just arrived. They were in the President's suite at the Governor's Inn. We had stayed there plenty of times. Nice, but she didn't need to do that. They could stay here at our house. She was probably showing Vinny around town, doing their thing. They had a ten-year-old, Scott, where they lived in Chicago for most of the year. Sounds like they didn't bring him along.

I called the front desk. They were not in their room, so I left a message. They'd want to be in on this Robbie Robertson thing on Wednesday. I was nervous, so many people over for dinner. I thought Robbie was just going to get a quiet family night. He'd meet Tim and Sharon and everyone, not to mention my wife Jennifer at her studio. A party. I wondered if I should forewarn him. No need. I'd fill him in at the Gallery when he arrived.

To top it off, I had a huge week at school. I was grateful for a fabulous staff. We were a well-oiled machine. Good people, working hard. The kids were great. We had our usual behavior problems, family issues. Nothing out of the ordinary. Our sector of poverty lingering in an ever more expansive and expensive city, which was the main problem.

Jennifer woke up as I was about to lie down. We dressed for outside and headed down to speak with James. How to deal with the kiva thing. I filled her in on Jimmie and Sharon being in town.

James was expecting us. We thanked him for all his efforts for making the camping trip such a huge success for the kids. He was concerned for Karen and Brandon. The situation was heavy on his heart. Ours too, I assured him.

He went first. Leave it be. Let the kids mull it over in their own way. They may talk about it, between themselves. They may have another vision, but he promised to not attempt any more initiation. He showed them the kiva because he felt he should. That was all. He didn't apologize, he wanted us to understand as parents that we had a responsibility. Like having a child with special needs, these kids had special needs. We needed to be alert. He was lecturing us. Jennifer took it in stride. I was feeling resistant. The truth was that he was right about it all.

As far as the vision itself. He had no idea as to the meaning. It would be made clear as time decided.

Then he brought up Robbie Robertson and Wednesday. He said it would be a special day. He wanted to witness it. Robbie was carrying special gifts. All the mysticism in the world that James had brought to our lives was in this visit, he said. It was time, he kept saying. Julian's time. I told him about Sharon being in town, just as I had told Jennifer on our walk. He seemed like he already knew. Stephanie's time. He said it over and over.

Then a knock on his door. I got up and answered it for him. It was Julian standing there. I was startled, as was he. I let him in.

"Uh, James, Steph has been telling me you wanted to talk with me. We didn't get a chance in the car or up camping. I thought I'd come down." James and Julian looked at me and Jennifer. We were not welcome. I smiled and we thanked James again for a wonderful weekend. He got up and hugged us. Then he went to his stove to fix Julian some cocoa.

We didn't have our usual big Sunday dinner. It was a quiet night. Louise had made some homemade chicken soup. We helped ourselves and ate where we wanted to. Jennifer and I ate alone on the veranda, watching the sun go down. Bundled up with our mugs. The kids were doing homework. Later I could hear Julian strumming away on "Ophelia" well into our dreams.

Jennifer

I was a bit of a commander on Monday. I had an impromptu meeting with the staff at 10:00. Everyone agreed to come in. It was unusual. I wanted to know how things were going with Samantha and her show. Turns out Samantha was in Albuquerque and hadn't come by the Gallery to help with her own exhibit. She was only returning calls sporadically. I was going to call her. Matthew was not due to give us a presentation on Frank's work, the *Kid* book and art, until next week. I had him give it a try anyway. He was impressed with the drawings. His initial reaction was to set up a small display, even a show.   He liked two of Julian's drawings as well. He recommended that the book be especially highlighted as a new medium. The various pages could be shown separately without compromising the book itself. Probably a twenty-page art show. Everyone liked it as they looked at the photocopies. I gave the green light. Buy a spread of advertisement for next month. We can about talk other promotions later. I'd tell Frankie. I let everyone know about Robbie Robertson arriving on Wednesday afternoon. They were accustomed to celebrities from all walks of fame visiting and were not sure why I was making a big deal of this one.   I told them about Julian's band, now called Retro Sky, performing in their little studio for him. There may be a bit of a crowd. Sharon, most likely, among them. That brought some murmuring. I finished by telling them that my Paris show was good to go. I would finish my final painting today. We could begin shipment to France in two weeks. Most of the paintings had already been shipped. Just this one, and one other I held back. They already knew the proper packaging and coordination with the people in Paris. The show would open on Friday December 15. I would need to get there at least three days earlier. Make arrangements for my flight and a hotel near the Musee de Orsay where it was taking place. I wanted first class. This was a priority this time. Even for me. Especially for me. Plan for my family to arrive on Thursday. Go ahead and make those first class, too. Let's splurge. I knew that the Museum was footing the bill on some of this. Wasn't sure how much. Didn't matter. The schedule would be a strain on Danny's duties as principal, but he was good with those dates. Arrange a flight home out of Rome after the new year. I'd make the hotel arrangements while we're there. Don't worry about Rome accommodations, but buy Eurail passes for the family, one way to Rome on Monday the 18th. We'd be at the opening weekend in Paris then head out. We had family plans in Italy. Everyone in the meeting looked around and knew their assignments. I thanked them. They were familiar with my style of management and were ready to go. They were incredibly reliable.

I got a hold of Samantha at their home here in Santa Fe. She was sheepish about the weekend, thanking me for all we did for Brandon and Karen. I bluntly asked her what was up. Would she please come over to the Gallery? Today. She reluctantly said yes and apologized. She'd be there in an hour, she promised.

I called the Governor's Inn. Left a message for Sharon. Just as I did, I could see through my glass window in my office that she was walking through our main entrance with Vinny at that very minute. She was stunning. Vinny was a tall, gregarious guy, saying *hi* to the staff. Looking up at my self-portrait. Sharon providing the background.

I got up and we hugged and loved each other up. I brought them into our conference room and filled them in that I might have an important visitor soon. All about Robbie Robertson on Wednesday and Julian and Retro Sky. About the many talks about acting with Steph. Vinny was smiling and having fun with all the news. We got caught up on their lives in Chicago. Vinny's shows in Miami were a big success. Sharon wanted to extend their stay through the week. Be in on it all. Spend time with Tim and Shelly. See how Steph did with try-outs. Vinny was fine with it. His mom was watching their son, Scotty.

I offered again to have them stay at our place. She thanked me and said again that they were going to stay with Tim. We'd catch up.

Sam walked in. Sharon and Sam had met several times and they hugged. We introduced Vinny. They were off to the O'Keefe Museum. Vinny was excited, he had

never been to New Mexico. He hardly knew who
Georgia was. That would have to wait for another time.
I went back into the office and handed them guest
passes to the O'Keefe before they left.

Sam collapsed in the chair across from my desk. I could
tell she was about to break down. I kept it business at
first. She complied, was appreciative of the show. She
would go in and make it right and do whatever needed
to happen with my staff. She promised. I loved her
work; we just needed her input. She understood and
apologized again.

Then I came around and hugged her and told her that
Karen was having a tough time. It was good to be with
her in the mountains. Brandon loved the horseback
riding, seeing the blue heron, the cook-out. He had a
blast.

"I know. He told me all about it. I'm so sorry I wasn't
there with him."

"What's going on, Sam. I'm worried about you."

"We may have broken up last night. I got back from
Albuquerque and Karen confronted me. I've been
seeing another woman for nearly a year. An artist down
there."

"Oh, I'm so sorry. Jesus, Sam, this is so tough."

She was holding back tears. "Damn. I love Karen. Really,
it's just a physical thing with this woman. We will never
be a couple. She doesn't want that. I don't think I do.
We have sex a lot. It's nice. I enjoy it. I got carried
away."

"Wow, is that how you told Karen?"

"Yes. It's all about the sex. Nothing else. No love, really."

"Did she say anything?"

"All she said was 'Get out.'"

"That hurts. She's hurting. You know that."

"No doubt. Of course."

"Well, do you want Karen back. I mean do you love her still?"

"Yes, like I said, I love Karen. I don't know, we've been together so long. Look what happened with you and Danny. Years ago. We both have messed around. A lot. Always together, though. This was different. Still about sex."

"It wasn't just sex with us, Sam. You know that. Karen knows that. Danny knows that."

"Oh, I know. God, I know. I'd run away with you in a minute, Jennifer."

We both smiled.

"Karen would run away with your husband even quicker."

We smiled again

"And what you did that day, over at Shelly's house, was the best thing for our marriage," Sam went on, "you put a stop to it."

"Had to."

We hugged.

"What do I do, Jennifer?" I was going to offer her a place to stay, and she stopped me.

"I'm going to get a hotel room. I need to do that. I'll try and work it out with Karen."

"I'm glad to hear that. I think Karen will come around. It will take time, if that's what you both want."

"It's what I want."

We sat quietly.

"Can I come Wednesday for the band thing. With Robbie Robertson?" She was laughing now through her tears. "I'm a big fan. To dinner, too?"

"Sure, of course. And if you get lonely in your hotel, the guest bedroom is yours. Sharon is staying at Tim's."

"Really? You think Danny would be okay with that?"

"Absolutely. Come on, get your stuff and I'll get you situated. Fuck staying in a hotel room. That's the last thing you need. I have a lot of work today, but I can get you over to your room this morning. You go in and talk with Sally, then we'll head over to my house."

We made a quick trip. I filled-in Louise that we had a guest. Louise was more and more like grandma, maid, honorary wise one, cook, everything wrapped into one. She could easily live in her own house. She was happy here. She had privacy. She liked being useful. She loved the hustle and bustle of the kids. Kids she never had. The kids loved her. Worshipped her.

Then I went into my studio and stared at my final painting for one last time. I had been thinking about Frankie's comments about character and a message. I knew exactly what I had to do. I needed to add another layer of texture. I used various objects and pasted them in carefully. Broken seashells mostly. I blended them in. I used fresh oil. I wanted the emotion to come from a vast ocean. I layered in the suggestiveness. New color blending into my humanity. Vulnerable. I was making

the message very much about vulnerability. I hoped
they saw it. It was what I felt. Deeply.

By the end of the day, I knew I was finished. I never,
ever asked for immediate feedback, if any feedback at
all, but I got the excuse to bring in Sally and hear how
things went with Sam. I let her into my studio, which I
never did with the staff.

She stood there, trying to respect my space, hardly
looking at the enormous canvas. She filled me on Sam,
all was well. She thanked me for 'wrestling her in.' The
show would be a great success for Samantha, and for us.
I turned and gazed at my work. The paint still wet. The
light perfect. Sally, who is also a very good artist in
acrylics, about half my age, dared to look. She tilted her
head and took in the entire thing.

"What do you think?" I wanted to hear but was hesitant.
She moved forward slightly and looked closer.

"Go ahead. Take a look."

She moved very close, examining it like a true curator. A
true artist. I could tell. It's why I hired her.

Then she came over and hugged me. That startled me.
"I get it. It's so different for you. It's so different from
the other pieces you already sent over. It will stand out,
you know. Your show will be controversial as it is. This is
unique. I don't know if I can say *love it* because it's a
message piece, more than even the others. It's moving.
It's - this sounds like a bad word - it's *merciless*. As the
viewer takes it in they have no other choice but to listen
to you screaming, to feel your pain."

She hugged me all over. "I never, pardon me for saying
this Jennifer, imagined you feeling such pain."

I hugged her back. I was crying. Again.

Then it dawned me. This painting was all my visions all my KNOWING wrapped into a psychological, spiritual release. Accumulated release. It was healing. At attempt at healing.

"One more thing," Sally looked nervous to talk. I encouraged her.

"You are my boss. You have given me an opportunity of a lifetime. You are also my role model. I have studied your work. I have had the honor to see so much of your genius up close and personal. You are always kind and caring. You can be a tough boss; you know what you need have done around here. You are letting me see this today, to be in here is an honor. I just want to thank you. On a personal level, I mean."

I realized how aloof I am as an artist. It must be that way for me. I know that. This tiny crack, this breaking through, meant a lot to me. I thanked her and hugged her and didn't let go. I was thinking of Georgia. How I missed her. Maybe Sally was being sent to me by Georgia. I'd think about that.

"Say, Sally, how is your artwork going? I've haven't seen anything in a very long time. Maybe since you were hired."

She pulled back. "Can I show you something?"

"Absolutely."

"Okay, I'll bring in a piece I just finished last week. Tomorrow?"

"Yes, please."

Julian

Every fiber in my being was getting ready for Wednesday. We rehearsed every second we could find on Monday and Tuesday. We decided to play "Ophelia" first. I had Robertson's lead guitar nailed. Nice riffs. I loved playing it over and over. Levon Helm's vocals were a change of pace for me. That hillbilly, mountain sound. I struggled. I worked and worked on it. I recorded it and listened to myself. We arranged Mel's backing. She and Frankie were becoming synchronized on their acoustics. Stu made the Rick Danko part easy enough. I wished we could use an organ. I wanted the lead guitar for Robertson, though.

Then we'd follow with "Beyond Belief." We had that down pat. No problems.

Mel wanted to do the Everly Brothers. I liked that. We sounded good. All the acoustics. If we needed to play more, we'd do "Here Comes the Sun," while we had the acoustics tuned up. Mel on lead vocal. I hoped he stuck around for it. I had no idea. Honestly, we had fifteen good songs ready to go. We could do the Pretenders. We had several 50's songs, Jerry Lee Lewis and Chuck Berry. Our other Beatles stuff. I could do Dylan. Lots of Dylan. Same with Elvis Costello. I wasn't worried about running out of material.

Dad let us get out of school about an hour early. He and Mom would greet him at the Gallery entrance. We'd go around back and set-up, get things ready. Sharon and Vinny, Louise, James, Tim and Shelly, probably Karen and Sam. Steph. We barely had enough room. It was a big deal for us. What a group. Add in

Mom and Dad and Robertson himself. I prepared a specific seat for Robbie. I even put a reserved sign on it. Overkill, I knew.

Everyone was trickling in through the Gallery side door. No one came in through our outdoor side entrance except Stephanie. Lots was going on inside the Gallery. Introductions. I could hear Vinny, he could be loud, laughing with Robertson. Damn, my heart was racing. Then Robbie Robertson came in. He was shorter than I imagined. Famous people always were. Except Vinny, he was taller. Sharon hugged me. Mom and Dad hugged me. Tim was in the back talking with Steph already. James and Robbie seemed to know each other. Robbie, he told me to call him by his first name, as we shook hands. He introduced himself to the others in the band. Everyone settled in and found a seat. Sam and Karen, along with Brandon, snuck in at the last moment and sat on the floor. Robbie laughed at the sign on his seat. It was quiet. Ready to go.

I counted off and we went into "Ophelia." Robbie grinned from ear to ear. It's a long song and Robertson's foot was pacing the beat the entire time. Alo and Stu had it down. My voice was smooth. I went into the guitar jam and played it understated like he did. Nice and easy. He looked impressed. Melanie was raising her backup, we finished strong. Everyone cheered. Robbie stood up and shook my hand. He was pleased.

"What else you got?" he asked me.

"We have a lot. Whatever time you have. We're ready to play."

"Go for it." He said.

I switched over to bass. Stu grabbed an acoustic. We did a quick sound check. Then Alo and I did this thing we worked out and bang, right into Elvis Costello. Fast. Robertson looked stunned. I was sweating and it dripped down my nose, rattling off the lyrics, pounding the bass, Alo driving me.   Mel on keyboards doing the reverb. There was incredible energy coming from the amps. We were done.

"Oh Jesus, that was great," Robbie said. "Keep going." We went back-to-back with Everly Brothers and Harrison acoustic vocals. Melanie stole the show. She was really finding her groove and I was staying up with her. She was that good.

Everyone was clapping hard.

Robbie kept saying how good we were. He was 'honestly, very surprised.' "One more, then I have an idea," he said.

I had no idea how much time we were taking. It didn't seem to matter.

I decided on "Isis." Kind of risky, it's so long. I moved over to the keyboard. We all chatted a bit in the band. Made sure everyone was on the same page. I put on my Bob Dylan, hesitated because I knew Robbie had played with Bob for years. Probably this very song.   And I let it rip. Syncopation, lyric, vocal chord changes. Power. It was all me, really. Alo pacing a driving drumbeat. Mel's back up and acoustic helped carry me through. It was all story, all lyrics. I banged away. My voice bent and tortured like Dylan's. I felt it. My eyes were closed for most of it.

I wrapped it up with a fury. It was dead silent. Then applause. Robbie stood up and put his hand on my back. "That's something Julian. I mean it."

"Look," he continued, "Can I use your Fender here?" I nodded. He tuned it some more, adjusting the amps, turning to the band. He showed us chord changes. We took it in. He told me to stay on keyboard. He adjusted the settings, giving it a full organ sound. He started to strum slowly the progression. I recognized it as "Shape I'm In." Then he started in slowly, still turned, facing us. He was checking each of us, going over each part. We did this for about ten minutes, he was humming the lyric, speaking them once in a while.

Then he turned to everyone listening. "Let's give it a try."

He counted off and nodded his head to Alo. The drums led in with Stu on bass. I climbed in with the swirling organ sound I remembered from the song. Robbie took the lead, he made my guitar sing, just like he was singing. *You don't know the state I'm in* ... Melanie took over completely on back up vocal. Robbie looked over at her and smiled. They found the connection. He nodded and the two of them started singing together. It was fun to hear. Then he lifted his hand and was counting down as we went softer. We were finished.

His smile was enormous. Sweat pouring down his forehead. It was hot in there.

Robbie went over and hugged Mel. He shook our hands. "That was fun," he said to everyone.

Mom came over, looking like she was in shock. She shook my hand instead of hugging me. So did Dad. So did everyone.

We all headed to our house for dinner. Robbie didn't seem to notice the small crowd that gathered to go eat. Steph gave me a big kiss on the cheek before I got in the car.

Everyone was hustling to put together our Mexican feast, usually for Sunday nights. Even Robbie was following Louise's orders, helping with setting the table. Stories abounded. Sharon, Vinny, Tim, one after another. Even Sam and Karen chimed in. All hilarious stuff. Liquor started to flow with the adults. Sharon was smoking in our house, which mom abhorred, but then so was Vinny. Robbie lit up. James had his pipe. A full-blown party. Immediately after our lengthy meal, toasts were made, clean-up, dessert. Mom and Dad motioned for me to head to Dad's office. Melanie was in tow, as was Robbie. We all found a chair and Dad shut the door.

"Robbie and I need to talk about some things about our conference, but I wanted to thank him for everything."

"Pleasure is mine. Thank you. It's been great fun." He turned to Mom, "And thank you again Jennifer for the tour. I'll get in touch as far as the painting I bought. Shipment."

She thanked him again.

I got the hint. I thanked Robbie again for his time, for teaching us a song. I told him how much I love his music.

"You nailed 'Isis,' by the way." He added. "I'd encourage you to find some gigs. Get out there. Play in front of people. You are more than ready. Here's a number of my friend. His name in Al, from New Orleans. He can help you when you are old enough and ready to leave Santa Fe." He handed me a torn piece of paper with the number. It had his name and number on it too. That caught my eye especially.

"And you, Melanie, I wanted to tell you how special your voice is. I loved singing with you. You two make a good match. Do you write? Your own music, I mean?" Melanie answered, "We try. Julian comes up with melodies, riffs. I have tons of poetry. We try."

"Keep it up. You guys, Retro Sky is it? You're good. Still garage band rough. All you need is more time. Nice cover sound. You already have the knack. You will want to expand into your own songs. Stay with it."

We shook his hand and left the office. I spotted Karen and Sam way over in our alcove with Brandon working on a long-forgotten jigsaw puzzle. Mel and I headed down to my bedroom as the impromptu party raged upstairs.

She fell on my bed, and I shut the door and locked it. We started to make out. Laughing how great everything went. We were so happy. I had her bra undone, enjoying every second, every inch of her fullness. Then the touch of her pussy. A sensation I never experienced before. The unzipping. The hand sliding under her panties. The pubic hair. The wetness. The electric impulse. She undid my pants and I gasped. She had me in her hand, sliding up and down. Fast. I had an orgasm almost immediately. She held on to me as my middle finger found her opening. Her hips rocked slightly. Her thighs grasping on to me. Her mouth was pressed against my ear, wet and panting for breath. I don't know what happened exactly, but I thought she probably had an orgasm too.

We put our clothes back on and stretched out on the bed. We kissed. We smiled. We held hands. I noticed her rubbing my knuckles. We fell asleep.

There was a knock on my door. I panicked for a minute. It was almost midnight. I got up and opened the door. It was Mom. She said she'd take Mel home. Everyone had cleared out. She relayed that James said something about wanting to talk with me sometime this week when I could.   I kissed Melanie on the cheek and fell back asleep.

Stephanie

The day of tryouts. Mom and I had been over the lines for days prior. Even Sharon quickly read them over with me. Sharon dressed me. Frumpy dress, glasses. She helped me sing the lines. Tim was there with Shelly.   I was getting help every which way.   My dad drove me to school early. I asked him if Karen had spent the night. Seemed I heard her talking with Mom before we left. She was having personal problems with Karen and might be at our house for a few days, maybe longer. I hoped that whatever it was, worked out because they both were like family to me. When we arrived at his office, he had me sit in the time out room where kids go that get in trouble. Don't worry about the lines, he reminded me.

Don't worry about anything. Be the librarian. He shut the door. I sat there quietly reciting my lines for the umpteenth time until the bell rang.   I had a hall pass out of my first period. I was scheduled to try out in the Senior Hall English room first thing.

I walked in. I did not know any of the three teachers. My freshman drama teacher was not involved with the play production. They introduced themselves. They had a large camera on a tripod to film me.   One of them, a man, I think the lead teacher, said he was glad I chose the option of wearing a costume.   Did I need my lines, the text? No. There was nothing other than a soliloquy and a song and I had them memorized.

I went behind the curtain as they instructed and then entered. I felt my presence as Marion. Not as a 14 years old. Not Stephanie. I was a mid-twenty-something in Gary, Indiana. I delivered the lines, no, they were not lines, they were the stirrings of my heart. I sang them. I started softly. The tones came easily. My confidence rose. Not my confidence, Marion's. Emotion spilled out, raw energy. I was done.

All three applauded.   The man in charge, Mr. Willow, I think, told me I just set a very high bar for everyone else. One of the ladies asked me who my mom was. She asked the question in a vague fashion.   I replied that she was a painter. An artist. I did not say her name.   No one responded.   I could go change my clothes over in the bathroom. They wrote me a pass. I would know the results first thing in the morning.

"You did very well," one of them said as I left the room.

I ran to the bathroom knowing I did the best I could ever hope for. Exactly like it. Even better. I tore off the librarian garb and got into my jeans and tee-shirt. I looked at the mirror and said *way to go*. I wanted to doubt myself, think I didn't do well. But I knew that I had. I was smiling all day.

Mom picked me up from school, wanting to know how it went. I told her I was great. She went on and on that when she first tried out for a role she thought she had bombed. I asked her if it was wrong for me to feel confident. *Not at all* she affirmed. It's just that I was way ahead of where she was way back then. She knew I had done well.

Julian had gone down to the cottage to talk with James. When we got home, I wandered down there, too. I was curious. When I got there, I spied in the window, and they were on his big leather chairs drinking cocoa. Smoking his pipe. Laughing. I decided to let it go. I wandered over to my rock. The stream was layered with thin ice in the shade. I sat and stared at the water flowing silently underneath. It was how I felt. Flowing life underneath my chilly exterior. I sat there a very long time. The sun was going down. I saw Julian walk back up to our house. He didn't see me alone in the trees. Julian was well on his way, I knew. It's like I KNEW it as a fact. Not a hope or wish for my brother. Retro Sky would be playing soon.

Instead of going home, I made the trek over to Tim's to let everyone know how I did. To thank them. Sharon hugged me. And hugged me again. She was pouring on the love. Once I found out tomorrow how it went, call them. Use Dad's phone. Good or bad. Call. Come right over after school Tim insisted. We will talk.

During third period science class, I was sent to the office. My heart raced. Here it was. I was directed by the secretary to a conference room. The three teachers were sitting around a table with about six other kids. The kids were all much older. They looked like seniors to me.

Mr. Willow, that was indeed his name, congratulated all of us. We had been selected for the fall performance of *Music Man*. I wanted to scream. We looked around at each other and smiled. All the others who had tried-out had been called down already and were told that they had not been selected. Rehearsal began next week. They would last until 7:00 pm. We went around the table and introduced ourselves and the grade we were in. Five seniors, one junior. And me. A freshman in one of the leads. We talked casually for about ten minutes then he had us talk about our character, the play, anything about *Music Man* that we wanted to say. We each took turns. Everyone stumbled at first.   As we got going we liked our character. The boy playing Harold Hill, his name was Gary, was thoughtful looking and had been in several plays already.   He looked directly at me and said he could easily fall in love me, flirt with me, like in the story. Everyone laughed, me included.   He was cute. Smart looking with his glasses and haircut. He had an athletic build. Once the laughter settled, I realized that I was the only one that had not said anything. I looked back at him and said something like *you realize that I don't like you at all*. He quickly retorted*, not yet anyway*. Straight out of the play.

I ran to Dad's office. He was not in. I asked his secretary if I could use the phone. Shelly answered on the first ring. I got the part. I could hear Sharon scream in the background. Tim got on quickly and congratulated me. I then hung up and called Mom. Her direct line in her studio. I got the part. She started crying. She was always crying when she is happy. I hung up and called James. Same thing. He was very happy for me. Then home to Louise. Same thing. I waited for Dad at his circular conference table. He was late from his last meeting. Cheryl would tell him. I better get to class. We had a big 'pow-wow' at Tim's house that night. Sharon was on a roll. Mom laughing, watching Sharon in all her exuberance. Dad sat quietly over by Shelly. Vinny and Tim were playing pool, eavesdropping. Julian and I were snacking on food. Listening. First the 'brain trust' was going to plot out my future. Step one. I had the part at the high school. Do my best. Shine bright on stage come November. Step two. Keep working on the scripts. Read, practice. Get help with Tim, Mom, Sharon, Dad, anyone. Everyone. Keep working on the scripts. Step Three. Dad spoke up. What about Eagle's Nest? *Sound of Music* in the spring. Try-out for one of the girl parts. Everyone loved the idea. I hadn't heard that one. My mind started thinking about *The Sound of Music*. Step Four. Mom had an idea. She said to listen carefully, it will take some time. Tim and Vinny put down their pool cues. She had an idea for a script, a rough written outline. Working title, *Purgatory*. She wanted Vinny to work with her on writing the final versions. Even though he's a comedian, he writes extensively and well. He also has a good grasp of history. Vinny took a bow. Picture Fellini. Black and white. Post WWI, northern France. Maybe Lorraine. Washed out lens. Silver toned cinematography. Sharon plays a single mom, turned prostitute to survive the extreme devastation of the region. Men are gone, dead, or severely wounded almost everywhere. Burned out buildings. Poverty. She has a daughter, Steph's age. Destitute. Should the daughter become a prostitute for survival? She'd bring in good money at her age. Steph fights with her mother. In comes the nun who runs the local orphanage. Hundreds of kids starving. Jennifer plays the nun. She takes Steph under her wing, to join the order. Help at the orphanage. Steph is drawn to the nun, to the kids at the orphanage. She does not want to become a nun, however. Conflict arises between nun and mom. Battle over the well-being and soul of the daughter. A low-level circus and traveling entertainment troop comes to town. Puts up tents for what will be about ten days. Steph hangs out with performers, meets the organizer and leader. He's an older, cantankerous man, worldly wise. He takes to Steph and wants her to train on the trapeze, make her a performer and star. Steph fights it out with her mom and the nun. When the circus leaves, so does the daughter. She's gone, emancipated from both mom and nun. Good and evil.

I love it. Absolutely love it.

Tim speaks up. We wouldn't have to use too much dialogue. Steph would be acting by way of survival and body language. Most of the hard dialogue is with Sharon and Jennifer.

Sharon goes over and kisses Mom on the lips. She lights a cigarette. "I'm in," is all she says.

Vinny said the story writes itself. Jennifer should have co-writing credits. He's sure he can put it together. We could sell it to Phil, the studio, by March. Take it to various producers about the same time. Tim could do a scouting tour of northern France with Shelly and a small crew. Head out after Jennifer's show in Paris. Shelly said she'd love to travel to northern France in the winter. Julian put his arm around me as we sat on the couch. He put his head on my shoulder. "Sounds great, Sis."

Applause. More drinks. Mom lights a cigarette, realizing that we've never seen her smoke. Julian and I just shrug. No worries. Mom feigns guilt and takes a drag and a swig of her whisky. Sharon is way ahead of her. They are definitely in their own world together.

Phase Two. Brother Julian. Mom takes over. That was incredible with Robbie Robertson here. Like a huge greenlight for Julian. For Retro Sky. Step One. Get the band set up at Jimmy's Bar. Play there for as long as it works out. "I'll take lead getting them lined up," Mom says. "Wait." Shelly interrupts. "Can I take on the manager role until we go to France? All of you have work. Sharon and Vinny will leave in two days. Tim is on the road. Jennifer you got tons going on. I can make calls, run interference, do promotions." Mom said absolutely. It was a great idea. Julian liked that too.

Removed from Mom. Seemed more professional.
Onward with Step One. Shelly takes the lead. Step Two.
Shelly can do this, too. Get photos. Get a demo going,
too. High quality. Find studios that will listen to it.
Maybe on the West Coast. Decide on the right sound.
Step Three. Have Julian and Mel write some songs.
Include some original material. Live and on the demo.
Step Four. Mom was going to make these calls, but
maybe it's best if Shelly does, she thought. Call Francine
at Jimmy's. Set up a try-out. Get some dates lined up.
Then call Sarah Johnson at *Today in Santa Fe*. Get them
on the air. She will love it.
Anything else?
Dad spoke up. "I haven't told Jennifer yet, so forgive
me." It was quiet. "I got a call from Bishop Sheehan
right at the end of the day. I know we haven't finalized
any plans for Rome and driving over to Abruzzi, but the
Vatican will be sending us a formal invitation to attend
mass in St. Peter's on Christmas day, extending a
pontifical greeting the following day. Of course, I will
miss Christmas mass with the outreach I am doing here
in Santa Fe and in this region, but Bishop Sheehan was
happy to cover. It seems the Vatican is *smiling* upon our
efforts. Vinny spoke up, congratulating Dad, yet asking
him about being a lapsed Catholic. And what about
Sharon and Jennifer and the three kids. None of them
are baptized. Dad said to not worry about that. The
Vatican is aware.
Mom went over and hugged Dad. She was proud of him
obviously.
The Pope, I thought. I was stunned. Everyone was.

Sharon clicked glasses with Shelly and Tim. "Here's to a prostitute in northern France, meeting the Pope in Rome!"

CHAPTER SIX

The great Mark Twain was talking to Karen about Samantha. His only advice to her was, "Don't allow someone to be your priority while allowing yourself to be their option." Certainly, Karen heard it in a dream.

Jennifer

Karen arrived in my office early. She had gotten
Brandon to school   I had spoken to Samantha at coffee
this morning, letting her know that Karen wanted to see
me.   Sam filled me in that the reconciliation was not
going well. Karen did not want counseling and was not
believing Sam that things were over with the other
woman. She was sounding more and more like divorce
was ahead. I asked Sam flat out if things were over with
the woman in Albuquerque. She had not seen her, but
they had spoken on the phone. That was it. Or so she
said. I believed her.
I offered Karen coffee and a bagel. She needed to eat.
She was losing weight, not in a good way. Karen was
looking for a friend to help her clarify what to do.   I
urged counseling. She was stridently opposed. I asked
her what it took from Sam to convince her that the affair
was dead.   She said it might not matter. She may never
believe her. Then I got to brass tacks.
"How many times did you and Sam fool around. During
your marriage, and before that. Like with me and Danny.
How much sex did you have with others?"
"Too many times. I agree.   I'm equally to blame in
setting this up."
"Did you ever. This is between you and me. Did you
ever sleep with someone else?"
She hesitated. "I know I told you no to that question.
Most of our excursions were together. But yes, I did."
"When was the last time?"

She bowed her head in shame. "Three years ago. I slept with a guy. His wife, too. A threesome. It was a big real estate deal. We were celebrating and it got out of hand."

"More than once? More than the celebration?"

"Two more times."

"Has Sam slept with anyone else you know of?"

"I know she has. We were messing around with a couple, two women, about seven years ago. Brandon was new to us, just adopted. We were still partying hard. We had been with these women several times. We made a vow to clean up for Brandon. Which we did. We didn't drink hardly. No more pot binges. No more coke. But Sam went back to them twice. She told me. For whatever reason it didn't bother me at the time. I was focusing on our new baby, our child. Sam turned it around quickly after that."

I took Karen by the hand. "I love you, Karen. I love Sam so much, too. You know that. You two have been great friends. But you two have been playing with fire for a very long time."

"I know."

"Do you love Sam anymore?"

"Not sure. I love sharing parenting with Brandon. I love when we are quiet at night. Being at her side. But I don't know if I can make love anymore. Not just her. Me. I feel, strangely, ruined or something."

"I get it. I understand."

"What do you think - Other than counseling. I don't want to go there now."

"I think you two need to take off together for a few days. Go to the mountains. Plan to grind it out together; well, you know what I mean. Make or break time. We can take Brandon for a few days. I will talk with Danny. Louise too."

"Really, you'd do that?"

I hugged her. "I think you both need to find out. Decide. Make a vow. No phone calls. Just the two of you or you break up."

We had Brandon at our house that night. He thought it was an adventure. They took off for Durango. For three nights unless they came back early. Danny was glad to help. Same with Louise. There was a big problem, though.

Jimmie, our old friend from high school, and his wife Denee' were coming to town. Thankfully they had a bed and breakfast lined up. Sharon was sticking around but Vinny had to go. Tim was leaving. I wanted to spend two good days with Sharon before Jimmie arrived. Sharon and I had made plans in Angel Fire already. Top of the line accommodations at the Thunderhead Resort. The snow reports were decent up there.   Danny laughed about us running off. So did Louise. It figured, they both said. No problem though. Brandon's an easy kid. Get him to school and back. Louise can still drive.   Two nights.   Danny felt he and 'grandma' can handle it. I told him I owed him one. Or two. He said, "Deal." Sharon rented a car. A driver. She was doing it right. We had the best gin and tonics right there in the back seat. Packs of cigarettes and great pot if she felt she could talk me into it. No other drugs, she promised. It didn't take long before were smoking a joint. She had all 90's dance music piped in. Stuff I had never heard of. My paintings were finished. The kids were well on their way and taken care of. Danny was fine, fine as can be. The Gallery was primo, like this ganja. Sharon took off her bra and threw it out the window. Her silk blouse, she said, was all that was needed to feel good. I wasn't there yet. I could chain smoke, finally. And the gin and tonic, chilled precisely, were going down nice and easy. Our suite was enormous. We each had our own room and private bath. An enormous refrigerator fully stocked. Great sound system. Top of the line accommodations. A five-star restaurant lined up. Dancing till 3:00 am at the Club downstairs. Skiing all day tomorrow. All day the next day. If we were up to it. Shower and a very expensive dress. We ordered prime rib cutlets, crab legs, salad. Starting with a chef's recommendation of wine. We didn't even check the label or cost. We took two hours to eat. We laughed. We told stories. Sharon got me updated on the business. She hated it more than ever. She was pissing off people left and right. Especially the press. She'd go on talk shows and promote her latest movie and yawn. David Letterman told her that she was either the biggest bitch he ever met, or the greatest actor he ever met. Or both. She loved Letterman and took him out to dinner and apologized for her disconnected attitude. Don't take it personally she tried to convince him. *I hate doing this schtick.* Her bank accounts were overflowing. She owned a jet now. Three houses. Chicago was home base. New York. And a little place still in So Cal. Her 'people' rented it out. It was sentimental. She had deals in the works for more but rolled her money into other investments – like with Jimmie's tech stocks. And Land. Not houses. Plenty of Land. She owned acres and acres. Thousands of acres. Montana. Idaho. Colorado. California. Washington. Prime, mountain land. All in the west.   Making movies was still her passion but it was harder and harder to find great directors and studios that would leave her alone. Vinny was a great husband. He was amazing in bed. She loved being a mom and wife. She still wanted to have a fucking great time. She missed me. Terribly. She wanted to do the WWI movie with me and Steph. Steph wasn't ready. We both knew it. *Who gave a fuck,* she said way too loud. With Tim directing and with us talking her through her scenes, she'll do fine. She's fit. The naiveté will work in her favor. Vinny will write the perfect script. But there you go. He's never written a script. But he's a hell of writer. Why the hell not?

I took it all in and was drunk on my ass. The pot was intolerable. I had no resistance. And she wanted to go dancing. She lit up in the restaurant. It was one of those places that was trying to change. No cigarettes. She didn't cause a scene. We left.

The Club was loud. Too loud for me. Crowded too. Too many people recognized Sharon. That was a bummer. No fucking autographs she said a few times. They got the message. She danced with a few guys. No one really. I danced once. One of the local press took a photo of her and he asked her who the new guy was? She said it was not a guy, it was a girl dressed like a guy. She hoped he'd print it.

We found a place where we could hear the music and still talk. It was semi-private. She lit a joint right there in the booth. We got higher and higher. I had to change to water. I couldn't stand up. No more alcohol for me.

Sharon was tired. I could tell. We went up to the room and got into comfortable clothes. I put on quiet music. I called room service for a pitcher of lemonade of all things. With lots of ice. We had plenty of snacks.

We calmed way down. Sharon ordered decaf. I quit smoking; it was bothering me. We laughed and coughed. We were out of energy. Skiing was going to be difficult. Sharon slowed way down and started talking to me like when we were kids.   She missed our easy ways. She had taken off all her makeup and jewelry. I liked the person with me.   We cuddled on the couch and reminisced. She said that we had a plan for my kids. She needed a plan. She wanted out of Chicago, but Vinny was happy there. She wanted to live on a spread like we did.   She missed Colorado sometimes. She saw how I quit acting for so very long and that was alluring. Maybe. Maybe she'd have the courage to do it someday. Right now, it wasn't the money, it was the art, the acting. She was an addict to the process of 'becoming.' One painting after another – she used that analogy for my sake. I understood.

I told her that we would ski tomorrow, but then let's check out of this place, rent a jeep, and go stay at a

cabin or some isolated bed and breakfast. No drinking.
Maybe some pot. But sober.

She loved it.

Skiing was okay. The snow had a thin base. We had fun
in the sunshine, easy runs. The fresh air was
rejuvenating. We were ready to go by 2:00.

We checked out by 4:00. A jeep had been sent over.
We got in and Sharon drove north. We had no
destination. We got off the highway at some small
town. I asked a gas attendant if there was a place to
stay. He had never heard of a bed and breakfast. Maybe
it was his broken English. A customer overheard me,
and he said there was a fishing lodge about ten miles
east.

Sharon was game. We found the place. Not too many
people fishing this time of year, the man behind the
counter said, looking over two gorgeous women in a
jeep. We took two adjoining rooms. He had some 7-ups.
Bags of chips. A crappy TV in each room. There was a
small restaurant across the street. They specialized in
homemade tamales.

We went over and quickly became two of four total
customers. The tamales and a beer weren't too bad.
We talked until 8:00. It was warm next to their fireplace.
We smoked a bit, drank another two beers slowly. It
was our agreed limit. Sharon was dreaming about life
without fame. It would get to be funny and then
equally sad.

Over in our room we found a movie, about a third of the
way through. It was a WC Fields movie in grainy black
and white. We laughed, or at least once or twice when

he caught us off guard. We appreciated the old drunk. His get-up. His vaudevillian gig and how he became famous. He was quick. He could be funny. A lot of his delivery didn't fly any more. It didn't age well. We both felt sorry for him even though he was long dead. No one was that dry anymore. Sharon did a WC moment, not bad at all, and said she liked her martini dry like WC Fields was professionally dry. She started crying. I held her. For a very long time until she went to sleep. Sharon wanted to take a walk in the morning. There was a path that led to a stream which we followed into the woods and along a few cabins. The stream was frozen in most locations. It was pretty in there. Sharon reached to the heavens and breathed deeply. Neither of us smoked at all that day. She came over and held my hand then put her arm around me while we walked. We never talked much as fresh air was doing the job. We ate old fashioned bacon and eggs and hash browns and wheat toast and lots of coffee before heading home. During the drive Sharon talked about cleaning up her act. Her intention was to change her routine. Work out. Hire a trainer if need be. Take care of her body. Sean Penn had been asking her about helping with a foundation reaching out to those in need on a global level. Penn was married to Robin Wright, who Sharon liked very much. Admired her acting as well. Sharon realized that Penn was a volatile person like herself, talented, similar in too many ways. Her intention was to stick close to Wright and the causes they fought for. She was done with the 'lifestyle.'

Woody Allen had been asking her to play a supportive role in his upcoming film. Allen was known for his ensemble casts. He also worked quickly, so the part would not be that demanding. A lot of fun, given that she had not done comedy in a few years, and was leaning towards accepting the role. She would play a married woman who suspects that her husband - who would be played by Jeff Daniels, and whom she liked a great deal - is having an affair and goes to odd and hilarious extremes to find out whether he is or not. Perfect for Sharon.

When we got home, Louise let me know that Karen had arrived and quickly cleared-out Brandon and his things. Sam was in the car the whole time.   Quick in and out and a big thank you relayed to one and all. Brandon had been a great kid. No problem at all. He and Danny hit it off.

Sharon asked if she could take over the guest bedroom for two more days. She wanted to take walks and meditate before heading back to Chicago. She'd be ready to be a full-time mom at that point. Of course. *Mi casa es su casa*.

I took a deep breath and took a nap. Jimmie and his wife Denee' were in town, looking to have dinner with us that night.   I begged Louise to help me. We'd prepare a nice homemade meal of pork chops and baked potatoes, big salad. I'd pick up some fresh bakery bread and apple pie.   A total of eight. She's a life saver.

I slept much longer than I wanted. Danny and the kids were home.   I took a quick shower and dressed nicely for the evening.   I kissed Danny and ran to the kitchen to roll up my sleeves and jump into fixing dinner. We already had the pork chops in the freezer from the best butcher in town. Louise had set them out and they were curing. I made the salad and put it back in the fridge. Danny wanted to jump in the car with me to the bakery. "Karen called me. I didn't want to talk about it inside," he said.

I listened carefully.

"Their getaway went well. Karen was allowing Sam to move back into their extra bedroom. She was terribly blunt with me. They had not slept together. Yet. They have too much to throw away right now, but Karen was still wary. She needed time and effort from Sam to build back trust."

"Sounds like a good move. Karen is taking responsibility, too. That's a good thing. Maybe I can talk with Sam sometime." I changed the subject. "I've never met Denee', do you know if Jimmie has business to talk with us, or is this just for pleasure?"

"I met Denee' a long time ago. They were passing through New Mexico, headed to Denver. It's always business with Jimmie. I have no idea what. To be honest, I have no clue what he's up to."

"Sharon and I had a good time. Partied a bit too much. For me, anyway."

"Predictable."

"She had a bit of a breakdown. I'm worried about her. She's staying with us a few more days. She's trying to settle down. Clean out some. You know how it is, Danny, this business gets to you. She's one tough kid."

"You sure you want to jump on that bandwagon again?"

"No, I don't. I want to act. I think if we can get this screenplay written and film in France. Stay out of L.A. and New York. Protect Steph. Have Tim run the thing. Sharon and I can have fun with it. Don't you think?"

"I like the plan. You've thought it through. Seems like the best way to go for all three of you. I like it. You know, one step at a time. Let's see how Steph does on this *Music Man* play. I'm going to stay far, far away as principal. I don't want to look like I'm sticking my nose into it. I'm already worried about the deck being stacked with your reputation, me – her parents perceived as pulling strings. She's a freshman and gets the part. You know and I know she earned it. Perception is all. You understand."

"Oh, yeah. No doubt. Whatever. Steph is going to have to learn and fight her way through it all. Same with Eagle's Nest if she tries out for *The Sound of Music.* You know she will. I can't have anything to do with that either. I mean, she will have to act her way into the role. Of course, I'm not stupid. I can help her get an audition. Then I'll let the dice roll. It's up to Steph. I'll start readings with her soon. Work with her. You understand."

"I sure do. We're on the same page."

Julian

Alo and I were working nonstop on the Beatles' "Rain." We already had two Beatle's songs in our set list, two of which were George Harrison's. I had been obsessed with this song for years even though it was terribly difficult. The rhythm section is complex. I also realized that this song was heavily dosed with studio manipulation and that accounted for much of it. Alo's drums and my bass eventually found that strange relationship making it possible to move forward with John Lennon's vocals. I found a solution to the backward masking in the George Martin production. I had Melanie come in a step behind me on backup. Blending, intentionally and slightly off key. We found it. No one in the group was all that excited about the song. We had added plenty of dance songs, so I was being selfish with this one. Like "Isis," this was my baby. Frankie asked if we could try a song, and he wanted to take a more complex lead on guitar. It was a hidden gem, The Guess Who's "No Time." It was a favorite of his mom's he said. I worked hard with Frankie on the very difficult bridge, which he was bound and determined to master. For a change I'd play a simple acoustic. The vocal dilemma was nearly identical to "Rain." Of our complete repertoire this was the only song where Frankie would also contribute with vocals. I sang lead, using Melanie and Frankie on one microphone blending the delayed backup. The same strategy of repetition, attempting to conquer the wizardry of early studio manipulation. Repeating *no time, no time, no time*, over and over was sounding so good to us we rehearsed it repeatedly. I was happy Frank pushed for us to do it. It gave us the final two songs we wanted for going live. A total of twenty-five songs. We were ready.

Shelly was doing a bang-up job as our new manager. We had a nice promotional photo worked up into flyers. She had passed them around to restaurants, posted in windows, prominently displayed in various busy locations in Santa Fe. It was a black and white picture with the exact same stuff we'd wear on stage. We used the Railroad District setting right outside the Gallery, situated under a southbound sign to Las Cruces. Most of us held one instrument or another, except Mel had her arm around me, practically hanging on me, dressed in a black bra showing through her sheer white blouse, decorated with her blond hair, lots of jewelry and makeup. Her usual. Alo turned slightly askew facing an oncoming, imagined train, with his long black hair blowing slightly in the wind. Stu, with hands in pocket and the largest smile of all of us, replacing his Dodger cap with a conductor hat lent to us in the office. It would stick, forgetting – on purpose - to give it back. Frankie, his blackness blending into the shadowy composition, unshaven, the oldest, toughest looking one, no smile at all. He looked intimidating. Not as young as we all appeared, each one being in high school. I looked the youngest by far capturing that Elvis Costello clone demeanor that I wanted, especially with the Ray-Ban sunglasses I had on. I still liked my hair longer than Elvis, pulled back behind my ears.

We were scheduled this coming Friday and Saturday nights at Jimmy's Bar. We could barely squeeze into the far end of the place, seating capacity around 60, if it was full and if the bar stools were taken. We could use a donation jar but weren't getting paid. Okay by us. Shelly had arranged for us to be on the local news anchor Sarah Johnson's *This is Santa Fe*, on Monday bright and early. A small problem came up. Sarah told Shelly she could only sit two people comfortably on the small set. The band was unanimous it would be me and Mel and our photo of our entire band would be shown to the viewing audience. Mel and I knew we'd be interviewed and promote Retro Sky's engagement next weekend during the first segment, cut to a commercial, then be asked to play a song. With our acoustic guitars we could easily do our Everly Brothers song.

Mom and Dad's friend Jimmie from high school and his wife stopped in for dinner on their way to Denver. Jimmie is a nice guy. I've met him a few times growing up. Strange mannerisms, excited about everything. He has a computer company in northern California that I know that we invested in, Grandpa did too. They've made a lot of money from what I could gather. Jimmie explained over dinner how the stocks had split, recommending that we roll it over. Sharon was at dinner and was writing a check to Jimmie. Even Louise wanted to expand the small investment she and George had made a few years ago. Very fun time, as they told stories of high school. Dances, things like that. They all left and went over to the Gallery to show Jimmie's wife around.

Steph and I lounged around. I read one of her scripts with her. A mid-west plains story during the dust bowl. There was a role for a fifteen-year-old alone with her mother and grandmother. All the men in the family had died tragically. A survival story in Oklahoma. I read all the parts except the teenage girl. Steph gave it her all.

She was also studying her lines for *Music Man*, which was my cue to retreat to my room.

I could watch TV, having finished my science homework. Instead, I listened to a lot of the music by the Band. Robertson's visit had a big impact on me. We were now using both songs, "Ophelia" and "The Shape I'm In" as part of the act. I liked Robertson's style, his vocals, his guitar work. While I preferred the upbeat new wave sound these days, the Band was the perfect example for us to grow into. His style, the Band's style, was comfortable and fun.

I called Mel. She lived far from our house, over near the hospital where her mom was a nurse. Mel could drive but didn't access to her mom's car very often. Her mom drove the two blocks to work and was gone a lot. I realized that I'd never been to their apartment. I'd only met her mom a couple of times. Mel and I hardly saw each other except at rehearsals and at school. We wanted to go out. Do something some time. Melanie had been out with several guys during high school. She was 'robbing the cradle' being with me. Her older friends made fun of her. She laughed, made light of it. I could tell, though, that she wanted to find a way. Maybe she could use Frankie's old car, except he was dating, and we didn't want to double date. With her history with Frankie, it would be way too awkward. Stu didn't have a license even though he was old enough. Mel and I talked a little about sex. She was still a virgin, even though I thought maybe she wasn't. She seemed sophisticated, a senior after all. It didn't bother me either way. Of course, I was. I wanted to change that status and so did she, for both of us. We danced around the possibility. Mostly we talked about music. She was smart and knew her stuff about singing. I really appreciated that about her, the ideas she came up with. While I knew I was in charge, even though I was so young, no one ever challenged it because I played my instruments so well and sang well too. Mel was challenging it a lot. She could stand toe to toe with me, especially vocally and with her age, she seemed like the leader a lot of the times. So far no tough issues or real arguments. I handled the instruments, and she handled the vocal arrangements.

When I went to bed, I thought about a conversation I recently had with James. He talked about the kiva when we went camping. The stuff me and Steph saw. The two buildings. The airplanes. The crash and fires. Vivid. I could see it when I closed my eyes. He told me to talk to Dad about it if anything like that vision ever happened again. Nothing to worry about. It seemed like he knew something he wasn't saying. He is a mysterious guy anyhow. I like that about him. Dad can be that way. Like something is always going on his head. James can see it. Mom too. It's not just an adult thing.

Then there's Sharon. I love that woman. She's the most special person in our lives and she feels like family. Not because she's the greatest actress in the world or famous. None of that. I don't even see her that way. She has that same vision, like she can look right into me. She is absolutely the funniest person there is, I can see why she married Vinny. I haven't seen him perform his stand-up. I wonder if the two of them could do an act together. Sharon could do it, no doubt about it. She probably just does not want to. She is that way. We all know it. She does what she wants.

I got up early. Like always. Dad was wishing me luck at the studio. Louise was going to tape it. He was out the door. Mom had me eat cereal, double checked what I had on. *That funky tie*, she'd say. Sharon was leaving later, right after. She climbed in the back. We picked up Shelly, then drove over and picked up Mel. Lord, she had on striped pink and polka dot purple, her purple bra, every earring in every piercing in both ears. White pants. Her hair flying all over. And the makeup. I shivered and smiled at the same time. I loved it. Mom and Shelly rolled with it, all smiles, too. Sharon was saying she wanted to look just like Melanie. Her new hero.

Sarah Johnson was very friendly and professional. She knew Mom and Sharon. The crew were in awe when we all walked in. They didn't expect Sharon. Neither did Sarah. Sharon yelled really loud, *this is about Retro Sky, nothing about me or Jennifer, none of it. Let's keep it that way*. Ordering them around. Sarah got the message with a big smile, hugging everyone.

The makeup lady had no idea what to do with Mel and her own made-up look for the show. Sarah said to leave her alone. She dabbed my face with powder, that was about it. Shelly gave Sarah the photo and flyer for a close-up during the promotional portion of the interview. Then we were situated in chairs in a cramped studio, given clip-on mics and a quick sound check. Our guitars were tuned and given sound checks for after the commercial. We would stand up for that portion.

About ten minutes later we were live. All I remember is that we laughed a great deal. Sarah made us sound like the new sensation of Santa Fe and we hadn't even played one gig yet. She loved the photo and we talked about each guy. We talked about what Retro Sky meant. Music everyone out there will love. Promise. Stuff to dance to. Stuff to move to. Stuff to listen to. Me and Mel were exchanging sentences just like lyrics. Sarah was great wrapping it up, promoting us for the weekend. Commercial.

A different make-up person quickly patted our faces, helped us stand and get our marks. Mel and I strummed a bit and did a sound check for the soundman.

Sarah quickly introduced us and the Everly Brothers song … which we sang like a dream. We looked into each other's eyes during most of the song, nailing every inflection. Mel kissed me on the cheek at the end. Sarah came out clapping, saying *Retro Sky at Jimmy's Bar, this weekend, see you there!*

Mom, Shelly, Sharon, hugged us. Great job, all around! Sharon was headed to the airport and needed to catch a plane. She apologized; she wouldn't be able to see us premiere at the bar. She gave me a big kiss on the lips and gave me that look like I was the greatest person in the world. I thanked her as she left. A cab was waiting. I thanked Shelly a lot. It all worked out well. I looked at Shelly, realizing that we had found a manager. Or she had found us. She and Mom drove us over to school, where Dad asked to meet him in his office. He quickly received an excited summary from all of us and then he was off to a meeting with a parent.

Danny

Jennifer was getting up at 4:45 every morning. She'd usually be greeted by an overnight FAX from Vinny, updates on his script of *Purgatory*. She'd fix coffee and work it over with a red pen, making long edits, contributing in her collaborative way. I'd find her hunched over at the kitchen table furiously making notes, adding dialogue, writing new scenes. Once we'd all headed off to school, Jennifer would rush next door to talk with Tim about ideas for filming each new scene. Stephanie was up by 5:30. Unheard of for her to be up that early. The two of them would work for nearly an hour going over *Music Man*, discuss Steph's rehearsals, then they'd read one of the nearly thirty scripts that were boxed downstairs. They had set up a camera, the whole thing. Steph was taking it all extremely seriously. Having her mom engaged now created a rapid change around the house. With both of them it was transformational. Jennifer was what I had remembered her to be as an actress. Steph was finding that same internal persona. *Music Man* was for Steph a steppingstone to where she was now getting the green light to go. Her seriousness and *professionalism* were certainly not the qualities of a freshman in my school. I had my secretary go down to rehearsals from time to time and sit in the back and watch. She'd give me updates on how things were progressing. Cheryl was never given to exaggeration or hyperbole, so when she would tell me that Steph was amazing, I trusted it. Cheryl would say things like *I never knew Steph had such a beautiful voice*, or *even the older kids are following her around up there.*

I met Bishop Sheehan at his office. He handed me the parchment from the Vatican. Formal paperwork and arrangements for Christmas. He was happy for me. For our family. He was willing to take on the holiday ceremony we had planned for the native nations. He was a serious man at heart. He offered to hear my confession, my thoughts and worries and aspirations. He would lead me in prayer. I worried about his health afterwards.

I went over to Jimmy's Bar on that Friday afternoon before everyone else. I spoke with Jimmy and Francine about the set-up. They were optimistic for a large crowd. Several regular customers, new faces, even lingering tourists, were asking about Retro Sky. *Just kids*, they'd say. A few had heard about Jennifer being involved. Shelly, Tim's wife. Even Sharon's name popped up. Of course, that all bothered me, and I wouldn't say a word to Julian. This was his thing and God knew he was good enough. Literally, God knew he was ready. I thanked them both and headed to grab a bite to eat and pick up James. The rest of the gang were on their own.

James and I ate at his cottage. He had made vegetable and lamb soup with homemade bread. I had quickly changed and relaxed in the comfort and warmth of his abode. James was moving slow, yet excited to see the band. He brought up the vision of the kids', the buildings falling.   He told me he wouldn't be there for the kids afterwards.   It bothered me when he talked like that. Fate setting in. That kind of thing. Resigned to what he had seen in them. What he had seen in me and Jennifer, for that matter.

When we arrived, it was mayhem.   A line trying to get inside the local bar. I guided James to the rear entrance where I knew we could get in.   Jimmy was excited to see us peer inside, quickly guiding us to a table where our entire entourage took up three tables.   The bar was packed.   Drinks were flowing. Pizzas rushed out to tables.   Shelly was up at the front, ready to introduce the band.   Jimmy joined her, welcoming everyone. A new sign was etched into the front of Alo's bass drum, *Retro Sky*. Julian walked the few feet over to me and leaned in and whispered something I wasn't sure. It was too loud.

After Shelly did the intro, naming each member - calling Alo, Freebird - Julian waited until it became reasonably quiet. Then bang. He hammered his keyboards, and they went right into Jerry Lee Lewis's "Great Balls of Fire." I had never heard him play this before. His voice sounded so mature, so powerful. No hesitation.   The band kept up. Melanie would dance with her tambourine.   The place was hopping with what little room was available.

A few more dance songs, then Julian changed up to more of the thoughtful covers.   The audience remained raptured.   Sweat was running down Julian's face as he took his guitar and ripped into Elvis Costello.   This was my son.

On and on it went. As Mel and Julian began to create their unique harmonies and sway together, the mood changed considerably. Jennifer reached over and held my hand. Both of us incredibly proud.

They took a break after about an hour and half. A scattering of standing ovation and chatter. The band released to go to the bathroom or grab a Coke. Julian went out the back with Melanie, holding her hand. They were talking seriously.

I followed them out to the alley. Curious. They were laughing and kissing. Embarrassed I had shown up. I congratulated them and as I was going back inside, Julian thanked me back. "I told you,"He said.

Melanie did the intro for the second set. They went into their Band repertoire, back-to-back songs. Less dancing to finish up. Julian then slowly, deliberately delivered "Isis," singing in a crying, tearful tone. It was moving. The Beatles songs soon followed, each of the three. "Rain," eerily their own sound. Julian looked peculiarly like John Lennon as he sang. They were going on three hours, and they all looked haggard and exhausted. The crowd wanted one more.

Bo Diddly left them raucous. Melanie shined taking the lead vocals, almost relieving the worn-out Julian.

Then they were done.

The feeling was a good one. Steph was the first to get up and give her brother a kiss. The band was all smiles as patrons asked them about this and that. Stu, I noticed, had that shy demeanor beneath his smile. Where'd he get that conductor hat, I wondered. One of the women at the bar went over to Frankie, obviously

flirting, offering him a drink.   Here we go, I thought.
Alo disappearing into the crowd. Mel standing out most
of all in her wild costume.

Julian plopped down at our table. He hugged his mom,
James, thanked everyone.   Tim's presence was creating
an enormous stir, but Julian didn't mind.   He had
performed his heart out.

We stayed up late that night.   Somewhere around 2:00
am I slinked off to bed. Jennifer joined me. We
whispered in our bed how happy we were.   We'd do it
all over again the following night.   Julian had left the
nest.

I went to early mass that Sunday, taking Louise with me.
She was exhausted from the late nights, as was I.   Music
rattled inside my skull. Sitting in the silence, gathering
my center. During communion, my being reflected on
two buildings, like towers in the sky.   They were images
within my kids. I was frightened. Planes toppled them
in a strange purpose. I prayed that Julian and Steph
remained safe. I did not understand.   I had been in
moments like this before, this I KNEW.

Jennifer

I brought James with me to the Gallery, gathering the
staff quickly. They had not seen James in a long time, so
there was a sense of reverence and congeniality before
we set forth on business.   James always liked
Samantha's work and was pleased with the finishing
touches on her show.

Then I asked Matthew to go over the work-up he had done on a possible display of the drawings and the book of *Kid*. James, in his usual manner, asked for cotton gloves. He carefully put them on, and we all left the room to give him time to look over Frankie's drawings. Eventually, James asked for a donut and some tea, which we scrambled to retrieve. With careful consideration, he said that he'd never seen anything like these. While it would be easy to dismiss them as comic book format, he was drawn to the unique perspective, and the storyline.

"Is this really what you want to do?" he asked me. Asking the group.

"I think so, James. We are always looking for a new direction. I think this is it."

He looked at Matthew, the youngest of our staff.

"Well, James, it's nothing like we've ever done here at Rio Blanco. Santa Fe is getting out of its southwest image to a degree. Modern stuff is showing up. Not abstract, per se, but like this. I think it's worth a try to give it a display, a bit of advertising. Nothing to sell, unless Frankie has more."

"He has more," I replied.

"And these two," He pointed to Julian's drawings, "They're good. Not as good as Frank's. Not sure we should display these. They're a different style. I'd go with just the *Kid* then see how it flies for an opener."

I appreciated Matthew's frankness. He didn't hesitate even though Julian was my son. I agreed with him. So did James. That mattered the most to me at that point of deciding.

"Let's do it. Matthew, you run with the design, making the space, a place to look at the book. The pages are removable, so let's cover them and do the usual protection. Run it in our next flyer, but not with Samantha's individual announcements."
He nodded his head.
"Also, go ahead and get ahold of Frankie. He'll get a kick hearing from someone in the Gallery. Handle it how you like. Invite him over. Or take him to lunch, get him out of school. Make a big deal."
"Sounds good. You know, I saw him and the band Saturday night. They were incredible. Julian has a voice. And can he play! He's been at it since he was seven, I think you told us. It shows. And that girl, Melanie, is that it? She looks like a star already."
I smiled. So did James. Everyone agreed. They had all been to Jimmy's Bar for the opening performance of Retro Sky.
I retreated to my studio for several days. I read scripts and thought of Stephanie's progress. *Music Man* would be premiering in a week. She was more than ready. My memories of my own development as an actress were skewed. Thoughts of Sharon and me in high school. The several plays in college. Jumping into dinner theater. Steph was on a different, high-octane track. I didn't know the end game back then. Steph was looking at Sharon's and my careers and was absolutely determined and focused.
My routine was to turn on some jazz, take out the conte crayons and pen and ink, some heavy-duty paper, then try my hand at cartoons. I made up a character named

Norah, around nine years old, who lived in a busy apartment complex in New York City. She was independent for her age, making observations about life around her. The adults in their serious demeanor. The children who lived near her. Some older, most younger, even infants. I did not worry about the storyline yet. I was getting the drawings down. Having fun.

I used a ruler, creating blocked diagrams. Moving from square to square. She had two or three friends who became regulars. Another girl, named, Suzee. Suzee's dog, Muffy. A doorman named Mr. Morrison. I set aside most of my training and years of successful oil painting to make imaginary sense of a kind of joy stirring inside of me. Because of *Kid*, I wanted to let these childlike characters out in vulnerability in a large and foreboding city. I was trying to find my voice all over again.

Sam and Karen came over for lunch. I had asked them to drop in at their convenience. I catered-in box lunches, situated in our meeting room. After discussing Samantha's show and how wonderful it was coming along, I broached their personal lives. I wanted to know how it was going. I was prying, as their friend.

Karen had agreed to couple's therapy. They had found a nice psychologist who was familiar and known in the gay community. One step at a time. Things were nice at home. Excellent parents together. A routine back in full swing. Separate bedrooms still. Time would tell.

I hugged them, giving them my love as I walked them to their cars. They had arrived separately. Realizing that they had missed Julian's band at the Jimmy's Bar they apologized profusely. They promised to make Stephanie's performance of *Music Man*. No worries, I assured them.

I was not sure if this would last with them. Karen seemed so hurt. Sam was making herculean efforts, especially for her. Hope was in my heart.

Late one night, after dinner, I grabbed Stephanie and brought her over to the Gallery. She had no idea what I was doing. A surprise.

I turned on the lights, went into my office, turned the dial on our large walk-in safe, motioning her to sit down. I brought out my Oscar for best actress in *Hull House*. She had never seen it. Ever. I hadn't seen it in nearly ten years. I had it wrapped in velvet, stored in a mahogany box.

Steph carefully took it from my hand, examining it. It was heavy. I sat by her and told her stories of the film, working with Sharon, with Liz Taylor, with Vinny, even before he and Sharon got married. Even Tim had a small role. We were in Chicago for all the filming. It was hard work. My dedication to the vision of Jane Addams was all that I cared about.

She remembered every scene in the movie, recalling pieces that I had forgotten. She could recite lines verbatim. My reaction was to hold her hand in approval. Once again, she asked why I gave it up. Painting, my true art was calling. And I had twins. I wanted a quiet life with my husband. He was doing well, successful. We had money. I hated the scene in LA, in New York. Sharon handles all that well, but even she suffers from the day-to-day torment of fame.

I told Steph in no uncertain terms that if she wanted to be an actress it was not about the gold statue she was holding. It was about creating, just like we were practicing every morning. She understood. I could tell she understood.

"I want to be like you Mom." She said softly. "Not to win an Oscar. Look around here. You have the greatest paintings in the world. You have Sharon as your best friend. I love you as my mom. You are a wonderful mom, but this is who you are too." Holding the gold statue.

"I know. That's why I've finally given in. That's why you're here tonight. I'm here for you in your pursuit of your own dreams."

We worked tirelessly. Her desire, her driven direction was rubbing off on me. I wanted her to be good, to find her voice. I pushed her, which pushed me.

Sally, my assistant, knocked, and came into my office with the painting she had wanted to show me. We place it up on a viewing easel, studying it. She had found a crude format in the desert, almost understated, muted in color, relying on texture. Barren subtlety. Yet I could see the layering and time. The more I looked, the more I enjoyed and appreciated.

Sally did not belong to the Women's League, which was an unusual hire for me. I was taken by her resume at Art College in Kansas City, where I had once visited in high school as a possible college for myself. She explained that she shunned politics and activism, given entirely to her painting and wanting to establish a career in Santa Fe. She was inspired by my own career and hoped to get hired – which I did. Gut feeling. James liked her too.

As I stood there looking over her painting, *Beige in Beginnings*, I would look at her face, her demeanor, knowing that she was special.

"Look, Sally, I like this a lot. Let's give it space on a wall in here. The main hallway. How much? Is it for sale?"

"I haven't thought about it. I don't think it rises to the level of what we are showing. Certainly not your stuff, or Sam's. I'm just not there yet."

"Nonsense. I decide what we exhibit. I've seen your other paintings and I would agree with you. This, however, is worth a run.   How much?"

"No idea."

"For sale?"

"Sure."

"Let's go with $500."

"No way.   The most I've sold my paintings for is $75, at a college art show."

"Give it two weeks. It will sell.   Maybe sooner. You sure you want to part with it?"

She waited, looking at her own work carefully. "Yes, okay."

"Keep up this style for the time being. You wait. Watch and see."

"Thank you, Jennifer. That means a lot."

Here at Rio Blanco, I was finding my stride.   I kept painting. Talking to clients. Working with the staff. Reading over scripts, making notes for Vinny and *Purgatory*. I spoke with my old agent Phil and thanked him for all the scripts he was sending us. He had his hands on copies of what Vinny and I had been working on for *Purgatory*. He wouldn't tell me how he got them, but I suspected Sharon right off. He loved it. He rarely said that right off the bat. And he repeated it.

"It's an artsy movie, you know. Black and white. Bleak post-WWI France. Won't make any money. But, honestly, I can see you and Sharon in these roles. She's always a big draw no matter what she makes. Amazing, that friend of yours. Let's get Stephanie a test."

"Look, Phil, I appreciate it. I do. She may not be ready. She still hasn't had opening night for her high school debut, for god's sake."

"I know. I really know all that. I don't care. And it's not Tim pushing me around to do this. I want to see her in action."

"Come see her. I know how much you despise rinky-dink theater."

"Not a bad idea. Don't tell her. When should I come out?"

"This Friday is opening night. Give her a few nights to warm up. It's playing for three weekends, Thursdays included later in the schedule. Matinees on Saturdays and Sundays."

"I'll fly in with Tim. He's in L.A., headed home on Friday to see her. I'll wait till the Sunday matinee, how's that?"

"Sounds good. I didn't know Tim was going to be there for the opening. I won't tell Steph."

"Good idea. If it goes well, let's schedule a quick trip to a studio lot. Do the whole shebang."

"God, it makes me nervous. But I agree."

"Say, Sharon went ahead and is working with Woody Allen now in New York."

"I thought so."

"I doubt she'll make Steph's play. She will be busy for several weeks."

"Not even Woody Allen can keep that girl under control. She'll be here. Knowing her, she'll be here for the closing show that final Sunday matinee. Wait till the very end."

"Yeah, you're probably right. Oh, and I thought you should know that the gossip is that she and Jeff Daniels are already making this Allen film one of his funniest. I love it when Sharon does comedy. No one really appreciates her for it. That Gleason film of hers is still my favorite and no one talks about it."

"It's a great one. No doubt … no pun intended," as I realized the nick name of Gleason himself.

"You know, I saw Sinatra at a luncheon right before he died a few years ago. He asked about you."

"No way."

"Absolutely. He loves Sharon. Always has. I think that Rio Norte was one of his favorite movies. He told me that. He thought you two were *damned tough dames*."

I smiled.

Then we hung up. I'd see him soon, this Sunday.

"Someone is here to see you," buzzed my phone from the front.

I was perplexed. No name. They know better up there.

"Okay, who is it?" I asked.

"One of Julian's friends, Frank. And his mom."

Another smile as I got up to go greet them.

We went into the small room of his display of *Kid*. Frankie was ecstatic. Matthew had taken him to lunch, gone over everything with him. Showed him the display before it was officially opened. He and Julian had talked at length about it. I explained that I didn't have the opportunity to speak with Julian yet. His mom was thanking me over and over. She had a look of hope and joy, standing there with her nametag still on from work, like a new day had dawned, as she said, "That band, Retro Sky, is Frankie's life. And now this. I can't believe it."

"He's sounding good. Did you get to see them?"

"I made it Saturday night. I was speechless. Still am." As she hugged her son. I paused to take note of the huge relief in her eyes. A single mom, moving from town to town trying to make ends meet. Frankie being in and out of trouble. Prayers answered I suspected.

"Me too. They were so well rehearsed, worked so hard. Sounded great." I finally responded.

"I'm saving the notice your Gallery printed up. And I have a flyer of the band, too. I'm already Frankie's number one fan club."

My day was complete.

CHAPTER SEVEN

There's no such thing as an original sin. Elvis Costello

Julian

A big night. Jimmy's Bar was charging a cover. It was only five bucks a head, but we'd get two bucks on each ticket. That's fifty or sixty dollars each night. We were getting paid seemed pretty cool.
One problem tonight was that Steph was opening at the high school. Mom and Dad asked me if it was okay to miss our third night of performing.   No hesitation was

my take on it all. I only wished that I could see her. I'd see her on Sunday at the matinee.

Shelly had Sarah Johnson there from *Today in Santa Fe*, cameraman in tow. They'd make a tape and show it Monday morning. Sarah asked me a few questions before we started. How'd we like playing live? What adjustments did Retro Sky make for tonight? How it felt being young kids in a bar? I answered with quick smiles and gusto. Had no idea what the words were.

We opened with Prince's "Purple Rain." I ripped my guitar to shreds. The place was on fire. Melanie and I were on all cylinders singing in harmony from the opening. She wore all black with black lipstick and heavy black eyeliner. Knee high black boots. She turned me on. The rest of the crowd too. Sticking with more recent stuff we followed up with "Burning Down the House" by Talking Heads. Alo was ferocious on drums. The crowd was already moving in their seats – if they remained in their seats at all - frantic looking. After Mel took over with Blondie's "Eat to be Beat," I realized she was stealing the show. All the older guys with beers and shot glasses going crazy over her. She looked at me and smiled, nodding her head. We flew right into our normal set, going back to earlier dance tunes and then album rock. By our break, I was sweating terribly. We all were. The lights were hot in that place with no ventilation. It seemed to me they were breaking fire codes, people crammed everywhere.

We already knew that the Beatles numbers were becoming crowd favorites. Our covers of "While My Guitar Gently Weeps," "Here Comes the Sun," and

"Rain," were so uniquely ours, changing the arrangements and instrumentations, they remained easily recognizable. This was only our third night in front of an audience, and we were learning to think quickly on our feet.   Mel and I would read each other's minds and trade vocals whenever we wanted. We had two microphones, but we shared one sometimes, making it more intimate. The crowd liked it when we did.

What helped during every song, is that Stu and Alo were terribly strong and carried the dance tempo that made everyone move.   Frankie was better and better on acoustic, which he could match with me and, or Mel. When I took bass, which was on only two songs, Stu wasn't bad on acoustic either.   I impulsively motioned Frankie to play electric on "Isis," which he had never done, not even in rehearsal, while Mel shook a muted tambourine. I was trying to find Dylan's bridge without a harmonica, which none of us could play. The song took on such a psychedelic tone, it didn't matter much. It was always about me and Mel when I sang those lyrics, *Isis oh Isis, you're a mystical child, what's driving me to you, is what's driving me insane,* everyone knew who I was singing about as she would take up the harmony looking right at me. It's such a weird song to be playing live, but I insisted. The crowd seemed to like the slower momentum after several hard-core dance numbers. They'd sit and listen and space out and sip their drinks. Cigarettes being lit.

We had a standing ovation around 11:00, which had not happened the previous weekend. Not like this. We were so damn good, I thought. I couldn't believe it.

True, we were all underage, but we'd been together for years, working hard in the studio. And all of us had been playing music since we were five or six years old, maybe even younger. Alo, no doubt earlier. I told Sarah all of that when she turned on the camera after it was all over. I remember having to wipe my face repeatedly of the sweat and the light of the camera made me wince.

Shelly took me and Mel back to their house. We'd be meeting up with the family and everyone that went to Stephanie's opening. They'd been there for about an hour, already having a good time. A festive atmosphere. Everyone bragged about Steph's singing. Her poise. Mom said over and over how proud she was of Steph's composure. Tim was effusive, hugging Steph as if she were his own.

Steph and I hugged. I pulled her outside on the veranda, a blast of cold air filling our lungs. She excitedly told me all about it. I watched her express every phrase, hints of makeup still on her face. Not once did she make a mistake, she told me. She not only knew her lines, but the entire script. Her timing and emotion were exactly what she hoped for. I was happy for her. She was transforming before my eyes. A young woman. Her auburn brown hair blowing in the cold wind. She was *determined*; found in those pools of dark eyes. She reminded me of mom. Sharon, too. That look. That's my sis. My beautiful twin sister.

The party was breaking up. Mom, Dad, Louise, said goodnight, congratulating me on our night at the Bar. Steph had already headed back. Shelly told Mel she could stay the night. Mel called her mom and then we went downstairs. We were still wired from the night, so we turned on a movie in their basement playroom. An old John Wayne western. Tim came down and acted all fatherly, yet proud of us. Shelly showed Mel where she could sleep.

We were alone with Sprite and popcorn. It was dark and we didn't even bother to change the channel. We made out. I practically had her naked when we stopped. We listened. I got up and looked up the stairs. No one. It was completely dark in the house. They were in bed, clear upstairs on the second floor.

We both knew what we wanted to do, but we were missing that one important item – a condom. I told Mel to hold on. I'd look around the guest bedroom master bathroom. They had a huge first aid closet, packed with everything. Sure enough, I found some KY jelly and a tiny box of three condoms among a douche container and a large box of feminine napkins. All of it behind another box of tampons, a rolled-up heating pad, a bag of cotton balls, a large bottle of aspirin – there it was, that very packet of condoms - I had found gold.

Mel was naked when I returned, cuddled under a blanket. The TV was off, with only the dim light over the pool table on the other end of the room. She told me to take off my clothes. Our nakedness was a fulfillment of great expectations. She had a solid body. Not thin, not fat. Almost muscular. Her firm butt was all that I hoped for when I reached under her to grab her tight to me. Her blonde hair was shiny in the dim light. Her blue eyes piercing me with a kind of pleading. I asked her about our virginity, and she made me stop talking, kissing me hard. Her tongue pulling me in. The sensation of entering her was tight and uncomfortable at first. She guided me slowly until I couldn't take it anymore. I let loose with everything I had, holding back nothing as her wetness increased and I was sliding faster and faster. I realized that her face was buried in my chest, pulling hard on my neck and shoulders. She was gasping. Then we collapsed.

I woke up at 3:20 am. I saw the glow in the dark clock above the mantle. I panicked. I should be home. I went to the bathroom and cleaned up. Then I woke up Mel and told her I should go and that she should move to the bedroom. She wrapped the blanket around her, kissed me, and then I quietly hopped up the stairway. It was dead quiet. I was glad they didn't have a dog. That's all I could think about for a second. Then I tip toed to the sliding glass door and made my get away. Running in the freezing dark night, I noticed the blazing quarter moon, hovering over me. Luckily I had been on this path numerous times, illuminated by the night sky. I stopped for a second and looked back. Their house was dark. I was the happiest man in the world at that moment, only wishing that I could go back and get into bed with Melanie. I saw a small porch light on at James's cottage in the distance. An owl or something flew overhead. Then I made it to our house. We never locked the place. I found my room, then my bed, staring up at the ceiling. Unbelievable. Simply unbelievable.

I went to the Sunday matinee of *Music Man* with a form of hangover absent alcohol, full of torrid music. My larynx was sore. I sat in the back of the auditorium with Mom's agent, Phil.   He wanted to go alone and at the last minute I joined him as I jumped into his rented car, a BMW Roadster. He took notes on a tiny pad. Phil was very professional looking. Polished.   We hardly talked. When we did it was mostly about Mom getting back into acting.   He did ask about Retro Sky, wanting Shelly to get a demo together.   Maybe some film. Maybe he could help. It wasn't his thing, but he knew some people.

Steph was wonderful.   She looked all the librarian, stuffy, eccentric. The conceit and condescension poured out of her in a reserved tempo as Marion. A perfect role, I thought, given that she could sing these songs well. And that she could slide into being in love, more expressive, center stage.   She was more than believable, I thought. She looked twenty-something to me. Intimidating at times. Flickers of Mom. I could see it.

Phil took me to a coffee shop afterwards while he made some calls on his new mobile phone. He said pretty much the same things that I was thinking. He liked what he saw.

When we got back to Tim's house, Phil went on about how much he hated the theater. He'd never been to a high school play he complained. He was all an act, I thought, he had a great time. He was provoking Tim. Mom just rolled her eyes. Phil, however, gave a measured positive review of Steph. *Let's get her in front of a camera right away*, he said. Dad agreed, as Mom waited for his go ahead. Phil had already set it up in two weeks after the play finished – that following Monday.

Everyone was realizing that the machine was at work. Stephanie would be excited when she got home. Tim wanted to fly her out himself on that Sunday, right after the finale. No use in waiting. Phil reached into his pouch and pulled out the latest version of the *Purgatory* script. *I want her to do the readings in here that I've marked.* Mom took it out of his hand and quickly read through the notations.

"Who's going to read the other parts?" She asked Phil.

"Standard people in the studio. I'd rather you stayed away. You know that. At least for now."

"Yeah, yeah, I agree."

"I'll go with her," Shelly said, "We can stay in a suite near the studio. Only for a couple of nights. I can show her around."

"I'd love to show her around too," Tim added.

Mom and Dad conversed and agreed that it was the best plan. I was glad they were letting her go. The painful arguments they had had in the past were vanishing. Steph looked exhausted, surprised to see Phil in the living room. She asked me right away if I had seen the play? Had Phil seen it? Yes, yes. She was great. I congratulated her, telling her I didn't know she had such a strong voice. I wasn't the only one who could sing she needled me.

Dad came over and hugged her. He then told her about the trip to L.A. A screen test. Shelly and Tim would take her. Was she okay with Mom and Dad staying back? She cried with delight, hugging him. She then ran over and hugged Phil, who looked completely taken by surprise. She wouldn't let him go. He looked at her closely through his expensive glasses. *Just like your mom* is what I thought he mumbled.

I was watching Tim most of all during this scene in his own home. It was more and more evident that with he and Shelly having no kids of their own, this was their own progeny. My sister. And me. They had adopted us in their own way.

I walked back to the house with dad. I traced the steps I had run after losing my virginity. Dad put his arm around me like he did countless times, saying hardly a word. Pulling me tight. I was nearly as tall as him now. His face was red from the cold air, his breath releasing frosty exhales. It always seemed to me that dad was in prayer or in a mystical place. I knew he was a golfer, a coach, my principal at school, but he seemed different from all of that. A kind of silence only Mom seemed to get through to.   His knowledge of the music I liked to play influenced me a lot.

"When are you going to start playing your own stuff?" he asked me.

"Me and Mel are working at it. We're close."

"I can't wait to hear it.   Can I suggest something?"

"Yeah, sure, Dad."

"I love when you play the hard driving stuff. New Wave, you call it. Or Punk. Maybe you should listen to some Rap. Look for a street sound."

I listened.

"I was thinking of talking with your Mom about having you go out to New York and visit Sharon. She's filming right now, busy I'm sure. Maybe Vinny can show you around some clubs. Listen to what's going on out there.

Of course, he's probably in Chicago with their son Scott. Anyway, Santa Fe doesn't have what you need."

The entire idea was so new. I let it sink in.

"I also thought you should take Stu. I can't let you go with Mel; I already can see your brain moving. But someone in the band go with you so you can talk with about it."

"What about Alo?"

"I don't know, it's up to you. I don't think it would work if too many of you went out there. I mean you're all underage. I'm not even sure if you can get into any clubs or venues."

"Yeah, you're right. I'll ask Stu. We can talk about bass lines. The core structure for us. You're sure, Dad?"

"No. Not at all. I still need to talk with Mom. Sharon and Vinny. It may not work out. Just a thought."

"I like it. Maybe when Steph goes to L.A. We'd be missing school."

"You know the principal, don't you?"

Stephanie

The play was going well. I was getting along with the cast. While I did everything Mr. Willow asked, I was sticking close to Mom's guidance and Tim's direction. The characters around me were fuel to my very being as a young librarian. I didn't even pay much attention to the crowd, the orchestra, the entire production. I absolutely focused on my persona of who I am in the moment. I sang my heart out. I was in command. I'm sure the kids felt that I was aloof, not breaking into the

hub-bub of gossip and even the fun they were having. I
went along. I enjoyed them. Then I read more scripts
at home.

Sharon came to my last performance on a Sunday
matinee. She tried hard to be inconspicuous but that's
impossible. She sat in the back with Tim and Shelly and
the family. They were an enormous distraction without
even trying. Not for me, but for everyone else.

I nailed it. No nerves at all. Everything was measured
with precision.

I hugged everyone after the show. I made a quick
appearance at our after-party for the cast. I had
achieved a goal and was proud and happy for the
triumph. For all our success. But I was anxious to get
home.

It was then that I received the news. The surprise. I'd
be leaving in about an hour for L.A. Mom urged me to
pack quickly. Tim, Shelly, Sharon would be going with
me. Sharon asked Woody Allen to hold off on her
shoots until Wednesday. She was nearly finished
anyway. She wanted to be around for my screen test.
Not only that. Julian and Stu were going with us.
Originally the guys were going to go to New York, but
things fell through with Vinny. He needed to remain in
Chicago with their son, Scott. Sharon and Tim would
watch over the guys as they visited some clubs and
studios, get a taste of the recording business. They'd
visit the beach, too. We'd all be back on Thursday
morning. Stu was in a world of make believe. Taking a
trip on Tim's private jet with the most famous actor and
actress in the world. Staying in luxury. Visiting who

knows what. All he had to do was pack a bag and bring his bass. I think Stu had a bit of a crush on me. That's okay. He's a nice kid. I was headed elsewhere.

We landed at LAX around 11:00 pm. Two limousines took us to the Park Avenue Hotel near countless studios in Culver City. I shared a room with Sharon, attached to Tim and Shelly's. Sharon told me over and over that she was looking forward to a slumber party. She ordered lots of food and sweets. Julian and Stu were next door. I could hear their stereo almost immediately once we were settled.

Sharon and I read over our script for the morning. My test was set for 10:00 am, at a small studio about three blocks away. Sharon was going to have me play it two or three times before we put it all away. She was smoking and sipping wine, which was okay by me. She told me about a hundred stories about acting, being on location, different actors and directors. She wanted me to meet Jane Fonda most of all. Jane had started her career in her teens, like so many. They had met years ago in L.A. and had become good friends. Sharon went through my performance on *Music Man* with precision. She noticed every detail. My singing, she told me, was very good and would only get better as I matured. What she wanted most of all was to coach me in front of a camera. That was an entirely different beast than being on stage. My acting was understandably body movement, gestures, and inflections. In this movie, I'd need to act with extreme subtlety. Each rise of emotion was to be detected by the camera. She wanted to see the clips tomorrow to see what my instinct was like. She assured me that there was nothing to be nervous about. This was going to be for Tim's sake, as director, most of all. For her and Mom. To find out what they had to work with in me. Relax, be the girl lost in northern France struggling with her destiny. With her mother, the convent, the circus world. Be honest about those feelings, as they arise. Don't worry about the camera, it will do its work.

I hardly ate when we got up around 8:00. Sharon was on the phone with her son, singing him a song, laughing. She'd be home soon, she promised. Sharon and Shelly were going to walk me over, it was that close. Tim had left with the guys to visit Island Records, then drive over to Venice Beach even though it was way too cold to swim.

The women left me alone with make-up people. Costumes were arranged. It took nearly two hours to finish the entire process. The director was a woman, kind, but all business. Not much chit chat.   The actresses were the same way, hired by the studio for these kinds of tasks. Two cameras – a handheld and what I thought was probably a standard studio camera. Lighting was adjusted constantly. Make up changed, reapplied over and over. In and out of this costume into another.

I had no problem finding myself in character. I was draped in the destitution of the time period. My feelings ran to a wounded bird seeking survival. An internal instinct leading me through every syllable. Every glance, every crease in my face. Every gesture and movement. The hunger within. The director and other actors seemed impressed. Mom had told me that she laughed and had a great time during her very first screen test. Not me. I hardly smiled. Maybe never. There was no room for happiness in this burned-out world of a destroyed Europe. I had to get angry at my screen mom once and this pressed my ability. I felt a slow surge, ever progressing, keeping it as bottled up as I could muster. And then the script called for tears. I stayed as far away from melodrama as possible. I let a tear drip because I had to. Nothing forced. Another one came gliding down my cheek. I could feel it in slow motion. Like a silent movie in black and white. The director let me stay in that place for an eternity before she said *cut.* It hurt deep inside of me. The woman playing my mom embraced me and said *good job*. I had to do the scene again. Different lighting. Different everything. It hurt even more the second time. And then the third even more. The pain was eternal, refusing to explode. When we were done, I found a chair and really cried. I had never done that before. The director told me we were finished. I needed to come back the next day. Tim wanted to see the dailies tonight. We'd work outside tomorrow, like a location shoot. Get some rest.

The three of us went to an expensive place via limo. Lunch in a private booth. They ordered me a 7-up and a shot of whiskey if I wanted it. They were kidding. I ate light even though I hadn't eaten breakfast. A salad.

Tim met us back at the studio to view the clips. Julian and Stu had visited the studio, even laid some tape of a riff with their two guitars. Something Julian was working on. Someone over in the engineering room put in drums. Julian did an overdub on a vocal. All very rough.   They were now on their own over at the beach and would have a car drive them back to the hotel in time for dinner.

The four of us sat in darkness. Tim had a controller to play the film back and forth, over and over as he pleased. He had a small table and light for taking notes. I sat far away, in the back with Shelly. Sharon was next to Tim. They were brainstorming quietly together.

There I was on the big screen. Color photography, yet I looked silverish in the dirty dress and beat up shoes. I could resurrect the feeling of that girl that was me. I grimaced. Tim would mercilessly play, rewind, slow down, speed up. Sharon was talking away in his ear. He was agreeing or adding or changing the subject all at once. It would get silent. That was the hard part as a long stretch of film would grind away and all I could hear was the dialogue. My voice. Close ups were murder too. My thought was how forlorn I was. Or the character was. Strength was in my dark eyes. In her dark eyes.

After an hour and a half, I saw that my armpits were drenched from nerves, just sitting there.   Tim left the room. Nothing said. Shelly followed him. Sharon came up and sat by me and hugged me. Her head fell on my shoulder.

"We'll do fine my sweet Stephanie.   This was much better than what I saw in your high school play.   Tim's happy too.   Rest easy my lovely girl. I love you."

I laughed in relief, holding on to her. Tight. "Really?" She smiled, looking up.

"I mean, be honest, please. Not as my Aunt, or Jennifer's daughter. Please." I pleaded.

"Look, Steph. You want to be an actress. I'm here with you. I'd take you home if I didn't think this would work. You did well. Rough around the edges which is all well and fine for this part. You are well on your way. I'm proud of you. Listen. I'm going to treat you like a fellow actor from now on. I'm a bitch to work with. I demand perfection. From myself. From Tim. From your mother. And I will from you. You will need to work your fucking ass off from here until the final take. You will hate me. Just remember, it's not me you hate. It's your goddamn screen mother you hate."

"I don't think I could ever hate you Sharon. I love you. You are my idol. That sounds corny. It's true."

"I love you dear. You know that. You mean more to me than most human beings on this damned planet. I'm just warning you. You will hate my fucking guts once you run away with that circus."

I smiled. I got it.

At dinner Tim and Shelly finally spoke up. They gave me kind comments, encouraging me to the fullest. Tim held up two pages of notes. He was eager to get to work back in Santa Fe. He'd have me in front of his tripod more often. Shelly urged me to stay strong. I was going to work with three of the most powerful people in the history of movies. No room for hesitation. I'd find time to have fun, like they did, but when I needed to break down. Well, when I needed to break down, I needed to go to her. Stay away from Sharon and Jennifer, my mom. And especially Tim. Go to her first and she would provide a buffer, a sound board before I reacted or lashed out. I wouldn't be able to do it all the time. Just remember that once filming starts, sometime next year, she will be in the same trailer with me. The entire time. Not with Sharon or my mom. Her.

Julian and Stu were telling hilarious stories about Venice Beach. Crazy things with weightlifters and drug use, skate boarders, colorful artwork, graffiti. The laughter loosened me up again. Honestly, though, I was only thinking about what was going on with me.

Tomorrow they wanted me working for three hours, minimum – it would turn out to be all day. All the filming would be outdoors. They would use both black and white and color formats. I was beginning to falter. Overwhelmed.

They must have sensed my reservations. Maybe my fear. I had been brave. They saw that. Shelly gave me a pep talk in a makeshift, enclosed tent, early in the day. I had on full make-up and costuming. I knew my scenes. Not a lot of dialogue, plenty of action and movement. I worked with other actors all day. Most scenes were of just me. One, running frantically to catch a horse-drawn flat rig – which was not actually there – was done ten or eleven times. Different angles; side, high and low.

Lunch was a boxed sandwich and an apple. I drank a lot of water; I was terribly thirsty. I sat alone wondering how much all this cost. Expensive I was certain. All for a movie that I wasn't sure I belonged in. Tim, everyone, was doing this for me. Shelly arrived with a big smile. She had seen several cuts from the day and was happy as could be. That lifted my spirits. It gave me a shot for the afternoon.

Sharon showed up in full costume. My heart raced in panic. She looked every bit the prostitute mother in the script. She scared the shit out of me. She stood far from me, intentionally staying away. The acting director had me read my lines. Another actor took the role Sharon would be playing. We rehearsed something I had memorized ages ago. Finally, I was brought on a specific spot, and the director called *action*. Sharon entered. I had the first line. It was like another person was speaking. Sharon went into her lines, moving about naturally. I kept up with her. Barely. The scene escalates. I was trembling, doing my very best to be her daughter. Begging to not go into *the business*. Sharon looked deep into me, grabbing my arm, she looked like the horrible woman on the pages. I was hating her. I found the hatred and responded, shaking, fighting tears. Brave as possible. A long pause. Staring at each other. A stand-off.

Cut.

Sharon walked off to her tent and didn't even acknowledge me. The director said something like *nice job*, but I ran to Shelly's arms as she whisked me to our tent. I was shivering.

"You did marvelously, you really did. Take a deep breath."

I did. Over and over.

"Your first scene with Sharon. Not many people can take it. Tim even complains how tough she is."

"Oh, Jesus. I've never felt that way in my entire life. I tried, I really tried. I did everything I could to stand up to her."

"You did. You were great. You won't have to do that scene again. At least not today. You'll do it a lot when we get to France. That's another day."

"Thank God."

"You're not done though. Listen, you got Sharon one more time." She handed me a script and turned to a late scene with her and the nun from the orphanage, who would be played by mom. I knew the scene backwards and forwards. A lot of it is me stuck in the middle between the two of them. Two powerful women having at it. The dialogue was almost unbearable. My lines squeezed in here and there, fighting for my own destiny.

"Listen," she was saying again, "do you know Robin Wright, the actress?"

"Of course. You know me, a big Madonna fan. She's married to Sean Penn now. Why?"

"Well, she's on set down the street, on another movie. She's friends with Sharon. Anyway, she's playing the nun in a few minutes. She graciously dropped in. Wanted to see what was up. She'll be dressed in the habit, the whole thing. Go with it, like you would. She will introduce herself later. Sharon wanted you to face the moment raw."

"Fuck." I murmured.

It was a different location. I makeshift looking building painted as a backdrop to a church. We'd be outside along a pathway. The camera was setup on a movable track as we walked. The director had me walk along the path, alone, explaining each sequence, where the three of us would stop and start up. Did I understand? Yes. Places.

Action.

Robin Wright appeared from behind the building door taking me in her arm. Sharon followed. They were arguing. I caught the phrasing immediately. I looked at her powerful face, her blue eyes. She was like a savior. She was enveloping me. They were having at it back and forth. Sharon getting the best of Robin. I spoke up as we stopped. I was on the verge of yelling, fighting the two personalities. They responded in kind; in a way I cannot describe. To have both Sharon and Robin looking right at me, heated, carving their vision into my soul, their expectations, I bore ahead with my lines. My emotions. I was fighting them both. The rage continued in powerful restraint. On and on, as we reached the end of the path. It would be where I hear sounds from the carnival. I ran.

Cut.

I stopped running. I was panting. Not so much from running but from the exhaustion. I looked up at the sky. It was overcast in L.A. Perfect for the scene I thought strangely to myself. I could hear murmurings behind me refusing to turn around. I kept breathing. Gathering myself.

A gentle hand found my shoulder. Unfamiliar. It was Robin Wright.

"That was fun, Stephanie. I'm Robin Wright."

I turned fully to face her and shook her offered hand. She looked sensitive with that smile of hers. Unique to her.

"I hope you don't mind me stepping in. Sharon and I go way back, and I agreed to help this afternoon. Anything for her. She's helped me countless times. Besides, it's a pleasure to meet you. I've never met your mom, but I love her work. Her painting mostly. Or even her paintings, I mean to say."

I understood.

"Nice to meet you. I have to confess, I'm in a bit of shock now."

"Sure, you are. So am I. It's a tough scene."

"Well." I paused. She waited patiently. "Thank you. I mean, this is all new to me. I'm in awe of meeting you. And under these circumstances, even more blown away."

She laughed slightly. That kindness again. She looked like the first professional actress I ever met. Sharon, Tim, Mom, none of them counted. None of the few I met at parties. This was different.

"You'll be fine, Stephanie. Sharon is headstrong believing in you. Just trust that. Trust yourself anywhere near how she does, and you'll be fine."

I thanked her again.

"When your mom takes this role, I'll be envious. I'd give anything to play this part. It's a gem. Your mom and Sharon's husband have done a bang-up job on this script."

I didn't know how to respond. I was worried maybe Mom would back out. I knew she had reservations. Maybe this was all a contingency plan.

Robin read my mind. "Don't worry sweety. I can't take on that role right now. Your mom will do this far better than I could. I've seen every movie, every scene where she and Sharon are together, and there is no combination in the world that is better. Not one. You will be in great hands. Like I said, I'm more than envious."

My mind was racing as Sharon arrived. She had a big smile, hugging Robin. Thanking her profusely. They were obviously friends. Sharon barely acknowledged me as we headed back to our tents. They were arm and arm. I trailed in back, like the lost teenage kid in the script. I was already the character.

I sat in my tent, eating an orange, getting out of my garb. Cleaning off my makeup. Shelly was chattering away how great I was. I barely believed her, thinking she was only building me up. Robin Wright peeked in, asking me if she could come in.

"Of course," Shelly responded, pointing to a chair.

"I wanted to say bye to you both. Say hi to Tim for me. I have to get going." She shook my hand again as I stood up. We had an awkward hug. Shelly stepped outside; she must've sensed that Robin wanted to be alone with me.

"Sharon talks about you all the time whenever I see her. Your brother, too. Julian, right?"

I smiled and nodded.

"I remember being a freshman in high school. You don't seem like a freshman to me. When the camera rolled, you seemed older. I sensed that in you. You were great."

"That means a lot. Thank you."

"Look, this is going to sound weird, me being married to Sean, but I hear you're a big Madonna fan."

I lit up. Of course, I was.

"Look, there's an informal gathering, cocktails late up in the hills. It is a Tuesday. Probably just sitting around looking at the views and listening to music. Eating barbecue. I think it's a record producer's house. Sharon was going to take you and your brother up there before she caught the red eye back to New York. You should go."

I wasn't processing well. Sounded good.

"Madonna will probably be there."

Air escaped my lungs. We hugged before she departed. Tim and Shelly did not go with us. They were headed to a dinner with potential producers. Sharon would take us to the home of a man named Peter Fontana who owned the famous Chrystal Record Company catering to cutting edge sounds. An informal gathering. Dress casually. Jeans, warm jacket. She was going to leave around 10:00 for the airport and we three would have a limousine back to the hotel. We had to swear we'd be good on our own and check in with Tim and Shelly when we got back, probably close to midnight. We were only fourteen, and Stu was sixteen, after all. I felt like I was about nine years old, nervous as could be. More nervous than filming or anything. Meeting Madonna.

Julian and Stu were making fun of me, although they seemed excited about meeting her too. Sharon was cracking up making jokes about it all. She still hadn't said anything to me about our filming that day. I had this eerie feeling she was trying to teach me something. To not rely on her constant reassurance. She wasn't cold, exactly. There was a purpose in this.

Peter and his partner Jonas greeted us warmly. Their home was decorated in bold décor and bright colors. We drank pop, while Sharon immediately lit up a cigarette and took a whiskey sour. Two or three others were mingling, as my eyes darted around to try and spot Madonna. Nothing. I could smell barbecue coming from their enormous veranda. It was cold outside, but someone was preparing delicious food.

Madonna strolled in from a back room with whom I presumed to be her new husband. Sharon hugged him and brought him over to me. My heart was racing. She introduced me to Guy Ritchie, a British director. He was polite with a heavy English accent. He shook all three of our hands. Madonna lingered where she was, laughing about something with someone else. I could hardly stand it. Guy Ritchie in turn introduced us to Madonna. Casually, like we might not know who she was. She was beautiful. A constant look of having fun creased about her. We shook hands, looking into each other's eyes. She asked me about filming that day. I was stupid quiet, muttering that it went fine, having no idea how she knew about my day. Guy was particularly interested. Wanting to know more about Sharon and my mom and Tim and the project. About Robin being there.

Madonna kept looking at me in curiosity, waiting for more.

We all found seats. Madonna right next to me. She put her hand on my knee and patted me, urging me to speak.

I told them about it the best I could. I am not at all sure what I said. Guy did most of the speaking. Sharon got up and left, taking Julian and Stu with her to meet Peter, to discuss recording and the music business. She was doing this for both me and Julian, I realized. Then Guy got up and left, for no reason that I could tell. I panicked. Madonna and I alone on the couch. She was so friendly. Almost like a lost girlfriend. So *normal*. I told her I liked her latest album, *Ray of Light*, just like a typical starstruck fourteen-year-old fan. She was gracious. She asked about my mom, saying she owned one of her paintings. That she'd been to the Rio Blanco Gallery. She was excited that Mom was getting back into acting. Then she asked me more about living in Santa Fe.

I also told her about riding at the pueblos. I mentioned James, whom she had met at the Gallery. I was relaxing. We talked more about horses, about the native friends in my life. That made her curious, asking about the culture. We were having fun, as she turned into a more comfortable position on the large couch, facing me, setting down her wine. She brought up her newfound religion, the Kabbalah, a kind of mysticism. A mysticism she found to be remarkably like the native culture of the region. I said more and more about James, and Bill, before he died, and about the ceremonies we had been to as a kid. The rituals, the dances. It was like the two of us were disappearing into a conversation mystical in and of itself. We'd exchange one thought after another, all associated with *another*, a force in the universe, we both understood on an instinctive level. People were eating food, mingling. We were left alone. Madonna kept talking to me when I wondered why. We were both going on and on about spiritual concepts in New Mexico and how they matched up with the Kabbalah. At least that's how she saw it. I told her how James and I would smoke a special pipe and he'd chant. She urged me to go on. I told her about the vision Julian and I had at the kiva. Two buildings high in the sky. Planes like birds. It was an eerie image I could not get out of my mind, my dreams. She grabbed my hand in empathy. *Trust it*, is all she repeated.

The night wore on and I didn't get to speak with Madonna again. Not even say goodbye. She and Guy left after a quick bite to eat. Julian and Stu were listening to music and talking energetically with Peter and Jonas downstairs in their music room and home studio.
Sharon left, grabbing a ride to the airport. We hugged. She looked me in the eye and said to watch carefully the film clips tomorrow with Tim. Listen closely to what he had to say. Nothing else. She was gone.

I was alone as the other guests left. I sat in the upstairs, on the same couch where Madonna and I had sat just an hour ago. It all seemed so surreal. Like a moment in time flashing from somewhere else. The music on upstairs was orchestral. I was lost in it. I put on my jacket and went outside and sat, looking over the giant city lit up aglow.

During the ride home Julian played a tape Peter had given to them. It bothered me. I liked the silence. They were excited, as Peter had arranged for them to go to his studio tomorrow and see what's going on over there. Bring their instruments. I was happy for them. Looking at Stu, especially, with his giddiness. This was Disneyland for him.

It was for me too. Tim and Shelly were glad that we were back to the hotel. All went well. Finally, everyone went to bed.

In the morning Shelly took me to meet Tim at the studio. We'd watch the dailies. Julian and Stu got a ride over to the studio. It was fun to see them get into a limo with their guitar cases, sunglasses on. They looked like famous somebodies getting away in a hurry. A scene from a Beatles movie I had seen as a kid. Too bad Melanie wasn't here. She'd fit right in. Alo and Frank, too. Someday.

Tim had breakfast for me. Preparing me for what would prove grueling. He made long lists for each scene. He never placed judgments like *good* or *bad*, rather what was working and what wasn't. All in terms of production. Angles, lighting. He rarely addressed my performance per se. He was studying me intensely. I was doing the same.

When I saw the scene of me and Sharon alone, I had to admit that I was deeply moved. It was impressive, I thought. I didn't even see any changes that needed to be made. Tim was writing rapidly on his little notepad.

Then the scene with Robin and Sharon. Moving, walking. The camera on track. The escalation. I thought I was right on target each line. I loved the black and white. Again, no changes needed. I was proud of myself.

After nearly two hours, Tim moved me to another room, well lit. Fruit on the table, a choice of soft drinks and ice. We went to the bathroom then settled in.

Director to actor. What did I think, he asked?

I told him my impressions. I thought I had done well. That all of it was a good start.

He agreed, then reached over and asked again, what I needed to work on.

"Well, Tim, I was ready. I had my lines, the marks. All of it. Even my emotions and execution. I was acting on impulse. It was overwhelming."

"I can see that. In some ways it works because of your character. We have a lot to process because you and your character are going through similar moments in time. I don't want to lose that. But I want to erase your own trepidation and tap into the character purely. You are so close. I don't need to direct you towards technique. You have good instinct there. The camera accepts your delivery."

I wasn't sure what he was getting at. He went on, "you are so young, Stephanie. This is new to me as a director. And you're a teenager. I'm dealing with emotions within you that are confusing, just like the scenes, the movie itself. Like your own life. There is an overlap I am struggling with."

"Tell me about it." I said almost sarcastically.

He laughed. "Look, ultimately, this trip is a huge success. It gives me the green light to go on. You did a great job Steph. Better than I could hope for. I've moved beyond all that already. Sharon and your mom will be ready. I have no doubt. I mean ..."

I interrupted, "God, Tim, let me say something."

"Sure."

"I have never been through anything like that in my life. When Sharon and I did that scene, it blew me away."

"Let's watch it again. Slowly this time."

We walked back to the viewing room, and he cued it up. We went through it inch by inch, almost in slow motion. We'd stop and examine each line from both of us. It was fucking good. Then we did the same thing with the scene with Robin and Sharon and me. It was fucking good too. I had to say it exactly that way. Sharon had done something to me. I could see it unfold right there on the screen.

"You're right kid. I know it. Jesus, I know it. She has that effect. Just wait and see how much better it will get. I know you can't see it now but trust me. After we rehearse, get to France, get down to business and it's the real thing, Sharon, your mom, you. The right cinematography, the sets, you know what I mean. Well, then you will see what fucking *good* really looks like."

Shelly rejoined us and took me around the studio, introducing me to some people they had to speak with. I was tagging along. I'd walk in hallways with famous people's photos. Academy Award photos. Original movie poster drawings framed in bold lighting.

We climbed into a limo and went to pick up Stu and Julian. The boys were seated in a small studio with their guitars as we entered a sound control room. They didn't know we were there. A guitarist was working with them, who the engineer told us was Mike Campbell of the Heartbreakers, who were recording with Tom Petty down the hallway. He dropped in to listen to what they were fooling around with. They were jamming to some piped in drumming. Julian was singing into a microphone as he sat there. Lyrics I had never heard before. Campbell let loose with a riff that even the engineer was blown away with. Julian was backing him on his Fender. Stu was moving impressively up and down his bass. The three of them started laughing when they finished. Mike got up and shook their hands, waving up at us in the booth and then he left.
I never saw my brother so excited. He had written his first song, something he had built with Mel. It was now on tape.
The engineer did a few maneuverings on his massive control board. Replayed the mix, then released a small tape, handing it to Tim. We exited and went into the sound studio. I hugged Julian from the side, congratulating him. Then Stu, who was still in that perpetual state of amazement. Tim yelled up to the sound room asking to hear it again. The engineer smiled and piped it into the studio. We listened closely. It was loud. It was explosive. The two guitars battling. I could hear Campbell's guitar taking over with authority. What really grabbed me were the lyrics. Julian was impressive. He sounded like Strummer of The Clash, I thought. Twist

in his accent or delivery. I wasn't sure. Not quite Costello. Stu's bass was powerful, reverberating in the room. He beamed. Tim raised an eyebrow in approval. Shelly was clapping. This was her band now and they had a demo. She'd need to get the rest of the band worked in when we got back.

We took it easy that night. Pizza and sitting around on the veranda. Our flight was going to leave at 6:00 am, so we went to bed early. I was exhausted. I smiled before leaving this world.

Plane lands a little before 9:00 am, Santa Fe time. After dropping off Stu, we get home and shower; we had left that quickly. Louise is there, knowing better than to ask too many questions but she always wears her curiosity on her sleeve. Julian filled her in on everything. I went to my room. Right away I took down the Madonna posters. Time to get over fandom. The teen thing. I knew her now. A friend, I told myself. In fact, I looked around my room and wanted to get rid of the entire junior high feeling. I wanted Mom to help me. Maybe do an O'Keefe thing, like she would do. Or maybe native feel. Nothing other than understatement. I was learning.

I wanted to talk with Dad in the worst way. I needed to see him, but I didn't want to go to school. We were excused that day anyway. I got my bike out, bundled up and made the long trek into town. To see Mom.

The Gallery was always busy it seemed to me. Tourists arrived during all seasons, all times of the year. Clients. I checked out Frankie's display of *Kid*. It was so cool. I really liked it. Note to self: let him know that I liked it. One of Mom's employees, I forgot her name, recognized me. She congratulated me on *Music Man*. She had seen it last week. I thanked her as she was going to take me to Mom's office. I asked to see Samantha's exhibit first. She gave me a private tour of the collection, which impressed me a great deal. I wished I could paint, or was interested in art. I never was. Mom never pushed it. We'd do watercolors and crayons, all of that growing up, but it wasn't my interest. I was always into movies, books and I liked school. Dad was my mentor and tutor on so much of my learning. And riding. And skiing — which was Mom's thing with me.

Mom hugged me tight. So glad I was home. We went into her studio for more privacy. I went on and on like a little child. One story after another. We drank cocoa. My excitement was contagious as Mom kept urging me to tell her more. Every detail. She laughed so hard about me meeting Madonna. I exaggerated it a lot and she knew it. I did try and tell her about the mystical stuff, Madonna's religion. Mom understood right away. She understood the connection.

Mostly we talked about the screen tests. The long hours. Sharon, Tim. Meeting, working with Robin Wright. The script and my role. My impressions. I thought I was good. She took it all in, listening carefully. I could tell her mind was whirling. Her professional mind, not just my mom's mind. She asked about details. The locations. The guest director and actors. Costumes. Lighting. Cameras. She was curious about the handheld camera and how I did with it. I was conscious of who I was in my role and was never, ever affected by the peripheral. She was glad to hear that. Even taking a deep sigh. That part was never an issue I assured her. She said something like going from high school stage to film was a big leap. Her prep, Tim's prior help here in Santa Fe were perfect. She got up and went to her office and came back with the latest edition of Vinny's script. It was near completion. We went over the scene with Sharon and Robin and me. We read it again. It was slightly different. Longer, a lot longer. I was sitting closer to my mom doing this and she didn't feel like my mom. This was a person getting ready for a race. A thoroughbred. I knew that metaphor from being around horses. Mom reminded me of a stallion over at the pueblo. She had that exact same look in her eyes. As she read aloud, her mind was racing out on the arroyo. A different persona altogether. It frightened me a little. Like Sharon had. Like I was losing people I loved the most in the world. Maybe that's why Dad always seemed like an anchor. Stable. We read right there, went through it twice. When she would look directly at me, I saw Mother Superior, a French nun. Connected to God. My future in the balance. I knew who I was in that very moment. I was bound for the circus.

CHAPTER EIGHT

Con Cristo riassume in sé tutte le gioie; vive la gioia perfetta promessa alla Chiesa: Mater plena sanctae laetitiae.Ed è con buona ragione che i suoi figli sulla terra, rivolgendosi a Lei che è madre della speranza e della grazia, la invocano come causa della loro gioia. A Christmas blessing from the Pope.

Danny

I was heading back to my office after making sure everything went well at the bus lot and parent pick up area. School was out and everyone was darting home. I dropped into the gym, said *hi* to Billy and watched him do his opening drills with the basketball team. I missed coaching. They were starting off undefeated, looking tough. Billy said a few words and we laughed about old times. I then poked my head into the wrestling room. Our team was weak, but I had hired a new coach from Texas. We had won our first meet.

Down the hallway, the pom-poms were practicing. I said hi to Mrs. Wheeler, our PE teacher. She was a great lady, a great teacher. She was taking maternity leave soon and I was having a tough time finding a long-term sub.

Over to Chess club. A big draw, maybe forty kids. It did my heart good. Tables full. Concentration at each one. I sat at my desk, wondering which phone calls to return first. All were parents. All were concerned about their child's grades. The problem that I was having, was getting parents and teachers to talk with each other directly. They both wanted me to intervene, bypassing the easiest step of all.

I called each one, giving them the extension of the teacher or teachers, they needed to speak with. If it didn't go well, I'd get involved. Let's try that first I encouraged. I rarely heard back from a parent after that initial call. But it was time consuming, hearing their particular issue, being patient.

Then my appointment showed up. My senior science teacher, Mr. Bonham. I was pissed off at him and tried to restrain myself. I wanted to give him a chance. He was a tenured, experienced teacher who was well liked by everyone. The kids especially. But he wasn't following any of the guidelines I wanted in terms of lesson plans or attending meetings. He had a cocky chip on his shoulder. I posed my concerns calmly, waiting for his explanations. He didn't have a good answer, avoiding eye contact. I reiterated my expectations in no uncertain terms. This was a meeting I did not want to have again, I told him. I asked him if it was a meeting he expected us to have again. He shook his head *no*. I told him to have a good evening. Don't forget to be on time to our meeting Thursday morning. He promised he would. I'd have to wait and see.

I was tired. It was getting late. Then I saw Stephanie come through the front office. My heart leaped to see her. I jumped out and went out and hugged her. Cheryl had a big smile on her face.

"Steph's been ditching school," I said. "I need to have a talk with this young lady." Escorting her into my office, sitting down at the small meeting table.

Steph was all smiles, telling me how she rode her bike to Jennifer's Gallery, then over to see me. Her face flush with the cold air. Then she told me the countless stories of being in L.A. – which I imagined were word for word what she had already told Jennifer. The Madonna one was the most exciting for her. As she told me about Sharon and the filming, all of it, my heart slipped into the dawning of show business back into our lives. I was fine with it, yet already missing the years behind us, relatively quiet and solid.   The writing was on the wall. I was happy for the kids, for Jennifer.

Stephanie looked so animated. My little girl rapidly becoming a young woman. I was listening to her mannerisms more than her words. How quickly they grow up. The cliché is true.

I organized a few files and looked over my agenda for the next day, then closed shop in the front office. Cheryl had already gone home.

I loaded Stephanie's bike into my trunk, and we headed home.

Julian was equally upbeat when I arrived.   Dinner was ready, a delicious stew Jennifer had whipped up, and homemade tortillas.   James joined us, sitting next to Louise.   He was brought up to the house by Julian so he could share in all the news of the trip. James was delighted. Always appreciative to be part of the family. Steph asked me and Jennifer if she could go to the Pueblo this coming weekend. She wanted to ride with her friend, Luyu – she called her Lu.   Luyu was probably Steph's best friend. She was probably nineteen or twenty, dropped out of school years ago. Lu worked hard with the horses, practically lived in the stalls.   We said sure.   I loved that she went over there so often growing up.   James usually took her, but he didn't drive much anymore.   I would drop them off. James always went with her and stayed with the elders.   She said she needed some time alone.   Sounded exactly like her mother. Jennifer smiled at me and reached over and rubbed my knuckles.

Jennifer and I had taken advantage of the kids being in California. We were louder than usual, making love every night they were gone. Once in front of our blazing fireplace. Even though it was a Monday night. We drank way too much wine for work nights. Maybe that's why I was dragging.

Julian went over his stories again. Probably for the countless time. He had told Louise everything. Then went to James's cottage and told some of the same stories. Then Jennifer got home. Again. Now me. He showed no sign of slowing down. We did all go downstairs to listen to his demo tape on our stereo system. He filled us in on Mike Campbell – which probably impressed me the most of all the stories I was hearing – and the engineered sound mix.

Our stereo is state of the art. Julian had designed it and bought the various components about two years ago. It had cost plenty. We all enjoyed our various music and took turns with our choices.

Then it started. All electric with two guitars, a blistering bass, and what sounded like a drum machine to me. The two guitars traded licks building to Julian's vocals. I listened to the lyrics carefully. They sounded street-inspired, like they were about living in the inner city in desperate times. Julian had listened to me. Campbell's bridge riff was so good, I wondered if Tom Petty would appreciate that it was on this ragamuffin demo of an unknown band named Retro Sky. We all listened to it again, chiming in on the chorus, *only the pavement knows my name only the pavement sees my shame.* It was catchy stuff. Julian said Shelly was going to find a way to take the demo and work in Melanie on backup, and Frankie on acoustic. The hard part was to remove the drum machine for Alo. Maybe Alo could play some tambourine. Anything to contribute. Julian wanted to make sure everyone was credited. Shelly thought there was a sound studio downtown somewhere. None of us knew where. Probably someone's garage.

We all went to bed late. School night, after all. Reality setting in. I walked James back to his place using a flashlight. The lighting down his path was not good. Jennifer and I lay in bed naked, talking. I left the bedside light on and gazed into her dark eyes. Her hair flowing on the pillow. We talked about the kids' lives and discoveries, all occurring in only a few days. Changed. My wife, too, was changing. I knew her to be like this nearly a decade ago. This part of her was returning. Parallel and in unison with everything else going on. I understood my role, my job. I was the hub of the wheel. Jennifer closed her eyes and fell asleep on my arm. I pulled back the covers, admiring her body, adjusting her to roll over, making her comfortable.

I didn't fall asleep for a very long time. My brain running through my family life, all over again. All that was going on at school. Things I needed to do before the semester ended.

And I needed to plan our trip to Paris and Rome. We'd be leaving soon. Luckily Jennifer had already arranged flights and accommodations in Paris. She'd be leaving December 12, three days before us. She had an art show to get ready. I wanted to see what I could do with the kids in Paris when Jennifer was busy at the Museum.

Rome loomed large in my mind. The Pope had sent me a private note, a blessing, for Christmas and our upcoming visit. The Holy Days would arrive soon. Sometimes I would go down and sit in Billy's coaching office when I needed a break from the chaos in the front office. I was hurriedly doing the teacher observations I needed to do before Christmas. I'd meet with teachers, offering positive encouragement mostly, a recommendation or two. I had a great staff. Meetings piled up. As I sat there I looked out through the coach's window at our state championship banners hanging down from the gymnasium rafters. Two of them were when I was coach. It seemed like ages ago already. Billy had framed pictures of all the teams we had coached hanging on the walls. I'd look at each one recalling the kids, the players. The good times.

When I walked the hallways, I loved sitting in on a class, taking in whatever was going on. Participating. No agenda. Listening to the teacher, the students. My favorite was going to the special education department and participating with whatever they were doing. I knew all the kids with an I.E.P. by name. I was in full support of mainstreaming, but some kids needed extra support and came down here for specific classes, like speech therapy, or motor skill development. Or a more low-level math instruction.

I carried a walkie-talkie if Cheryl needed to get ahold of me. I stayed out of the office as much as my schedule would allow. I was in Mr. Vaitaitis's music class, mixed band and choir. I'd sit in back and enjoy the purity of the music. The innocence. Stephanie was in this class, but I was there for all of them at that moment.

The art room was my favorite. I would take off my jacket and hang it up and put on a smock and sit at one of the tables and do whatever project they were doing. Watercolor was my favorite.   I would spend an entire class period in there if time allowed.

I was known as a highly visible and accessible principal. The kids knew me, talked with me freely. Teachers, too. I drew closest to the kids who were at risk, usually the ones that got into trouble, or had tough family lives.   I'd sit with them at lunch, checking in.   Or go out to the playground where kids hung out and played basketball on warm days. Or just sat around in their coats on picnic benches on cold ones.

I knew that I was keeping an eye on Julian's band, keeping it as part of my routine.   I'd have a copy of their schedules in my notebook. Frankie was in his science class when I made my rounds.   I went in while he was working on an experiment with his lab partner. I made my way over and congratulated him on his display at the Gallery. Shook his hand without disrupting the class. He's a big kid. I wondered if he ever played sports. Stu was in language arts. They were taking a test. I stood over his shoulder to see what he was writing. Something about the novel *Tom Sawyer*.   That Mark Twain did a nice job describing Tom's relationship with Huck. His handwriting was strained. I knew he struggled. I tracked down Melanie in business class. She was blowing a big pink bubble with her gum. Not really listening to the teacher talk about a typing test next week. Her hair was up in a beehive wrapped in a blue 'doo-scarf'. She had on orange lipstick and a bright yellow sweatshirt that read *En Vogue* FREE YOUR MIND on it. She saw me and waved, everyone noticed. That was Mel, I thought. I nodded and left. I knew it was serious with her and my son.   I wasn't sure how serious. I liked Melanie even though she was a handful. She was a good student, but I knew she could be a great student if she applied herself. The band, Retro Sky, and Julian were all she cared about now. I could see that. She was her own person already, no doubt. She was a senior. The oldest in the band. How was she going to treat this situation, graduation looming?   Julian had three more years of school. College was never on her lips. I knew her mom couldn't afford it even if it was not an aspiration of hers. My mind was processing what she should do after high school.   I was being a surrogate dad. I knew. I was aware. Maybe a job and the community college.   Keep taking business classes. It bothered me. Alo was at lunch.   I sat with him and his friends from the reservation. One of the kids kept calling Alo, Bird. Bird this. Bird that. Alo was a happy kid. Nothing bothered him. He always wore the same new clothes I had bought him. He was perpetually drumming. With his hands, with pencils, with his fingers. A rolling soundtrack in his head. I'd ask him who did a particular song in 1958, a top ten hit, and he knew who did it and who played drums.   He got about 90 percent of my trivia questions right. I'd ask him a quick one in the hall, answering, *Little Richard, Charles Conner on drums*, he'd say without missing a beat. Or another, *The Rolling Stones, Charlie Watts, too easy Mr. Tomasetti.*

Once back from L.A. Shelly had immediately gathered the band over at a recording studio in one of the local DJ's basements. They were not able to remove the drum machine background, or remove anything at all from the original tape, but they were able to add in sound. Melanie and Frankie played their acoustics, deciding to let Julian's vocal stand alone. They also decided against tambourine, opting for an additional native beat underneath the existing drums. Just off beat enough to give it additional edge. They were ready to market their first demo.

And they had a new gig. An upcoming weekend at Maxwell's Bar and Grill. It was larger than Jimmy's, seating about 100. Cover charge would be $5.00. Maxwell's had an actual stage, with additional speakers. Hard to believe that Jennifer and I had our first beers in Maxwell's way back when we first moved to Santa Fe. Eventually I was called back to the office. Something always came up. Another problem. Another question. Another phone call. The janitor needed to talk to me about installing new lockers for our expanding population. A curriculum question from a board member. A line-item budget estimate for the superintendent. I was good at it. I took it all, full speed ahead. Like the captain of the ship, which I was.

Late one afternoon, I went over to the Archdiocese offices. Bishop Sheehan was back in Albuquerque. His secretary, sister Michael Rose, had an itinerary for me sent from Rome. Dates, contacts and phone numbers, arrangements for stay. Even recommended restaurants. Rental car information, although a car was going to be provided when we arrived at the train station from Paris. Then there were two hefty packets – one for me and one for Vinny.   Both were marked confidential and sealed. I assured sister Rose that I would Fed Ex this packet myself and speak with Vinny personally on the phone.

I sat in a leather chair and quickly opened my packet. It was a historical and genealogical study of our family origin in Abruzzi, in the town of Castiglione Messer Marina. I could tell that it contained copies of documents, translations from the Italian. Charts. Dates, manifests. Archival value. It was extensively researched by the Vatican historical office. A gift from the Pope. I wasn't going to read it now, save it for later. My dad back in Denver would want to hear all of this right away.

Julian

We didn't need to make many changes to our set for Maxwell's. The song selection was just fine according to the owner. Shelly recommended that we talk a little bit more, interact between songs. Melanie and I agreed. We'd clown around, talk about each song, the original version. We did add our new song, agreeing we'd call it "Only the Pavement Knows." No Mike Campbell, so I tried my best to cover his lead. It would take a lot of time to reach that level. Melanie had a love song – which we both wrote, "Into the Clouds," which was simply gorgeous. She played it solo on her acoustic. We had a long talk about what to do with it as a band. We'd go round and round with one idea after another. Finally, I decided. She'd do it solo. We'd announce one more song, then Melanie would lead us into a break, asking beforehand for the single white light on only her. All of us would exit to the rear behind a divider that led to the kitchen. She had no hesitation. It took a lot for me to get to that point. I was the leader. Everyone understood that. It was the correct decision as it turns out.

Our entire first half of the Friday night showing was a huge success. There was more room for dancing, which most people in the audience did with exuberance. It was a lot of fun for Mel and me to talk about a bit of trivia regarding our song selection. We'd highlight someone in the band. For instance, giving Freebird, now evolving into *Bird*, kudos for a drum solo. That kind of thing. We were more relaxed this time around.

At the break, the four of us stood silently inside the kitchen with the dishwasher of the restaurant humming in the back corner, straining to hear Melanie sing her solo out front. The audience was dead quiet. Her guitar was clean and sweet. Her voice exhibiting her potential range. Her song was part soul, part street wise, part sentimental. It was sad. The standing ovation we heard was incredible. Mel slid back through the partition, flush with excitement. We all hugged her in the steamy heat of the kitchen.

We finished that night going much later than we thought. We played "Twist and Shout," sounding more like the original 1951 Top Notes, or a Buddy Holly version, rather than the Beatles hit. I took lead vocal, but Mel and Frankie – on one microphone – were chiming in with the fast-paced dance feel. Bird was driving the tempo, like always. It was all corny in our way of handling it, but the crowd seemed to like it. Then we finished with our song, "Only the Pavement Knows." It was the only song that was not a cover thus far and even though I introduced it as written by Mel and me, they listened attentively, uncertain how to react. I'm still not sure how it was received because the final ovation was more for the evening than the song itself.

In impromptu fashion we praised Alo and Frankie and Stu, sending them out the backway, ready to say goodnight, saying we had one final encore. Mel and I sang our Everly Brothers tune, making lyrical love to each other and to the audience in that dreamy fashion. Mel didn't play her guitar, instead she used a cloth covered, muted, tambourine keeping subtle beats. We'd only tried it a few times in practices. It heightened the mesmerizing effect.

As the two nights progressed and eventually ended, I was concerned that Mel was stealing the show. Sure, I was on target and blowing the house down. The band sounded wonderful. No complaints. She just had a way, a feminine mystique, attractive and bold. I spoke with her about it on Sunday, taking a long walk out by our house. It was terribly cold, almost teeth chattering cold. We hugged and kissed; we had no problem with each other. She understood what I was saying, though. She liked how we were evolving as a band. How she and I were together now. That meant the world to her. It meant the same for me. We settled into the fact that the audience loved her. They liked me a lot – some of them loved me. They all loved her. That was okay. We laughed because we knew so much of it was sexual. She had sex appeal. I'd find my own attractiveness, a different kind of allure. Maybe a little more personality and confidence as the leader added to my already supreme composure with my own musical ability. It would come. It was already beginning to show itself. Ultimately, the music of Retro Sky was all of us together. Dad sat us all down one night while he and Mom went over the rapidly approaching Christmas break. Mom would leave for Paris three days before we left on December 12. She would be making sure everything was in place, doing promotional work for the Musee de Orsay and her opening. Tim and Shelly would be there for the opening then they were headed to the north of France to scout out locations for filming *Purgatory*. Sharon wouldn't make the show. The Woody Allen film, now titled *Undercover*, would be premiering sometime in the new year in New York. Vinny, she and their son Scott would hook up with us later in Rome. We'd spend a few days in Paris, doing the usual tourist stuff. Eiffel Tower, the Louvre. Stephanie wanted to hang out by Luxembourg Gardens and the college district, near the Sorbonne. Where all the young people were. I liked that idea, adding that I wanted to see where Chopin lived. Cindy, my piano and music teacher, fed me a steady diet of Chopin when I was ten and eleven. Essentially, I was classically trained before breaking out into rock and roll. Cindy was always fine with my preferences, but she's always kept up my jazz and classical work. Even now, she'd assign me a tough Beethoven piece when I was trying to write my own songs. That's how she was. Anyway, it would be a whirlwind visit, then headed by Euro-train to Rome. Dad perked up talking about celebrating Christmas in the Vatican. We had a personal invitation from the Pope. Our lodging was arranged for all of us including Sharon and her family. We would not have much time in Rome, though. Only three nights. We were renting cars to travel to the region where Dad and Vinny's families were from. It would be an adventure, out of the way, especially in winter. Hopefully the weather would cooperate. That would be a weeklong road trip, which sounded more fun than anything else. *The primitive countryside away from cosmopolitan Europe*, is how Dad phrased it. We'd fly back from Rome just after the new year, 2001. It seemed official that we were beginning the dawning of a millennium.

Mom talked about the art show, her excitement for us to see it. To see the famous museum. For all of us to be in Paris in the winter. She made what I thought to be a formal statement that she was getting back into acting. We all smiled, knowing it already. She rambled about the north of France and probably going back in May to start filming. Mom was jumping the gun because producers weren't even lined up. With Tim and Sharon there'd be no problem. She didn't mention Steph, exactly, but we knew she'd be involved.

Mom was really proud of Dad when it came to her thoughts on Rome. None of us were Catholic, but we knew it was important to Dad. I mean, who wouldn't be excited to meet the Pope? And at Christmas? Mom was hugging Dad, like a dream come true. For us to share an adventure, driving to the east coast of Italy, was going to be the most fun of all. I rarely saw Mom that animated. We were all ready to get the semester over with.

I'd miss Melanie. Part of me wanted to ask if she could come, but I knew better. Melanie was terribly jealous. Her mom had to work a lot at the hospital over break, so she'd be alone a lot. We had made tons of notes for songs, even several arrangements. I urged her to use the studio with the guys and put songs together. I'd be fine with it. I had contributed my share. Part of me, unsaid, was worried that she was going to take over. She could practically read my mind, grateful that I was giving her the green light for her to take on our new songs with the guys. I would always be able to change things when I got back, she said.

We had two long intensive rehearsals before the break. Our list of new songs had twelve complete tunes. Four did not have names to them yet. Melanie and I had written all of them, most of the lyrics were hers. We even agreed on the arrangements for each. I played piano on eight of them, singing lead on seven. I would play bass on one, moving Stu to acoustic.

Which reminds me about Stu. His mom had thanked my parents profusely for the L.A. trip. Here she was stopping by our studio, which no parent ever did, to thank me personally. Stu was embarrassed, explaining that she was there to pick him up, but could she drop in. No problem. He introduced her as Arlene.

"Julian," reaching for my hand, "I can't thank you enough for including Stuart on the trip to California." I realized that I had met her during the hub-bub of our first night at Jimmy's. Her facial features looked just like her son. She was an attractive woman, petite; hard to believe she was a mother of three kids. I introduced her to everyone in the band. She was like a super-fan, even though she knew all of us from one time or another, except Alo it turns out.

"Look, I know I'm out of line," as she was pulling a tape out of her purse, "but I love the songs you do of other bands. Really fun. These two songs really mean a lot to me, if you could listen to them some time. Maybe they'd fit in somehow. Stu told me you were trying to write your own music."

I was about to respond, and Stu looked like he was going to grab her and throw her out. Then she went on, "don't worry, they're just from other bands, you might recognize them. It would be fun to hear you play them some day."

Melanie butted in, taking the tape from her hand and going over to the stereo. Mel said, "Sure, let's give it a listen. I'm curious." She was smiling at Stu to put him at ease.

"Chicago is my favorite band," she said as the song started. I sat down listening to the beat. I did not recognize the song. Alo was quietly copying the drum lines on his kit as it played. Frankie was figuring out the chord progression on his electric. It wasn't a very difficult song.   Melanie had caught onto the lyric, humming then singing along, *old days good times I remember ... memories seem like yesterday ... old days,* over and over. Stu was staring at me, waiting to see how I'd react. I grinned and hugged Arlene.

"Sure, this is an easy one.   Mel can sing it. She's already got it. Stu, you want back up?"

"Vocals?" He replied, knowing he seldom got to sing. Never got to sing.

"Sure, Mel and you can work it out while I'm gone.   I think it will go over well with our growing fan club." I said that tongue in cheek.

Everyone chuckled. Alo spoke up, "I know this song. My uncle loves Chicago. What're we going to do about the horns?"

Frankie spoke up, "I'll take the lead, if you don't mind, Julian. I think you could do a lot with the keyboards on this one.   Fill in on the horn sounds."

"I like it," Mel, added. "Stu on bass, I'll play acoustic. We can sing at the same microphone." Stu looked scared shitless.

"What if you put a tambourine on the kit?" I asked Bird.

"Way ahead of you. Perfect."

"What else is on the tape?" I asked Arlene.

Mel hit *Play*.

The song started with a deep studio fuzz, ocean sound. *I'm not in Love, so don't forget it, it's just a silly phase I'm going through ...* caught my attention. I had her start it over again about a quarter of the way through. Mel and I had eye contact during the entire song. I stood up and went over to her, pulling my long hair out of my face and eyes, back into a ponytail, taking off my glasses. I put my arm around her as she hummed into my ear. She was grazing her hand over my black sweater with the whole Yoko Ono sound about mid-way. I just didn't know how to copy the deep fuzz and background vocals as we listened even more closely. This band, whoever it was, had technology I was unsure of. I was digging the lead vocal and piano, the whole denial lyric thing. I hit rewind, looking over at Stu and Bird to give it a try the next time. Frankie was going to figure out the chord progression again.

Arlene told me it was a band called 10cc. I had never heard of them. None of us had.

I turned it up and stood behind Mel in a slow movement, swaying, singing softly into her ear, copying the lyrics as it played. She would hum the fuzz backing vocal, whispering to me that she needed to run her microphone through a guitar amp to get the same effect. I kept singing *I'm not in love, no, no, I'm not in love, so don't forget it …* embracing her tightly. She sank into my chest.

We played it over and over, realizing Mel would sing, *be quiet, big boys don't cry, big boys don't cry, big boys don't cry* during the bridge. Then I cued up the band and turned the tape on again. Each of us playing our instruments softly, attempting to align with the original. The bass runs a wonderful gamut and Stu already had it down. I was struggling on the electric piano and the way the fuzz was echoing. My heart raced singing the lyrics, completely engrossed with Melanie. She stood over by the stereo with her jeans and boots, a big plaid winter shirt, her long auburn hair straight – parted on the side, looking older without makeup or any jewelry. We smiled at each other. We had this one already.

Arlene stood there amazed during the half hour or so we spent on the second song. I was good with the first one, leaving it to the band to figure out. I was far more ecstatic about the second one. I asked Arlene if we could keep the tape. She might as well have asked for my autograph with the look on her face. "Stuart," I called him, "your mom here has great taste." He was relieved. He and his mom took off, taking Alo and Frank. Arlene would give them a ride home.

Melanie complained a little bit about how both songs sounded too corny for us. We'd play them anyway. Give our own special flavor.

I opened the door and looked to make sure Mom wasn't in her studio. I grabbed Melanie as I turned on the song. I had a rubber in my backpack, stored away for this possibility. We fell into that dance, taking off our clothes. The song ran out, as we fell to the small couch. We fucked like we wouldn't be seeing each other again for a very long time.

Lucky for us, we were clothed and getting our stuff together, when Mom knocked on the door. I forgot that she was going to take me home. She happily said she'd take Melanie home, too.

Once we dropped off Mel, we said our goodbyes. I kissed her. I'd call her but we were leaving in a few days, and I knew we weren't going to be able to get together. Too much going on around the house.

Mom was quiet. I knew. She had seen us. Or had an idea. I just knew. She usually had a lot to say. Or asked questions. Nothing. I did not know what to say or do. I wasn't going to turn on the radio. I couldn't even bring myself to ask how her day went. Or about the trip. She didn't even look excited. Something was up, and I had a pretty good idea. Maybe I was being paranoid. I doubted it.

Finally. I mean finally, she said something.

"Um, Julian." She paused as we waited at a red light. Light snow was falling. Her face was racing for the right words. "Julian, we probably need to talk." Another long pause.

"Okay," I mumbled.

"Well, I don't want to embarrass you. And, I probably shouldn't even say anything ..."

"You saw us, didn't you?" I filled in the gap.

She didn't answer. She nodded her head *yes*.

Long silence. We were near home at that time. I hated the silence. When she pulled into the garage, she turned off the car and looked at me.

"Look Julian. I'm not going to lecture you. I'd be a hypocrite if I did. I just want you to know that I'm concerned for you and Melanie. That you're careful. You know what I mean. I love you. I love you both. And I need to talk with your dad about it, too. You know that."

"Yeah, I know Mom. I want to say I'm sorry. It doesn't feel right to apologize. But I'm sorry. I'm mostly, like you said, embarrassed."

She was looking directly into me. It was my mom, this I knew, but she was someone else. Like an older friend. An experienced, wise woman. Wisdom was pouring out from her eyes. Not judgment. Not anger. A kind of love I'd never seen from my mom.

"We're careful, Mom." Is all that I could muster before we got out of the car.

She went inside, presumably to talk with Dad about it all. I stood in the cold garage for a moment, looking at the packed suitcases standing there. Mom would be leaving tonight for Paris. I forgot that too. She had a late flight, lay over in New York. What a way for her to leave home. I shook my head and went inside, expecting whatever may come from Dad.

Louise was chatty fixing dinner, Stephanie was too, helping her. They didn't even notice me come in the house. Mom and Dad were gone. Probably in their room. I wanted to get it over with. Instead of burrowing in my room, hiding out, I sat in a big cozy chair in the den, looking out through the big picture window. It was still snowing lightly. I loved watching smoke come out of James's cottage. It seemed peaceful. I was lost in the scenery when dad tapped me on the shoulder and he and Mom took me into his office.

Dad shut the door. "Look, son. No one likes this conversation. You don't and we don't. We are your parents, you know." I smiled. "We have been where you are, you're just a bit younger than we were when Mom and I started dating. We were in love at your age. I'm not saying you and Melanie are in love. I know you care about each other. Lord, we ..."

I spoke up, "I know, you want to make sure we're careful. I get it. We get it. I appreciate it, I do. We are. I promise."

Mom chimed in, "You've heard all this, Julian. Pregnancy is a tough road at this age."

I didn't have to respond to that.

"I have to be honest, Julian." Dad pulled his chair closer to me. Mom remained standing. "We like Mel. Love Melanie. I want you to have a conversation with us and not be defensive. I want you to be a man, talk straight with us."

I had never seen him be this way. Not exactly this way. He went on. "Mel is a senior. She's graduating from high school. I don't hear her talk much about plans. About school or college or work. I know her mom doesn't have the financial options as some kids' parents have."

My mind was racing to where he was headed.

"You have three years of high school left. With your talents you could go to any college in the world. You have options. Choices."

I was cringing inside.

"Mel, as far as we can tell, has the band. Has you."

He let it sink in. He didn't go any further. I was glad. He was showing a degree of mercy. It's like he was not going to insult my intelligence, allowing me to put two and two together.

I stood up and went to his office window. It had the same view of James's cottage, but from a slightly different angle. I was taking in the askew perspective. How should I respond?

Mom came and stood by me. She was staring out the window, too. She didn't say anything. She put her arm around me, is all.

Time stopped. None of us said anything. They weren't going anywhere. I was tumbling all of it my brain. I did not have an answer.

I spoke anyway, "Love? I'm not sure, really. I'm so young. Melanie is the first woman in my life. She's not a girl, not like at school. We have fun. We are so damned great together with our music. I really like her. I love her in so many ways. Physically too. Obviously, now."

They were listening carefully. I did not feel any judgment. Or anger.

"I hadn't really thought about after the school year. Mel never talks about it. She talks about maybe doing a road trip with the band over the summer. Maybe Shelly can supervise, organize it. I don't know what else Mel is thinking."

"Julian, I don't think Mel *is* thinking of anything else." Mom said.

I turned to them, maybe ready to cry. I wasn't ready for this kind of reality. "I'm not sure what to say to you guys. I really love you and appreciate that you are here. I haven't even begun to think about what to do after college. I just got to high school for fuck's sake."

They smiled without a wince.

I went on, "I don't want Mel to get pregnant. I don't want to get married. I don't want to miss my opportunities in life, like you said. What I do want is the music. I love Retro, I love what we're doing. We sound great, I think. I can hardly believe it. And I love that

Melanie and I share that. She is so incredible. So good. You've seen her. You've heard her. You've heard us." They shook their heads in agreement. Mom had a tear in her eye. A tear dripped down my cheek.

Dad came over and put his arm around me. "Julian, we are with you. Keep talking. Keep staying in touch with the reality of it all. Talk with Melanie about her plans. That you're a freshman with your own life, too. That doesn't mean you have to break up or anything. Just be a grown up, if you want to do grown up things. And I'm not just talking only about sex. I'm talking about having a band, traveling. Taking responsibility for yourself and taking responsibility for *your* band. Being responsible with Melanie."

He was cutting right through me. Challenging me instead of scolding me or making me feel guilty or any shame. I guess he's right. I am a man now, like it or not.

"And we are always. Always here for you, Julian. Talk to us. Don't wait for us to confront you if something is going on. That's the most important part. Yes, you are growing up fast, but you are our child. You always will be."

We had an awkward group hug.

Mom went back into the kitchen and kissed everyone. She and dad hugged, going out to the garage. She said she'd grab a bite at the airport and apologized to Louise. Dad was taking her to the airport. He'd be right back. *Damn,* I thought. She's going. Next time I'd see her will be in Paris. At least we had some kind of resolution.

CHAPTER NINE

When good Americans die, they go to Paris.   Oscar Wilde

Jennifer

This is not the image I wanted stuck in my mind for an unbearably long flight.   I would have a one-hour layover in Denver, then a two-hour layover in New York, totaling over seventeen hours.   I was one of a few lucky ones, flying first class.   I asked for a glass of wine and a steak sandwich. To be followed by several more glasses of wine, I assured the waitress.
Earlier in the day, I did a walk through the gallery like I normally did. Checking on receipts, business for the day.

Wishing everyone a Merry Christmas as I prepared to leave. I was already packed at home, ready to go. I went over to my office, did a last-minute check in my studio, hearing what I knew right away to be muffled sounds of Julian and Melanie. Passionate sounds. I dared to tiptoe over and open my door, move slowly over to the window. They were naked on the couch right by the window I was peering in. No doubt about the activity they were engaged in. I quickly moved back to my office and waited. Waited until I felt it was safe. I needed to get home.   Julian probably forgot I was leaving for the airport.

I finished my sandwich and wine in record time. Even the stewardess was a bit surprised, asking me what else I'd like. I hadn't even paid attention to lift off. I told her I'd wait till we left Denver. We weren't switching planes, just filling up the plane, re-fueling. Not even deplaning.

I curled up in a blanket and tried to sleep. Succeeding to a degree, not even aware of passengers getting off in Denver, new ones boarding for New York and some on to Paris.

I had brought a novel by Barbara O'Neil, whom I had met once at an art show. I liked her a great deal and made a note to read her work. I wasn't going to get to it on this flight. My mind was racing. I listened to music, mostly classical. Slept for several hours. They had an in-flight movie which I was not interested in either. Was my son, my fourteen-year-old son, a freshman for god's sake, already having sex? I was in motherly denial. Sure, I got it. I lived it, practically. It was not Melanie's fault. Only that she had such a womanly body, fully developed, *everywhere*. All over Julian. All the time. I tried. I really did try to blame her. I couldn't. Then I wondered about Stephanie.   I raced through all the boys I knew in her sphere. I looked for clues in everything she may have said.   Or anywhere she may have gone. Nothing. She talked about boys. Liked a few over the years. Nothing. Surely she was not sexually active. I needed to talk with her.   Have *the talk* in Paris. Right away. I also wanted to blame the entire situation on Sharon.   She was always a walking sex pistol. No, I couldn't find the rationale. I couldn't blame myself.   Or Danny, either.

Eventually I did not blame anyone. No guilt.   Nothing wrong.   Human.   Relax. Julian will be responsible. I had visions of Cynthia and John Lennon getting pregnant, with, of course, Julian Lennon, having to get married. My mind would not relax.

In New York we had to change planes to Paris.   There was an enormous photo of downtown Manhattan.   I stared at it for a very long time.   The World Trade Center, two towers. They looked strangely like the description of Julian and Stephanie's vision back in the kiva.   They mentioned it from time to time.   Another image I couldn't shake. In fact, it bothered me so much, I found a pay phone and called home, collect. Danny answered.

I assured him right away that I was fine.   How were things with Danny? He said fine.   The kids were getting their suitcases out, starting to lay out stuff for the trip. They were excited and wanted to start packing. I asked him a favor. When they entered the terminal for their Paris departure, take a long look at the enormous photo of the Manhattan skyline. It's right above the escalators, they won't miss it. Danny was perplexed, wanting more. I told him to not say anything but look at the World Trade Center. See if the kids notice anything, but make sure they get a good look. He let go of his curiosity, assuring me he'd do it. He told me he missed me already. He loved me. God I loved him, wishing he was with me at that very minute.

I slept almost the entire flight. Arriving mid-morning in France. I was happy for the lush breakfast of eggs and muffins and plenty of coffee they served about two hours before landing. I had slept through dinner.

A limousine picked me up at Charles de Gaulle airport taking me to The Plaza Athenee'. I had the top floor suite, three bedrooms, three bathrooms. Plush overlook of the River Seine, the Eiffel Tower within throwing distance. Elegance in every detail. I had no commitments until this evening's private showing for the board members of the Musee. Cocktails and hors d'oeuvres Meals in the hotel were comped. I unpacked, took a shower. I put on walking clothes and shoes heading outside. I had no idea where.

As I was leaving my phone rang. The front desk had patched through a call from the Director of the Musee. He wanted to know if everything was satisfactory. If I needed anything. A car would pick me up for the short ride about 7:00 pm. I thanked him for everything, looking forward to meeting him in person finally. He offered to take me to dinner first, but I said that I had plans. I didn't have plans, but I wanted to get out and see the City of Lights on my own for a few hours. Besides, I had budgeted for some very expensive clothes. For the show, for being in Paris, for Rome. Time to get started shopping. Seriously.

I found my way to the Bershka, the Anthropologie, and the Elsa Mode, buying both formal wear and two nice outfits for the Vatican, shoes, three pair, and four scarves. I had them driven and delivered by car back to the Hotel. I had never done that before, wondering if they'd arrive safely. Or just disappear into the city.

I ended up touring the Picasso Museum. I had never been influenced by the master. Perhaps some of his earlier phases moved me. Seeing his work in person, studying them up close, changed my mind. I was terribly impressed, wondering how, being an artist myself, Pablo had not swept me off my feet, like so many other women. That look in his eyes, in every picture, screamed romance and danger, and creative energy. I was immediately in love with him. I asked him what he would think of my show opening down the street. He told me that he loved the passion. That's all that mattered. I wanted to jump in bed with him. And, like so many other women, fuck him until he was finished with me.

I walked and walked. It was cold. Not terribly. I sat in one of the thousands of street side restaurants and drank tiny cups of Turkish coffee. Sipping as people rushed around. One of the women sitting nearby was smoking and she saw me staring, offering me a dark cigarette. I obliged, lighting up. We tried to carry on a conversation, but her English was only slightly better than my terrible French. We enjoyed, no, savored our drinks and each inhale. She offered me another. I tried to explain that my show was at the Musee and she was impressed, unbelieving. She conveyed that she'd try and make the show's opening tomorrow. We agreed on around 3:00 if she could make it. Her name was Ailes and I repeated it over and over, wanting to remember her if she showed up. She was slightly gray at the temples, her brown hair pulled back tightly with a simple brown wool hat and matching scarf. Her coat was large and warm, dark blue. I took a mental photo as we said goodbye.

I took a nap. Cleaned up again, adorned myself for the *very important people.* The ones funding all of this. The ones who were paying me.

When I arrived, I was greeted with reserved politeness and warmth. Reverence might be the word. I was not used to it. I sipped a white wine, which was delicious and ate what was probably too many crab and lobster pleasantries on a cart. And the sweets. My lord. I hadn't eaten dinner and I could've feasted on what was being served. I was introduced to probably fifteen people. Then we toured, as a group, each of my paintings, all exhibited on the second floor. The presentation, the curating, the lighting, were all phenomenal. I was truly impressed. My works screamed in their size and emotion. Stylistically powerful. I was startled that I had done all of these. It was the first time I viewed them as a collection. They were speaking softly in French, serious conversations.

Our guide assured me that everyone was very positive, even overwhelmed.   There was a writer for a city paper, I had no idea which one, who was taking notes. He asked me a specific question about the final one I had completed, the one with seashells, and I told him I credited a friend of my son for the idea, the inspiration. He raised his eyebrows. I realized that he took it the wrong way, like I was romantically inspired. I tried to explain, eventually leaving it alone. Let him print what he wants to print. The gossip was going to fly.   Go ahead, tell the world that an underage boy inspired all my new work.

Various members were congratulating me, shaking my hand. A few giving me a slight hug. Or a kiss on the cheek.   I was glad. Everyone was happy. The interaction I had with people ranged from questions about my family to more thoughts or questions about each painting to my thoughts about being in Paris.   It went well until several began asking me about my acting career. When was I going to return to film? It made me realize that in Santa Fe, the general populace had steered clear of that question by now. And in my trips to big cities in America, I just didn't get asked very often. I was a cult figure of sorts in France, is what they were trying to tell me.   A kind of Greta Garbo hiding in the Indian Territory of the Wild West. Everyone there honestly liked my paintings; I was certain of that. Or at least they didn't want me to doubt that at all.   What was clearer, however, is that everyone wanted a glimpse of Jennifer Braxton, actress.

The show was opening to the public the next day. They showed me various articles and photos of advertisements and posters of the monthly promotion. One of the posters pissed me off. It called me the *Academy Award Winning Artist*. Oh well, they were marketing, and it was true. I don't know why it surprised me.

They expected a full house. I was not expected to be there all day, but to make appearances for two groups of large contributors to the Musee. I was glad to do it. One group was to be there at 3:00, so I made note to look for Ailes.

I knew that Tim and Shelly would see the show tomorrow as well. They were going to be unannounced. Undercover. Sometime late before closing, which was around 8:00. Hopefully they'd call me at the hotel first. The family would arrive from the airport later in the evening. Probably around 11:00 pm. I doubted that Tim and Shelly would hook up with them because they were leaving immediately the next morning for Rouen and various towns in the north. They'd want to hit the hay and catch an early train. The kids would be tired, too. Anxious to get going on their Paris adventure. My commitment would be finished by then. We'd go see my exhibit after breakfast then off to the tourist locations. The day after that would be over by the Luxembourg Gardens, *the college district*, is what Steph called it. I saw that a Chopin piano recital was scheduled at one of the small churches near there and I guessed that's where we'd end up. Unless they found music where the college crowds hung out.

Then on Wednesday we had to leave. A quick turnaround. Catch the early train to Rome at 6:48 am. Twelve hours, with one fifteen-minute stop somewhere along the way, I forgot where. We probably wouldn't even sleep the night before, as Danny had arranged sleeper compartments. *God Bless him*, I said aloud, looking through the car's back window.

I told myself I wasn't going to do it, but I had the car stop at a small, corner vendor for cigarettes. I planned on staying up late on my hotel porch and look at the lights. The Eiffel Tower was blazing in wonder, right there out my door.   And drink plenty of wine stocked in my suite's fridge.

When I got back, all my clothes, boxed and in shopping bags sat in neatly near my closet. I remembered.

From then on, it was heaven, it was very late on a big, padded couch outside, warm blankets, smoking the brown cigarettes I asked about at the shop. Cold air exhaled mixed with the savored tobacco. The wine was divine. I ordered crab cakes remoulade to be sent up. Two large plates. I watched the river flow in a meandering winter fashion, reflecting various lights, movements and stars. Cars going by on the street below. It was active well into the night. I was drunk. I had jet lag. The exhibit was going to be a success. I felt great.

Stephanie

Arriving in New York, we had to move quickly from one terminal to another. I was hooked on a new book everyone was talking about, *Harry Potter: Sorcerer's*

Stone. Dad was engrossed in his friend John Nichols' book *On the Mesa,* and Julian was reading, or re-reading, Elvis Costello's autobiography. We hardly said a word on the flight.

Before I left, I picked up a catalogue at our school counseling office on the Sorbonne, which I was dying to visit. Truthfully, I wasn't much into the tourist things in Paris. It would be exciting, being in the great city. I just wanted to be on the campuses, the gardens where I read that they hung out. Julian agreed with me, he wanted to see the same things.

Dad was hustling us through the airport. We were taking a long escalator upward and Dad asked us to look at the wall size photo of the city skyline. Wasn't it incredible he stated? It was impressive, the size mostly. I didn't think much of it. Julian stopped at the platform bending his neck, looking upward at it. Dad was standing next to him. I was wondering what we were stopping for, we were in a hurry I thought.

"Steph," Julian called me. "Look up there on the upper left side. See those buildings?"

I looked carefully. Two buildings, nearly matching. Nearly parallel towards the sky. Something inside of me was scared out of my mind.

"Looks like the vision thing we saw in the kiva, don't you think?"

I stared a long time. I also saw a plane to the upper right. It was a very strange sensation.

"It's the World Trade Center." Dad informed us.

A few people were slowing down trying to see what we were so interested in.

"Damn, Steph, this is freaky.   I think this is what we saw."

"Me, too." I mumbled.

Dad had a look of concern, but he knew we had to get going.   I had a small, cheap, instamatic in my purse and quickly took a picture of the picture.   I also made a very indelible mental note.

We were unable to fly first class from Santa Fe, but we did to Paris.   They had a film in our cabin, *The Truman Show* with Jim Carrey.   Somehow all three of us had missed it when it was in theaters.   It was fabulous.   Funny, but it had a great moral to the story about our world and each of us finding our way as individuals.   I liked the final line, *that's all folks*, taken from a cartoon I thought.   We loved everything about the movie.   Even Dad went on and on about it afterward, and normally he didn't say much about movies.   He thought Ed Harris, who was one of his favorites, was equally as good as Carrey.

The food was reasonably good, and I curled up and slept the rest of the way. Awaking late at night upon landing, I looked around the dark cabin.   Julian was zonked.   Dad had a look of impatient expectation.   He wanted to see Mom; I could tell.   Passengers were collecting themselves in their seats, so I did the same.   I needed a shower.

Taking a car through Paris late at night is a mesmerizing experience.   I loved the lights, the wintery glow.   The massive expanse of the city.   I looked hard to find the Eiffel Tower, knowing Mom would be in a hotel right near there.   Julian was talking to the driver about the music on the car radio, which I didn't recognize. Dad had the overhead pin-light on in the front seat, reading something about our itinerary.

Julian and I had a reasonable grasp of French. We were both in third year French at school. It was the only class we took together. We had a good exposure to Spanish growing up, both of us good in that language, too. So, we picked French for our junior high elective. Julian was showing off, I thought, so I smiled, turning my attention back out the window. There it was, far to the right, I could see the singular structure, lit up and marvelous. A beacon of arrival.

Mom was up, of course, anxiously waiting for us. She smelled of cigarettes and was obviously a bit tipsy. It was getting past midnight, but we were all hungry. She ordered whatever we wanted. I couldn't believe I had my own room and bathroom. Our accommodations were nothing like I'd ever seen. Julian darted to see his room and drop his large bag. Dad and Mom slipped into their enormous suite. Living room size. He was as surprised as we were.

Food arrived and we stayed up talking about Mom's show, what she'd done so far in Paris, until almost 2:00 am. No hurry. We could sleep in. She had to be to the show at 11:00 am and again at 3:00 and then Tim and Shelly would probably drop in the Musee at around 7:00. The Musee was within walking distance, but we could take a car if we wanted. She'd be busy going back and forth.

I got up around 10:30. Julian was wide awake, showered, dressed, watching a local TV show. He was ready to go.

So was Mom, she had to leave. She was going to be busy with something, so dad was going to wait and head over in the afternoon. Julian wanted to *just walk around.* I was a surprised that Julian left with Mom. They were going to walk over to the Musee together and he'd wander around and come back on his own. Mom and Dad seemed fine with it if he was back to the Hotel by 1:00.   They made sure he had the phone and room number, address written down. *Just get a cab if you get lost*, is what Dad said.

Dad had sweet rolls and coffee going. I grabbed some orange juice, thinking about what it was I wanted to do. I looked out the window with Dad and he pointed over to the American Cathedral of Paris, asking if I wanted to take a walk in about an hour.   We'd be seeing Notre Dame tomorrow, but he was wanting to visit the Cathedral.   I said sure and got cleaned up. It looked cold outside, so I put on warm clothes.

Walking with my dad through the streets of Paris was a special moment.   Just him and me.   He pointed out architectural points of interest every step of the way. He showed me where the underground subway stations were. I had never been inside a cathedral. Or even a big church. The church dad went to in Santa Fe was tiny, and poor in the scheme of things. This was overwhelming.   A smattering of tourists wandered through, but beyond the rope it was getting crowded for late mass.   I could tell Dad wanted to stay. I was never pressured to go to church, but I agreed that we should go to mass.

It was a theatrical affair. Robes and ceremony and music, all in French. I had no idea, really, caught up in the medieval-like history of it. I went up to communion with my dad even though I wasn't baptized or even a Catholic. He didn't mind. I even sipped the wine from the chalice.

Dad was in deep prayer after communion. He was like that. He reminded me of a priest sometimes. So introspective. Intelligent. Thoughtful. I could see why Mom loved him so much.

We took a long walk going back a different route. We approached the Theatres des Champs-Elysees and dad said we should go inside. It was open. Where we had just visited his domain, we were now visiting what I hoped to be mine. It was a marvelous venue of ancient time. The theater. I could feel the history. It was in me. We walked around on our own as I took out my little camera and took pictures of the marvelous stage, the balconies. My imagination ran wild. I picked up a flyer, reading that the stage was used primarily for opera these days. Even more intriguing I thought.

We reconvened, all four of us, going to the dining room before heading over to Mom's exhibit. I needed to eat. We all did. Julian cheated and had gone over to the Eiffel Tower. He didn't go up but wandered around the area. He enjoyed all the music in the city. People playing instruments on countless corners. It was cold outside, but the festive atmosphere was prevalent. Dad and I had not seen any musicians, so it must be around more tourist areas, he said.

Mom was in her glory. Her show was amazing. I told myself that this was not the mom I grew up with. I had seen her work my entire life. This was special. She also showed us around the other exhibits. It was difficult to move from one painting of Van Gogh to a Renoir, to a Picasso, to a Monet, Degas, Cezanne, endless. Overwhelming. Oddly enough, the one painting I liked more than all the others was by someone named Alfred Sisley, *Snow at Louvecienne*. Mom could tell I was taken by it. She whispered to me about the composition, the sky, the mood. How incredible it was. She knew quite a bit about Sisley, his life and work. She was in agreement with me, which made me feel good.

At 3:00 she met up with several people who contributed to the Musee. There were press there asking questions. She handled it all with poise. A lady, dressed in a brown coat and hat, with a colorful scarf, went up to Mom and shook her hand. It was not out of the ordinary, but the woman was obviously not part of the entourage. Mom broke away from everyone crowded in the lobby area by her exhibit and brought the woman over and introduced *Ailes* to us. Mom said she'd be right back, disappearing with the larger group. Ailes attempted English and Julian took over in French. Ailes looked impressed. All three of us began a crude conversation in French. She was a naturalist writer, who worked for a national magazine. She spent most of her life on scientific expeditions, reporting on animal life, habitats, that kind of thing. She was divorced, she said, with two kids who were grown and now both lived near the Atlantic coast. She liked Mom's exhibit very much, explaining how they had just met the day before. She then asked about us. Dad was trying to follow our conversation and answer her questions. I'd interpret from time to time. Julian talked about Santa Fe and the band. I told her about acting in *Music Man*. She seemed delighted by everything. She mentioned that she had graduated from the Sorbonne and my heart leapt. I interrupted and told her that it was the one thing I wanted to see while we were here. She said she was glad to show us around. We agreed on Tuesday at 10:00 am. She wrote down the name of a brasserie near Luxembourg Gardens, within walking distance to the University. Dad approved. Julian was equally interested. We invited Ailes to spend time with us that afternoon, offering to take her to dinner. She declined graciously, looking forward to Tuesday. She saw that Mom was overwhelmed and sent her wishes and compliments, wanting to talk with *Jennifer* more.

Tim called our suite about the time we got back from grabbing something to eat. He and Shelly were in a hurry, would meet us at the Musee shortly. There were still quite a lot of people touring the various floors, Mom's exhibit, staying until closing. Tim was recognized immediately. I felt bad for him. All he wanted to do was see Mom's exhibit and get going. People were taking pictures. Then Mom was recognized more fully as an actress, an obvious friend of Tim's, and because of a local Parisian news cameras reporting on the exhibit, it turned into a fiasco. Dad escaped, showing Shelly around. Mom tried hard to pry Tim away from the paparazzi and growing crowd.

Unsuccessfully. Julian and I stood and watched in shock. This was not New Mexico.

We barely got to spend any time with them, then they sprinted out. Mom was furious. Part of it was her fault, she said. She had not alerted the Musee that Tim was coming. They would have arranged better access, security. It was all too impromptu. She knew better. We walked the city for hours that night, taking in various areas we knew nothing about. We hoofed our way up the hill in Montmartre with Sacre-Coeur lit up in Christmas colors. There was an ensemble playing Christmas music, all the musicians bundled up warm. It was late, chilly, so we kept moving, stopping once for hot drinks at a tiny little shop, the aroma of pastries overwhelming.

Mom figured out how to use a pay phone, calling Tim at his hotel, making sure everything was okay. She was feeling terrible about the evening. Tim said that he knew better as well, don't worry about it. He took the blame for the madness. Mom wished him good luck on his movie scout up north. She couldn't wait to hear what they discovered.

Mom was pleased that we would be meeting Ailes on Tuesday. Again, she took the blame for arranging a meeting with her at the Musee, not thinking of her other commitments. She was *dropping the ball*, she repeated. Dad said *nonsense, everything was fine*. *The life of fame* he lamented with a smile.

The next day was the whirlwind, taking in every tourist stop we could think of. Mostly we walked. A few times we took the underground. Eiffel Tower, up we went,

taking pictures on a windy clear day. Spectacular views.
Notre Dame, crowded, lines of tourists, especially this
time of year. We did not go up into the stairwell,
overwhelmed enough by the vast interior architecture.
Back over to the museum area taking advantage of
passes that mom had to enter the Louvre. None of us
were very excited to go in, a bit overloaded on art
already.   Seeing the *Mona Lisa*, struck at how small the
painting was, gorgeous expression, reworked over and
over; that alone was worth the visit.
We ate somewhere in the Left Bank where we could see
the river from the window. Julian and I drank white
wine with our salmon.
Resting in our Hotel all of us slept, moving slow for the
evening. Mom and Julian looked into the Chopin
concert he wanted to attend tomorrow by the Gardens.
There was a different piano recital at the Chopin
Museum, which still had tickets for tonight. We decided
to give it a try, which would free up our evening over in
the Latin Quarter. Or Dad talked about going to *Les
Reservoir* tomorrow for dinner and live music. We'd ask
Ailes what she thought.
Julian loves Chopin. Probably his most influential
composer. I think it's because Cindy trained him on
piano at such a young age, almost all his recitals
included Chopin. I enjoyed the sounds in such a
wonderful atmosphere, happy for him. It was a small
affair, maybe thirty people in attendance, it was that
intimate. The performer was a large woman, maybe in
her late twenties. *Margarite* I think was her name.
During the intermission Margarite went around and

spoke freely with those in attendance.   Julian and she hit it off, as he shared his background in piano. She invited him to play the Bechstein Grand piano once her set was finished.

People were filing out at the end, which was a fabulous time, when Julian was waved up front.   We moved up to the vacated front row.

Julian took a seat at the piano, warmed up for an awkward moment, then proceeded into one of the numbered piano pieces Margarite obviously recognized right away. Several people stopped and found a seat once again. My brother gets lost in his music. I saw it all the time. He swayed, his long fingers gliding on the keyboard.   His long hair parted, nearly to his shoulders, moving with his time. He was having fun. He made a mistake or two, which made Margarite and Julian smile, but he moved forward, determined. They talked for a moment about Opus 11, I think, and Margarite went over to another piano nearby. The two of them started up, and Julian asked if they could start over.   Then they found a common tempo, playing a wonderful duet. I had never heard anything like it. Mom and Dad looked choked up. I know that I was.

That moment alone made the trip amazing. Memorable. Ailes was already seated when we arrived. She was drinking coffee smoking a cigarette as we all gathered in chairs around her. It was a tight fit. Her suggestion was that we walk through the Garden, take in the morning, then we could tour the Sorbonne. She and Mom were talking away about her show. We ordered drinks, but Julian and I were ready to get going.   We sat and talked about his performance again. How incredible it all came together. Dad was all choked up recalling every moment for about the third time.

I loved the park, the people running, bundled up, moms with kids, groups of friends, older people who struck me as spending much of their day here. The large pond and fountain, even in winter. Sculptures everywhere you walked. It was a vast expanse.

The entire atmosphere of the college was spellbinding. The students who were still hanging around on their Christmas break, wandering the ancient buildings. Mammoth library. Classic lecture halls. The measured language and simple conversations, much of which I was overhearing and comprehending. Ailes had received her science degrees here and was currently working as an adjunct for The National Center for Scientific Research. Since I was interested in drama, we walked the fifteen minutes to the Meisner Studio. Not much was happening, but I enjoyed seeing the facility. The stages, the make-up and costume rooms. The secretary gave me a packet for application, which I would need to submit by my junior year.

Ailes wasn't sure how serious Julian was about studying music, but she had us walk the extra distance to the American Conservatory. It was a premier music school in Paris and extremely difficult to be accepted. Second only to the Paris Conservatory, which was quite a distance away. Julian would have to begin the process as soon as possible, for either school, and that would even be for a freshman entrance four years from now. Julian perked up hearing the pianists practicing, working hard, even over break.   The various music rooms, concert venues, were startling.   It was obviously a very exclusive place. Again, we picked up a packet in the front office.

During all of this, Mom and Dad walked arm and arm, enjoying the various sights and changing atmospheres. The opportunities we were being exposed to. They chatted away between themselves, occasionally asking Ailes a question.

Ailes was being extremely generous with her time. More than any of us would ever expect. Mom insisted on treating her to dinner, going wherever she wanted. Dad asked her about *Les Reservoir* on the other side of town. She responded favorably, accepting our invitation. She needed to go to her place for a rest, take care of some personal business. She escorted us to the nearest subway station, which was difficult to find, explaining how to get back to our hotel. She agreed to meet us at 8:00.

I couldn't believe we were already packing. Such a quick visit to Paris. This suite, my room, such luxury and we hardly stayed here. We had no idea when we would get back, wanting to stay out late on our last night. We had to leave by 5:15 am to get to the train station, so who knows.

What a blast. Live music. Dance music. Great food. I gorged on lobster, sharing bites of steak with Julian. Back and forth, dipping in butter. Ailes was animated in her conversation with Mom and Dad, while Julian and I acted as interpreters for some of what any of them were trying to say. Ailes was asked by an elderly gentleman to dance, which she readily accepted. Mom and Dad went out on the floor too. A young guy, probably in college, hadn't shaved, expensive clothes; I could tell he was with a large group a few tables away, came over and asked me to dance. He asked politely in French. We danced three dances. He realized that I was American, and way too young for him after only a few minutes. I didn't even catch his name as we strained to find conversation. We danced one slow dance and I realized how strong he was, how excited I was. It was a nice moment, his smile, whatever cologne he had on. Something inside of me awoke. A sexual energy I don't think I had ever experienced before. I turned it aside, seeing that Julian was into the live music, studying the band, how they presented themselves.   I urged him to ask someone to dance but he wasn't interested.

We left around 11:30, thanking Ailes profusely. Dad inviting her to our house if for some reason she ever made it to Santa Fe. She seemed interested, wanting to see the desert and meet James, who both Mom and Dad spoke about quite a bit. She reached into her large bag and handed Mom a collection of four or five newspapers, explaining that they had reviews of her exhibit. Mom thanked her, almost sarcastically given that it was the press, as they smiled. Ailes assured her they were good reviews. We hugged, kissed on the cheek, and headed away in different cars.

CHAPTER TEN

The area off the west of the Tiber River was once an unsettled marshy region. During the second half of the 15th century, the Apostolic Palace and the Vatican Library were completed. Once the Sistine Chapel was finished, Michelangelo Buonarroti was commissioned to paint his timeless mural on the ceiling in 1603. More importantly, his grand sculpture, the Pieta, was installed within Saint Peter's. It is the supreme piece of art in all human history.

Jennifer

The rattle of the train, zooming across Europe. I'm jammed into this tiny sleeper bunk, barely able to move, much less rollover. But I'm grateful to sleep, or at least try to sleep. Danny is above me in the top bunk, snoring away. I was able to hear the kids in their bunks next door a few hours ago. It's quiet now. Pitch black, although it's probably gorgeous outside. We got about three hours of sleep at the Hotel before darting off to the train station. Each of us raced to find a place to sleep once we were moved into our cabins.

I turned on my overhead light, careful not to disturb Danny, as it glowed in a slender tunnel upon the newspapers I began to unfold and attempt to read. They were all written in French. I stumbled through each one, happy to decipher favorable opinions on the *magnificence of the vision*, as one phrase seemed to say. One of the articles was alluding to my *male muse*, a friend of my son's. From what I could tell the reporter – who I remembered distinctly - did not extrapolate any age of the young man, nor anything other than a bit of humor. That relieved me.   It was all innocent enough. My thought was how strange things unfold. I was happy for the huge success of the show. The money, the notoriety. Not just for me, but the Gallery. How much fun we had in Paris, wishing to go back. It was all too quick. The kids had a great time and I'm enormously indebted to Ailes for her generosity of time. I will urge her to come see us. To stay with us.

One visual of many, was of Steph dancing, slow dancing, with that older boy last night. He was probably in his twenties. She looked so grown up. Mature. With what happened with Mel and Julian, I still wanted to chat with Steph.   Just seeing her in embrace with that very handsome French boy, reinforced all that I wanted to say.

I couldn't sleep. I quietly put on my loose travel clothes and slid out into the narrow walkway, taking those articles with me. The brilliant light blinded me. I swayed in the speed, finding my bearing to the bathroom, first, then to the dining car. I ordered a coffee and half a grapefruit. My numb brain taking in the South of France as it flew by. The dining car was nearly full of chatting families, lone travelers.

A handsome man with a thick black mustache, dressed in a gray business suit approached me, apologizing for the intrusion. I was slightly self-conscious, knowing that I looked as frumpy as I could. His English was very good, probably an Italian by virtue of the accent. He recognized me as *the* Jennifer Braxton. He was quickly explaining that he had been in Paris on business and attended my opening at Musee d'Orsay. He liked my paintings very much. I thanked him, inviting him to have a seat, apologizing for my appearance, that I couldn't sleep. The waiter retrieved his coffee from the table he had occupied. His name was Matthew DiPietro, an international attorney for trade issues. He lived outside of Rome. He also liked *Rio Norte* and *Hull House*. I thanked him again, not wanting to talk about movies. Mr. DiPietro motioned to the crumbled papers on the table, asking me if those were reviews of my exhibit, then asked if he could read them. I handed them to him. He read and spoke fluent French. He had a big smile, relaying specific quotes. I was embarrassed.

I told him of our plans in the Vatican when he asked of our journey. I slipped, mentioning that we were meeting my friend Sharon and her family, which he guessed rightly was the famous actress. He was impressed with the entire scenario and our planned travels. He handed me a business card as he wrote his home number on the back, apologizing for interrupting my *solace*. He did not want to intrude any longer – even though I thought I was being most welcoming. He urged me to call him if we wanted any travel advice for Abruzzi. His home was about forty miles from Rome in that same direction if we wished to drop by on the way. He'd love to have all of us over any time, day or night. His wife had died two years ago of breast cancer. His kids had moved away, and he lived alone. He'd love to have us, he repeated and wished me a pleasant day.

Small towns. Villages. Train stations passed. Farms mostly. Until mountains covered in snow surrounded us, making the windows frost. My eyes took it all in without registering much. I was exhausted. Realizing that I had stored up a great deal of anxiety over the exhibit, uncertainty about a future film, the madness of travel, balancing family, my mind was trying to synchronize with my body. Sleep.

Which I finally did.

A priest met us at the Rail Station. Danny had already eaten a small dinner with the kids, allowing me to sleep, holding them over until later. I didn't mind. They were excited, rested, ready to go. The priest had bright red hair which stood out on his long black cassock. He was originally from Ireland with a heavy brogue. I had a tough time understanding him. Father Byrne informed us that Sharon, Vinny and Scotty had arrived earlier in the day and were already situated at their suite at the

Roma Sogna Infinito. Julian asked the meaning of the words, which he told us was *Rome Dreams Infinite*. Rooms were provided by the Vatican, as we were the holy father's guests until Tuesday the 26th. He would gladly help us with transportation anywhere in the city, answer questions, give directions, be at our beck and call. He too was staying in a room at the *Infinite*. Rental cars were arranged and ready for pick up that morning. He had our driving instructions printed and ready at our suite.

One of the problems was that we slept most of the day and were terribly antsy. No worries, Father Byrne would take us for a late meal in Rome. We could walk around near the *crypts and catacombs*, which would keep us out of the direct evening cold, and even do the three-hour walking tour. The car was not a limousine, exactly, but it could seat eight. Comfortably. He was aware that he was assigned to seven guests.

Our accommodations were extraordinary. Sprawling. We could see the Basilica lit In splendor, right out our patio. Sharon, Vinny and Scotty were across the hall. We set our stuff down and went over. Hugs, kisses, a great deal of joy and excitement. Scotty was ten with a cheery personality. He looks Italian, like his father, with his mother's spunk. He and our kids would do fine, regardless of the age difference. Scotty had a *real camera, a Nikon*, he said, with rolls and rolls of film. He was ready to take plenty of pictures. All in black and white he added, like he was a professional photographer.

Every time I see Vinny, I am reminded of how big of a man he is. Probably 6'4", a barrel of a chest. Great shape. Thick, black, curly hair. Dark complected, a heavy beard he shaves regularly, permanent laughter lines on his face. A jovial, quick-witted guy. No wonder he does so well in stand-up comedy. And he's strong enough to stand up to Sharon. The toughest job he has, I would say. Sharon melts into him, curled into his embrace half the time. I love it.

Sharon told us that she was glad to be finished with working with Woody Allen. Hush hush rumors circulated that he was a womanizer, couldn't be trusted. She found him to be a soft-spoken, dry-humored, gentleman with a clear vision of his movie. He gave Sharon a great deal of latitude with Jeff Daniels. She predicted it to be a success. She loved comedy, wondering why she ever returned to the godawful demands of drama. She said it loud enough to needle me and Stephanie. She knew where Tim was at this very minute. I already sensed her excitement about the whole idea.

Danny and Vinny loved talking about Italian food, Italian history, our planned travels to the coast, their shared heritage, their strong mothers and extended families, and more about food. Food. It was always the center of their laughter. Vinny brought out Danny's extemporaneous talents. They could go on for hours with one-liners. Danny played the Groucho set-up and Vinny would hit a homerun. Like it was in their blood. They'd cry laughing so hard. Danny needed this trip, the wear and tear of being a principal was showing and he was only in his second year.

And food we found. Father, I would call him father with a twist and Sharon was needling the poor man, who was probably only in his early twenties. He knew exactly who he was with, dreading the rapier wit of everyone, including the kids. We were good natured with him, loving him truthfully, but no one, except Danny, could get over calling this 'lad,' *Father*. Steph asked him his first name, politely of course. Seamus. Seamus Byrne. We started calling him Seamus with our own poorly executed Irish accent. He eventually lightened up about it. We hugged him. No harm. Anyway, Seamus took us to an enormous Italian restaurant where they had live violins and an accordion, while cheesy love songs were sung in Italian by an old guy on stage. Straight out of the Mafia. Or a bad rip-off from *The Godfather*. Vinny got up, without being asked, gently took the microphone and started singing. It was so damned funny. I spat up. Scotty was taking pictures. Sharon got up and joined him. The place was about half full, laughing, joining in on the festivity.

We ate so much pasta, ravioli, seafood soup, bread, and more bread and butter, fresh and hot. Four bottles of wine. I'm certain that all three kids were wasted. I was. Sharon had a wicked mouth when she drank. She promised Vinny she wouldn't smoke either. At least not around Scotty. She grabbed me and we went outside and snuck a cigarette. She was saying *fuck* this and *fuck* that. All in a good way. She wasn't even complaining or upset about anything. We hammered our full glasses of wine and three cigarettes each, our teeth chattering. She needed the vacation too.

We bypassed the walking tour, unable to walk at all. We'd do it the next day; it would be warmer anyway.

Julian

I was terribly drunk. Stephanie and I were taking advantage of the situation, ordering whiskey sours, practically drinking a bottle of wine on our own. No one noticed. Dad was blitzed. Mom was falling all over Sharon. Well, they fell all over each other. We were being nice to Scotty, but he was running around the restaurant with his ridiculous camera. The restaurant was getting a show from three actors, counting Vinny. It was pandemonium. The poor priest, Seamus, was mortified, doing his best.

Steph and I were telling each other about who we would like to have sex with at school. She was all into some of the seniors. She came right out, slurring her words, that she wished the guy she danced with in Paris would've taken her home to his place and fucked her senseless. I spit my whiskey all over the tablecloth. I didn't dare tell her about Melanie. She asked me instead. She said she knew. Just knew. That's all. Good for me. Good for Mel. She was bluffing. Not really. I couldn't even bring myself to deny it. I made up a fantasy about some girl cheerleader, a junior we both knew, that I was *wanting*. She raised her eyebrow and said *really, what would Mel think*?

As the night wore on, the restaurant was moving in weird directions. Sharon was up dancing to the old guy singing and I tried to figure out how old she was.

Probably early forties. She and Mom and Dad were all the same age. Vinny, I think may be a couple years younger. Sharon looked so damned hot. Not for her age. Just damned hot. I grew up with her as my *aunt*, or special relative. Now that I had a tiny glimpse into the world of sex, I saw her differently. She turned me on. I wanted to feel guilty about my emerging crush or lust or whatever it was, but I couldn't. I mean, she was seen by millions of men in the world, probably even tens of millions, as the sexiest woman in the world. In fact, she was ranked the number one sexiest woman in the world something like four years in a row. I'd seen countless pictures of her nude. To this day, the sex scene in *Rio Norte* was the biggest turn on of my life until Melanie and I hooked up. I was looking at her dancing out there and visualizing the same sex scene. Insane.

Stephanie caught me staring at our wonderful aunt.

"She's beautiful isn't she?" She asked.

I couldn't deny it, "She certainly is," almost sounding like Stan Laurel in an old movie.

"Well, stop it, brother. Your blood is boiling. I can tell. I mean, good ol' Auntie Sharon is tying one on, having a great time.   If you are tempted to go out there and dance with her, you'll embarrass yourself with that fucking hard on in your pants." She laughed.

I actually looked down; I was that drunk seated in my chair. She was right. The waiter brought us our third whiskeys and we said *cheers*. Clinking our glasses.

We sat there, quietly, eating an Italian lemon ice with dabs of honey, sucking on our wine or whiskey or whatever glass was looking best at that moment in time between bites.

"What do you think of that photo in New York? I mean, the World Trade Center. Those two buildings were exactly what I saw in the kiva."

I tried to focus. "Exactly. Weird, Steph. It kind of scares me. The plane in the photo too. Like it was moving."

"I know, I know. It freaked me out." She paused. "I love James, I really do, but what the hell. I mean, during our whole life, especially when he gets on the res, or with Bill when he was alive, or I see him with these old people when I go riding, and it's like he's some kind of spirit rider or from another world. You know. You talk to him all the time."

"I get it. He's incredible. When I look in his eyes, I know what you mean. He sees right through me. I'm used to it. I wonder if we should talk to him more about what we saw in New York."

"I agree." I waited to say the next thing. "You know, Steph. I don't know if I should say this, but I get the exact same feeling around Mom and Dad sometimes. Mostly around Dad."

She turned to me, even grabbed my hand. "You are absolutely right. Dad and I went to this church in Paris. We went to mass and ..."

"You did?"

"Yeah, yeah. Anyway, he gets that same distant look as James."

"This is even stranger, but when Mom is painting, I don't see her paint that often, but she gets that same look."

"Oh and when she's reading our scripts! Jesus."

I was thinking about what she was saying, not sure how to respond.

"Oh, get this, Julian. When I was doing my screen test with Sharon, well, she had that look. Like from another world. It scared the living shit out of me."

I looked back over at Sharon dancing with Vinny. Lucky man.

The next several days were a whirlwind. Seamus proved to be an outstanding tour guide. He took us everywhere, we saw everything. We ate constantly. Gluttony, I'd say, became our deadly sin. If I were going to go to confession, which Dad was going to do before our papal mass, I'd confess to being a pig. I ate more gelato than anyone except maybe Scotty. At first I only ate chocolate, eventually trying every possible flavor. We spent four hours doing the catacombs, which was incredible, overwhelming amount of skulls and gory stories. I was glad we waited to see them during the day. The entire Coliseum wore me out, listening to each detail of gore, of ceremony, this fact and then another. I was touristed out quickly. The Forum, The Spanish Steps, The Pantheon, were all a blur. I was mostly watching the people. I had noticed lots of beautiful women in Paris. Rome was crawling with them. Every Italian woman dressed nicely. Aimed to be pleasing in her appearance. Even though it was wintery out and everyone had warm coats and hats on, there was a sexuality about the entire city. Religion, sex, history, death, all at my fingertips. And they were loud. In Paris, everyone was notably restrained, spoke in hushed tones, private. Not here. Their hands moved their body language spoke wonders, their inflections said more than the language itself. Anywhere and Everywhere. We slowed down one day. We had to. Steph and I had been drinking almost as heavily as the *adults*, because we could. And they didn't mind. Eating light salads. Sleeping in the luxury of our suite. Dad had been getting wasted with Vinny. Mom and Sharon were trying to sneak cigarettes between countless bottles of wine. Dad and Vinny started smoking cigars, so mom and Sharon did too. They were like little kids back in high school, acting like they were getting away with something. I could almost visualize them in high school. Scotty stayed back sometimes, or lots of times, usually at night, watched by a nun, Sister something. So, me and Steph got trashed. My sister could hold her own. We'd do shots of some Italian liqueur, nearly fainting. In fact, she was able to walk much straighter than me every time we measured our abilities after such grand accomplishments. And I puked twice. She never did or lied about it.

Anyway, we did have a 'down day.' Mom and Dad went out by themselves once. A couple afternoon date. They were trying to fit in a bit of romance I guessed. Lots of sleeping going on. We had a warm, heated swimming pool. Practically to ourselves. A therapy pool and hot tub, warm and relaxing. So here we go again, Sharon wears a bikini. Mom and Steph in modest bathing suits. Sharon in a bikini. A black bikini, to be specific. Probably a designer bikini. Something she modeled most likely. She looked like she was 18. I could hardly stand it. I even tried to *not look*.

Seamus took us on a full day tour of the Vatican. A private tour. St. Peter's. The Basilica. The underground. It was remarkable, I had to admit. It was my favorite part of the sightseeing. Seamus made it extraordinary. Dad went to confession in a side enclave in another side chapel, with one of the on-site priests. We waited. Vinny made a joke, then confessed to all of us that he should probably go. He wasn't even a believer anymore. Vinny went into the adjoining confessional cubicle then came out a long time later. He walked far from us and knelt on one of those 'kneelers' and was saying his penance, I presumed. Sharon, dressed in festive layers, eventually joined him, kneeling by his side. Mom was doing the same with Dad in another pew. Steph told me that God would never forgive me for fucking Melanie, so don't bother thinking about going to confession. I couldn't believe she said that right there in the holiest place on earth.

When I saw the Pieta, my life changed. Seriously. I had never seen anything so amazing. Mom's work, O'Keefe's work, the artwork in Paris, nothing was close. I loved the Sistine Chapel ceiling, but this sculpture blew my mind. Seamus let me get close, beyond the ropes. Mom put her arm around me, in the same kind of wonder. I felt like crying. Mom was, I think. Even Steph was moved. It made me want to believe in Jesus and the crucifixion. This said more to me than any preacher or church service. Seamus whispered all kinds of facts and stories about the Pieta. I didn't really listen. Something was happening inside of me.

The next day was the Sunday before Christmas. We had all agreed to not give gifts to each other. This was the gift. Being here. Being with each other. We were all *blessed* enough in life to have anything we wanted. Even Scotty agreed. In fact, we celebrated *not* giving gifts. We went to mass in a chapel somewhere within the Vatican grounds. A celebratory mass. The Pope would be saying mass in St. Peter's the next day to an invited group. A bit of overkill in my mind, but whatever. I was fine with it. Dad was in his glory. He beamed. The remaining six of us were happy for him. This was his time.

Danny

My confessional was a pouring out. Not so much of specific sins. Not that at all. I cried to God of this life we had led. Since high school. Since moving to Santa Fe. Our marriage. Having children. The visions. All those visions. The seeing the knowing. Now the kids. I KNEW. I was pouring out my blood to God in this changing, ever changing sense of destiny. I was uncertain of life in its entirety. In all of God's Grace. The priest did not speak very good English, but he tried hard to show mercy. God's mercy. He asked me to pray. Not specific prayers like the Our Father or the Hail Mary. He blessed me and prayed for the Holy Spirit. For me to pray for the Holy Spirit.

Jennifer knelt by me in the pew. She whispered her love for me, holding me tight. She understood me. She cared about me. I was grateful for her. I was blessed by the mere fact that we had each other. That we were on this journey together. Life's journey. That we had our children. We had everything in the world. All because God had made it so. James seemed to get it. Bill had understood. They tried hard to convey the mystery.

As we settled into Christmas Eve, drinking nothing but spiced tea, listening to Christmas music, mostly in Italian, surrounded by Christmas lights. Vinny sat by me glad that he had gone to confession. He wasn't a Catholic again. He was just glad. Sharon was singing softly, holding her son. The kids looked exhausted and were in bed before any of us. Seamus told me that we would be escorted to mass at 8:30 am.

The Pope was magnanimous. Full of grace. Celebrating the birth of our Lord in this cavernous place of worship. There are no words beyond overwhelming. Father Byrne wanted us all to go up for communion. Vinny could take part, along with me. The others, he advised, were to ask for His Holiness's blessing instead. The Pope was a short man, clothed in celebratory garments, radiating joy. He embraced my family, one by one. Slowly, with purpose. He did the same with Sharon, with Scotty. Vinny took communion. As did I. Consecrated. My heart was full.

Our evening was spent within the Vatican at a large, decorated hall. The Pope was not there, but special guests from all over the world attended. Christmas music played live by a string quartet. The actress Ashley Judd was there, who Sharon had befriended on the set of one movie or another. Ashley was a devout Christian, a Baptist I think she said, but being from Kentucky, she was familiar with the writer Thomas Merton, who had lived his life at the Abbey at Gethsemane outside of Louisville. Merton, she conveyed, was an important writer in the Catholic tradition that she greatly admired. She had done retreats at Gethsemane, saying with a smile that she may be a Catholic at heart. This being only one of many papal visits for her, she spoke freely with us about her faith and attraction to the many humanitarian outreaches of the Church. She was also a hard-core activist, which was Sharon's shared passion. As Ashley, Sharon and Jennifer sat and talked for a good hour about activism, movies, being in Rome, I was stunned at their combined beauty. Not merely physical beauty but their radiant strength. I listened from time to time, wandering away occasionally in the very informal atmosphere. Looking back at them I saw Stephanie pull up a chair and join the conversation. The three women were obviously welcoming her to their pow-wow. It struck me as terribly symbolic, these four women, Stephanie now included. A coterie of magnificence. I liked to think that this too was from God.

I asked Father Seamus to wake me at 3:00 am. I would bundle up and walk the grounds with him to a chapel of contemplation, attending Matins, the nightly vigil. From there he would show me the private libraries where I wanted to do some reading of Augustine before attending Lauds, the morning prayers of sunrise. Both services were heavily attended with guests, which surprised me to a degree. Mostly of one order or another. I may have been one of the few lay attendees.

Ashley attended Lauds, draped in a veil, blending in with the others. I barely recognized her. We did not actually catch mutual recognition.

Jennifer was dressed in a warm wool, simple long dress she had purchased in Paris, especially for this occasion. Julian wore his same suit and tie. Stephanie wore her same Christmas dress with a beautiful jacket. Sharon, Vinny and Scotty were dressed conservatively as well. I changed into a dark suit that I had purchased weeks ago for this meeting. New tie as well.

I was nervous. I think everyone was because there was very little talk as Seamus recited protocol of the proceedings. We would be eating breakfast with His Holiness and his immediate staff. Probably fifteen total. Feel free to ask the servants for anything you would like. Normally fruit, eggs, bread and ham are the staple. A pastry of some sort. Pope John Paul is a jovial soul. Not given to much formality. Spartan only when he needed to be. Yet it is best to be deferential. Wait for him to speak directly to you. He will inevitably bring about lively conversation, especially since you are from America and relatively famous. Although he is not readily knowledgeable about movies or the art world, that kind of thing.

Seamus informed me that the Pope wanted to see me first, alone, prior to our breakfast gathering. We all walked through the grounds to the private apartments. Everyone gathered in a comfortable dining area. Coffee and orange juice, tea if requested, were served. Seamus took me down a long hallway to an office. A private secretary, a priest with a long Italian name, then escorted me to the Pope, who was sitting at a side desk reading. He had on glasses, so I did not readily recognize him. His all-white habit was instantaneously familiar. He stood, offering his hand. Seamus advised me to kiss his ring if I was comfortable. Not required. I embraced his aged hand, bowing, kissing his ring. He embraced me calling me Daniel. He blessed me on the forehead, offering me a seat. His English was excellent, brushed with a Polish accent.

His demeanor turned very serious. He gave me a synopsis of Native American History in relation to Catholic missions, the Spanish conquest. He looked pained. He wished to convey to the people for whom I advocated that God's Love was for everyone.

He stopped there. I knew that he could not ask for forgiveness on behalf of the Holy Church. Nor bridge the injuries of centuries. He turned his back to me, staring out the window at the snow-covered gardens. He then guided me to a table, where we sat down. He held my hand, thanking me for my efforts in New Mexico and the region. He had heard good things from Bishop Sheehan. He opened a file with photos of pueblos, native villages of the area. He traced images of Indian children and mothers, families with his index finger. His reverie was unbreakable. I sat quietly.

The Pope grabbed my hand even harder, looking me deep into his eyes. My heart was racing. I could see his predicament. It was not time to do anything formally. A part of me was heavily disappointed. I have no idea from where this emotion welled-up, but I was holding back a tear. He knew this and sensed it. We stood and we embraced.

Love these children, he commanded me. There was authority in his voice. *Love them as you do, Daniel.*

Back inside the dining area, the Pope entered with gusto and good cheer. He was hungry, he said. There was laughter. No formality at all. He went to each of us in our group, asking our names, looking at us carefully, a blessing on the forehead. He was particularly engaged with Scotty, asking about his camera. Scotty must have been given instructions because he asked politely if he could take pictures. Seamus was about to say *no*, I could tell, but the Pope agreed immediately. This was obviously a break in protocol.

Servers brought platters of food, serving as we requested. I barely noticed or tasted the food, watching the interactions of everyone. John Paul was carrying on a conversation with Vinny, at one-point spanking *Vincent* good naturedly on the wrist. Another comedy routine, I smiled. Scotty took photos of our family, his family, all of us with the Pope. Even Ashley Judd and her friends. I was glad that he did. I hadn't even thought of it. I quickly asked for a photo with me and John Paul alone. It was impulsive. Sharon, Jennifer, Ashley and Stephanie put on veils or scarves over their heads and had a group picture taken with the Pope. Very serious expressions had by all. I knew that Sharon was behind it one way or another. Probably a subtle dig in there somewhere. Sharon was close to many of the activist nuns fighting for equal rights within the Church. Advocating for women priests. Wasn't going to happen, but Sharon thought she, herself, would make a wonderful priest. A joke she often told to annoy me. John Paul was soon whisked away by an entourage of several prelates. He waved goodbye.

I was irritated as we loaded up the rental cars, thanking Seamus for the abundant goodwill and generosity. We asked what we could do to show our thanks and he said that he would probably be the representative sent to Santa Fe if the situation developed favorably. Perhaps we could reciprocate. Gladly we assured him. I knew what he meant by the *current situation*. It would not improve unless the Church moved from its silence considerably.

I was also irritated that I had agreed to meet someone Jennifer had met on the train to Rome from Paris. A lawyer of all things. I tried to look on the bright side. It was about 10:30 am. We'd make his home in about an hour. He offered lunch and promised to have us on the road by 2:00. Everyone was happy for the quick stop. We'd have to eat anyway, and why not with a local? Abruzzi was a little over three hours from there and we'd be fine.

I asked Vinny to drive our car with the guys. I was tired. Exhausted, wanting to drift off and meditate on the entire trip. It had been a wonderful, once in a lifetime experience. Jennifer was driving the other car. We made sure we had directions, glad we could skirt the city of Rome itself, getting on a highway almost immediately. The estate of Matthew DiPietro was sprawling. We could not even see his home from the entry gate. Being alone, as Jennifer explained, I expected a small bachelor home.

He did have one servant, a maid and gardener combination. She greeted us at the door dressed in winter garb, winterizing something outside. Mr. DiPietro then came to his door with a messy apron and good cheer. He was cooking us lunch. A feast.

The dining area was massive. The table set with china, heavy duty earthen ware, and silver. He had been breathing the wine, pouring everyone a glass of Castelli di Jesi. I deferred, thinking I should be driving when we left. Sharon said she would abstain, which shocked all of us. She also said that she had already drunk way too much during the week. Which, again, did not seem like her.

Matthew was a giant Maria Callas fan, playing her music softly on an old fashion reel to reel that he had programmed. His collection of opera was stacked from floor to ceiling in his nearly two-story library, just off the entryway. He quickly showed us around the six-bedroom estate, various sitting rooms, dens, family rooms. Impeccable rococo design. Like a museum. We were afraid to sit down.

On a very large oak table, he had old maps and Italian documents spread out. I took out my Vatican packet of my family heritage and Vinny did the same for his. Matthew put on glasses, examining the various pieces. He was excited, able to trace both of our heritages to the same town, practically cousins. He had found almost the exact things that the Vatican had. Vinny hugged me calling me *Cousin Danny* with a heavy Italian accent. Everyone perked up with this development.

We had reservations to stay in the seaside village of Pescara that night, which he said would be fine, but he had planned for us to stay at the home of the mayor of the town of Castiglione Messer Marina for our final two nights in Italy if we so chose. Matthew assured us that their home, while modest, would easily accommodate all of us. And the mayor wasn't really a *mayor* as we thought of it. More like a local councilman. In actuality, the man and his family had a century long sheep and wool operation in the hills.

Other than asking Jennifer and all of us how things went at the Vatican he seemed disinterested in our time in Rome. He never asked about art or movies. He seemed interested in Julian's conversations about music. Matthew had a grand piano in the house and Julian agreed to play a piece of Vivaldi. The sound reverberated beautifully inside the mansion. Matthew was happy we had visited him. Simple as that.

True to his word, Mr. DiPietro had us on the road right at 2:00. We were stuffed and more than anxious to get there. Vinny gave Matthew a business card with his agent's name, mostly for stand-up comedy gigs, but asking Matthew to call if he was in Chicago or the States. Jennifer thanked Matthew profusely. It was a chance meeting on a train and now they were friends, she emphasized.

Sharon took the wheel of her family in one car, and the four of us piled into the other. I was looking forward to the drive.

CHAPTER ELEVEN

The past could be jettisoned, but seeds got carried. Joan Didion

Stephanie

Pescara. *The capital of the region*, so read the sign. A sprawling ocean town, we settled into our hotel, a simple place on the beach. It was winter. I could only speculate about this place as a summer resort. No one was around. Everyone seemed to like it that way. Silence only punctuated by the foggy Adriatic coastline. Cold and foreboding.

Sharon wanted some family time to herself, and we agreed to spend two nights here and then head up the mountainside road to Castiglione. Nothing much to do but rest, which was fine by us. Dad made the calls and arrangements. Then we were given keys to our rooms to an almost empty building. The manager gave us all the largest rooms available, at reduced cost, even on different floors. It was funny when I walked into my tiny suite and saw two bedrooms and a bathroom to myself. I set my suitcase and backpack down wanting to start on *Harry Potter's Chamber of Secrets* looking forward to curling up by the window looking out at the vast gray ocean, when mom knocked on my door. She wanted to know if I was interested in taking a long walk on the beach. Just her and me. She wanted to talk about *Purgatory,* the script and the movie, and *some other stuff*. Of course, I was interested, finding my warmest clothes and darted off with my Mom.

It was cold, no doubt about it. But we were energized, walking along the vacant cement path running parallel to the beachfront. We walked in silence for a good while. Probably miles. Mom made some comments about Paris, all the sights in Rome, her joy in meeting the Pope. I agreed, patiently, waiting for the movie to come up. She informed me that she and Vinny had finalized the script as it was now being marketed to producers in L.A. She felt they already had more than enough backing but were waiting for final contracts. Tim and Shelly had found a perfect location between the town of Amiens and the Belgian border, securing government cooperation on the local and national level. *That was fast,* I thought.

Filming would most likely start at the end of February. My heart raced. Tim used the same casting company he always used, but they wanted Ashley to play the trapeze artist and Robin Wright to play one of the nuns.   They were small roles, but they wanted an ensemble look. With the mysterious collage of images that they were after, 1960's style black and white film, existential art theme-look in silver and gray, changing the title to *Purgatorio,* late 1910's - early 1920's era poverty in a devastated post-War setting, burned out buildings, dead horses and livestock, shattered villages. It would be either a disaster at the box office, or at least a cultic movie for those curious about the cast.   I was so excited I couldn't stand it. My character name was going to be changed to Manon. Mom explained to me that the name meant *bitter,* and it symbolized the awful choice she had to make towards the end. From here on out I was Manon, rolling the middle *n* in pronunciation. She also wanted to make it a family affair. Vinny would play a barker at the tent of horrors in the carnival. Tim would make several appearances as the ringmaster. Shelly would be in a scene as a prostitute.   Even Scotty would be an impoverished boy in the crude wooden stands hollering in delight at the elephants. Quick cameos for the most part.

"This is where it gets tricky," she went on. "I want Dad to come. I know he has school, but I want him in it. You know the scene when an old, crippled man is walking down the road as you and Sharon are headed to the crematorium to identify a dead *worker*?"

"Yes, I remember the scene."

"And the man drops dead, collapsing on his cane."

"Yes, yes, it's quick."

"I want Dad to play it. With makeup and rocks in his shoes, he will be fine, hobbling along. It's shot from the back."

I laughed. "That would be wonderful. I have no idea if he would ever leave school for that."

"I haven't even talked with him about it.   He could do a quick shoot and fly back. Probably three days, tops.

Hardly worth it, maybe. But I want him there. Mostly to see you."

"It would be fun." I was so afraid to talk about my role. The reality of all this.

"Then Julian. I have a good scene for him too. We need a blind piano player with rudimentary sunglasses, a surviving French soldier, drinking wine from a dirty glass. Smoking a cigarette. Terribly young. He'd play the new jazz on a broken down stand up in Sharon's parlor. In the *house of ill repute*, so to speak."

"God, Mom, that's so cool. It's not in the script, is it?"

"It is now."

We reached a distant pier. It, too, was vacant. We walked out on the shaky boards as the icy water splashed in mild waves. The gray wind was merciless. Seagulls complained overhead. I could hardly see a half mile out a small fishing boat of some kind, its lights blinking, in and out of fog.

"Steph, this is a big deal. Sharon and I feel that you are ready. It will be hard work. I'm worried about you, though. Working with her, with me, will be a terrible strain. Because we are your family only makes it worse, not easier. Believe me. It will be so difficult for me to deliver many of those lines to my daughter. I will always be talking to Manon, don't forget it."

"I know Mom. You know, like I've said, when I was with Sharon in L.A., and when you and I read sometimes, it really scares me to death."

"It should. We have a bleak and horrid script. This is the opposite of so many of the formulaic things out there. It's dated by the approach we are taking. No one would touch this thing if it weren't for Tim directing. Mostly because of Sharon. She's automatic. Honestly, it's amazing to watch that girl. I think of when we were on stage in high school and now. She has magic, that kid."

"Mom, you underestimate yourself, you know. I mean, everything I see and hear, especially on this trip, is that you are an icon over here. They will come in droves just to see you reappear."

She smiled, hugging me, turning us around, heading back.

"Anyway, this is going to happen, Steph. We will use your last name Tomasetti in the credits. Most people will figure out quickly that you are my daughter, even with my different last name. We are not going to publicize it at all. When we promote the film, you often won't be there. And we will try and avoid any situation with you and me together. We don't want to sell it as a mom-daughter thing. Not at all." She took deep breath, exhaling the moist air. "We have lots to figure out with your dad. Our film and travel schedule mostly. I'm not worried about school; neither will your dad. You get straight A's anyway. You will need to join the union, have a tutor on set. Phil, the studio, they will take care of those things for you. Phil wants to be your agent. You good with that?"

My mind was trying to wrap itself around these things. I agreed with another shake of the head *yes*.

"And a contract. You will make a good amount of money."

I hadn't thought about that.   I was frozen. Literally and figuratively. We were getting colder as the wind picked up. We still had a good distance to go.

"Steph, I want to be blunt. I want to talk with you about sex."

More to process.   I had no idea where this was going.

"I don't see you with a boyfriend, really. Or even all that interested in guys. You've had lots of boys interested in you. You went to junior high dances. But I look at you and you're already a beautiful young woman."

I thanked her, shivering in her arms.

"I can't pretend that you will stay a virgin, I hope you're a virgin." She waited.

I nodded *yes*.

"All I can emphasize, in this birds and bee talk, is that you are safe. Always be safe. Protect yourself. Talk with me about protection. Condoms, birth control, the pill. Don't hesitate.   Be in charge of your body and emotions. It's not easy. Believe me, I know."

I did not want to know. My mind could not go in that direction.

"Also, you see the pleasure and allure of sex. Sharon is a prime example. You know that. And Madonna. You even met her. You can see her magnetism along with her normalcy as a woman. You know what I'm trying to say."

I wanted to throw a dart into the conversation. Not be a passive teen. "You mean like Melanie?"

She stopped dead in her tracks.   She was evaluating the origin of my comment. What did I know or not know? What could she assume? Mostly, she knew I wasn't really being a smart-ass, just that I was correct. Should they even be talking like this, its Julian's business, not theirs. I could read her mind.

"I don't really want to go there." She finally said. "I need to have the same talk with Julian. Probably your dad. Melanie is definitely a strong-willed young lady; I will give you that."

I was disappointed. I wanted to pursue the speculation, find out details, if there were any.

"She sure is." That is all I could say. And I had successfully deflected the attention off me.

Mom walked me to my room. We were on our own for a day or two. Read. Sleep. Rest. Stay warm. Watch Italian TV. I could call room service, or we could eat as a family, or I could eat with Julian. Mom and Dad were going to take advantage and be alone. I knew what that meant. Do Not Disturb. Julian wanted to read, as well. He was also working on lyrics. Music for *Retro Sky*. Walking with Dad somewhere later.   They'd probably have *the talk.*

I thought about sex. What Mom said. The college kid in Paris was the only time I was with a boy in person and really felt a burning desire. I liked boys in school but never felt the way I had dancing with that guy. Playing the librarian, being with older guys in the theater, even then I wasn't all that turned on.

I fantasized.   I felt like a woman. It blended into the actual filming of my character, Manon. Manon was certainly sexual. I could tangibly feel it in her persona. Having a mother who owned a brothel. Seeing nakedness, hearing fucking, even seeing fucking all her life. The men. The lesbianism mixed in with the working prostitutes. Their attempts to find love and connection. Escape. The soldiers called back to the hellish front. The alcohol. The laudanum. The opium. The addictions. The war. The endless, relentless noise. The trauma. The smoke. The bombings. The starvations. The death tied into sex. The desperation of sex. The human anguish to bond with someone else, especially in horrific circumstances. She was savvy to them all, to all of it. The very young vulnerable Manon had managed to keep her virginity in such a world. Maneuvering through the insanity. Pulled in the opposite direction towards celibacy and the convent, was excruciating. Sex as survival. One extreme or the other. An impossible choice.

And I, Stephanie Tomasetti, a freshman in high school in the dawning 21st century, was certainly aware. More than aware.

Julian

After my awkward walk with Dad, I grabbed my backpack and headed up two floors to Steph's room. She let me in, in her PJ's wrapped with blankets, returning to the couch by the eastward facing window. The hazy ocean filled the panes. She didn't even say anything, returning to her book. She was engrossed. I grabbed an Italian fizz drink from her refrigerator, making myself comfortable on another couch. I was in gray sweats, still shivering from being outside.

"So how was it?" she finally asked, setting down the book.

"Was what?"

"Your walk with Dad?"

"How'd you know we took a walk?" I felt perplexed, or irritated.

"Mom and I had the same walk. We're fourteen now brother, it's time for the facts of life talk. They were working in tandem." She smiled. I smiled back in unison. "Yeah, only several years too late." I added. We both laughed then. Then I added, "Damn, Steph, I hope you aren't, well, you know."

"Don't worry brother. Mom was being cautious. It was a nice conversation. I appreciated it."

I was stirring on the couch, trying to rearrange my body, my mind.

"What about you, Julian? Did it go okay with you and Dad?" She asked me.

"Sure." I wasn't even looking at her. I came up here to her room for a reason, though. I knew that and she also knew that. She could read my mind. I wanted to talk about Melanie.

I waited. My drink looked good, so she got up and made one for herself with ice. She was adding ice to her glass self-consciously because we had heard someone in Paris criticize Americans for using ice all the time. *Too fucking bad*, she was thinking. She liked ice.

"Steph, you and Mel are good friends, right?" There it was. I asked.

"Sorta, I guess. She's older than me. Well, us. I don't really know her that well. She's very cool. A lot of fun. We get along well. Always have."

"She acts like you're her best friend sometimes."

She thought about that for a long time. I looked at the painting above the mantle uncertain why anyone in their right mind would put that in here. It was an ugly modern art deco rip-off, reproduced from the 1980's. Then Steph answered, "Come to think of it, Mel has talked to me a lot about her mom's divorces. How she doesn't even really know her dad. Or dads. How she has distant relatives in Las Vegas." I didn't know how to respond. "I was glad she sleeps over," is all that she could seem to add.

"You're the only one she's ever talked to about that stuff."

"Really?" She sat up and looked more closely at me. I was still struggling somehow.

Then I said, "Yeah. One thing I've learned about Mel is that she's all show to everyone else. All the makeup and clothes and colors. It's a show. She's lonely at her apartment. Her mom is never home. Always working or dating someone. I think I'm all she has. The band. You." She listened closely now. "I'll be more aware when we get back. I like her. We should do more things together. Just I'm not into music like you guys. She liked horseback riding that day. Maybe I'll take her to the pueblo with me."

"She'd like that." Pause. "I slept with her, Steph. You already could guess. Dad could tell. He didn't say it outright. You know, the whole be careful, contraceptive thing. He was spot on talking about Mel, worried about her graduating this year. Worried about me."

The little girl in Stephanie wanted to scream or say *yuck* or make a crummy statement about me having sex. The emerging young lady in her, the one I was beginning to see clearly, said, "I assume you were careful, used a rubber or something. I'm glad. You did, didn't you?"

"Yeah, of course." I answered emphatically.

"I think Dad's right. You and Mel have something serious going now. Tough spot. You're still too damned young brother. You need to have a good long talk with Mel, is my thought."

"That's what Dad said. I don't know about love. I do know I feel alive with her. Maybe more. We have a blast singing. The band is the most important thing in both of our lives."

"It shows. You guys are incredible. I mean that. You two blow me away. The whole Retro thing is amazing, Julian. I really mean it brother."

"Thanks. I'm glad you're there, around with us." I waited. "I think you mean more to Mel than you let on or realize, Steph."

"Like I said, I'll be more in touch with her when we get back."

We tried to read our books, but it was impossible.

I asked about the filming of the movie *Purgatory*. She gave me all the details of *Purgatorio* – and the name change. She wasn't supposed to say anything, but she told me Mom's ideas about casting. Everyone involved; Dad even; Scotty even; Shelly even. Then she told me about my part. I had snot come out my nose I laughed so hard. I rarely laughed that hard. I usually had a sly kind of laugh, or mischievous laugh, or chuckle. This was from my gut.

"No fucking way am I getting in front of a camera!" I practically yelled.

"Oh, come on Julian. It would be so cool to see you made up as a young blind soldier. Your dark glasses. Drinking from a dirty glass, smoking a hand rolled cig. Jamming away on a crappy piano with some kind of Charleston thing. A prostitute near you at the piano. Maybe even someone famous. Maybe even Sharon. Now that would be something. Huh?! You and Sharon in a scene. You'd have a blast."

I was smiling, considering it. I liked it. I'd always have Sharon on celluloid, I seemed to be telling myself. Not the Sharon I grew up with. Not Auntie Sharon. THE Sharon Preston, on the covers of *Time* and *Glamour* and *Vogue* and so many others including the *Sports Illustrated Swimsuit* edition – three times; in the August 1996 *Playboy* with a full three-page profile of nude photographs, a serial treatment in *Life*, two unauthorized biographies. I could see my mind in gear. I could see myself up on the screen with Sharon looking like a turn of the century prostitute, in black and white smokey haze, smoking a cigarette, hand on my back swaying with the primitive jazz. That wicked smile of hers. That all-knowing tunnel in her eyes. And me at the piano where I am most comfortable. Most sure of myself.

"What about you, Steph? You ready for this thing?"

"Ready? Maybe not. Maybe so. But I can't wait. It will be something."

Our drive up the winding road was part dirt, part paved. It was snowing moderately. Sheep dotted the hillside. Then acres and acres of dormant vineyards. A few large herds of horses, then cattle. More sheep, everywhere. Climbing until we spotted a primitive castle like structure with a crucifix on the spire. A church. It was the 12th century landmark we hoped to find.

The village was not big at all. Houses were either spread out or stacked on top of each other, like a distant idea of an apartment complex. Our population summary said 950. I had no idea where anyone was. It seemed desolate to me.

We parked in the courtyard where we had been directed by the mayor. It was windy, freezing. Luckily the snow was letting up. Not deep at all. It was a Saturday, but we went into the Church for warmth, if not for anything else. Inside, the early Middle Ages remained intact. Nothing like Rome. No hint of the Renaissance or even anything in history. This was another time period still existing in the present.

No one inside. We sat in silence or whispering. Scotty was taking pictures. That was about it. Dad eventually got up looking for someone. We were supposed to meet the mayor here. Sharon and Mom started walking the stations of the cross, carved out of wood, probably hewn from nearly a thousand years ago. The crucifix of Jesus on the cross above the stained-glass window, was probably older. The window may be more modern, a replacement. Hard to tell.

A short, hobbled man walked through the front door, took off his hat and gloves, dipped his hand in the holy water, making the sign of the cross. He motioned for us to follow him, through an interior door, into a small meeting room   A place we could talk.

He introduced himself as Miguel Romano. He was aware of Matthew and our arrangements. He would show us our quarters shortly. His English was terribly strained. I felt bad for him, searching for words.

Today he was going to show us the cemetery, which we would have to drive to, the common grave marked with honor just outside in the courtyard, and the town hall, where various plaques and books recorded the local history.

When my dad shook his hand and thanked him, the man cried. Literally began crying. He repeated our name Tomasetti, Tomasetti.

Another man came in, he was looking for us - his uncle Miguel primarily. He was Luigi Romano. He would act as interpreter. Luigi hugged his uncle and told him that everything was okay. Or at least I assumed that was what he was saying. Luigi asked us to get bundled up. We were going back outside. First he urged us to use the bathroom, help ourselves to water from the sink. Cups sat lined up on a shelf. We scattered for water, waiting to use the single bathroom. Or went back into the church and looked around.

Outside, the snow had stopped. A sliver of sunlight shot through a cloud heavy with the sea far below. Luigi explained why his uncle was crying. He showed us the large, rectangular formation in the ground, sweeping off a thin layer of snow. It was a common grave from roughly 1660. The exact year was not given. It was the year Napoleon III invaded Chieti and all of Abruzzi. He slaughtered hundreds. The Tomasetti family led the resistance.   Along with the Calibrasella family, Vinny's family, they were lined-up and shot. 27 names were carved into the marker.   15 Tomasetti's, 9 Calibrasella's, 3 Romano's.   The old man knelt in the snow praying in Italian. Vinny took off his hat, looking at his notes and his now damp file, finding his great-grandfather's name. And several others. He looked shook up. Dad could not find his great-grandfather's name and asked Miquel, via Luigi.   Luigi stood up and hugged Dad. Then he came over to me. He was looking at me closely through his damp eyes, cataracts visible. He asked my name, I could tell. I said *Julian*. He hugged me tightly. He used his old, rugged hand, running his fingers through my long hair.   Mom introduced herself, and Stephanie, then everyone else. The old man hugged Steph, still with tears running down his cheeks.

He mumbled something to me, and his nephew laughed slightly while interpreting.

"He's asking if you are coming back to claim your town." Dad and Vinny had no idea what he meant.   Luigi was or was not serious, we could not tell. "This is your town. It probably still is, legally. It belonged to the Tomasetti's. Truthfully, I have no idea.   Uncle, here, believes it's yours."

We laughed. Especially Sharon. Vinny made a joke that he could say he owned the town when he did stand-up comedy here.   No one really laughed. The absurdity, the ridiculousness of it.

Luigi asked us to follow him in our cars. The drive was about five minutes. He put his uncle into an old white VW van.

We got to a cemetery out in the middle of nowhere, perched on the hillside. A mausoleum in the middle. It was eerie walking through the gate with grave markers and statues hundreds upon hundreds of years old. Scattered in no discernible way.

Luigi brought us to a memorial about 15 feet high and 8 feet wide. A block of cement with saints and a crucifix plastered here and there, narrowing towards heaven. It sat like a discarded immobile ton of memories waiting for us to arrive. Dead grass clung to the sides. A dead vine along one side.

Here is where Dad got very emotional. The large plaque read Nicola Guillermo Tomasetti. No date. Buried here was the 'leader of the community,' interpreted into English. He was The Godfather.   Luigi explained that the Tomasetti's were slaughtered but one boy of five years old was smuggled out, along with three women of the family, two of which were Calibrasella's. Two Calibrasella boys also survived and were smuggled to Naples.   Vinny was rapidly reviewing his file, nodding his head. The Tomasetti boy ended up in Genoa, where he grew up, marrying a girl from a seamstress family in the region. He took the name of Nicola. They had six children there, then immigrated to New York during a famine.   They had five more children in America, then the twelfth in 1899, who they named after Nicola, the enshrined patriarch. Carrying on the name, Nick then came to north Denver at the age of nine, fleeing the crowded tenements with an older brother and sister via train to live with the enshrined Mother Cabrini in an Italian commune of sorts. That was all they knew of the history, and they weren't even sure of the last part. They did not know about the heritage once Nick arrived in Denver. Dad confirmed the last half of the story, from Genoa forward. Dad had no idea of what preceded Genoa. Neither had his own father, Richard, son of Nicola. Now himself, Daniel, and his children, Julian and Stephanie in the line.

The mayor brought us to Luigi's home. His wife, Carmella, was a large happy woman. Could not speak English at all. Vinny and Sharon were shown a room with only two small single beds. Scotty would have to sleep on the couch. Our entire foursome was shown another room with only two beds, where the four of us would have to sleep. For two nights. We looked at each other in a tiny room not even large enough for our suitcases. Luigi offered to have Stephanie and I sleep on what were two cots over in the church meeting room. We jumped on it.

Luigi's house was a short walk. We'd head over after Carmella fed us. She planned a feast, to be served next door at their neighbors, the Vaira's. The Vaira's had an extra bed that Luigi and Carmella would use. We had displaced our hosts.

We had eaten well on this trip, but nothing as wonderful as this. Fresh lamb, cooked with special spices from their garden. Various vegetables mixed in handmade tomato sauce, covering a ravioli structure I had never seen. Homemade bread. I mean real homemade bread.

Their own wheat. Salad at the end. Honey caked pastries filled with cream.

Steph and I giggled quietly in Mom and Dad's room, wanting to talk about everything. We grabbed our warm clothes, extra blankets, our books, and dashed into the black night.

We found the cots. Army cots it seemed. It was not as cold as we feared. Steph and I talked and talked about this whole unreality, finally falling asleep well past midnight. I woke up, unable to find the bathroom, wandering into the church, like stepping back in time. The sensation was like being in a spaceship, flying at Mach one. I saw the two buildings again, above the sacristy door. Like the photograph in the LaGuardia airport. I quickly creeped back into our sleeping area and woke up Steph. She was angry, but I pulled at her. She stood there with me staring at the vision. She saw it too. A plane or planes collided into the vision. The two buildings. Sweeping them away. We shook. It was insane. Like seeing a movie flash on the wall near the sacristy. Then disappear.

We were frightened this time. Not perplexed. Frightened. I turned to the side chapel where candles burned for the remembrance of the dead for the closing year. A saint, I had no idea who, looked directly at both of us. Steph said something like his face looked like flesh and blood. Like he blinked as he spoke to us. We were freaking each other out. *To those to whom much is given, much is required*, he seemed to be repeating. Steph said she heard the same words. We held each other, both of us confused and scared out of our mind. I had peed myself in a slight trickle.

I got up early in the morning. A heater was blaring, so it was comfortable. I went back into the church, examining the image of Saint Peter carefully. The candles still burned. Above the sacristy door. Nothing on both counts, no indications of what we had seen. I cleaned myself the best I could and went outside. The breaking sunshine was brilliant. I could smell the sea air in the distance. Sharon was outside sneaking a cigarette. I strolled over. She offered me one, and I laughed. She smiled too, throwing hers into the snow.

"Come on, let's take a walk, Julian." She put her arm through mine, directing me who knows where.

"Quite a trip," she said, bowing her head, her beautiful hair falling, putting her expensive wool hat back on. "Can you imagine that Vinny and your dad are like brothers? I still can't believe it. The whole story, you couldn't make it up." We walked a few steps, "Quite a trip," she repeated.

Little did she know, I thought. *A trip*, exactly. We didn't talk much. Short observations of this or that. She was happy for Vinny. Looking forward to filming. Loved my band. That kind of thing. She was warm next to me. I was in love with her. I rapidly forgot the madness of the night before. Of this town. My town. I smiled to myself. I was in love with Sharon. We walked and walked. I was the luckiest man in the world. Next to Vinny, of course. I looked at her lips, into her eyes when she talked.

She stopped me, turned and faced me. "What's going on? Tell me. I can tell. I've known you since you were in diapers. Tell me."

Speechless. How could I tell her that I wanted to kiss her? Absurdity in the craziness of my entire world. She hugged me tight. "You're missing that girlfriend of yours, huh? I get it. Melanie, right?"

"Right," I said.

We turned around and headed back. She put her head on my shoulder, her embrace, her hair, again. I wanted her. I was full head over heels in lust, maybe not love at all.

Mom greeted us. She was bundled up and wanted to walk, too. Sharon went back inside, kissing me on the cheek.

Mom and I walked for nearly an hour. Not a word, until she told me about the acting idea. I told her that Steph had already told me. She didn't seem bothered by that. She asked me if I liked owning this town. We laughed again. She knew I was out of sorts; I could tell. Not just Sharon and the vision thing, my life seemed to be like that spaceship at Mach one. I wanted to go home.

We spent the entire day visiting with each other. Talking about our experiences over the past two weeks. The Pope and what he was like. Our hosts were terribly impressed and interested, wanting every detail. We ate good food, drinking a lot of coffee and tea. Luigi showed us around town, to the town hall where there were some more historical markers of both the Tomasetti and Calabrasella families, then over to the Romano family farm. Lazy, relaxing day.

It was New Year's Eve. 2001 was soon upon us.
We barely stayed up past midnight. No TV. No fanfare.
A quick sip of wine. A toast of good cheer. No one was
drinking anymore. Kisses and hugs. Sharon kissed me
on the lips, like everyone else.   Damn. I couldn't stand it.
It was all my issue. My problem, all in my head. She
wasn't doing anything.
We loaded up, thanked Luigi, the mayor, everyone, and
left early the next morning for a 3:20 pm flight out of
Rome. First class back to New York. Steph and I would
look at that skyline photo in the terminal one more time.
Very closely.

CHAPTER TWELVE

Each morning I wake invisible.
I almost know what it is to be seen.
Now I know that I am seen
Because I have a shadow.
I clothe myself until even the shadow had substance.
From Solar Eclipse

Stephanie

Mom and Dad were shook-up when we told them on the
plane about the vision in the church, how it matched our
vision in the kiva. We'd talk later, they both assured us.
Once in New York, we said our goodbyes to Sharon,
Vinny and Scotty, as they were off to a different
connecting flight to Chicago. The four of us practically

ran to our connection for Denver. We stopped and stood in front of that enormous cityscape photograph of Manhattan. Yes, those two buildings, the World Trade Center were exactly what we saw.

Dad chatted with me and Julian a bit during our quick layover in Denver. Mom listened closely, letting him speak. He thought James would be good to talk to as soon as we got home; that he and Mom had some things to say, too. We'd do it first thing in New Mexico.

We practically invaded James's tiny cottage. He welcomed us home. He expected us. Water was boiling for tea. We found chairs around his practical kitchen set. He lit up his pipe, offering it to us. We all declined, although I wanted to take a puff or two.

Julian did the talking, reminding James of the vision at the kiva what seemed like ages ago and told him of the vision in the church in Italy. He would mumble or chant under his inhale and exhale of sweet-smelling smoke. His response was that the two of us inherited. No not inherited. We're the beginning. We're offspring. Daniel was the first, Jennifer joined, Sharon brought into the orbit, like the moon reflection. Julian and I looked at each other making no sense of the gibberish.

Mom took James's hand, wanting to talk. She explained that she and Dad had had visions in their lifetime. That James and Bill had known of them. Time as a continuum. They could *see*. They *knew* things. The reason was uncertain most of the time.

I asked what kind of visions that they had had. Dad talked of time bending, of bad things happening. Sometimes in the past then averted and changed.

Sometimes of the future, stuff they still could not comprehend. Of good things that would change, too. We sat there a bit incredulous. It was nonsense, explaining nothing. Julian and I melded into a stand of our own. Dad was this responsible, even-keeled guy, a principal for God's sake. His Catholicism was his own thing, but not like this. Mom was successful on every front. They were not the type to fall for this mumbo jumbo.

James spoke up with authority.

"I will not be here to understand these visions you have seen. Just *Know* they are real. For now, it is for you and Julian to see them unfold into history. This is not your responsibility. It is merely a baptism of sorts. It is a confirmation. Your Mom and Dad can help you get through it."

"You sound like you're dying." Dad said.

"I am not dying. Not now. But I will be taken to the Spirit when this is made manifest."

Jennifer patted his hand. They held hands, the two of them.

James went on. "Do not be afraid of anything. Your Mom and Dad know this. Get on with your lives. The blessing is being poured out in overflowing amounts. Like an ocean. Do what you need to do. You will be fine."

Then he added with ease, looking directly at me, "I'd like to go with you and your mom to the pueblo this coming weekend. It will be cold to ride, but you should go and ride anyway. I will be staying at the pueblo for a long time."

I felt frightened.

He quickly added, "I'll be fine. Don't worry about me either. I have a ceremony to perform."

He got up and put his hands on Julian's shoulders. "You have other things to do. Play your music. You will be traveling again soon. Let it go for now."

"And you, Danny." He was looking at Danny like a son. "Just relax, will you? You've had quite a trip. Go to your church with Louise. Pray, as you will. You are a rock. Love is with your family, Danny."

He asked us to leave. He needed to rest. "Here," he said, offering me the pipe. He knew I wanted to take a puff. I did it right there in front of Mom and Dad. I passed it to Julian, and he did the same. James then handed the glowing pipe to Mom and then she passed it to Dad after she exhaled. Dad took a deep inhale, then handed it back to James. We were *smoking pipe*. It was his way.

Mom and I rode mile after mile. We were dressed in warm clothes, taking food and water. Our horses strong and swift. Both were long hair, black Morgens. We were as free as they were. Mom was free of her art show in Paris. We never spoke of the movie, or of any visions. Or of Rome or Italy. Rarely of anyone at all. We spoke only of the trail, the wintery views of pinks and whites and nearly terrifying sunrise and sunset. The parcels of food we consumed, dried and minimal, some fresh fruit. Canteen water from broken iced streams. The wildlife and dormancy of the desert. For two full days it was only us and our horses. We were left alone by the reservation.   We slept in a crude cabin.   Mom was beautiful in her braids, checkered warmth. I felt fully alive. A woman, like her. She would braid my hair like hers. Occasionally we would sit on a rock or log, looking over the horizon. Not even a word spoken. The sun moving overhead. The cold breezes. A sound of a hawk. A jagged ledge we followed or into a valley below.

Danny

I returned from late mass with Louise, secluding myself in my office.   I gave Julian a ride to Melanie's apartment on the other side of town. I'd have to go get him around 7:00.

Computers were an issue in our school, as well as districtwide.   We only had two in the front office until Jimmie got us a deal from his company in Silicon Valley. First an installment of twenty-five then fifty units.   We were working hard to put email in place, but it was still an unreliable means of communication, so I had to rely on what was becoming old fashioned handwritten, mimeographed memoranda.   With my agenda book and master calendar in front of me I examined duty rosters, meeting schedules, district trainings, sports schedules, teacher evaluations, conferences, board meetings, just about every commitment I had down. I was in a slight panic being gone the entire Christmas break. Julian mentioned his phone conversation with Shelly, who already had a concert gig lined up in Albuquerque and wanted to try to book Retro Sky in the I-25 corridor of towns from Trinidad to Pueblo to Colorado Springs to

Denver. Shelly was gung-ho, forgetting that these were kids. Maybe their parents, like me for one, would have something to say about it all. Julian was a good student but the band, not so much. Missing school will be a problem that I will have to deal with head on. I could only imagine.

My main concern looking at the calendar was the filming of *Purgatorio*. It was sounding like Jennifer and Steph would need to leave in February and stay through early April. Steph would be getting tutoring, and her grades were excellent. No worries. How in the world Julian and I were supposed to fly out for what was going to be one day of shooting was sounding ridiculous? Jennifer assured me that the studio budget would handle it. Money wasn't really the problem. Time was. Besides, I really wanted to do something special for Jennifer when she was done. Over our spring break, take her somewhere. It was another item I placed on my growing list of things to do.

Cheryl was an amazing secretary. We met every Monday bright and early, and I looked forward to tomorrow. I was going to be jumping on the fast track and I needed her to run interference.

I called the bishop to fill him in on our trip, the Vatican, the Pope. To ask him how the tribal mass and celebration had gone. He was incredibly upbeat, for him. He said that the attendance at the native Christmas celebration was overwhelming. Festive. The elders were appreciative. He asked me every detail of our trip, including into Abruzzi. We talked for almost an hour and half. He was mostly pleased that John Paul was seemingly relaxed and enjoying our visit. I withheld my frustrations and even anger that the Church was not moving forward on the policy front, or willing to make any commitment to recompense. Bishop Sheehan was sharp as a tack and picked up on the matter anyway. I was not going to let the matter go, but I was at a loss as to what to do next. For now, I'd let it *be in the hands of God*, so to speak. I would continue my educational outreach to the community; it was where I was having the most success anyway.

Vinny called me. They got home and settled back in Chicago. He thanked me, was already reminiscing about our trip, especially our familial bond in Abruzzi. It was pretty cool, I had to agree. Sharon's premiere of Woody Allen's *Undercover* was going to be February 2nd at the Lincoln Center. All of us were invited. I told him that we probably wouldn't make it. In fact, with the kids' school and the upcoming filming in northern France, I would only let Jennifer know. He said that Sharon didn't expect us to attend. She hated those things, and so did he, but she liked Woody and Jeff. Vinny doubted that he would go, wanting to stick close to Scotty. Besides he had steady comedy work in the Second City.

We had missed our twenty-fifth Columbine graduation reunion this past summer. One of the many letters in our stack was from a good friend of who I played basketball with my senior year, David Cabrera. David was recently remarried, to a lady named Linda Valario. The Valario family had a rich heritage in the Taos area, hundreds of years old. This intrigued me because I had heard of the Valarios several times. I even think James was familiar with them. They were returning to Linda's family horse ranch of fifteen acres, a training facility of 51 stall barns, a half mile track, and ranch house which was now empty. David and Linda were inviting us up to visit when we could get the chance. He missed us at the reunion and wanted to arrange a visit. Either direction, their house or ours. I'd run it by Jennifer, I really wanted to see them. Steph would go nuts when we told her. I had one of the new computers in my home office, a gift to shareholders in Jimmie's company. The telephone dial-up connection, was terribly slow, making all kinds of creaking sounds. Once I got on the internet, which, to be honest, I really didn't know what that was, my directions told me to 'choose a search engine.' I was lost. Two new ones, Google and Teoma, were recommended. I got on Teoma and typed in hotels in New Orleans. I found several names and locations in the French Quarter. We could get decadent when Jennifer finished filming. It would be the surprise I promised.

Julian

Melanie and her mom lived in a small apartment about as far from our house as you could get in Santa Fe. Close to the hospital. She took a bus to school. Her walk from our rehearsals, at the Gallery, was about two miles. One of our parents usually gave her a ride. I had never been to her room. It was heavy duty with music lined posters of bands like the B-52's, the Cure, the Psychedelic Furs, Eurythmics, plenty of photos of

Chrissie Hynde – who was her hero. She had a small stereo on a cinderblock bookshelf loaded with books. A large album collection in wooden crates surrounded the room. We played the radio on a local station. Easy going native sounds mixed with yoga tantric stuff. Melanie had on loose white sweats and a baggy long sleeve tee-shirt. No bra. Her hair straight and beautiful in that strawberry blondness I loved. I already wanted to be naked with her.

We were alone on a Sunday when her mom worked a twelve-hour shift. Our being alone was like an exclamation point at the end of a sentence. Abruptly real.

We kissed for a very long time, taking breaks to talk about my trip. About her Christmas. No family. Just her and her mom. New Year's she was with some friends of her mom's. Boring. She drank some beers. She missed me. I missed her. I knew we were more than likely going to make love, so I brought a condom. Two.

I wanted to talk to her first; stemming the passion was not easy.

In fact, it was impossible. I slid her tee shirt off and enjoyed her breasts more fully than I ever had. Full light of day. Her nipples wanting me. I sucked on them for who knows how long. I would switch back and forth, while she ran her fingers Over my scalp.

My clothes came off quickly. She was grabbing hold of me, her grip sliding up and down, easily. Softly. I think she already understood how sensitive I was.

When her pants came off she had no underwear. I cupped her pussy, caressed her hair and her opening.

Her legs spread inviting me.

Our kisses were deep. I hardly used my tongue, as she pressed her lips hard against mine, her mouth barely open attempting to breath. I loved more than anything grabbing her full firm butt with my right hand, pulling her close. And me inside.

I think we both fell asleep or drifted to the strange music. Our nakedness like sweetness. I could not get enough of feeling her, caressing her quietly. Gently.

She did the same.

She went to the bathroom and put on her baggy shirt, cuddling close upon return.

"Mel, I thought about you so much on our trip."

"Me too. It seems like you were gone a long time, Julian."

"I wrote a ton of lyrics."

"Me, too. The band sounds good. We have a lot of good riffs and arrangements for our new stuff. I think you'll like it."

"Can't wait."

"Of course, you can change it. Do what you want."

I waited for a long time. Went to the bathroom. Put on a tee shirt. Then asked, "Mel, this is your last semester. You have any idea what you want to do?"

She sat up leaning against the back wall of her bed. She didn't have a headboard. "No idea. The band. I thought about the community college. Maybe nursing like Mom. I don't know. Why?"

"It's a natural question, I think. Just that I have three years to go."

"I'll have to work. Mom needs the money. Maybe I can work at a veterinarian clinic. I like animals."

I didn't respond.

"It is weird," she went on, "to be the oldest one in our band. All of you will still be in school next year. Does it worry you? Should I be worried?" She had a touch of panic in her voice.

"Not really. To be honest, my parents asked while we were on vacation. Don't get me wrong, they like you a lot. You know my dad. He's concerned."

"Look, Julian." She pulled her legs up close to her chest. Defensive. "If you need to break up or something, I'd understand."

"No. Not that at all." I hugged her. "We should talk about it though, don't you think?"

"Probably."

"I love Retro. We'll keep going as we are. I think Shelly will do us good getting us gigs."

"I hope so." She had a tear in her eye. "I get it Julian. I mean it's a long time. You have homecomings and proms and dances. Parties. You can't be hanging out with an older chick. I can't be going to high school stuff the next three years. Fuck, you'll probably have another girlfriend or two or three before you graduate. Then college, or wherever you want to go. I mean you said you visited that music school in Paris. Fuck, Julian, you can do whatever you want. I can't. I'm stuck here."

She started crying very softly, a pillow over her mouth. I hugged her tighter.

"You're dad's probably worried that I'll get pregnant and trap you." She stopped crying and had a look in her eyes that scared me. She was going to hurt me first before I could hurt her.

She couldn't do it. She embraced me and whispered, "The problem is, Julian, is that I've loved you for a long time. I'm way too young. Jesus, you're way too young, for me to say that. I'd never do that. Get pregnant, I mean. I promise. I am on the pill and haven't even told you. Mom and I thought I should after my sophomore year. I still want you to use a rubber. I don't want to get pregnant. No way I'm going to pull myself down even further. No way."

"This is going to sound crazy, but I have to ask you. Let's say money was no issue, what would you do?"

"Honestly?"

"Yeah."

"I'd like to study business. I was always good in math. I like the idea of being in real estate or in a bank. Of course, music is my passion. That's all I care about. But if I could, I'd like to manage our band. Not like Shelly, but the finances, the money flow."

"You'd be good at it, and I could care less about it. Then do it. Enroll tomorrow. Here in Santa Fe. You can start in the fall."

"I'd have to come up with some money. Work first."

"No. I'll get it. Just tell me how much." I paused. "Melanie. This is important. You should go to school in the day while I go to school, and we would have our usual times to rehearse."

"No, I don't think I can do that. The money, I mean. I appreciate it." She got up and put on her sweats, going into their kitchen and grabbing two Cokes. She put on a new radio station. Dance station. Upbeat.

"Retro Sky is going to take off, Mel. We will be traveling a lot. On the road and you need to do something flexible. You will make a tiny bit of money. Not much. I already have a lot of money given to me over the years; all saved up. You know, we should talk to my parents." She cringed as I went on, "Really, Mel. I know they are looking out for all of us in the band. Let's keep the band at the center. For sure. You will be the main draw; we both know that. The crowd loves you. But you need to do something you want to do, too. At the same time."

"Ah, Julian. Don't say that. You are the best in the world. Don't be modest. You rock the house down. I can hardly believe it ... I'm open to talking to your mom. Your dad is our principal. Not sure about him yet." She smiled.

We talked more about our music. I was relieved to have that discussion over and talk songs, lyrics. Once we finished our can of Coke, I wanted to use my second condom. I was staring at her eyes. Her mouth. She knew.

I laid her face down on the bed and slid off her pants. I took off my clothes and lay on top of her, stretching my chest over her back, reaching under her shirt cupping her nipples. My erection was firm on her butt, then she arched her hips upward, and I was aligned with her spreading legs. She was reaching up for me with her right hand, guiding me in. My face buried in her long hair as she rocked me hard, making me kneel up straight, grabbing her hips and butt, pulling at her as I came. It felt like I had an orgasm that would never stop. She was too, I think. Her sounds were different, even longer and louder. I collapsed onto her breathing fast. Her body moving up and down with her lungs.

We lay quiet almost falling asleep again.

"I was wondering, wanting to ask you something about our image for Retro. Should I keep wearing bold colors, make-up, that kind of thing? I was beginning to think maybe I should go with straight blond hair, jeans and black leather vest, almost mountain hippie thing. With my boots. You guys all look so laid back. Even your Costello image comes across as more intense than anything else. It adds to the sounds we're playing. Elvis was sorta retro, retro anyway."

We were laying face to face. I loved when she didn't have make-up on. At least with me; alone like now. She looked Irish or Welsh or someone from a distant British Isle. When she wore bulky sweaters and those wonderful jeans, that's all I cared about. On stage, she was someone else. I liked that person, too. I didn't know how to answer, but I tried. "I think the audience likes the contrast, the disconnect you bring. You stand out. I get nervous sometimes that it takes away from our band. From me. It's my own ego. I don't want to be your front band." I grinned. "But I'm very much aware how they love your stage presence. I'd go with the extreme for now."

"Don't worry about that. I've said that before. You are the power, the electricity in the sound. We're a good team. You know, when you take a solo and I'm doing back-up or just on my acoustic, I watch the audience

carefully. You are spellbinding, Julian. Don't forget that.
It's *Dylan-esque*, as you'd say."
We'd only seven or eight performances. Not many.
Enough for us to get a sense of our direction. Our image.

We kissed then got up to find something to eat. She
complained that there was never food around. She
liked to go to the deli in the strip mall near the hospital
and eat salads. Read, look out the window. Watch
people go in and out of the hospital. She lived on yogurt,
salads and a sandwich lunches at school. Our walk was
only two blocks. Hardly anyone was in the deli. She
ordered a small cobb salad with a roll. I ordered an
Italian sub with chips. We both drank water. Bottled
water was now the rage, although I never really
understood why we were paying for something that was
in the drinking fountain.
Dad picked me up about the time we got back. Melanie
gave him a big hug, telling him that she loved my stories
of our trip. He asked her about her break. She didn't
have much to say. Her mom worked a lot. She worked
on lyrics and some new songs. Met with the band three
or four times. She read several books. The Harry Potter
series. Dad told her that Stephanie was into those too.
On the way home, I told Dad about my talk with Mel
about her wanting to study business after graduating
but didn't have any money. Melanie understood my
concerns – his concerns – about graduation. Dad was
relieved in his tone, asking me if it was okay for him to
talk to her tomorrow at school. He had an idea, getting
her hooked up at the counseling office. Streamlined for

application next fall. Maybe even call her mother.
That's the way my dad worked.   Jump right in. I was
fine with it.   Relieved that he didn't even bring up the
fact Melanie and I had been alone all day in an empty
apartment.   He was already well past that, I assumed.

Jennifer

Danny and the kids got off to school. I accidently slept in,
worn out from a weekend of horseback riding in the
chilly air.   Stephanie is a driver. Amazing on a horse and
in the wilderness. What a great time we had, I thought,
sipping my coffee. Louise and I talking about everything
over the holidays.   She had spent most of the time with
her sister's family in Flagstaff, returning late last night.
With Danny's blessing, I gave her all the Vatican
memorabilia, the papal letter, signed and embossed
with an official seal. We had a few pictures, looking
forward to Scotty's documentation in black and white.
She lamented that George was gone for all of this. I
gave her a skeletal outline of the trip but had to get to a
meeting at the Gallery.
The staff had taken a great deal of time off during the
holidays, making do with a rotating shift. We had a lot
of tourists, plenty of sales, so I had not planned that very
well. We went around the table sharing our Christmas
stories, giving each other late gifts, small things, mostly
jewelry. Matthew got a lot of leather bracelets because
he mentioned once in a meeting that he wanted one.
He got more than one.   Samantha's show was a huge
success. She and Karen were in the Gallery a great deal.

They even helped answering customers' questions on other artwork for sale – most of the paintings from the Art League. Sam sold all her work – the ones for sale, anyway. We'd be closing her show this week.
Lots of questions on the unusual art book – graphic novel - on display. Everyone recommended that we move it into a more prominent area. Which I agreed with.
Then I announced that I was going back into acting for a long trip in the north of France. I'd be with Tim and Sharon on a film. I intentionally didn't mention Stephanie. I said that I'd be hiring two more associates on a trial basis. Temporary for now, which could expand into long term if things went well. Trudy would run the ship, per usual. I would later pull her aside and give her a raise. We'd draw up an agreement making her the official manager of Rio Blanco Gallery. She was that good. I'd remain owner and CEO, if there was such a thing for us. Sally had sold her painting on Christmas Eve for the asking price of $500. She was still in celebration and the staff clapped for her again, even though they had already congratulated her over the past week. Sally was beaming. I told her, there in front of everyone, to bring me three more works – new ones. I wanted to keep the momentum going, for her, and for us. Everyone was in good spirits, doing well in their personal lives as far as I could tell. I paid them well, giving them professional opportunities in the area as they grew as artists themselves. I was grateful for them. As I was leaving the meeting, Trudy, handed me a note, her face looked stunned. It was a typewritten formal

letter on expensive stationary. It had Arabic insignia and family crest. Highly unusual. Signed by someone in Saudi Arabia, a prince or something like that. He was offering me a cool million dollars for my self-portrait. I stared at the note and read it twice. No way this was serious. Trudy asked me if I was going to handle it or if she should.

"Please write a note of thanks but decline the offer. You sign it. I don't want to answer this myself."

"Wow. I don't think I could turn down a million dollars."

"It's not the money, Trudy. I'd never sell my work, especially our Gallery *moniker*, to someone in Saudi Arabia. You know how they treat women over there? No way."

"I guess. But it is a lot of money."

"I know. James bought it for $500 in my first exhibit. I was straight out of college. That was a lot of money. More than a million dollars to me at the time. That painting belongs here. I have no idea where it will end up, but while I am alive, it's not for sale."

"I get it. I'll take care of it."

I went to my office and grabbed mail, phone messages. Overload. Escaping with it all into my studio. My cartoon-like paintings staring at me, taking me by surprise. They were telling me, ordering to keep going. I smiled. They'd have to wait just a bit longer. I had to sort out my business first.

I worked all morning, wired on great coffee and too much sugar from an éclair I should not have eaten. When I finally felt like I was on top of things around here

I went out and watched Matthew move the graphic novel into a larger studio. Frankie could be proud. It was groundbreaking. I had no idea what to do about selling it if I got an offer. I'd have to ask Frank, talk to him about it. I also wanted him to look at my own drawings, story board. I'd be curious. I'd show Matthew more later. It was all too new for me.

I had to decide what to do about Sharon's opening in New York. I had not met Woody Allen, which made me tempted to go. I couldn't, I knew. I'd be leaving for France again in no time. Before calling her, I wanted to return a phone message from Gene, the owner and director at Eagle's Nest Dinner Playhouse, where I got my start as an actress. I hadn't spoken with him in years. I was curious.

Omaha, the longtime secretary over there, was happy to hear from me. We chatted for almost a half hour. I missed her. A wonderful lady to have around for struggling new actors. Always encouraging.

Gene got on the line, "Jennifer. Thank you so much for returning my call. I really appreciate it."

"No problem." We exchanged pleasantries about the holidays. He said he was doing well. The Playhouse was doing well. He liked the current crew a great deal.

"I have the strangest favor to ask." He finally got to the point, and I interrupted him.

"Gene, I'm not acting in theater anymore."

He was laughing. "Oh, I know. I know better. No, it's a terribly selfish request."

"Shoot."

"Well, as you may know I went through a divorce three years ago."

"I don't think I knew that Gene. I'm sorry."

"It's okay. Anyway, I've been dating a lady, an agent who is relocating to Santa Fe. Oh, and by the way, Karen has been a huge help with us finding a place. Anway, ..."

I interrupted again. "What kind of agent?"

"Mostly in the music industry, but a few actors. She's getting out of the business, though. Wants out of L.A. for good. We're not getting younger, you know."

"Music business, huh?"

"Yeah. Like I was getting at. I don't know how to reach Sharon and I read about the premiere of the Woody Allen flick. My girlfriend, Rhonda, was asking me if we could go? We'd never been to a premiere, and we were going to New York and catch Broadway anyway. I'm like barging-in by asking. She's a huge fan of Woody's. No harm to ask, right?"

I was thinking. I knew Sharon could swing it no problem. That was not the issue. I wanted to bargain.

"Gene, I'll call Sharon. It shouldn't be a problem. I can get you two passes. February 2nd, right?"

"Yep. God that would be wonderful."

"But .."

"Oh shit, here it comes. But what?"

"Well, two things."

"Oh fuck." He said laughing into the phone.

"It's about my two kids. The twins. Julian and Stephanie."

Silence.

"We'd like to meet Rhonda. Julian has a band, Retro Sky. Tim's wife has been acting as a manager of sorts. They've played at bars around here."

"I think I saw a flyer or something.   I had no idea that was your son."

"They're good Gene. Not saying that as mommy of the lead singer. I promise."

He was thinking.

"Sure, we could have dinner or something. Rhonda would love to meet you and Danny. Shelly too.   Tim if he's around, of course. What else?"

"Stephanie. My daughter.   She was in the high school play as Marion in *Music Man.*"

"No way. Like mother like daughter. How old are they?"

"Fourteen."

"Wow. You must be proud."

"Absolutely. I see you're doing *Sound of Music* in April. When are tryouts?"

"End of the month.   I'm not directing though. I have a part-time director filling in from time to time. He's from the college. Nice guy. Brett Hodges. He's good. Why, you want Stephanie to audition?"

"Checking it out.   Curious."

"Liesl or Louisa?"

"Her personality fits Louisa.   I'd like to see her audition for Liesl, though."

"Bigger role."

"Exactly."

"Well, sure. Have Stephanie come over, meet with Omaha. She'll roll out the red carpet for her."

"Thanks Gene. I appreciate it a lot. I'll get back with you about dinner with you and Rhonda, have you out, okay?"

"That would be great. I don't think I've seen your place since ages ago."

"I'm calling Sharon now. I'll get you confirmation on passes in New York. Lincoln Center, I think."

"Thanks again. We'll talk soon."

Sharon was not always easy to get ahold of. I had to leave a message. She'd get back with me eventually. I appreciated that about her. After all these years, her fame, well, our fame. What happened with Danny and me years ago on the *Rio Norte* shoot – which that alone would've killed any friendship. Oddly, never affecting me. If anything, I felt even closer to Sharon, even Danny. I probably needed psych help to figure that one out. Having kids, all of it. Our sisterhood was closer than any bond. Closer than my own sister. I looked forward to acting with her again. It was like she challenged me like no other person in my life. I think I did the same for her. She said that all the time. I was concerned about Stephanie and the dynamics of this entire project. We were putting all the best people in place for this movie. It was a risk going the art film route, we knew. Even then we were getting the absolute premier backing, acting, film crews. The studios were snapping to Tim's direction. He was a reliable commodity and when you put Sharon's name on the marquee, even an off-the-wall movie like this one will be a draw. I think the entire idea that I was somehow an icon in Europe was not a secret to the producers because they were banking on it. They almost didn't even care how it sold in the United States. Plans for French, German, various language subtitles were already in the budget. Sharon and Tim got off on thumbing their noses at the run of the mill shit. I was happy for the protective nature for my comeback picture, and mostly for what it provided Steph. I was certain that Steph could not even imagine the heavy hitters surrounding her. I was nervous for her. Not that she'd bomb. Somehow I wasn't worried about that. Not even sure why I was so nervous. Motherly protective instinct.

My attention turned to the artwork I had started weeks ago. Conte crayons, pen and ink, a ruler. New York City apartment complex. I shuddered to think of the World Trade Center picture in the airport. My caricatures, nine-year-old Norah, her friend Suzee and dog Muffy. Bright colors. Bold. I was not even sure where they came from, it had been so long. Norah staring at me, questioning where I was going with her? She'd been waiting patiently. Again, I didn't worry about a story line, taking a few hours to work fast on various blocked scenes. Action stuff. Emotions. Fleshing out these three main people before me, and Muffy seemed just as much human as the two girls.

Sharon called me back. We laughed when I told her about Gene and his girlfriend wanting to attend the premiere at the Lincoln Center. Sharon was glad to get them passes. VIP. Tell Gene they'll be waiting for him when they get to New York. She didn't want to give Gene her number, which I understood. What we found funny is that he had a new girlfriend, speculating what she would be like. He was a tough one to peg. Neither of us had met his first wife. The entire agent scenario possibility for Julian, and Steph auditioning for the play ramped-up Sharon. She was all gung ho. She thought Gene was ballsy to even ask for an invitation, but who cared, if it helped the kids. She gave me kudos for bargaining with him. She understood that we couldn't make the Lincoln Center. *No big deal*. Vinny wasn't going either. Sharon didn't really want to go. She was doing it for Woody, the producers. Now she had a reason to go. Twist on Gene and his lovely Rhonda. *Look out*, I thought. Maybe I should even warn them. *Nah*.

I went out into the Gallery and found Matthew. He was on the phone. I waited, looking at a painting from one of our League artists. I liked it. More than I remembered from when we accepted it. I was surprised it hadn't sold.

I asked Matt to come with me to my studio. Everyone gets a shocked look on their face when I talk about the studio. It is so off limits to everyone.

He took a seat and I shut the door. Suzee, Muffy and mostly Norah drawn in countless scenes. Big, bright and almost overwhelming. I asked him to look at them, tell me what he thought. I had hidden the ink and crayons. He had no idea they were mine. He was suspicious though. He was in my very private studio.

I waited.

Nothing.

"Well?" I prodded.

"You mean for our Gallery? Not sure what to say.
They're not exhibit material."
"I get that. What do you think of the characters?"
"Who's the artist?"
Damn, Matt, don't ask that. "A friend of mine."
"Well, it can't be Frankie. Not his style at all. Maybe
another kid from the high school?"
"Maybe."
He got up and looked at them more carefully. "Unusual.
I mean you have these bright figures with lots of
personality, in the dark setting of the city. They stand
out like action hero types. Maybe for kids."
"Exactly my thought," I said.
His face betrayed him. He knew that I drew them.
"A lot different than the Paris stuff, huh?" I asked him.
He was hesitant. "Sure are, Jennifer. I've studied your
painting almost my entire life. Everything in this gallery
is top notch.   Not that this is not good, I just have no
idea how to square this with, well, who you are."
"Matthew don't worry about it. I have no idea either.
When I heard you talk about Frankie's book and the
entire genre, I wanted to try something completely out
of character for me. In an odd sorta way, these people
you are looking at, up there, have a story to be told. I
don't even know what it is yet. I want to tell a story."
He smiled, almost laughing. "As an artist, I'm happy for
you. You have done in your career what no other artist
has done in a long time. Especially any American artist.
This new direction is terribly fun. If you're asking my
opinion, I'd say go for it. Keep going."

"Thank you, Matt. Please do me a favor, okay? Don't mention this yet. Let me keep working on it for a while longer. I'll show everyone if I decide it's worth it."
We shook hands politely. He had a big smile on his face and left.
I heard Julian unlock his studio and the muffle of his stereo turn on. Even though it was wonderfully soundproofed, I was able to vaguely listen in if I wanted to. I thought the music was Dire Straits, *Sultans of Swing*. Julian went right to work, teaching himself Mark Knopfler licks, copying each note and chord on his Fender. That was how Julian did things. Others were entering saying *hi,* getting situated. They had probably talked at school, jumping into their rehearsal. Stu and Freebird were quickly chiming in with Julian with the drums and bass.   There was a knock on my outside door.

"Hi Frankie," I greeted the rough looking kid in front of me. Unshaven, messy hair.
"Um, Mrs. Tomasetti, um Mrs. Braxton, hi."
"Call me Jennifer, please."
"I don't know. Really? *Jennifer*, okay."
"Come in."
"I wanted to thank you again for all you've done with *Kid*. I just saw the new display in the show room. It's cool. Not sure where you got a picture of me."
"Shelly gave it to me. From some photo session you did with the band. We just cropped it. I wanted to ask you, Frankie, if you want to sell *Kid*? I mean if someone wants to publish it?"
"Sure. That would be amazing."

"Okay, I'll let people know it's for sale if they ask. Now that it's in a prominent location in the Gallery, I would guess something will happen."

"Those are cool," he said pointing to my drawings. Shit, I wasn't ready for him to see them. I was embarrassed like a first-year art student. He got up and looked closely. "This one," pointing to Norah, "Is really fun." He was laughing.

"What do you mean?"

"She looks tough, in a comic book kind of way. Like for kids. You do this?" he asked.

"Yeah. I did. Playing around."

"Cool. It's not like your stuff in there." He was referring to the Gallery.

"No, sure isn't."

"You should put captions. Tell a story, you know."

"I think I will."

"Maybe they're like a dynamic duo, Batman, Robin like, with a dog with extra sensory ability. Like he knows where bad guys are."

I smiled. "Or like crime solvers, I was thinking. Help the police."

"I like that. They look like crime solvers. That's New York, right?"

"Yes."

"Make a fictional city. Like Gotham. Give it another name. Kids won't think it's just New York then."

I liked that idea. "What else?"

"Just write a story. A quick crime solution they solve. Put it in bubbles like they talk, you know. It won't take long. Maybe twenty pages worth."

"How many drawings?" I asked.

"Depends. Some full-page ones. Some quarter pages. Maybe fifty, total drawings, at the most."

My mind was working.

He asked if I had any story ideas. I wasn't sure. Maybe a bank heist. He interrupted. "You should solve a kidnapping. They look like they were going to help someone kidnapped for a ransom. Blackmail someone important. Like a senator."

My mind processed some more. "Would kids get that?" He waited to answer. "Maybe you're right. Depends on your age level. They can read. Sure, they can get it. Don't do murder, these characters look too cartoonish for blood and mayhem. It can be scary, should be scary, but not murder. Fights and stuff are good."

I hadn't thought that far. He was thinking fast.

I thanked him and changed the subject, "How was break? The music?"

"Break was tough. Mom and I fought. My semester grades sucked. Oh, Sorry. She threatened to take me off the band if I didn't get better grades. Fuck. Oh, Sorry. Again. Anyway, the music sounds great. Mel is good. Great, really. She writes some mind-blowing lyrics. I think Julian will dig it. I think I'm better on guitar lately, even over the past few weeks. Cindy helped me a lot. I hung out at her house, just playing guitar. Listening to stuff with Billy. Old albums. Bird is cool. Stu is too. They dropped over there too. We get along. Anxious to get going on these songs."

"I should let you go. Thanks for your thoughts on the drawings."

"No problem. You're not bad. You should try and sell some of your stuff." Frankie had a huge smile.

I thought I should wind things up, get home and get things ready for dinner. I could drive back in a few hours and pick up Julian. Lately Danny has been picking him up after his long stretch at school.

Then another door knock.

It was Shelly.

We talked about the holidays. She filled me in on her trip to north of France with Tim. The success of it all. All things green light for the movie.

"I have two weekends in Albuquerque lined up for the band if their parents are good with it. We can stay in a cheap motel. Both venues are geared for concerts, non-alcoholic and alcohol tags. Proof of age kind of thing. Bigger crowds. More money, too."

"Wow, Shelly, that's fabulous news! Have you told them?"

"Not yet. I thought I'd run it by you."

"Their parents will love it. All we have to tell them is that expenses are paid. We'll foot the bill for food and the motels. Don't tell them that. In fact, we should have a big family meeting at our house. Talk about the future of Retro Sky."

"That's a good idea. That's nice of you to pay. I can help too."

"You've done a lot! And so quickly." I hugged her.

"Let's do the meeting at my house. That way I can establish myself as a manager of sorts."

"Sounds good."

"I'll organize it. Oh, and one more thing. I'm going to work hard on getting bookings along the Colorado cities going northward to Denver. Trouble is that time off from school. Travel time, driving time. Probably Fridays, maybe a few Thursdays. What do you think?"

"Might be an issue with Frankie. His grades. Anyway, let me work on the principal. Hold off on that news for the time being."

CHAPTER THIRTEEN

I want to live darkly and richly in my femaleness. I want a man lying over me always over me. His will, his pleasure, his desire, his life, his work, his sexuality the touchstone, the command, my pivot. I don't mind working, holding my ground intellectually, artistically; but as a woman, oh, God, as a woman I want to be dominated. Anais Nin

Danny

One thing, among many, that I love about our house is that we have two wings from the central bulwark of a ship like design. One wing houses Louise and her privacy. Sometimes she will disappear into her own world. Usually with church friends and activities. We are comfortable with her, with each other. I'm glad she is a part of our family. Her love is infectious. The kids have rooms on other floors. They have their privacy, too. My office is private. The remainder of the house is spacious, inviting, warm and friendly. Lived in. We don't have any space we do not use. Nothing like a formal sitting area that is like a show room. Then there is our wing. Jennifer and I have a glorious area. She designed it. Plenty of light, enormous views, space for our own world. A place to create. A place for us to fuck ourselves silly. Even after all these years we stumble upon a time when one of us, or both of us in unison, are so damn horny we can't stand it. We had a delayed reaction to Paris, Rome, being on the go. Not able to let loose. Which is regrettable because Paris was magnificently romantic, and we only managed one night to ourselves. Even then, we were slightly timid. Holding back ever so marginally.

Then tonight rolled around. Jennifer gave me a look. She was drinking one more glass than usual. A good wine, I noticed. Even on a work night, I imbibed. The kids went on and on about this or that. I barely took it all in. I watched Jennifer. I studied her body. She was being an exhibitionist in an extremely subtle way. Never overtly. She was luring me ever so quietly. Like fly fishing, gliding on a soft current. She even had on a sweater she knew I adored. I guessed that she didn't have on a bra. The space between her belly and above her knees, both front and back absolutely make me insane. I stare, wondering what she will look like, feel like, taste like. As if I had never experienced her before. The sliver of skin between her sweater and her loose warm corduroy pants, shown as she reached high to put away a serving bowl. She knew I could see and wonder. I knew she was teasing me.

Once she looked at me, stared at me. I froze at the confrontational look. The kids were still over at the table laughing about something. Louise was there too, telling a story. Jennifer was looking right at me, boring into my eyes. She mouthed the words; *I want you to fuck me.* I wasn't sure because she hadn't talked that way in years. Nor had I. We had settled into wonderful, loving sex. Even adventurous from time to time. But not like this. Not in so long, I couldn't remember. I wasn't sure and kept staring at her. She walked over near me at the refrigerator and said out loud, "hard." Then walked away, chiming in with the conversation at the table.

I sat and ate. I tried to act normal, like you do when you are high or stoned. Smiling, acting like you are paying attention, or have any idea of what is going on. I went through the motions of cleaning up. Everyone scattered to their areas, even saying goodnight. Terribly early to say goodnight it seemed to me. I refilled my glass of wine with a new bottle. Jennifer had taken the bottle to our bedroom. She was gone.

I did a walk through the house making sure lights were off. Killing time, mostly. I fumbled around in my office like a teenager waiting to see if and who was really going to get laid. Anticipation. Nerves. I knew I was in charge. It just didn't feel like it. Lust building. For a woman I had forgotten about. The *other* Jennifer. Like an animal I paced, telling myself to take my time. I paced some more. Nothing to be anxious about. She's my wife, for God's sake.

I went to our room. The bathroom light was on, the door closed. Music was playing. One of my favorites, a very old John Klemmer CD. I noticed she had stacked all the Klemmer music we owned into the auto play of the stereo.

I went to my walk-in closet and was mulling what to put on for bed. Pajama bottoms. A silk pair I hardly ever wore. The matching shirt, only three buttons. A purple, dark royal black blend.

The lights were dimming.

Jennifer stood by the reading light over by the couch in a maroon, nightgown. Classic, smooth. Sleek. She was sipping wine, looking right at me. The window curtains were open, the night sky, wilderness in the background. She stood there like a goddess commanding me to take her.

I went over to her, and we continued sipping our wine. We didn't even talk. We just looked into each other's eyes. It was like a game of chicken, who would break first. I knew it would be me and we played anyway. Finally, I sat down my glass, took hers from her and set it down. We kissed. I loved the taste of the wine. Her tongue. Her lips. We found a slow rhythm with the saxophone.

Jennifer's breasts, her nipples were against me. I told her to undo my shirt, which she did, looking at me directly, unbuttoning my shirt adeptly, sliding it off easily.

We kissed again, as she broke from my mouth, kissing my neck, circling one of my nipples with a finger. Her other hand sliding over the silk of my ass. Pulling me closer. My erection wanting to break through the silk of my pants, her gown, into her. She was sucking on the top of my chest by my clavicle. It almost hurt she sucked so hard. I was running my hand through her hair. I took off her top by merely sliding off the loose straps on her shoulders. Her breasts erect, I pushed her away so I could suck on her nipple. I bore down. Almost like I wanted to suck in her entire breast, wanting to emit pain in her joy. I looked up and her head was arched upwards, almost crying to the sky. Her two towers of sheer white pleasure erect against a still tanned body. I destroyed them with my mouth, my teeth, my tongue. Devouring them.

We stood up breathing hard. I took one of the glasses of wine, giving her a sip. I took a sip, then told her to take off her panties.

She slid her panties off slowly. Looking at me the entire time she bent over. She had a look in her eye like a wild cat. I told her to stick her fingers into the wine, which she did, swirling the liquid, putting two of her fingers in her mouth. Wine dripped down her chin. She did it again, and I took that hand, dripping with wine, and placed it on her pussy hair, getting her wet. She placed her fingers in again, and swished more wine on her pussy, sliding her fingers on the folds of the opening within.

I grabbed her down on the bed and devoured her clit, her wetness, engulfing her entire sex in my mouth. She was loud. Like the alarm sounds too early in the morning loud. I quivered in moans as my tongue thrusted over and over, swirling with her hips hammering at my face. She was fucking my mouth full speed. She went at it for so long, my neck hurt, my tongue hurt, my body was full of pain and contorted. Like a seizure. Then she seized, over and over. Her tone quieter now. Almost whimpering.

She lay there exhausted. I was still in my silk pants, a raging hard-on. My balls full and screaming in pain for release. Her pupils were reflecting the moon. Dark and black. She begged me to command her.

I took off my pants and came close to her mouth, watching her take me, pulling me hard into her. Urging me to thrust. Over and over.

I could not take it for very long. And pulled away.

I quieted down. Thankfully the music was quieting down as well. She was quieter, laying there beneath me. Her incredibly beautiful body waiting for me. I spread her legs wider, kneeling between her. Her hand gently grabbed my hard throb, almost telling me to settle down. Slow down. Relax. Gently stroking me. Sighs of relief in her breathing. In my breathing.

She slowly rubbed the head of my cock on her, up and down, causing her spine to arch, her hips to lift. Not letting me in. Then she pulled me close to her mouth not letting me kiss her. Her lips moving like a silent movie. *Fuck me Danny. Fuck me hard.*

And she pulled my ass gripping me digging into me as I thrusted over and over. She was holding me so tightly I couldn't breathe. Her legs and hips doing equally as much work as my endless muscle taut thrusts. Until I exploded. Tore into her womb. I was never this loud. Ever.

I was empty. I fell on her. We were trying to find our breath.

When I got up, the clock read 11:12. Jennifer was naked, asleep. I went to the bathroom, left in the dark, peeing. Getting a glass of water without turning on the light.

She was awake when I returned, grabbing the water from me. She greedily finished what I had not drank. We slid into our covers. Kissing for what was probably ten or fifteen minutes. No tongues. Not even with passion. Kissing, closeness. Lips wet. Appreciating each other. The meaning of life.

CHAPTER FOURTEEN

Fame, fame, fame, fame, fame, fame, fame, fame, fame, fame, fame, fame, fame ... What's your name (echoing) ... David Bowie

Stephanie

Tim and Mom and I met for nearly two hours. We went over the filming schedule. The flights. Train schedules. Other transportation. Details amassed. The list of names finalizing the cast. A woman named Estelle would oversee me the entire time.   She was the best in the business. A tutor in all subjects. A maid. A pseudo acting coach. Adept at maneuvering sets, and time frames, especially emotions. Readings. My driver. My personal assistant. She'd been doing this for ages. I'd meet Estelle in France. I would not room with Mom or Sharon. I'd be by myself, with Estelle next door. I could have access to Estelle day or night at any time. Mom was out of bounds unless I just couldn't take it. Of course, my mom and I would eat together, enjoy some of the sights and down time.   But not much.   Mom was focused once filming began. Rarely went out or socialized.   She'd be plenty of fun until they got down to serious business. Sharon was unpredictable. No one told her what to do. She knew the boundaries for most sets, most directors, but she did what she was going to do. Best that I didn't bother her.

The great cinematographer Michael Chapman signed on to work with us in Europe, which he rarely did. He was

adept at the black and white tones that Tim was after.
Chapman was also known to be the greatest cameraman
to work with young, inexperienced actors, as well as
seasoned pros.   Both DeNiro and Scorsese
recommended him to our project.

Polish costume designer Magdalena Biedrzycka was
difficult to sign. She was overbooked and finally agreed
to do *Purgatorio*, dropping a prospective Belgian film
that paid far less. Again, perfect for a post WWI film,
also a great deal of experience with young actors.

The script was set. Mom would be on-site, being co-
wrIter and able to do re-writes quickly.

Set design, lighting, all the particulars were coming
together fast. We would fly out the second week of
February.

Tim was in charge. He was my boss for the next few
months. I had never seen him talk this way.   He was
drinking whiskey. Mom sipped whiskey too. I was
wondering if I should ask for one. He went through yet
another script with handwritten notes in the margins.
Every word was intended for me. He told me to read all
of it. Take them to heart. Memorize them. He'd ask me
about them when we got to France.

He had Mom take me in another room and put on a
peasant dress. He took photos of me. Close ups of my
face mostly.   He said that I'd need to cut my hair. They'd
do it over there. It would be choppy, he warned.
Maybe darken it a hue. He wanted to do another screen
shot over there. He might like the washed-out
transparency he saw on the original screen tests. He
could take advantage of my natural color. He hadn't

made up his mind. He liked the way my breasts fit the dress, perfect for the part. My waistline and legs. My body was perfect for the profile. Slender. Not too well fed. My teeth were too pretty. A usual problem for actors trying to play a part under these historical circumstances. Make-up would figure that out for all the main actors. Mom took my measurements, wrote them down, along with shoe size. All of it would be sent ahead for a head start on production.

He told me that press releases would be leaked. Mostly in Europe. My name would never appear. Don't talk about what you're doing or where you're going when you're at school. *I'm going on a vacation with my mom*, that was a good enough line. My teachers will be providing work, standard district outlines and books for Estelle. Keep this low key.

As far as auditioning for a part at Eagle's Nest for April's *The Sound of Music*, go ahead and go over and talk with Omaha right away. Fill out the paperwork. I should be able to get an audition before I leave. I still have plenty of time. Don't say or write anything about the film. If they try to reach me at home for some reason while I'm gone, Dad will handle it.

Mom drove me over the next day to meet and talk with Omaha. A great lady. I liked her right away. I filled out the forms. Omaha told me that Brett Hodges would call me, the guest director, if she didn't, to set up an audition. Would be soon. She gave me a script. I didn't know which part to put down as my interest. Mom told me to put down Liesl and that I'd be ready to audition for Louisa as well. I wrote it just that way.

I strolled into the theater area as mom and Omaha talked. It's here that mom got her big break. Tim acted here. Unbelievable, I thought. I'd read about my mom being naked on this very stage for *Gypsy*. That was even more unbelievable. I walked down an aisle and moved around the stage. Mom followed down and joined me. She started singing in a soft voice, *let me entertain you*, on and on. She transformed easily. Having fun. Then she started into *the hills are alive with the sound of music,* both of us swirling as if on an Austrian hillside. Omaha stood up at the entry way and applauded.

As we walked out, Omaha said, *lord, I've missed you Jennifer*.

Mom and I had not been through the script in quite some time, but she wanted to look at Tim's notes. We sat in our playroom going line by line. She was focused, but I knew she was uneasy about something.

"Let's do this." She took the script and notes away so I could not see anything. "I'm just going to talk with you. Don't worry about acting or even being in character or being Manon. Be yourself, Stephanie. I'll say the things that Sharon, your mom, would say, and I want you to just respond like you would normally. And the scenes of me as the nun looking after you. How you would feel and act. Don't ever worry or even try to act. Let's just have the conversation of what you are feeling and what you are thinking and how you would handle each situation. Okay?"

I agreed.

The first time we went through the script took almost three hours. I struggled terribly, realizing a disconnect between what I was feeling and wanted to say and what Manon would say in my memorized response. Her lines were not even close to my reaction.

Mom pushed me harder the second time through. I barely got a bathroom break. Reading right through dinner. She was upping the pressure on me to express myself in the most honest way that I could. She stopped me about two-thirds of the way through and left the room bringing down a platter of food. We ate in silence.

"Explain to me, Steph, the biggest difference between you and Manon." Mom said, taking a bite of a sandwich. It was obvious to me now and I was afraid to say anything.

"Go on," she prodded.

I wanted to cry. Mom was showing no sympathy, peering into my eyes. I finally answered her, "Manon is on the edge of death, almost daily. Survival is perpetually seizing her existence. She lives day to day in a heartless, God-forsaken world. There is no escape. No hope." I had a tear roll down my cheek.

She took another bite of her sandwich. "Go on."

I raised my voice, "I'm a fucking spoiled brat! I have never experienced anything of how Manon feels. I've never gone without a meal. I've always had a bed to sleep in. Love is surrounding me ever since I was born. I have no idea how to be Manon. I can't do this, Mom!"

She didn't even respond. She ate some potato salad. No empathy, no encouragement. She wiped her mouth with a napkin. Then she finally said something. "Thank the good lord, Steph. There's hope for you now. I was worried. All of Tim's notes were gimmicks to get you to feel Manon. I have known all along that my daughter would never be able to feel Manon."

"What?" I murmured. "Why are we doing this if you knew I couldn't do this?"

"That's not what I mean, exactly. What I knew, what I know, is that you would need a breakthrough of pain and desperation to begin to understand Manon, to understand yourself. It will be tough, honey."

"What can I do? She's an entirely different girl than I am. I have the lines, I can do this entire thing, but I can't be her."

Mom didn't react. She smiled and took a drink of her water. "Let's rehearse from here on out without a script. I'll push you and I want you to dig into Manon. She'll show up for you. Don't worry about the lines. Keep responding to me over and over, with the feelings of imminent death knocking on your door. You die a miserable death at a young age. Or you become a prostitute like your mom. Or you become a nun in the convent. Work at the orphanage. Leave your mother. That's all you got. There is no freshman year in high school. There is no horseback riding or skiing. No cozy world. Not even a nice bed. You don't have shit, girl. Worthless in an uncaring world. Give your body to drunks and slobs for a few francs. Or live in miserable virginity and isolation proclaiming a faith you can't even find inside your heart. What's it going to be? Tell me. I mean it, tell me." Mom was dead serious.

I wanted to cry but I could feel Manon whispering to me. *Don't fucking cry. It's not worth it.* "Who is asking?" I finally whispered. "My mom or my prostitute mom or a nun or God. Who is asking?"

"Maybe Stephanie is asking Manon. Or better yet, maybe Manon is asking Stephanie."

I was awed by her insight.

"That's enough for tonight." She didn't hug me or say goodnight. She cleaned up, picking up our plates and glasses and napkins and left me alone.

Julian

Once Frankie got back from talking with my mom, we hit the new songs with full force. We had the stuff before I went to Europe, and all the arrangements they had worked on, plus new lyrics.

Shelly asked to say a word, announcing that she was going to host a gathering for all our parents soon. Alo's uncle, too. She had some plans for the band and wanted them involved. That got us pumped up even more.

This process was far more difficult than I imagined. Being a cover band was easier. All of us were adept at figuring out chord changes, instrumentation, arrangements, vocals. We were already able to recreate most of the earlier non-studio fabrications of an era. We had great lyrics to work with now. Bits and pieces of melody or guitar riffs or piano work. Even Bird and Stu could crank out original syncopation. Unique sounds. It was trying to put it all together that was the challenge. I read how a lot of great performers worked on their own then came together with the band and plugged them in. Avoiding too many cooks in the kitchen problem. Cliché, but true. Melanie had taken the liberty to work this way while I was gone. They had some finished songs, playing them for me. I liked them. They sounded good. Truthfully, though, I was pissed off. I didn't want to give up control. Mel was already fidgeting, reading my mind. I think the entire band sensed it. It didn't take a genius to figure out that I was in a position of response.

One of the songs, one that I had written the lyrics and sketched out a basic format for weeks ago, was the one I started with. Melanie had worked hard, fleshed out a nice sound during that time. I went to the piano and played it back solo, singing the lead. I then asked Stu and Bird to play it with me, the first few verses. Then again, Frankie on guitar. He sounded good. He'd been working on it, I could tell. Mel stood and listened, staring at me. That was it. I wanted to move on. Next song. I was intentionally being a prick leaving her out.

"What the fuck, Julian?" she said.

"Oh, yeah. You can play your acoustic."

"Jesus Christ. Is that how this is going to go?"

"Whatever let's do another song."

"Fuck you." She banged the door, heading outside.

I sat there at the piano. Cold. Stu whispered that I should go get her.

I reluctantly got up and found her outside in the field. She was smoking a cigarette. She didn't smoke very often, that I knew of. She was furious.

"Damn, I'm sorry, Mel."

She didn't respond. I tried to put my hand on her shoulder, and she pulled away.

"It's a great song, all that you did on it. I'm sorry. Let's do it again. I'm just protective, I wrote it originally."

"So, what. You change stuff I write all the time." She was angry. I understood why.

"You're right. Tell me, what would you like for the song?"

"Everything you said. I'll play acoustic. That's how I hear it. But you scrubbed my vocals. I don't even sing that much on this one. The harmony is quick and nice. I thought you'd like it."

"I do like it. I'm sorry."

"Julian. Let's do it your way. I mean it. You go in there and play everything. All the songs. You take lead. Play piano or fucking guitar. Or bass. Whatever you want. Just tell me what you want from me."

I stood there feeling helpless.

We went back inside. I told everyone that I wanted to do a duet. A new song I wrote in Rome. I went through it on guitar. It had a difficult twist in two parts, otherwise, an easy piece. Everyone had their part. I had asked Melanie to play some simple chord changes on the keyboard. Then I moved my guitar over by her to share the same microphone. I told her to take the lead and I would join in. I'd take the fourth verse as lead. We sang it once and her smile returned. It was sweet.

It was for her. She knew it. By the third try, we had it down.

We found four songs where all our parts found their place. Naturally. They just needed fine tuning.

I had one song that was intended for me alone. A hard rocking blitz of a song. I wanted to trade some hard blues with Frankie. Bird and Stu would know what to do. I really did not know what to do with Melanie. I didn't want keyboard chord changes underneath it. No tambourine. No back up vocal. I was not sure what to do. Melanie could read my mind and told us all to go ahead and play it that way. We ripped it up good. Sounded like I imagined. This is where I borrowed liberally from Mark Knopfler. Bird was really one hell-of-a drummer carrying the drive. The song did have a bridge and Melanie went to the keyboard and put the setting on bass saxophone and imposed faux horn, stretched out over the bridge, changing tonality in a subtle way. We played the song again and Mel merely sunk that sound-in on cue. It sounded incredible. Nothing we'd ever heard anyone do. It made it our song entirely. I kissed her. Stu clapped. Bird clicked his sticks. Frankie asked if he could smoke because Melanie had smoked outside. We all laughed.

Melanie took over on two songs. I was backup entirely. Both were perfect the way they were. No qualms.

Then Mel sprung one on us. She wanted Stu on bass. I could've easily insisted on playing bass but let it slide. She would sing a Capela. That was it. She hummed the song, so Stu could get the progression. It was a dirge, about her father dying. I didn't think her father had died.

When she finished I asked her where that came from? She wrote it for Frankie's dad dying in Iraq, she answered. Frankie looked shocked. She wrote it when she and Frank were together a long time ago. Now that we were writing songs, she thought she'd bring it out. Frank thanked her sheepishly. Then he went outside and smoked a cigarette.

That Thursday night Shelly had the band and our families over to their house. Tim was not there, but everyone knew this was Tim Prescott's house. A lot of whispering. She had sloppy-joe's and bakery fresh buns with chips and baked beans. Pop and a variety of juices. Delicious. Casual for all of us. Melanie wore a dress with her boots. A ponytail. I had never seen her dress like that. Always a surprise. Her mom still had on her nursing outfit, just getting off work. She looked exhausted. Dad wanted to speak with them afterwards. Stu showed up with his entire family. His mom was trying to keep two younger sisters in line. She apologized for not finding a sitter. Wasn't even an issue. They could play downstairs, watch TV. Stu's dad was in construction. He apologized. He didn't have time to go home and clean up. A burly guy with a huge smile. Frankie was getting a fuller beard. His hair longer by the day. I knew that Dad also wanted to talk with him and his mom alone, after everything was finished. I wanted to tell Dad that it would look weird for him to be having all these private meetings. Frankie's mom was drained, and I doubted she was up for it. It wasn't her work as a receptionist, I could tell. It was Frankie. Alo showed up late. His uncle was using a cane to walk. Alo introduced his uncle as "Red." Red was looking haggard, on the verge of dying. We all knew that he was a decorated Korean War Vet, had played drums his entire life. Life on the reservation had been terribly difficult. A beautiful older Indian woman named Rose had driven them in an old pickup. Rose was so in awe of the house, I wondered if she had ever been off the reservation. Both Red and Rose called Alo Bird, so I thought we probably should start calling him Bird. Strange, though, most of the kids called him Alo.

Cindy and Billy were there too. Dad and Billy were talking basketball right away. Cindy was our music teacher, of course, for years. She asked to be there, to help if she could. I think Frankie was mostly on her mind.

Shelly had handouts; a calendar of upcoming weekends and her intentions for taking Retro Sky on tour. She had lined up two weekends in Albuquerque. We'd stay in the Midnight Motel for two nights each trip. Meals were on the cheap. Mel would stay in her room and the four guys had two rooms. Expenses were already paid. Everyone looked around the room when she said that, but no one questioned her. The kids were going to have to follow her rules. Lights out by 1:00 am on those Friday and Saturday nights. Homework would be looked at on Sunday mornings. Books were encouraged. Boring otherwise.

Well into the next few months she planned on gigs throughout Colorado. She'd try and stay close to the I-25 corridor. Parents, of course were welcome at any point. Transportation would be provided by a van that easily sat seven, with a small, enclosed trailer for instruments, amps and suitcases. Shelly assured everyone that she was comfortable taking this on. She was excited about it.

Surprising there were no questions.

Then Dad got up and talked about school He would need written parent permission to excuse absences on those Fridays, and probably upcoming Thursdays. He had checked semester grades and kept updated on each band member. School was a requirement and he wanted to impose an informal eligibility requirement, like when he was a coach. Like Billy, standing right there, would impose on his basketball team. From here on out, if the band member fell below a C average, he could not go on the trip. If a band member got into any suspend-able offense at school, he could not go on the trip. The band would just have to figure out how to play without that person. Every person in the room knew that Dad was talking about Frankie. Frankie's mom, especially. I couldn't read her face. If she was grateful or sad or just plain exhausted. Dad's little speech eliminated any need to speak directly to her. Right now, everyone was starting fresh. That brought relief to her face. He'd check everyone's status a week from now.

Still no questions. Strange. The adults were more excited than we were as a band, it seemed. Red raised his hand after an uncomfortable silence.

"I was wondering if I could get a ride if someone goes and sees the band." He asked.

Everyone said they'd be happy to give him a ride. But no one said they'd be going to Albuquerque. Too much going on. Too many commitments. Even my parents didn't think they could make those weekends. Maybe my mom, she wasn't sure, maybe the second weekend. Red shrugged; he didn't have a phone anyway. Besides, he wasn't feeling all that well.

Shelly was surprised how easy the meeting went. The kids were hers, essentially, for life. Retro Sky was now in her hands.

Dad did manage to pull Mel and her mom into an adjoining room as things were breaking up for the night. I was sure that he was explaining to them that he and Mom would be happy to sponsor her in college as she graduated this year. Mel had been to the counseling office at his insistence. The counselor wanted to see the paperwork completed by Monday – that much I did know.

Driving to Albuquerque the following week, I made sure that we had our set lists ready. It was heavy on my mind. That we chose a good balance between cover songs and four or five of our new ones. "Only the Pavement" was our strongest, putting our best foot forward. It had been well received in Santa Fe. We were opening for a popular local band called HotBoxNero. They had a CD with a song playing regularly on New Mexico and Arizona radio stations, "Dance Your Jewelry Girl." They were a lot of fun, a dance band mostly. The 900 capacity Sunshine Theater was an old cinema gutted into a concert-dance venue. I had been there a few years ago for a Christmas concert. I chose a lot of dance songs, to kick it off.   I nixed "Isis" because the crowd would be younger, I guessed. Mel sat by me in the van watching me make a list, scratching out songs, adding songs. She told me to keep "Isis." She urged me to play it after four or five fast songs. Mix-in that Doors feel. Play it on with the electric keyboard, like I do. They'll love it, then wheel off into "Beyond Belief."   It would be a good showcase for me. Then towards the end we could do our duet "All I Have to Do Is Dream." She looked into my eyes. I knew I had left off "Into the Clouds," her solo, and "Dirge for Daddy."

"Where do you want them?" I asked her.

She didn't answer. She snuggled close.   "Julian, I don't know. I'd like to do them. I know we only have an hour. Maybe just one of them, please?"

"How 'bout this?   Let's have you do "Clouds" tonight, then "Daddy" tomorrow. See how you feel. Jeeze, we have another two hours of songs we could fill. Easily. We can even change up our set for tomorrow night depending how it goes tonight."

"I appreciate it. Where in the set?" She was using an index finger gliding down the list. "How 'bout here?" About half-way.   I liked it.

After checking into a dive of a motel, we went over to the theater to drop off our gear, set-up, make a sound check. We'd do another check later. Nerves abounded. Stu looked far more nervous than any time down in Santa Fe. I was glad Frankie got clearance to go. He was the rock for all of us.   No nervousness at all. He had nearly a B average at the moment, so as we all knew, he was capable. Alo acted like he was on a vacation, laughing with Shelly. No pressure there. I was the one most nervous. We ate hamburgers and drank shakes. We went back to change and clean up. Most of us laid around watching motel TV. Stu was with me. Frankie and Bird in the other room.

Mel was made up with her usual black boots, combined this time with bright pink pants, polka-dot purple blouse, black lipstick. A yellow scarf. Funky as hell. I loved it. We were sitting in front of a mirror in her bathroom where she had moved a chair. We were scrunched into the one plastic chair. She took out some white make up, took off my glasses, and smeared some over my face, like in pantomime. She got up and found Shelly's hat, with a broad, colorful band. It was only a little bit small on me.

"Do Dylan tonight. You know, *Desire*." She urged. I looked in the mirror, wanting to get rid of the glasses, ditch the Costello for now. But I couldn't see, literally couldn't see without my glasses. I'd have to figure that one for a later concert.

"Get rid of the tie. Let's find you a colorful shirt." We went to my room. Nothing. She didn't like any of it. Then we went over to the other room where the guys were hanging out. They laughed when we walked in. My make-up. I asked Frankie if he had a colorful shirt. He was laughing, looking in his suitcase, retrieving a purple shirt. His mom had told him to wear it. He was thinking about it. I was going to borrow it for tonight, if that was okay. He threw it at me and told me to not get make up on it.

When we got to the venue a doorman showed us the Green Room. He told me I could put on make-up in here, I didn't have to put it on so early. Melanie told the guy I wore it all the time. He looked at her, then me. He couldn't tell if she was giving him shit.

HotBoxNero showed up around ten minutes before we were to go on. They were all in their twenties. Much older than us. They looked around the room at our youth, our strange presentation, wishing us good luck. Mom and Red were at the door as we were about to go on stage. They made it after all. Mom reminded me that Dad had taken Steph and a friend of hers on a pre-arranged ski trip. My heart was racing and having my mom here was a good anchor. She saw my get-up and laughed. *Go get em, Julian*, I think she said, I was moving too fast.

The problem with being an opening band, of course, is that everyone is there to hear the main act. The place was about two-thirds full, more still coming in. It took two songs before the place settled down, then started moving and dancing. We cranked hard on the fifties, early sixties beat, as I sweat on the piano doing my Little Richard thing. It was fucking fun. All of us were in a groove of good times. The crowd picked up on it. By the fifth song we were exhausted, so was the crowd. "Pavement" fit right in. I had switched to lead guitar and we rocked hard. I saw a girl in front swirling her hair all over the place dancing so fast, almost dangerous on some guy's shoulders. It was like a mosh pit. When I went into "Isis," I had arranged with the light people to do a more psychedelic thing. I swirled the electric piano in Doors fashion. I could smell pot smoke. Cigarettes lit up. I did my best Morrison croon and cry, letting the Dylan imagery linger. The spotlight hard on my face, the white make-up glowing I imagined. Mel crooning an eerie back up vocal with her tambourine. *Mystical child*, over and over.

After a few faster paced songs, Melanie stepped up front with her acoustic and did "Clouds."   Solo. She sounded just like Grace Slick. I had not heard her do it this way.   The crowd loved her.

Our duets were perfect. The guys never missed a beat. We closed to a strong ovation.   I was very happy; all of us were, waving to the crowd as we exited stage right. The HotBoxNero guys, I don't remember their first names, gave us handshakes, congrats. Their leader told me to go back out there. Go ahead and do an encore. I sent out Stu and Melanie instead. Do "Dirge for Daddy." They looked shocked when I told them to go ahead. I watched from the wings as Melanie ate up the light, the rapt crowd. She brought the house down.

I gave her a big kiss when she came back to the Green Room.

"Thank you, Julian. I love you."

We only stayed for a song or two of theirs before we left. They were a good band but nothing better than us, I thought.   Mom and Red wanted to take us out for a real dinner.   Shelly was proud as could be. At dinner, she showed me the notes she had made on every song. She liked the mix. Maybe another dance number during the second half. I agreed with her. She kept telling us how great we were. Mom, too. Red had his arm around Bird, smiling. It was like this is what he had stayed alive for. The following night went much better in that we squeezed in two more of our own songs which seemed to go over well. There were even more people dancing which ignites our energy. We had not played "I Can Tell" the previous night and the crowd liked our Bo Diddley romp so much – and Melanie and I playing hard with the lyric - it was evident we needed to make it a staple. Melanie had insisted that if we did an encore, I should do "Rain" this time. With the psychedelic twist. Mel and I were sharing the same mic and we decided to do more of it. The crowd liked our interactions. We liked it too. I was going to ditch the makeup from here on out. Not a bad idea. Just that it itched and dripped with my sweat. I wasn't sure what my image should be. I had Costello quickly taking a back seat to Dylan, with Morrison tracking in my arteries. Those fifties' guys piano geniuses, showmen flaunting it all. I wasn't sure where I was going to land.

Jennifer

The countdown was on. One week before Stephanie and I were going to leave for France. We'd been working hard on the script. Not the script, exactly. The part of Manon. After her ski trip a few weeks ago, she became a recluse. She'd read. Do her homework. I saw her taking walks in the bitter cold. She'd go down and visit James two or three times a week. She did make a quick trip with all of us to see Julian and Retro Sky play in small venues in Alamosa and Trinidad. They were the sole band on a Thursday-Friday-Saturday stint, playing to small crowds of about a hundred, then two hundred. They were a lot of fun, though. Julian knew how to command attention. One hell of a player and singer. Melanie was like his true partner up there, almost a duo instead of a band.

Steph worried me, still. Her introversion was being exacerbated by the role. I'd seen this before. In myself. I left her completely alone, offering no help in figuring out her feelings, emotions, transformations. I'd check in on her during the flight. It was important that she did this in a kind of existential despair. No apparent salvation. Most of all, I stayed far away from talking about the final scenes, the circus. The way out for Manon. I wished, in a way, that she was unaware of the ending.

Sharon's premiere in *Undercover* was another hit. I don't think Sharon has ever suffered a flop. Woody Allen and Jeff Daniels, Jeff Goldblum, Annette Benning and Natalie Portman, the entire, star-studded ensemble received rave reviews. We saw it as a family when it finally reached Santa Fe. Hilarious. Louise was dying to have Sharon stay with us again someday. She had a million questions, as always.   Danny and Julian laughed, quoting lines. Steph, on the other hand, retreated even further into herself. I could see, I could read her mind. Sharon awaited her in France. The image of her stage mother, this giant of her destiny loomed. She not only had to struggle with the childhood love Manon felt, that Steph felt, and the raging appearance of hate towards her own mother that now possessed Manon; Steph was dealing with her own hatred towards Sharon now. An emotion terrifying her. And Sharon would pour gasoline all over it when we started filming. I knew her. It would break Steph, which needed to happen. I trusted my girl. She had me inside of her. She would find a way to fight. She would find a way to push Sharon right back. Deep inside, I was hoping that Steph would scare the living shit out of Sharon while the film was rolling. I liked *Undercover*, but no one pushed Sharon very hard on this one. She was good, no doubt about it. Always at her peak. Wait till we get to France.

We had Gene and Rhonda over for a quiet dinner. Just the four of us. Steph had auditioned for *The Sound of Music* that same morning and Gene sat in the back while Brett Hodges from the college ran the process over at Eagle's Nest. It was Brett's show.

"How old is Stephanie, again?" Gene asked.

Danny answered, "Fourteen. Why, you think she is too young to play Liesle?"

Gene was squirming in his chair. "No, that's not it. Well, maybe. Normally, yes, certainly. Damn, this is not my play. I'm sure I'm prejudiced here." He stopped.

"What, what is it? Did she bomb?" Danny continued running interference.

"She didn't bomb. She was good. I sure had visions of you, Jennifer."

"What'ya mean?" I asked.

"I remembered you auditioning, over twenty years ago, now, I think."

"Hard to believe." I said, remembering many of the details. "So, you think she might get a part? I'm just curious. If not, she'll understand. I really appreciate that you gave her a shot."

He didn't answer me right away. He took a stiff drink of the whiskey Danny had served him. "Jesus, I remember *Bob, Carol, Ted and Alice*. The heyday of *Gypsy*. The Nest never reached those heights again."

"Well, come on, Gene. Tim accounts for all of that. That kind of thing just doesn't happen very often." I insisted.

"True. Not all of it, Jennifer." He was looking right at me. He was looking older these days.

Rhonda changed the subject, thanking me for their fun trip, getting to see the premiere. They had met Woody Allen, Sharon was gracious, remembering all those good times at the Nest.

"So, you're doing a movie again?" she asked me, innocently. "It's been a long time. *Hull House*, wasn't it?"

My turn to not answer. I guess the news was going to come out sooner or later. It was still between friends. Even then, it would break to the public soon enough.

Danny chimed in, "Well Rhonda, it has been that long. Jennifer is looking forward to it. She and Sharon are close, as you already know."

"We heard rumors that Stephanie was going to be in it." Gene mumbled.

Neither me nor Danny responded.

"I got to tell you, Jennifer. Stephanie was so damned good in that audition; I couldn't believe it. She looked like she was thirty years old and had been acting her entire life. She was commanding. And she can sing. She is probably a better singer than you were back then Jennifer."

"No doubt about her singing voice," I said, "that good, huh?"

"If it's true she's doing that film with you and Sharon, and she gets a part in *The Sound of Music*, it's so strange, you know. Same thing all over again."

"Gene, I appreciate it. Please don't say anything about the movie." I said.

"So, it's true?"

"Yes."

"I have to ask you a serious question, then." Gene continued. "I won't say anything and won't have any say in the casting. That's all up to Brett. I gotta tell you, though. I sat through all seven auditions for Maria and not one was as good as Stephanie. I mean that."

I looked over at Danny. We both tried to decipher the idea.

"Problem is, she's so young. I tell you — if it were up to me, I think it wouldn't take much to get her to look like a twentysomething. She should play Maria."

"The lead? You sure of that or are you, I don't know, are you playing this somehow? I'm not going to get involved. And neither is Tim. Or Sharon. Guaranteed." I said emphatically.

"I knew you would think that." Gene said, "Believe me, she was that good. I know she didn't try out for Maria. I don't know. I'd put money on it that Brett will call her back to audition for Maria."

"We're leaving next week." I bluntly stated.

Gene took that to heart, contemplating the timing of everything.

Rhonda volunteered one of the topics we wanted to talk about it. She looked lovely in her styling dress, simple pearls. I loved her hair and told her so. "Your son, Julian? Has a band, is that right?"

Danny answered, "Retro Sky. What do you think of the name?"

"I'd go with Retro. Maybe by itself. I'm not sure of the Sky part." She said with authority. "Can I meet him?"

"I'm sorry, he's over at a friend's. A member of the band. We cleared the house out for tonight." Danny answered.

"Too bad. I wanted to measure him up to all that I've heard."

We remained quiet. Julian didn't even know about this dinner. "They've played in the area? Some clubs, I hear?" Rhonda asked.

I went over the details of the dozen or so engagements. That's all they'd had. She did not respond. She was thinking. "Can I hear something of theirs?"

"Sure," Danny got up and went downstairs. He came back with a tape of "Only the Pavement Knows" and another tape of their Beatles' songs, all three of them. The third tape was of "All I Have to do Is Dream."

Dinner was finished. I had everyone relocate to the living room with fresh wine. I'd serve dessert shortly. Danny put in the Beatles tape first. I forgot how unique they had made "While My Guitar Gently Weeps" and "Here Comes the Sun." Melanie was singing lead on that particular recording of the first one, and Julian on the second. Rhonda asked Danny to stop the tape. "Do they always cover songs in their own way? These are obviously Beatles songs, but they are so different. I like it. A lot."

"Not always," Danny said. "Their dance songs, the fifties stuff is almost exact. Julian's vocals are his own."

"And the girl. She's good. I like them both."

Then he played "Rain." She leaned back on the couch and closed her eyes. "How'd those guys get that stuff to sound like that? That's a tough song. The original is all studio-mixed, sound shifting in speeds, even backwards. This is cool for a such a crude try. Nice."

We smiled.

"Pavement" blared on the stereo. It was a tape from the sound studio in L.A.   "Wow, that's something powerful. I swear that's Mike Campbell on guitar, it sounds just like him. Is that Julian?"

Danny laughed. "You're good.   That was Mike Campbell. He sat in on a studio taping in L.A."

She looked impressed. "Let's hear it again. This is their writing, right?"

"Yep."

Rhonda walked around our living area, putting her ears closer to the speakers from time to time.   She asked Danny to stop and rewind and then start again.

Then she sat back down.   "Julian can sing. And that girl, like before. They can belt it. The rhythm section is extremely strong. Who are they?"

"Just a kid from Phoenix, in their school plays bass. An Indian kid from the reservation on drums. His uncle played his whole life."

"Can't believe they're kids. What else you got?"

Danny put on the Everly Brothers cover. I about cried. It was probably my favorite of theirs. I hated to admit it to myself, but Julian and Melanie sounded so in love when they harmonized. Even though this was a cassette made over at the studio, they sounded beautiful.

Rhonda excused herself to go to the bathroom when it finished. I went to the kitchen and prepared the strawberry shortcake. Danny came and helped me. We whispered to each other how good we thought they sounded. Proud parents. Gene went out on the porch. It was freezing outside.   He was in deep thought. Probably about Stephanie.

Rhonda bounded in. "That was a beautiful song. They're good. I would like to see them. When do they play again?"

"Not for two weeks. In Colorado Springs." Danny said.

"What about rehearsing? Where do they practice?"

"Oh, over at a little studio attached to Jennifer's Gallery. They'll be over there tomorrow."

"Can you ask them if I can sit in?"

"Sure.   They'll be excited."

"Just tell them I'm a friend of Gene's. You don't have to say much more."

Melanie arrived first, which was unusual. She came around to my door and knocked. She apologized right away, asking if I'd let her into the studio. I gave her a big hug. Not just for what she was doing in the band, but she had completed all her paperwork and application for business school.   She looked so different, her blond hair in pigtails under a red and green striped wool hat, a big brown sweater and brown jacket, baggy pants and tennis shoes. No make-up. I hugged her again.

While the guys gathered, Matthew knocked on my office door, bringing in Rhonda. He had given her the tour as I had asked. She was impressed, saying she had been here two times before – once a long time ago with her first husband, and once when she began dating Gene. I asked her to wait a second while I went and asked the band about her sitting in.

Rhonda sat on the beat-up old couch, watching carefully. I tried to be inconspicuous in the corner. No one seemed to mind or care, or even wonder why we were there. The kids were screwing around, laughing, taking their time getting down to business. Frankie looked higher than a kite, like he hadn't showered in days. His beard was now full, like a thirty-year-old. His hair in a bun. My worries about him and his grades went up like a red flag. Stu had been on a date. A Sunday afternoon matinee with a girl that asked him out. He was so excited. Everyone was giving him grief.

Julian got everything under control, looking over notes. He yelled out "Sultan," putting on his guitar. I had not heard the band play this yet. Julian was always trying to copy Knopfler. His lead guitar was wonderful. Melanie took the lead vocal, strumming her acoustic on the third verse – *check out Guitar George, he knows all the chords*, all the way into *they play Creole, Creole*, smiling the whole way. They finished. No fanfare or words. Matter of fact. Julian looked at his notes again. "Let's try 'Blast Blast.'" He said easily enough. It was a new one, I thought. Strange intro, Julian meandering on the electric piano. Bird clacking on the side of his drum in no discernable pattern. Stu picking it up. Both Melanie and Frank on acoustic guitars, amplifying a new rhythm. Julian singing a lyric pointedly about breaking up. The broken-hearted girl in the story ripping the guy to shreds for cheating on her. The phrase *blast blast*, taking different meanings in each verse. Sometimes a gun or bomb going off, sometimes the good times the guy had with his new fling, or the times he had with the girl he's breaking up with when they first dated. Melanie took over singing, right at Julian, what a jerk the guy was, and she'd been fooling around all along. He was never that good anyway. Get over it. Blast Blast. She was having a blast without him.

There were some giggles. Melanie liked the zing. Julian had written it for her. I noticed that they were trading off singing more and more. I looked at Rhonda, she was writing stuff down on a note pad.

Julian asked Rhonda, who she was. Almost rudely. She smiled, reiterating that she was a friend of Gene's and thanked them for letting her sit in.

"Why, does Gene want us to play at the Theater?" Frankie asked with sarcasm.

She laughed. "No, no. I just heard about you, about Retro. Retro Sky. I was curious. I really appreciate it."

"Something you want to hear?" Julian asked her.

She thought for a while. "I hear you do a lot of fifties, sixties stuff. Can you do anything by the Stones?"

Julian sat up right away and put his Fender back on. He spoke to the band for a good five minutes, playing with knobs on the amps. Stu and Iso shook their heads, playing out a rhythm I thought I recognized right away. They continued when he went over to Frankie, showing him the chord progression. He nodded his head several times. He and Melanie played over at the electric keyboard, where she was now sitting. He wrote down the lyrics for her. They went through a crude rendition of what was going to be obvious. Then practiced it quickly a few more times. Then Julian finally counted them down and he ripped into the guitar solo of "Can You Hear Me Knockin'" with Bird picking up the drums right away. Then Stu followed when Bird gave him the signal to go ahead. Julian amped it up louder and louder until Melanie broke into the lyric as Frankie took his cue. She was crying *cocaine eyes* with Mick's *aching blues*. Then Julian backed her up on the microphone, *Can't you hear me knockin*, over and over loud, *hear me singing soft and low*, the two electric guitars trading licks. Julian's hair down in his face.

Then they jammed.   Melanie playing the electric piano where I knew a saxophone would normally be. She was whirling the sound over and over.   Frankie looked like he was in outer space, keeping up with Julian. Julian turned to him and smiled.

Julian made a signal, and their sound went down low, and he took over on a guitar solo, which was making the studio vibrate.   Bird and Stu were looking right at each other, facing each other, copying their beat and direction. Mel hitting the keys harder as they sped up. Then Frankie took over. Julian quit playing, walking around with his head down sweat dripping on the floor.

He went to the microphone and said *yeah*, in a grunt, Bird taking a set of bongos shifting gears and then brought it all home as everyone jumped in for a finale. I was one proud mama.

Frankie went outside. Probably to smoke I thought. Mel laughed. Stu and Bird were clapping. Julian, turned to Rhonda, "You mean something like that?" He asked with a straight face.

"You have never played that before?" she asked.

"Nope. I've messed with the guitar. Keith's part. Open G chord. Done that before. Mick Taylor's riffs. I think Frankie's done it. Sounds like it, don't you think? I've done it lots of times. Melanie is no Billy Preston, but damned good, I'd say. She sounded just like Mick, too. But no, we've never done it as a band. First time."

"My god."

"What else you want to hear?" Everyone laughed. Even Rhonda.

"How long you guys been playing together?" She asked.

"Bird, not that long. But he's better than any of us." Julian said. "What, Stu? Six years? I forget. Maybe more. Frankie a couple of years, probably more. He was gone off and on. I don't know. Melanie and I since we were seven. Umm, let me think. Like almost every day. Our teacher, Cindy, gets a lot of the credit."

Rhonda bent over and shook her head.

CHAPTER FIFTEEN

I'm wide awake, I'm wide awake, wide awake, I'm not sleeping, no, no, no. U2

Jennifer

We boarded Tim's private jet around 4:00 am on a
Monday.   Danny was up helping us get to the airport.
Our goodbyes had been said the night before. The
entire week before.   Julian had returned from a
Colorado Springs trip with Retro Sky early on Sunday.
Rhonda had made the trip to see them. She had filled in
the band that she was a retired agent. She liked what
she had heard thus far. Seeing them play live for two
nights went well, Julian thought. So did Shelly.
I kissed Danny goodbye. We still had to work out the
timing of how he and Julian would be going to France for
a quick three days.   Probably in March.
Stephanie was sequestering herself more and more. She
went directly to a back seat with a blanket and pillow.
Our script readings – without a script - over the past
several days were intense.   She was even changing her
demeanor.   Eating less. I trusted it because I kept
telling her to trust it. This sucked for me, as her mother.
As an actress, I was starting to do the same with my
mother superior mode.   The orphanage administrator
scrapping for food for about 130 young kids.   Disciplined.
Fighting for their survival. In some ways, I felt my Jane
Addams character rear her head.   The passion for the
forgotten. Sister Marianne, my latest name in the script,
was younger, more faith based. She didn't have
financial backing like Jane had. Marianne was lean and a
fighter.   She would give Sharon's character, Madame
Rosette, a battle for Manon's soul. This would be a clash

that Sharon and I had never approached in our careers. The script, the human struggle was the life and death of a young girl. I knew, I had a deep feeling that the script would be ditched anyway. We had the words, the outline, the scenes, but Sharon and I would take over. It was up to Stephanie to rise to the occasion. It was her life after all.

Tim kept studying the minutia. Notebooks. Tons of drawings. It was his job, I understood that. What was odd is that he never asked me how I was doing with the character. I suspected he never asked Sharon either. We'd rehearse when we landed, but the actual acting wasn't even in his consciousness from what I could tell. Steph asked me to come sit by her. We were somewhere over the Atlantic Ocean.

"Mom, I haven't talked with you about my audition over at Eagle's Nest. It's a big distraction. Going back and doing a scene as Maria was not as hard as I thought. I was fine. I sang with gusto and fun. I was cheery. It felt easy somehow. I am in this plane flying to France with you, with the most famous actor in the world sitting right over there. About to act with the greatest actress in the world. No offense."

I smiled.

"And all I can think of is starvation. Death. Seeking escape. Desperation. I don't even care about Maria. I don't care if I get the part or not."

Inside of me I wanted to jump for joy. Rejoice. She was exactly where she needed to be.

"I can't read novels lately. School bores me. I don't pay attention. Mrs. Harrison in my Lit class pulled me aside and asked me if something was wrong. I didn't even know how to answer her. I wanted to answer *the whole fucking world is wrong*."

I thought I should probably engage just a bit. I said, "And I'm worried about the 130 kids of mine who did not have enough food. Many did not have shoes. We were sleeping three and four to a bunk. School was mostly working in our gardens, taking care of our cows and chickens. Singing and praying. Going to mass. Learning to read and write when we had time. I'd have a family or parents looking to adopt about once a month. That was it. Then you came into my life. You are helping me in the orphanage. You are looking for an answer. You don't believe any of the Church's teachings, and don't even believe in God, but you and I form a bond. You know all that, Steph. That's who I am now."

She shook her head. Resting it back on the pillow. "And when we get off that plane, Madame Rosette will want to get her hands on her daughter. Not because she loves you. Because you can bring in good money. Because of your age and your attractiveness, you are in danger. Severe danger."

"I know." She closed her eyes to sleep. I sat there for about an hour, dozing off. Then she stirred, looking at me. "I hate you too, you know."

"What?"

"Your trap is as bad as my mother's. As bad as Rosette's."

I hadn't thought of it as that extreme. I was mulling it over. She was right. It scared me. It would scare Sister

Marianne more. I put my arm around Steph and gently hugged her.

"You know Mom. I don't think there is one scene anywhere in this movie where anyone hugs me. It's another expensive commodity. Too emotionally expensive."

She closed her eyes, and I didn't remove my arm. I couldn't. My little girl fell asleep. I told myself, *I better not hug her again until this fucking thing is done*. I'd leave that up to Estelle as soon as we landed.

We landed in Brussels. It was snowing, gray, miserable. Tim was purposely keeping us away from Paris. We didn't even get to rest. That was true to form as well. We loaded up in a van. Not a car or nice limousine. A van. We had blankets and a terrible heater. Estelle was part of the entourage that met us at the airport. She and Steph talked for only ten or fifteen minutes, eager to get going. Estelle was a warrior, already ahead of the game. She motioned for me to sit in front, while she took Steph to the rear of the van. Sandwiches were passed around. An apple for everyone. It was nearly a three-hour drive to Amiens. Normally, I suspect, it's a gorgeous drive. We saw nothing except heavy clouds, sleet and clouded windows. It was miserable outside. Tim was delighted, I could tell. Exactly what he hoped for. He wanted as much gloom as he could get.

It was nice to get to a hotel, finally. Nothing spectacular, but comfortable. Warm. Decent food. Estelle whisked Stephanie away. She was no longer my daughter. She was Madame Rosette's flesh and blood.

Sharon called me in my room, informing me that she had arrived in Amiens the day before. *It's a godawful place*, she laughed. *Perfect, don't you think?*

Then she added, "Lord, Woody was all color and happy. Laughter all over New York. It was a fun movie. Now this. I knew what I was getting into, though."

"Me too. It's still a harsh wake up call. You know, Santa Fe, to this."

"Steph okay?"

"Depends on your point of view. On the one hand I've never seen her this way. She scares me a bit. On the other hand, I like it. She's almost there, Sharon."

"Good. This is going to be brutal. You remember when we did Helen Keller and we were warned we may not be friends afterwards?"

"Absolutely. We took it on full force."

"We survived, didn't we?"

"Yes. And *Rio*, too. That was difficult."

"Ah come on, Jennifer. You wrote this thing. You know how torturous this is going to be. God, I'm too old." She was lighting a cigarette on the other end.

"We'll be okay."

"I hope so. I mean, your daughter is walking into a buzz saw. I don't think there is anything we can do at this point. We can't go easy on her. You know that."

"I know. It's like playing in the NBA after playing middle school basketball. Or something like that."

She laughed. "Something like that."

"I'll see you at the reading tomorrow."

"Yeah, okay."

The reading was held at 6:00 am. Again, Steph was learning. Estelle had her fed and ready. They were on time. Good. We were all introduced, various actors sitting around. Most of us knew each other. Not a lot of chit chat that early in the morning. We had our scripts and plenty of coffee.

Tim asked us all to open to the third scene, in a playfield on the orphanage. Rosette shows up to bring back Manon from where she had run away. It was the first time that Rosette meets Sister Marianne. It was bothering him. He wanted to start there instead of at the beginning. Steph didn't open her script. Estelle stepped up from behind her and tried to open it. Steph said, "I got it. I don't want to look at it."

We all looked around. My motherly instincts wanted to jump in. Steph had said it, not like a prima donna, but with a sense of urgency. She really did not want to look at it. Tim flushed. Angry and perplexed.

"Why the fuck not," he said, right at her, climbing in her face. He had never spoken to anyone like that. Never that I could recall. Everyone froze. Even Sharon. Then Sharon grinned without anyone seeing her except me. She slowly opened the script. Estelle helped her find the right page. Steph was looking at Tim eye to eye. Defiantly.

We read the scene without much definition. Holding back any acting. Just reading. Steph read her lines without looking at the pages. Still looking directly at Tim. He We spent the day reading, discussing. Going through the usual motions, notations added here and there. The set guys and camera guys taking notes. We'd take a break and Steph would dart with Estelle to her trailer. She didn't eat or drink with us. Sharon did the same, but most of us hung out. This was supposed to be laid back. At the end of the day, there was clapping. A sense of readiness. We'd read for a few days, take the scripts and walk around. Do some stage rehearsals. Steph was ready to leave for the day when Tim practically ordered her to stick around. He wanted to talk to her. He looked at me and I just shrugged. I was out of this ballgame unless the coach sent me in. Everyone scattered. Even me.

Tim called me in my room late that night. I was in bed, near sleep, wide awake at the same time. He apologized for bothering me. He hated to bring me in on this already. He was exasperated.

"Ah Jesus, Jennifer. Stephanie is already being difficult. And not like I thought. It's not because she doesn't know what she's doing. It's because she knows exactly what she's doing."

"What do you mean? You sure you want to bring me in on this?" I asked.

"She's telling me that she wants to jump right in. She tells me, the director, that Sharon knows her shit, Jennifer knows her shit, she said *Jennifer*, and that this was a waste of time. We wouldn't use the script anyway. I about blew up."

"Oh God."

"I tried to tell her that this was for everyone, that the crew needed to know and hear this too. Work on the camera blocking process. She knows all that. I tried to reason with her." He was losing his cool.

"Stephanie said *fine* and asked to leave. She'd do what I told her. She promised."

"Okay, let's see in the morning. Don't call me again, either. This is your problem."

He laughed. Sort of. I hung up.

Stand up rehearsals went a little bit better. Probably because we weren't required to hold the script. Steph cooperated for most of the day. She easily pulled off the most difficult readings and scenes. We were almost done, when Tim asked if there were any questions. Several people spoke up. It was a good conversation. Lively. Steph raised her hand, in a sarcastic gesture, like the bad kid in the back of the classroom, and defiantly asked, "When do I get to say the stuff that I'm really going to say once the camera rolls?"

Everyone froze. I thought, *Jesus, she is going to get fired*.

I could tell that Tim was going crazy inside. He didn't know how to handle this in front of everyone.

Then Sharon spoke up and got right in Steph's face.

"Listen, you little bitch. You are going to do exactly what I say. And you are going to do whatever this man wants you to do?"

"You mean like fuck him, like you fuck him?" Stephanie was glaring in rage.

You could hear a pin drop.

"Exactly, little girl. If that's what he wants. Then that's what he's going to get."

Steph spit on Sharon, and Sharon immediately slapped Steph hard across the face. Steph went down in a flash. No tears. No words.

"All you are is a goddamn whore," Steph said softly, rubbing her face. Looking up at Sharon.

Sharon appeared as though she was going to bend over and help her up. Instead, she looked Steph in the eyes, glaring hard. "And that's what you are Manon. You better get that through your head." Sharon stormed off and out the door.

Steph slowly got up. Estelle rushed to help her up. Estelle was using a handkerchief to dab touches of blood on Steph's cheek.

"That's not in the script, is it?" Steph was glaring at Tim and walked away.

"It is now," he said with a smile.

For whatever reason, I was the happiest person in the room.

Danny

It was past midnight in Rouen when I was able to reach Jennifer from my school office, on the district long-distance line. She had been on a train, relocated to film at the Gothic church Saint-Maclou and the cobblestone village atmosphere. Tim had altered filming schedules, at least from what I could tell, largely because of Stephanie. Tim was proceeding to 'rein-in' Steph after several outbursts on Steph's part. I would've been more alarmed at the extreme stories Jennifer was telling me if not for her seeming delight and pride in our daughter. Honestly, I was disbelieving and horrified. I could not wrap my head around it all. Jennifer was taking it in stride, and I had to trust her professionalism on the matter. Sharon had stepped in with Tim. It was going to be okay.

I missed Jennifer terribly.

After we hung up, I looked at the stack of notes and files for my day. It had been an exhausting, demanding Thursday. I needed to let off steam. I told Cheryl that I was going to go down to the gym to the basketball practice. *Have a good night*. She looked concerned about me. The best secretary in the world. I was lucky to have her on my staff.

Billy had the team working on a defensive drill I was quite familiar with. I learned it from the great Jerry Tarkanian at UNLV, and we adapted *the Amoeba* to our own system years ago. I watched the guys, envious of my coaching days. I missed it. A lot.

I went into the coach's office where I kept a change of clothes, my work-out stuff, a survival kit of sorts for long nights of supervising games or facilitating conferences. I put on my basketball gear and looked in the mirror. I had been very good once. I was nervous about going out there as the guy looking back at me. A few pounds heavier and hints of gray in the thinning hairline.

The team had lost in overtime to a mediocre school, here at home two nights ago, ruining their undefeated season thus far. It seemed to light a fire in their intensity. Billy invited me to jump in when they started running fast break drills, press break options. The guys were ribbing me good naturedly. I was easily the slowest one on the floor. I was about to fall over after only fifteen minutes. My tongue dragging.

We split into half court offensive drills, 5-on-5. I was with the second team, taking on the starters. I found a groove, not running full court helped, scoring a bundle of points. Lots of oohs and *aahs* from the guys. Sweat was gushing from my pores, my shirt soaked. It felt wonderful.

When they broke up to shoot free-throws, Billy and I chatted about the remainder of their season. We'd lost two players from last year's state championship team and Billy was grooming two sophomores. He thought they might be a year or two away. I wasn't so sure. They seemed tough to me right now.

I showered and went home. Louise had told me she'd be gone so I picked up a supreme pizza for me and Julian. Julian was downstairs on his bass. I knew he probably had headphones on, and he was practicing riffs. This one sounded like Jack Bruce of Cream. I wasn't sure. As his dad, I am terribly proud, of course, but I am always amazed at how obsessed he is with his music. Ever since he was six or maybe even younger, he would sit at the piano for hours, practicing for hours. We never had to remind him or force him in any way. When we bought him a guitar, same thing, only he spent even more time practicing. With Cindy and the various kids that hung around, like Melanie and Stu, he'd play for even many more hours. Almost every day, all day. Julian never had the kind of grades like Steph, but he always made honor roll. He didn't like to ski or ride horses. Not much of an athlete except for hiking great distances, long backpack trips excited him. Our father-son relationship was strained because of his disinclination toward sports, and he hated golf, too. Which was my biggest interest. And I could not play a lick on any instrument. But I did know my music and albums and bands, and he readily shared my era of music with me. He loved it all. My role models in music were his, except he took them literally and played and sang and mimicked them verbatim, note for note. We could talk about music for hours. I was incredibly grateful for that.

We ate and drank 7-up, talking about Retro Sky and their plans. Rhonda was working hard to line up some more dates, maybe in Phoenix, work their way to California. Although she was not officially a manager or agent, she was working closely with Shelly. Their Denver concert at the Ogden Theater was their first 'big' concert, top billing, more money. It went well. They had received a small article in *Westward* magazine in Colorado, which gave them some attention. Frankie should not have been allowed to go on the trip, but I relented. I was reminding Julian that Frankie was 'ineligible' until he pulled it together. Julian shrugged his shoulders, not fazed by it.

In the meantime, they were back at the bars in Santa Fe becoming a regular at Jimmy's, every other weekend. A small regular following of fans was developing.

Julian brought up Melanie and her going to school next fall. She had been accepted, just that day, into the business department for the fall. I assured Julian, as I would Mel and her mother, that we had it covered. If she kept her grades up, we'd pay for her school. Simple enough. Melanie was very grateful. Julian was happy that it gave him some relief in terms of knowing what would happen with them in the near future.

I like Melanie. I remembered her singing, playing at recitals with Julian when they were only seven or eight or nine, all the way up the ladder. They grew up together. Melanie mostly played acoustic and classical guitars for Cindy's programs, but she was on piano occasionally. She was an outstanding singer from an early age. She and Steph would sing with both Cindy's programs and in school choirs. The two girls would be close from time to time.

Which brought my mind wandering mind back to my daughter. What the hell was going on over there? I knew that Steph was one sharp girl, stubborn and opinionated, but on the set of her very first movie? And with Tim? It baffled me. She wanted this more than anything and she was sabotaging an enormous project, and opportunity. Jennifer's attitude saved me. She did not seem that concerned. Jennifer had that sound in her voice like Steph was doing just fine.

Julian and I set a date for a four-day trip to France to do our parts in the film. We were laughing, the idea still seemed absurd. He would have to get a haircut, he was told, to play a blind, piano playing soldier. He did not seem to mind, wanting to look like John Lennon during John's close-cropped era. I was not wanting to fly all that way just to fall-down dead in a street for a ten second clip, especially when I was feeling overwhelmed at school. Seeing Jennifer and Steph would be great, but I knew the odds were not good about having any quality time. Julian and I would have fun flying First Class and being in a nice hotel. Great food. Make the best of it. I said an early goodnight to Julian and grabbed a cigar from my humidifier and a stiff whiskey. Sitting bundled up on the bedroom porch, my usual jazz selection on, was now my bachelor lifestyle. I was getting up at 4:15 regularly. I liked it that way. My reading list was nil. Staring off at the wintery stars, the moon in all its changes, blowing smoke from the wonderful tobacco, swirling and savoring each and every swig was my relaxation. Mr. Bonham, my science teacher, was getting worse and worse about following expectations, missing school more often, too. I was coming down hard on him. Documenting each infraction. All of them petty; he just seemed hellbent on self-destructing his career. Our conversations were not at all productive. I tried hard to make improvement plans, offer suggestions, even attempting to see if anything in his private life was getting to him. Nothing. The teacher's union was doing their thing. Fairly. No problem with me. One of many quandaries.

My efforts with the Catholic Church and our native communities were fizzling. Mostly because I had given up. I had told Bishop Sheehan as much. He knew and understood the silence of the Church was killing me and my efforts. I was expanding our educational outreach and programs on the reservations, however. Always a priority for me, our efforts paid dividends with school morale and success rates. That was about all I could do for now.

Our socio-economic imbalance was widening. More wealth, more poverty. Extremities in the student body. Class and racial-cultural divides forming, subtly. Our per capita income rising along with student at-risk ratios. I hated it and was doing all that I could with our staff, our counselors, our student body to hold on to cohesion. Staff meetings seemed to be dominated by this discussion.

Mostly, I had teacher evaluations to write, and they were due in April. They weren't hard to finish. I had all my observations and notes ready. The time demand and monotony of it loomed over me.

I got a late phone call. About 10:15. It was Karen. She was not happy, telling me that things with her and Sam had deteriorated again. It was she who had left this time. She was in a hotel room. I flat out asked her if another affair was involved. She was silent. That explained it all. I could tell she was 'feeling me out' looking for someone to run to. Or more specifically, someone to run to her. She knew Jennifer was out of town. I don't know, maybe I was reading something into it, but I doubted it. *No way* I was saying to myself. She was dropping hints about meeting up, *to talk*. Visions of our sexual encounter nearly twenty years ago was permanently etched in my mind. That image, high on hash and drunk-on our ass, entering her, the new sensation of *another woman*. Jennifer and I sharing the entire night, talking about the risqué nature of it all. It was all in the past now. Not to be resurrected, I inferred to Karen. I shook it off. I said she could come to the school if she needed to talk some more. We could meet in my office. She understood. I doubted that she'd come by the school.

That was a rough way to head to bed.

Stephanie

My cheek was feeling better by now. Estelle made me put ice on it almost all the time to make the swelling go down. The make-up people were not bothered in the least. I was getting close to Estelle. I had dug a deep hole with Tim, and I knew it. Only God knows what in the hell got into me. What is odd is that I still felt the same way, just that I came to a bit of my senses and shut up. Kept my stupid mouth closed. Estelle told me to shake it off. She'd seen it all before, and far worse. No big deal. Suck it up and do my job. She was right. I had a job to do, not just a character to play, to become, to be.

I must hand it to Tim. He would've fired me if it weren't for Mom and Sharon. I knew that. Instead, he changed the shooting schedule, and he was working almost exclusively with me. We were doing scenes of me remembering the War, the death of my brother and father on the front. Some of the good times as a child. They were good scenes. And two of my first scenes with Sharon after our little encounter in rehearsals. She was all pro, like nothing had happened. She did say something like, *how you doing kid*, as I sat there in my makeup chair. That's all it took to break the ice. They were fond memories of mother and daughter. Sharon's caring in those scenes were somehow cathartic for me.

Mom was sent off with the assistant director to shoot on location. Scenes with an archbishop, pleading for help. Seeing firsthand the War's devastation in a larger city as well. Asking questions about relocation for some of her children, and for Manon, at the orphanage. I missed Mom, secretly embarrassed by my behavior. I wished I could talk with her. I knew she'd have none of it unless I was on the verge of a breakdown. Which I wasn't. I felt strong. I must credit Estelle for saying simple things here and there. Not encouraging, per se, but words that kept me focused. She also made sure that I was eating, which Manon resisted. I needed the sustenance.

Tim had figured me out after those first two days. My guess is that Sharon, maybe Mom, somehow got through to him. He was dealing now almost exclusively with me, waiting to move on to the bigger, meatier parts of the film.

He sat with me for hours. He walked through the minutia, talking with Manon, not Stephanie. Pushing Manon to tell him, almost as if he were godlike, to hear her pleas. He had never directed a 'child-actor' nor taken on this big or expensive of a project. He was rising to the occasion.

One time, probably not accidently, Robin Wright approached me on set. She was hanging out, watching. She asked me how it was going in a matter of fact, almost cold tone. She said my cheek looked better. No judgment at all. *Stay tough*, is all she said, then left. It felt weird, like no one was all that surprised about what had happened at the beginning of this journey.

Soon Tim and I found a good rapport. I trusted him. Or should I say Manon trusted him. Part of the problem, I realized, is that Manon did not trust anyone at all, much less any man. She did not believe in God, either, or Tim, as director felt all too God-like. Manon was going to resist and fight every inch of the way. Tim wanted me to stay with that, don't let that go. It drove the movie. Channel it in the right moment. We were on the same page.

Then we had to film the first scene where my screen mother, Sharon-Rosette, has started hooking regularly. They've moved into a brothel and Manon is surrounded by the evening drove of clients and sex and drug abuse going on around her. It's a long scene where I must move through several rooms and floors, followed by a boom and two handheld cameras surrounding me, interrupted by numerous disturbing scenes distracting me. Tight quarters. Not a lot of dialogue, most of it dealing with close-ups and subtle feelings. It took hours to film. It culminates with Manon confronting her mother, who is high on opium, just been with a client, is naked from the waist up, smoking a cigarette, laughing with another man. It was far more difficult for me than in the numerous readings, or even what I thought would happen. There was more of a sensation that all hope was lost. For the first time in Manon's consciousness. This was not her mother anymore.

Sharon played it with her usual precision and disengagement. She did not see Manon as her daughter but as a potential co-worker, moneymaker. The subject is broached for the first time between the two of them.

Our rehearsals did not in any way predict my inner revulsion to the extent that I felt once I heard *action*. Not anger, exactly. More like I was going to puke. I stumbled on the first two takes, but on the third take I was in full force. Our interaction, not argument, hazy dialogue of realization, the prolonged scene wore on me, revolting me, culminated with me barfing all over the floor. All over Sharon's shoes. She rolled with it immediately. Sharon did not miss a beat. Tim kept shooting. Sharon showed no motherly impulse whatsoever. She was nonplussed, annoyed, with this young girl. The men in the scene laughed in drunken derision. They went with the scene better than I could react to. But I bore down and heard Rosette demand that I clean up my puke. It turned into a pathetic dawning of reality. This was more real than anything I had ever experienced in my entire life. I had never felt so terrible, so awful about who I was.

Cut.

Everyone applauded on set. Tim was happy. Sharon hardly said a word and was trying to shake the puke off her shoes. "That's a first," is all she could say as she got up with her assistant trying to use a towel. Estelle used another towel to wipe my mouth and the front of my ratty dress.

Tim said, "I hope it looks good because we won't be able to do that again."

Not one person asked me if I was all right.

I went back to my trailer and told Estelle to leave me alone. At first I wanted to cry. As I lay there staring up at the metal ceiling, I turned and took a drink of water from my glass. Then I smiled.   I knew that I had nailed it.

Tim never let me see the dailies. In fact, he never
mentioned them. This time he asked me to come over
to a viewing tent after our boxed dinner. I was getting
ready, putting on my warm coat and hat when Ashley
Judd appeared at my trailer door. She asked me if she
could walk over with me. She had just arrived, had
missed the first two weeks on another job. Her scenes
were not up yet, and she did not have a big role as it was.
It was an important role, though. Especially for Manon.
"How's it going?" She asked.
"Okay, a rough start."
"I heard," Ashley smiled, put her arm around me. Then
she continued, "You sure? I heard that today was
intense. You puked or something."
"All over Sharon." I smiled back.
We laughed softly.
"Mind if I sit in on this? Would it bother you?"
"If Tim doesn't mind. I don't always know the rules, you
know."
She smiled and hugged me tight. It was the first sign of
affection I had received during this ordeal. It dawned on
me. She was in character, too. Like everyone walking
around here. The realization freaked me out.
Ashley held my hand during the several angles and clips
of the one scene. Tim did not show me any other scenes
I'd done thus far. And there were plenty. Sharon sat on
the other side of the room. She barely acknowledged me,
giving me a kiss on the cheek when we practically
bumped into each other when we arrived. She looked

like Sharon, not Rosette. I wanted to run and hug her and talk and talk and spill my guts out to her. Her body language almost acknowledged me, demanding that I keep my distance.

It was tough for me to watch.   Nothing like any screen test or anything I'd ever seen of myself. That girl in those black and white grainy shots, with the frightening visions of raw sex and people shooting up and the raucous group orgy scenes, switching back and forth to closeups of me transfixed. Manon is in full view. Disturbing. Vulnerable and naked within. I was frightened for her.

When I saw the first view of Manon throwing up, it was a handheld closeup. The cameraman went with it like it was rehearsed over and over. It hadn't been, of course, but it seemed so revoltingly natural. I wondered how an actress could store up so much puke and not look fake. Then the other handheld view. Then the overhead view. Over and over. Tim and Mike, the cinematographer, were talking intently. Seriously about every detail. "Well, thank the good Lord, this is perfect. We don't need you to puke again," Tim finally said.

Sharon spoke up, "I like the first view best."

Tim and Mike agreed.   That was that.

Ashley walked me to my car. Estelle was waiting in the driver's seat. Ashley complimented me, looking forward to our two scenes. She was kind. I needed her.

What bothered me most of all, though, was her affection real? This is how Manon would feel about her. Was Ashley just a circus performer. A trapeze artist, recruiting me for the road? Or did she really care about Stephanie at all?

Mom, Jennifer, was back. We were jumping right into filming several scenes with her and me at the orphanage. Or in town, in the desolation of a bombed-out existence. It snowed hard once, painting our outdoor sets a bleak washed out white. Being in these countless scenes, and numerous takes, day after day, with this woman, this someone I did not really know, this hardcore nun, bitten by the stark reality surrounding her. The lives and deaths of children she was trying to save. Manon rapidly became her strongest ally and assistant. Manon was good with the kids. She was resourceful. She worked tirelessly.

But Manon did not believe in the God that Mother Marianne drew her faith from. Manon resented any God that would do this to her world, her country, her mother, her lost father and brother, to these kids. She admired and respected Marianne. She helped her with every ounce of energy she could give. That is until Marianne began to proselytize. Urging, insisting, that Manon join the order. Take the vows. Become as her.

Mom was beyond believable. I never once thought I was interacting with my real mother. That person that lived in Santa Fe was nonexistent. She was a painter. This was an altogether different human being. Someone other than the person of hundreds of readings we had done together. Certainly not the lady whom I had skied with or gone horseback riding with. I had never known a nun. I had never met anyone from this era, during this time in history. She was as foreign as a French religious in 1919. I admired her. I did not want to become her. I slowly began to hate her as much as Rosette.

During our filming, it was tough for Tim to change up the timeframe and sequencing of scenes. He steered clear of it as much as possible. He knew that I was not seasoned enough or experienced enough, or experienced at all, to be able to shift that quickly. My relationship with both Rosette, and especially Marianne, were evolutionary and needed to be linear. A progressive process of awareness and adaptation and eventual relinquishment.

The problem with Sister Marianne is that she was perfect. Where Rosette was now in the depths of hell, Marianne was pristine. The allure of her cage was clean and simple. Void of human want or will or desire. A vessel of heaven. Suffering was merely the ticket to another afterlife.

Manon wanted none of it. She did not want an afterlife, she wanted life now. And not the life of the hell her mother offered.

The scenes with Manon and Marianne were the most important of my life, my life as Stephanie. This was the woman that I wanted to be growing up. Jennifer Braxton, Oscar Winner, star in recluse. I was now acting with her. Yet it never once felt like acting, if I had any understanding of acting at all. She was not acting, it seemed to me. I loved this young woman, this person of vows and celibacy and rosaries, and a determined vision of some far off heaven. I once wanted to be this person. Not anymore. I needed to run.

When Dad and Julian arrived, it seemed too surreal. It shook me up that there was a reality from where I had originated. I understood Sharon and Jennifer's need for distance. I hugged Dad and Julian, happy to see them, but I didn't want much more than that. Mom would be my mom, ever so briefly, but it seemed just as surreal. She wasn't really being Mom after that first gathering. We never ate as a family the entire time. So very strange. Sharon never showed her face. It shocked me.

I never got to see them on set for their filming. I was discouraged from being there or was on a different lot altogether. Eventually I learned and saw Julian's hair was cut like a bad buzz cut. He wore a ragged wool corporal hat. He was blind in black glasses from the era. He smoked hand-rolled cigarettes, over and over, until they were finished with each take. He walked around like that, in costume, the entire time he was here. He banged out various songs on a 'shitty' upright piano, humming them for me later in the day. Three cameras, one right on top of his hands. One of the actresses flirted with him on stage and off.   Her name was Serena. I never found out where all of that ended. Dad was in good form. He laughed about walking with rocks in his shoes that were far too big for his feet, falling dead on the street. Hardly anyone in the scene noticing. His hat falling off. His ratty suit coat getting dirty and the costume people rushing to get him ready for the next take. Oddly, I think, that I was in that scene and they'd splice-in his quick appearance much later in editing. I ate with them two times, all provided by the studio. We never went out. Then they were gone. Terrible, I thought, that they flew all this way for that? And Mom, where was she? I don't even know if she stayed with

Dad or not. Dad said he slept alone the first night, but I have no idea the next two nights. Julian was having fun. That was a good thing. He loved meeting everyone, the extras, the young girls playing prostitutes or nuns. I couldn't wait to talk with him when this was all done.

CHAPTER SIXTEEN

A man can love two women, but only until one of them understands what's going on. Colette

Julian

Serena was twenty-two. She was studying drama at Center Univisitaire in Calais. She was in the graduate program, and this film was the first American film she had been in. Serena had short black hair, black eyes, slender, almost petite features. I fell in love with her immediately. She was eight years older than me, so I had no idea why we hit it off or what she saw in me. She knew nothing about music except a few of the French bands she liked.

Telling her the truth about my age, fourteen, was painful. She laughed; she didn't care. We went out to eat several times in Amiens. Once at a very fancy restaurant. She insisted on splitting the bill, which bothered me a lot because it was my understanding that this was very rude in France. She shook her head *no*. It was no big deal, common practice among the students. She paid half. Mom and Dad were probably spending time together - secretly for some reason or getting off on the whole clandestine thing – which was fine with me. Serena was familiar with the city, showing me around town. We'd go in shops and bookstores. It was cold outside, so we'd sit in a warm corner, drinking drink coffee - she drank tea - for hours. Once we drank wine and ate cheese and bread as our meal. I got drunk easily. My age was not an issue anywhere, or with her as far as I could tell. She had a boyfriend in school, who was two years older than she was. I had a girlfriend. We talked about that occasionally. Age differences. He sounded like a cool guy, potentially a very good actor. She liked Melanie, interested in the stories I told about her. Serena asked several questions. She wasn't all that impressed with

Retro Sky. It didn't register with her as anything other than a few guys clowning around on instruments. Even when I told her about playing live in front of hundreds of people, she rolled her eyes, like no big deal. That made me love her more.

We became very physical almost immediately. But she was firm about not making love. We'd go to a cramped flat that she was sharing, where she gave me a hand job once and I made her cum, I think, with my finger. All very fun and exciting. Her body was so different from Melanie's, I hated to compare, but it was my first time to explore someone different. Her thinness, her smallness. Her experience. Her maturity. She made me feel much older than I was. I told her once that she was breaking the law in American because of my age. She yawned then kissed me lightly on the cheek.

Then I had to go. Depart for home. Back to America. I asked for her address. She had a school email address, that I was not at all familiar with using. I gave her my actual address and home number. She kissed me goodbye with a nice smile. She said something terribly long in French and kissed me again ever so sweetly. I was distressingly sad. I had the distinct feeling she had had many of these quick encounters. That bothered me. I would learn to use email.

A sliver of guilt remained under my skin when we returned to Santa Fe. I thought only about Serena during the entire flight, dreading to see Melanie. Afraid that she'd see right through me. I saw Mel at school, who was excited to see me. Her sweater engulfed me.

Purple lipstick smack on target at my locker, kissing me in an almost violent attack. She wanted to know every detail of lights and cameras and movie stars and what was Tim like and Sharon and my mom and how funny I looked with my haircut. Over and over, she took off my winter cap, putting it back on, repeatedly, laughing. And asking the same questions all over again. What was it like!? I answered the best I could. Enjoying the stories of being the wounded veteran, so terribly young and blind, surrounded by prostitutes and whiskey. And I smoked cigarettes one take after another. I played the piano too well the first time. Tim wanted me to sound 'clunky.' I did my best to sound worse. He liked it. She never asked about anything else. If I met anyone on the set. Those imaginary questions that haunted me on the flight. She was happy as can be that I was back. I took a deep breath and relaxed.

Frankie and I talked for a long time over at the studio. He was always skirting around a C average, usually slipping below. He had gotten in trouble with his English teacher for cheating. He copied his girlfriend's homework and got caught. He was scared that my dad would find out. He hated school, that was that. I tried to tell him that he only had one year to go. Senior year was the easiest. Pull it together.

I walked away knowing that he was also smoking a lot more pot. Cigarettes all the time. His girlfriend was a stoner. Mom and Dad, even I, thought that his artwork, *Kid*, would help him turn it around. I wasn't sure if I should start looking for another guitarist, cut him loose. Or wait it out. Or just figure out how we'd get by with four members. I liked the last option most of all unless Frankie turned one way or the other. Just make up your mind.

About a week later, Frankie showed up to a rehearsal clean shaven. Clean clothes. Not so subtly showing off a new backpack with his schoolbooks and supplies. Like he was in kindergarten. He had a cough but was bright-eyed. He even had an idea for a song. It was okay. Nothing special. We all worked our way, our instruments, into the various chord progressions. Melanie sang it after Frankie mouthed the words. It was a terribly depressing song. About a fight with his mother, we could tell. I humbly volunteered a few lyric changes, so we had the right meter, a better rhyming scheme. I was trying hard to keep him engaged. He went along with it, asking if he could try singing back-up to Melanie. A mother-son kind of trade off, I assumed. We went through it ten or twelve times. It took up most of our afternoon. Stu and Frankie are in the same grade, and Stuart knew Frankie's girlfriend better than any of us. After about the ninth take, Stu asked Frankie if this song was really about a mother, or if it was about a girlfriend. It was sounding like the same person to Stu. Frankie just said, *take your pick*. I switched my electric piano settings to an organ sound, like in a cathedral. Jesus, the song was so incredibly sad. We now had "Dirge for Daddy" and this one, without a title, originating from Frankie in one form or another. Frankie was proud of himself. I liked his singing, at least for this song. Almost a Johnny Cash gruffness. He decided on titling it "I'm Gone, Too Far Gone." We'd sing it on

Friday at Jimmy's. I swear Melanie had a tear in her eye, looking at Frankie, trading lines, harmonizing the best she could with his crude voice. Frankie strumming chords on his electric guitar, holding the sound changes in tremolo. It was the only song that would get a standing ovation before it was finished that first night we played it. I got the sense that just about everyone in that place could relate. I had to find a way to keep Frankie in the band and not disappear on us. Music was working.

I asked the librarian to help me with the internet and with sending an email. She had to set me up with my own email address, teaching me about logging-on, a password. I wrote it all down carefully. Then I wrote a long note to Serena. I thanked her for everything in France. I enjoyed our time together. It was the best time of my life. She is amazing. That kind of thing. I told her that I loved her, and it sounded right out of "Isis." I could hear it. Damn, I realized, that was sung directly to Melanie.

I sat in front of the blank screen for nearly fifteen minutes, hoping she would respond. It would be nearing 9:00 pm her time. Then presto, response. My heart jumped. My first email. And from Serena.

She wrote a long paragraph in French, and I tried desperately to decipher it. It was listing all the fun things we did and where we went. Then she switched to English, as she was being funny. Talking about me being a cowboy again, singing with my guitar in the mountain prairie. Yodeling. Sweeping my beautiful girlfriend off her feet, riding into the sunset. I smiled the whole time reading it. She then signed-off, *je t'aime mon doux ami, Serena*. I re-read it a thousand times.

Dad took me to Melanie's apartment on his way to afternoon mass. He had slept-in, leaving Louise on her own with her friends. He was looking rough around the edges. Tired. I knew that he went on the road to Las Cruces with the basketball team where they won a tight one, but he didn't get home until 1:00 am.
Mel was playing Fleetwood Mac, doing her Stevie Nicks thing with a long black scarf. Hardly anything else on. We went right to bed. I let loose with all my pent-up urges and desires. I wouldn't say that I fantasized about Serena. That's too far. Serena was certainly crossing my mind. I let her image stay once or twice. Her smile, mostly. Not letting go. I came hard. So did Melanie. I tried to remember what it was like when Serena came on my finger. It was different. They were two very different women. I lay there with Melanie curled on my chest, trying to figure out how two women could be so different in personality, in sexuality. Sexuality, mostly. That is what I found most fascinating.
I turned and looked into Melanie's translucent blue eyes. I stroked her blond hair, seemingly redder once again in the sunlight. She grinned, hugged me. We held each other tight, naked. Tired. I stroked her butt, which I loved so very much. It felt like being home.

Danny

Karen showed up unexpectedly. Without an appointment. It was late on Friday. Cheryl showed her in once I got off the phone. She had on a business suit, as a real estate broker, an important person in the growing city. She kept in marvelous shape. She wore a pensive smile, almost as perfectly placed as her attire. She didn't ask any questions about me, diving into Samantha and her fighting with her again. I dreaded the conversation. Counseling had gone well until Karen broke down a few weeks ago and flirted with a couple selling a house. She liked threesomes. Karen was blunt about it. She liked her bisexuality. Again blunt. She didn't like the exclusive, snippy way of many self-indulged lesbian couples. She was on a tirade. It was only flirting she insisted to Sam and the counselor. Sort of. Making out. With both the husband and the wife. Karen was being honest in therapy and Sam went ballistic. Karen felt ganged-up on by the therapist anyway, even before this happened.

I sat quietly, shifting in my seat. Looking at the clock. School was going to end, and I needed to get out of the office into the hallways.

Karen saw my anxious look and stopped.

"Anyway, Danny. I know it's a long shot. I had to talk with you. I needed to see you. I have a room. I want to see you. No strings attached. I've never been able to get over our time together. We always flirted – I wanted to interrupt and say *she* always *flirted* – and, I have to say, I really want you." Pause. "To come over. Come see me. Just come." She smiled in that wily, unfettered, ever tempting demur way. She drove me crazy when she acted that way.

I shook my head. I stared at her lips. The intensity of her mouth. I knew how she could use that mouth of hers and she was advertising like a neon sign. I looked at her and I would lie if I said that I wasn't tempted. I knew she could be amazing, wild. I just couldn't do it. "Well, I'm in 303 at the Renaissance. I'll be there all weekend. Maybe longer. We can have a great time. Promise."

She got up and left, being all pleasant with Cheryl. Karen then turned and waved as she departed the building. I watched her walk, her sway from behind. She knew I'd be watching out the window. My heart raced.

I don't know how I got through the weekend. Friday night was unbearable. Julian was playing with Retro. Louise was out. I watched *Goodfellas* again, lost in the tough world of being *made*, the insanity of Joe Pesci, the narration of cocaine- infused Ray Liotta, marveling at DeNiro's mastery. A masculine world of not giving a fuck. The severe violence throughout stoking my adrenaline. I sipped whiskey which was not the best idea at all. Every ounce of energy inside of me was fighting to keep me chained to the couch, keeping me from driving over to the Renaissance. I knew beyond a doubt that Karen was waiting for me. Somehow I made it without going over there. Like fighting withdrawal symptoms. Saturday arrived and I was fine. The trip with the basketball team, sitting on the bus with Billy was all that I needed. He even allowed me to sit on the bench next to him, with the team. I slipped into coaching mode, teaching the guys at timeouts, that kind of thing. Billy only smiled. And we won. A close one, but we won.

On Sunday, after a rough night of hardly sleeping, I dropped off Julian at Melanie's fully suspecting what was going to happen with those two. I hoped repeatedly that they were being careful. All of which made my own internal struggle worse. I drove by the Renaissance, circling the block. Twice. Then I waved goodbye and headed home to go back to bed. I wasn't going to do it. I never did make it to church.

CHAPTER SEVENTEEN

That's a wrap.

Jennifer

Fifteen days, fourteen hours each. Demanding as hell. Grueling. I was in twelve of those days, Sharon was in eleven. Steph was in all of them. I broke down and approached Estelle and asked her how Stephanie was getting along. Estelle pulled me to an even more remote place, giving me a rundown on their schedule, the diet Steph was keeping, her sleep, general emotional state. "She's one tough little shit, your girl." Estelle said. "I know." I replied and thanked her for everything. We were all buckled in for the final stretch.

As expected, Sharon and I were like lightning bolts on screen. We were fighting over the destiny of her child, we got that. It was evident in the written script. What was not evident on paper was the sheer primitive law of the jungle. The claws were out, the fangs exposed. She would tear into me with her explosions. I would counter with all the righteous indignation I could find. To have an exhausted prostitute, strung out on just about everything, barely alive at thirty-something, threatening to kill a seemingly innocent thief – me - of her flesh and blood; while I reminded that woman that all hell awaited her daughter Manon if I did not save her. All of which added up to a raging fire. The sets ignited in reserved temper, sometimes burning down in utter destruction. That was all safe enough as far as movies go. Sharon had resurrected me, single handedly. What was yet to unfold was the appearance of Manon. Three scenes. All of which would require mental health professionals, even an ambulance if necessary. Hyperbole, I am certain. Yet not far from the truth. The first of the scenes was at the brothel. Mother Superior going to the house of ill repute to literally take Manon away. It was ugly, it was contentious, physically challenging, and certainly emotionally debilitating. Manon stood up to her mother in ferocious courage. I stood there as the camera rolled, the lights boring down on us, observing my daughter rip Sharon to pieces. They fought, they scratched and clawed, even punched each other, it was practically carnage. Tim could only stand to do two takes. Make up and costumes looked helpless to put humpty-dumpty back together again. I took Manon off into the night. Victorious Mother Marianne.

Scene two. At the central convent structure of the orphanage. It was the exact same scene that had been disastrously rehearsed on day one when Sharon had slapped Manon, drawing blood on her cheek. That was nothing it turned out. The argument was prolonged. The same spitting, the same punch, the same name calling. It was the same until Steph stood up, blood dripping from her lip. Her eye swollen. Steph hugged Sharon and wept. Except it was Manon hugging Marian. "I tried to love you, Mom. I really did. But I can't." and Steph ran away, outside the door into the snow. The camera followed her. Steph ran and ran, the snow blinding her from our vision. Completely unrehearsed. Tim did not have the courage to ask for another take. Sharon was out of character. Her final emotional. She was done. She started crying.

The circus. A colorful tent appeared in the field. Luckily it did not snow those days. Horses were everywhere. Actors dressed in colorful garb. Animals of all sorts. Even three elephants and a giraffe. Tim played the circus ringmaster with incredible gusto. Vinny hammed it up as a barker. Scotty running around in his ragged garb, delighted to be at the circus. A big band played. There were five more scenes to film. Ashley was in two of them, the trapeze artist, urging Manon to join them. She would make her a star, center stage. Two others were with Robin Wright, the nun who secretly helped Manon get away. I was in the final scene when she escaped the convent, running away for good. The final look from me to her, from her to me, waving goodbye. Manon had made her final bitter choice.

"It's a wrap!," Tim hollered.

Everyone clamored and clapped. Wine broke out. Food appeared. A party was planned.

I could not find Stephanie. I looked everywhere, realizing she was probably back in her trailer. I grabbed a bottle and practically sprinted to her location. Estelle was sitting in a chair, wrapped in a blanket, sipping wine.

"Not sure you want to go in there," Estelle said to me.

I paused for an explanation. She shrugged her shoulders motioning me to go ahead.

Stephanie was sprawled out on a recliner. She was smoking a cigarette. She looked at me and did not react.

"You think Dad will suspend me again?" She asked, grinning under her exhale.

I hugged her tightly, tears running down my cheeks. She hugged me back, heaving in her chest, letting the pent-up emotion finally flow. I was bent over her for so long my back was hurting. I found two plastic cups, poured us wine, and pulled up a chair.

"Give me one of those," I asked her.

She pushed the pack my way. I took a Marlboro and lit it up. We said, "Cheers."

Then the door opened.

"What the fuck, girls!" Sharon exclaimed. "Partying without me. Give me some." She found another cup and I poured her some wine. She lit up one of her own French Galois's, setting down the pack in case we wanted one.

Steph stood up. They looked at each other very carefully. It was then I noticed how beat up Stephanie was. Make-up on two or three facial bruises. Sharon pointed to two of her own. They laughed and hugged again.

"Let's get high," Steph said.

I about spit up.

I stated firmly, "No Way!"

Sharon looked at me, shaking her head with a big smile, overruling me. Sharon stuck her head out and asked Estelle if she could get us a joint. Sounded favorable from what I could gather. I decided not to cause a scene. We were already telling stories, regaling in that scene or another, when Estelle showed up with a bong and a baggy and two more bottles of wine. She then left, saying, *be careful it's powerful stuff they told me.* Steph did not hesitate. She poured some wine in the cylinder, sprinkled the ground plant into the bowl, lit a match and inhaled deeply. Her exhale was long and cloudy. She handed it to me. Was I her mother or a nun or did I have any say in this at all? I surrendered and took a long drag. Sharon hogged the bong for a full bowl of her own. She was moving fast in full force celebration.

"Steph," I said, "I am so proud of you. I never was sure what I should do. I am your mother, and it was tearing me apart watching you go through this."

"I hated you for it. I suppose that's the point, huh?"

Sharon chimed in, "Ah, Jesus, it's done. You were fabulous. You kicked the shit out of me. I've had a long career already. This one wore me out. You took me by surprise. But I have to say, after that first day, when I smacked you, I knew we were in for one hell of a ride." She took another drag off her cigarette, offering me one. I was pouring more wine. Steph was hugging the bong. Of course, it bothered me, but I decided to let it go for now.

"I suppose I should apologize or something like that," Steph was saying to Sharon, choking on her exhale.
"Fuck, no way."
We laughed.
"The press will have a field day with this one. Not very often you see a little kid, fourteen going on gold glove forty, going toe to toe in an honest to god catfight between mother and daughter." Sharon pried the bong away.
"I can't wait to see this thing when it's done. I never say that. Usually, I'm ready to put it to rest. I gotta see you kid." Sharon added.
"You don't have to call me kid anymore," Steph said.
"Guess you're right." She answered lighting the bong.
I looked at Steph through my stoned eyelids. It all hit me fast and hard. I was enjoying the buzz and flavor of the French cigarette and wine.
Tim and Vinny came in. Like a whirlwind. It startled me.
"What the hell?" Vinny said. "Why weren't we invited?"
They didn't even seem taken aback by my very stoned daughter.
Tim grabbed the bong and filled it. "I gotta say, Steph, I wasn't sure we'd get here. You are one amazing actresses."
"You mean like my mom?" She said, slurring her words.
"Not at all. Only you could play that role. I mean that."
She smiled. We all smiled.
"Steph, we will need to talk tomorrow. Or before you leave. I have to go to New York. I'm meeting Shelly there. I want to talk about press releases, promotions,

that kind of thing."

"Can we leave her out of it?" I asked.

"Really?" Steph asked, a bit hurt, or curious.

"What do you all think?" He asked.

Sharon and I waited on Steph. "Honestly?" Stephanie asked.

"Yeah, tell me." Tim replied.

"I'd like to do the big European tour. I know you are premiering in June at Cabourg, then in Moscow at the festival in June. You're targeting a European audience first; isn't that the plan?"

"Risky, but yes." He replied.

"The two of you can do the American stuff in between." She was talking about Sharon and me. Both of us shied away from that kind of thing.

Tim was contemplating it hard or was already too stoned to answer. I was too stoned to offer an answer. Sharon got up and walked around, taking a deep breath. "Let's wait till we see what we have in editing. That okay?" She looked right at Steph. Then at Tim. Then at me.

Tim agreed. I agreed.

Steph smiled with rapidly messed up features of the pot. She was way too high.

"Let's join the party," Vinny said.

We bundled up again, Steph changing into the warmest clothes we could find. She grabbed her wine as we moved out into the cold, late afternoon.

Everyone stopped and gave a roaring ovation and applause as our entourage approached the festivities. They were relieved and glad, I could sense, that we joined them. Me and Sharon stuck close, letting Steph soak up the adulation. She had been a recluse for so very long. Away from human touch, human anything. She was high, and drunk, laughing with everyone. I had not seen her smile in months. Ashley had to keep her from falling a few times. It was funny to witness. As her mother, well, I had mixed emotions, but to hell with it. She earned her adulthood the toughest way I could imagine.

Then, in what I thought was totally out of character, Sharon made an impromptu speech. She thanked everyone for the success of the film. She thanked Tim especially. She thanked me by name. She singled out Ashley and Robin, thanking them for squeezing in these appearances in this god forsaken weather. Everyone applauded.

Then she grabbed Stephanie and kissed her on the lips. She bragged about how Steph shocked her, shocked her mother, shocked Tim, shocked us all. They didn't have to hold her hand, even though Estelle did. Everyone laughed. Sharon made a joke about going fifteen rounds with Steph and it was a split decision. Everyone booed good naturedly. "Okay," she said, "Steph knocked me out fair and square."   Steph was crying through her smiles. She was so messed up she tried to talk but couldn't. Everyone applauded again. *Cheers* went up several times.

The plane ride. Steph could easily choose any seat in the cabin. To herself. Instead, she curled up close to me, snuggling under a blanket. I had my little girl back. I was about to tell her that she wouldn't be able to smoke and drink and smoke pot when we got back. She said *I know* even before I finished my sentence. Our stop in New York customs took longer than usual. The image of the World Trade Center stirred both of us.

"What do you think it means?" Steph asked in a sleepy way.

"I have no idea. We can't worry about it."

"I know. Just in my head, I guess."

"Me too. I'm with you. I understand." I assured her.

A steward brought us a couple of magazines, "Thought you'd like to see these," he said to us. "Welcome back to America."

The first was *Variety.*

Jennifer Braxton is back. Directed by: Tim Prescott. Cinematography by: Michael Chapman. Estimated Budget: $120,000,000. Starring: Sharon Preston as Madame Rosette, Jennifer Braxton as Mother Marianne, Stephanie Tomasetti as Manon. Guest appearances by Tim Prescott, Ashley Judd, Robin Wright, and Vincent Calibrasella. Release date: June 7-10 Cabourg Film Festival. June 15-17 Moscow Film Festival. July 3-7 The Old Chicago Theater.

With this powerhouse cast it's impossible to speculate anything but success. The question mark is the new and unheard-of actress, fourteen-year-old Stephanie Tomasetti. Can she hold her own with these heavy hitters? Word is that this grim, dark picture, shot in black and white, will be tough to swallow. An 'art picture' depicting the immediacy of post WWI France, and all the dire circumstances following the Great War.

Look out. We saw this in Hull House. We saw it Rio del Norte. Everyone is chomping at the bit. Why the delay of releasing this film in America? Why such a large distribution in Europe? Maybe the existentialism of the time, of choices made, will resonate better over there. Americans usually don't like dark movies. We shall see. The same thing was written in *Moviemag*. Standard release, but by whom. Neither mentioned a connection between Steph and me. That would happen soon enough.   Stephanie read it over and over. In *Moviemag*, she saw the photo of me and Sharon from way back in *Hull House*. A caption of my Oscar winning speech. Innocuous thus far.

Julian, Danny, Louise and James had the welcome mat out. They even had a Welcome Home sign over the kitchen entry. James was cooking his famous barbecue. It was a festive celebration.   Steph answered each one of Louise's million questions. I even had some of the pictures Sharon had given me of the Italy trip that Scotty had taken. Lots to talk about. Julian filled us in on the status of Retro. We'd plan on going to see them this coming Friday.

After dinner, Danny and I slipped into our bedroom. We sipped a gin and tonic made over dinner. He hugged me repeatedly. He hesitated, and I knew something was up. Karen had called. Twice. She was separated from Sam again. She was over at the Renaissance as far as he knew. She had dropped by the school office to invite me over. To *talk.* He quoted her with a sheepish grin.

"So, did you go over and talk with Karen?" I asked, getting closer to him, putting my arms around his neck. Staring right into his eyes.

"No. But honestly, Jennifer, it was tough. She was throwing herself at me."

"Like she always has, Danny." I kissed him on the cheek. "Like she always has."

"I know. Just thought I'd let you know."

"Glad you did." I kissed him again then went over and pulled the covers back on the bed. I removed my earrings.

"I missed you Danny. It's a long time to be away. I get it. I'm very grateful you came all the way over to do those scenes. It meant a lot."

"How many guys hit on you over there?" He asked almost afraid to bring it up.

"Way too many." I laughed. "Not one. I guess I'm losing my good looks. No one seemed interested in this has-been." I went to the bathroom and shut the door. Danny had stripped down to his tee-shirt and shorts, climbing into the warm bed ahead of me. I had on my warm flannels. We made love slowly and quietly until we both fell asleep.

Stephanie

I didn't go to school the next day. I gave all my files to Dad, tons of homework, stacked by subject matter, completed with Estelle's help. He'll give it to all the teachers. He'd find out what I needed to do for re-entry. Probably a lot of tests to take.

I went down to James's place and drank tea and *smoked pipe* for nearly three hours. We laughed and told stories. Not true: I told stories, he laughed and smiled. He fed me lunch, egg salad with celery on his homemade bread and lintel soup. With corn chips. His fireplace blazing, I'd get up from time to time and put on another log. He walked with me around the property, through the snow. It was sunny outside, glorious. Hawks flew overhead, screeching. He told me that they were calling me. He said stuff like that all the time. I held onto his arm the entire time, clinging to his big rawhide coat. He kissed me on the forehead when we got back to my house. No one was around. I lay in my bed and fell asleep again. I was still exhausted, still suffering jet lag; fatigued.

The next day, only a few people asked where I was. Mostly teachers. News had not surfaced yet. I was glad. I arranged to make up my exams. It was like I hadn't skipped a beat around there. Dad called me to his office. I got out of fifth period gym class.

"Gene called. Here's a number for you to call to talk with Brett Hodges, the director of *Sound of Music*. He wants you to play Maria." Dad said matter of fact. Dad's office area was packed with a lot going on. He was in a hurry.

"Wow," I replied, not ready for this yet.

"Oh, and you should call Phil, in L.A., before you call Brett. He's your agent, you know."

I knew. I forgot. He hugged me as I left. He then escorted a kid with a bloody nose towards the nurse's station. Dad looked like he was out for bear.

I asked Cheryl, who looked busy, if I could use a phone. She said sure, but that I better go to the counseling office.

Mrs. Carmichael was kind to me, but busy in her own way. She moved me to the conference room and gave me the code for long distance calls. She'd never do that with most students, I thought to myself.

Phil was happy as can be. He had heard good things, he said. He said I was remarkable. Tim told him. Sharon told him. Everyone told him. He'd get back with me about promotions. *What's up?* He finally asked.

I told him about *The Sound of Music*. Rehearsals started on Monday. He laughed, making a joke about Mom. I didn't pay attention. Then he made a crack about how much school I had already missed and was going to miss. I hadn't thought of that. He had to go, get off the phone. Someone had arrived. *Have fun*, he'd get back with me.

Brett was excited that I called. He wanted to make sure I was in on this. He wanted me as Maria very badly. I said *sure,* I told him, regarding my desire to take on the main part. Not all that excited, I truthfully told myself, I'd get there eventually. He took me for my word and told me he'd see me Monday at 1:00 for readings. Swing by and get everything I needed from Omaha at her desk. Full scale rehearsal would start Tuesday at 9:00 am. *What was I going to do about school* I asked him? He said I should talk it over with my parents. They'll excuse all the days I'd be gone. I guess he hadn't figured that I had already missed months of school.

I looked through my school locker and found the old script for *The Sound of Music* and went to the library. I ditched my last two classes. Sitting, reading Maria's parts. Highlighting them in pink, purple for the song lyrics. My mind was resisting this woman. She was way too goody-goody, and all the songs overwhelmed me. The vast amount of memorizing.

I had to change my attitude most of all. And quickly. I made the walk over to Mom's gallery. I found her talking with a customer, looking up at one of the few native works that remained in the Gallery. Mom, and James for that matter, were having a tough time finding an 'authentic' Indian voice these days. Pop art was the thing, she'd complain. She looked gorgeous in her comfortable clothes, her native look.   She was back to normal. No more sister whoever she was over in France. We went to her office, and I explained my predicament.

"Steph, you knew all this. Why is it a surprise?"

"I don't know. The reality of it, I guess. Next Monday already." I mumbled.

"Dad and I are fully aware. Don't worry about school. You'll be fine.   We can hire another tutor through the Actors Guild if you want. I have no worries about you."

"What about Maria?" I motioned at the script.

She laughed. "Well, she's wanting to be a nun. You'll be fine after all that you've been though." The look of humor in Mom's eyes was telling, since she had just played a nun, wanting my character to become a nun.

"Oh lord. Not sure of that. And all the singing."

"Welcome to dinner theater, dear."

"And my age? I'm fourteen? Maria is twenty-two, I think." I said.

"Steph, you look twenty-two with make-up. I've seen you dressed-up, mature. And after what you just accomplished. No worry."

I thought that one over. After this film I felt like I was thirty. I'd aged twenty years.

"Will you read with me this weekend?" I asked her.

"Sure. You know I will."

I relaxed a little bit.

"Steph, look at me." I looked at Mom and she went on, "Maria is in you. You will find her soon enough. Relax. Have fun with her. She will love you. This is a love story. A musical to sing and dance and enjoy. Maria loves you."

"She loves everyone." I said sarcastically.

"You'll have to bring something unique to her. You're so young, Steph. You really are innocent inside. Maria will want to celebrate your innocence. You don't have to be Manon anymore. She's gone. She went to the circus. She made a choice. If you insist on carrying this on, remember, you're in the circus now. Performing in the big top. A trapeze artist."

I smiled and hugged my mom. Here she was bouncing back with ease. Like her comeback was nothing. Come and gone. And I thought about Sharon. In a comedy with Woody Allen one week, then in a harrowing depressing drama with me the next. She's such a pro, she's probably already onto the next script. I still have bodily aches, literally, not to mention the emotional pains of it all.

Retro Sky looked and sounded even better than I remembered. In a few months of playing at live venues, they were more at ease, having more fun. Even clowning around in that dingy bar. Julian had that close cropped hair cut, sometimes putting on his French cloth cap from the set in Amiens, wearing those dated, wraparound sunglasses. Like he was blind. Frankie was cleaned-up, unshaven for only a day, a smile on his face from time to time. Stu, the withdrawn, steady guy, always focused on Alo's beat. A girl from school that I wasn't sure that I knew, and her family sat up front and Stu kept saying something to them between songs. Melanie was playing from the keyboard more often than I remembered, rarely standing. I wondered about Julian switching from instrument to instrument, changing singers and arrangements so often, always trying new sounds. New ideas.

Plus, I didn't recognize half the songs. They were playing their own music. I liked it. It took some getting used to. A nice variety, almost always catchy. People would get up and dance. I got up and danced with Dad and Mom. Fun stuff. Then switching abruptly to a few very serious songs. One almost made me cry as Melanie and Frankie sang together. I had never heard Frank sing before. Julian and Mel bantered a lot. They teased each other. They flirted. They acted like no one was around. The crowd ate it up. I was happy for them. Which made me wonder about my own life. I had danced with that guy in Paris, which lit a great deal of curiosity inside of me. I was ready to be more serious with guys. Not the junior high thing. Like my sexuality was trying to catch-up with the other maturation going on within me.

I went to school early Monday going around to my teachers to speak with them about my rehearsals at Eagle's Nest. They were all surprised, excited, encouraging. Most had graded all my work, pleased with what I had turned in. Test times could be arranged whenever I could get in. No worries with time off. Being the principal's daughter, a good student, they joked about it all.   Again, no mention about a movie or where I was for so long. They took the story of me being on a trip with my mom at face value. I was dumfounded that no one knew yet.

My Lit teacher assigned *Fahrenheit 451* as I browsed the "B" section in the library fiction section to check it out. As I found it, I saw Julian plop himself at a computer.   I was curious but did not want to bother him. He was typing away.

I went over and said *hi*. He was startled, almost embarrassed. I asked him what he was doing. He explained about email, the whole process.

"Who you writing?" I asked.

He hesitated. I could tell he was wondering if he should be truthful or not.

"You remember an extra on the film. Her name is Serena?"

I wasn't entirely sure I remembered her, even after he described her in detail.

"She gave me her email before I left France. I've been writing her."

"Do tell," I egged him on.

"No biggy. She's got a boyfriend at the University and..."
"What, she's a college student?"
"Well, yes, but ..."
"Julian, you bad boy."
"She's a friend. I like her. We had fun."
"Oh yeah. How much fun?"
"She showed me around Amiens. Coffee. That kind of thing."
"Sure." I let it go. "Well, that's nice you were able to do all that over there. I'm sorry, I hardly saw you. I'd sure like to know how to use this thing." Referring to the computer.
"I can show you sometime. How to set up an email. It's fun. Quick."
"I gotta go, do some things. Let's do it soon."
"No problem. It will take ten minutes, tops."
"First I have to figure out who I'd write." I smiled, patted my brother on the back. Sly dog. I was terribly curious about this Serena.

When I got home, Tim called me. Not Mom. He called me. He had been in L.A. working on edits. He was ecstatic. He wanted me and Mom to see some of it. Right now. He'd flown in to catch up with Shelly, take a rest, wanting us to come over. They'd have dinner. Sure, Louise can come.
We had to wait on Dad. He got home later than usual from supervising a wrestling match. He showered quickly. Louise was beside herself that she was included. Mom seemed nervous. Or maybe it was me feeling nervous. Projection.

We ate quickly. Pizza and salad. No alcohol. Sweet tea or pop. Tim was giving me shit about playing Maria in *The Sound of Music* and I started doing my Maria role, channeling Marian the librarian in *Music Man* like in my high school role. First it was Maria impersonating Marian, then vice-versa, hamming it up sarcastically. I had everyone in stitches. The nun telling the librarian to pull the stick out of her ass. And the librarian sticking her nose up in the air at the nun. Or something like that. Mom was keeling over laughing so hard. "What the hell," I said, "no one will be able to tell the difference." Tim situated us in assigned seats in his theater. He wanted to sit between me and Mom.

"I decided on Erik Satie for the music. Let me know what you think. Also, I've used a great deal of period piece sound injection. Stuff we've found and cleaned up from the time. War footage during the memory sequences. A lot of the street sounds and even in the brothel. Very subtle. Anyway, the sound is all embedded now. Editing is nearly finished but I wanted you to see it. Sharon told me to go ahead and do my thing, but I invited her."

The film started in cold black and white. No credits. No title. Soft piano, distant. Haunting. Mostly white with my gray image taking shape from out-of-focus winter light. I pull my short hair out of my face, turning towards Amiens from the field in which I stand. Light snow licks my cheeks. Hard to tell if I am crying or if it is snowmelt. I have no expression. I head back, it seems. I am mesmerized sitting there while I am watching. I never quite accept that the person, not a girl really, not

even a woman, almost a figment of someone called
Manon, is me. She speaks. She eats in small portions.
She sees death and destruction all around her.
Her mother is dominating. Yet Manon overtakes the
screen. She is filmed, often, from a slight upward angle.
Her imposition on everyone, especially her mother, is
formidable. Her mother's drugs and sexuality, her
mixture of lesbianism and the devouring of men, her
unquestioned authority over Manon, is clouded by her
heightened ability to stay one step ahead of the lurking
inevitability of despair in all the world. This is what
Manon understands and is taught about life.
Manon floats in the brothel, daily, as if a ghost. She is
not one of them or of anyone. She is merely *there*. An
observer of the hell she will soon be forced to enter. No
longer in *Purgatorio*.
Creeping on the ice of gravel, clothed in the black habit
of God. Framed by the Church. Licensed to slay the evils
that have beset the children of their province. Sent by
the Almighty in all starvation and cloaked in oaths is my
real mother – sitting two chairs over in this small
viewing room. She steals every second she is taken in
by the camera. Her voice. Her crucifix. Like the Angel
Gabriel behind her, statuesque in the background, Tim
had framed it perfectly. The symbolism unmistakable.
Mom hints of otherworldliness, barely to be looking into
the camera, as a child dies in her infirmary. In her arms.
No tears. No emotion. A knowing that the unnamed
child is but one lost battle in the continuing Great War
between heaven and earth. Or hell. Take your pick.

As Manon enters the life of this orphanage. This ward. This convent. This temporary stop-over into another world. They become allies. Yet it is soon realized that these two women have no such common faith. The God of Mother Superior is no God of Manon. Salvation is now at stake.

And Satan must be defeated. Rosette, up from the pit of damnation. As a serpent. The second half of the film is pure spiritual warfare of the most repulsive kind. It is not a movie whatsoever. It is a page out of Revelations. Even the cinematography is tinted slightly. We have descended into Dante's circle.

It is impossible to say who of these three women are the strongest. The girl, perhaps, has one edge. Her naivete. Her youth. Her pure innocence. It strikes me, at that very second, a quick scene I had forgotten that took at least twenty takes, I resisted each time, a look in my eyes, the expression, that I was absolutely *incognito*, unknown. Sharon and Jennifer were known beyond any question. Rosette certainly. Marianne as a resurrected Jesus once again on Earth. I was the center of every creature watching the film. I was that person in the audience. Awakening to a self.

It played almost like a silent picture. The pathos. It exhausted me all over again. Wrenched by that Damien sword.

Then the circus arrives. Tents and animals and people — real people — with personality and hope, arrive. The cinematography shifts once again. Almost color. I wanted to believe it was now in color. Even Manon is transformed by the mere seeing. I could swear I saw shades of red in the tents. Angels arrive in Robin and Ashley. Do they have a slight rouge on their cheeks, I cannot say? Manon to be ascended. In color or not. She will evaporate into the snow.

But first the deathly scenes of mother of blood and Mother of the Church. Sharon and Jennifer. Excruciating.

Manon makes her choice. The music prolongs everything, and the entire film hangs in the balance. She is gone. The film ends. Eventually, maybe never, the credits' roll in absolute silence. I see my name third in disbelief.

Everyone is hugging each other. I barely stand up. Julian is suddenly by me, whispering in my ear, how wonderful I am.

I make a crack about his scene, playing the piano. I never really recognized him. I certainly did not recognize Dad. Dying on the street as if it was a regular occurrence.   By that time in the movie, we are already numbed out to noticing.

Tim says, "I love this goddamn thing so much. It's the best thing I've ever done, and it will probably flop. I don't give a shit."

"Don't say that" Shelly butts in. "It's superb. People will flock to it."

Dad and Mom are embracing. Louise is bathed in a wet face. Blowing her nose.

Tim asks if he can speak with Jennifer and me alone. Lights go on. It's quiet.

"I love you two so much." He scratched his cheek, fighting emotion. "Whatever happens. I have no idea

how this will be received. I have some work to do, still. I am way too close to this. Just know that, okay?"
We nodded our heads.
"Steph." He couldn't speak. "I never imagined, honestly, that this would be as good as it is. You are so perfect. You never once were anything but honest in every frame. I was never, ever, watching an actress. Manon is, well, the reality, the truth in us all."
Mom hugged me tight.
"And Jennifer. Welcome back. My heart rejoices. I have missed you terribly. It is providence that you wrote this. That you paved the way on your terms. As you determined this to be for your daughter and your best friend. I am honored to have directed this incredible work. I hope I did it justice."
"Tim, no offense, but this film, in all humility, outshines anything you ever did in all those others. And I know that may piss you off. But it's true. You already know it."
"Yes, yes. No argument from me." He looked over his palm, rubbing it back on his cheek. "Oh, dear God in heaven. Sharon, oh, Sharon. Only she could play that role. Only she will be able to stand the scrutiny of the press, of the critics. She has taken it so many times. Even back to *Rio*."
"I'm not so sure, Tim. I think she's going to get raves on this one. People are tired of picking on her. She's overcome the world, so to speak. Plus, let's face it. She is fucking good. I am amazed. Once again, amazed."
I didn't know what to say. My mind was clearing. Just the images of Jennifer Braxton and Sharon Preston in what seemed to me as one of the greatest films of all

time, already, seemed certain. I was a mirage. I could not grasp that Stephanie Tomasetti played that role. Tim handed me a large manilla envelope. I opened it. A letter of congratulations from the studio. Another letter of endorsement from the Actors Guild. A third letter from my Agency explaining benefits, contractual obligations, percentages. I barely comprehended that one. And a check in the amount of $121,920.00.

CHAPTER EIGHTEEN

Listen to my story and everything will come true. Bessie Smith

Julian

"Julian, you there? What's going on, you seem distracted?" Melanie threw a wadded-up piece of paper at me, sitting at the piano. She hit me in the shoulder. I was definitely distracted. "Just figuring out something. What were you saying?"
"I've been listening to my mom's Janis Joplin album. *Best of* or *Greatest Hits*, I think. Reading this, too." She held up a colorful paperback, *Love, Janis,* by Laura Joplin, Janice's younger sister, Mel was explaining.   I focused and turned to her. "I have an idea. We've been working

on our new songs, playing them mostly - lately. I'd like to try a cover ... or covers."

I listened. The rest of the band settled into her train of thought.

"Maybe you could do "Me and Bobby McGee," like the original. Kris Kristofferson, I think. Country, folk. Acoustic. Just Stuart behind you. No drums or anything. I nodded. She had my interest. I liked his gruff rendition from what I could recall.

"Then I went to the library, over by us, near the hospital. They had all these great albums. Bessie Smith. Ma Rainey. The stuff Janis liked. I found the old Erma Franklin original of 'Piece of my Heart.' Fell in love with all of it."

She hummed a verse, adding some words. "Then I could come in at the tail end of 'McGee,' harmonize, then Bird kicks in the drums, Frankie adds the lead Big Brother style, and I do 'Piece of my Heart.' Let it fly. You come back in after the second verse and we finish strong. Not a medley per se."

I liked it. Melanie handed me the lyrics to both songs, she put on Joplin's take on each over at the stereo. It took us about forty minutes to glue it all together. I didn't have the Kristofferson version, so I guessed on the key, taking liberty with how I imagined Robbie Robertson might do it. Mel came in nicely, escalating, transitioning into the bluesy Erma Franklin, aka Joplin "Piece." My contribution vocally at the end was merely a tiny boost to where she had already taken the song. The second time we played it, I switched my acoustic midway, adding my Fender to Frankie's electric guitar.

It drove it even higher. Much better. Melanie's range was expanding. Evident to all of us. She had a hell of a voice.

Everyone was clearing out. I lay down on the couch, closing my eyes. Melanie came over and curled into me. "What's going on Julian? I can tell something's bothering you."

I felt like I should say something about Serena. Not sure why. Serena was telling me more about her boyfriend, Corbett, how serious they were, cutting short her emails. Greater distances in time between each one.

Melanie remained silent, lightly stroking my forearm and the top of my hand.

"Nothing really. I wanted to tell you about this girl I met in France." She sat up. I sat up and we faced each other. "Her name is Serena. She was an extra in the movie, going to college at the University north of Amiens. We had coffee. This is the hard part. We messed around. Just messing around … We didn't sleep together. She has a boyfriend. And I told her all about you."

Melanie withdrew and didn't say anything. "What do you mean, *messed around*," her voice quivered?

Oh fuck. Why in the hell did I open this up? I was mad at myself. I had no idea how to answer. Melanie looked terrified. Angry, hurt. All of it.

"Never mind." She said. "I don't want to know." She got up and went over to get her backpack. She was crying. "Melanie, please." I stopped there, then went on. "Don't go. I, we, need to talk."

She knelt on the floor, head down, like in a ball. Her crying softened. I went over and knelt beside her, embracing her. "Melanie. I am so sorry. It's been eating at me. I knew if I even mentioned it, I ran the risk of losing you. But I also knew that I did not want to lose you and it was better to be up front about it. If you want to break up with me, I understand. I really do. Damn, please don't, Melanie."

She looked at me through watery eyes. Her makeup smeared. She rubbed her nose on her sleeve and wiped her eyes.

"What if I told you I 'messed around' while you were gone?" She asked softly. Looking at me intently.

"I'd be hurt. Angry. Mostly hurt. God, I don't know how I would handle it. Like you didn't love me anymore."

"Exactly." She bowed her head. "I should go."

"No, no. Please. Come here." I pulled her gently back to the couch. I hugged her and now I started to cry. Once I started crying I couldn't stop. She barely rubbed my back. I attempted to look at her and her eyes were not engaging. She was being protective.

"Julian."

"Yeah."

"Let's give it time. I can't do this right now."

"Are you leaving me?"

"No. Maybe. I don't know. Like I said, let's give it time. It hurts, is all. A lot."

"Okay. I'm so sorry."

"That you told me?"

"Well, I wish I could tell you about it all, but it will sound like crap. And yes, I'm sorry about all of it. And yes, that I told you; that too. Maybe more if you leave me."

She rubbed her open palm over my stubble of a haircut, kissed me on the forehead and stood up. "Please don't call me Julian. I will call you. I promise. You deserve that much. I just don't know when." She left.

Melanie did not come to rehearsals the rest of the week. She avoided me in school, which was easy to do since the senior hallway was on the other side of the building. We didn't have a performance that weekend at Jimmy's, so I didn't see her then either. I broke down and tried to call. Four times. No answer. Two more times on Sunday. No answer.

I wrote her a long note and slipped it into her locker on Monday morning. I was even late getting to class, hoping to catch her. She never showed.

The band was now edgy. Monday was a waste of time. We quit early. If I didn't know what was going on, then how could they? What about the coming weekend? Should we get ready without her? I was frozen. I had no idea.

She called me that same night, about 8:00. My heart ripped through my chest.

"I need to see you. I don't want to talk on the phone." Is all she said.

I ran downstairs. Mom was the first parent I found. She agreed to drive me over to Mel's. They knew something was up anyway. "I'll be right over."

I knocked on her apartment door. Melanie answered dressed in gray baggy sweats. Her face pale. Her mom said *hi* then quickly disappeared.

"Should I tell my mom to wait? Or come back later? Or what? If you are breaking up with me, just say so." I said.

She went over to my mom's car and said something. My mom hugged her through the window, then she drove away.

"She'll be back in a half hour. Come inside." We went to her bedroom, and she shut the door. She sat on her bed, and I sat on the chair by her dresser.

"What's her name, again? The girl in France."

"Serena."

"In college, you said."

"Yeah, in the drama department."

"Did you fuck?"

"No."

"Do you write to her?"

"I have been. I learned how to use the internet at school. She gave me an email address."

Melanie was very quiet, pondering this.

"Still?"

"Not much. She's very serious with her boyfriend."

"Look, Julian. You are fourteen years old. You have a seventeen-year-old, almost eighteen-year-old girlfriend. You hang out with a French college girl in a fling on the other side of the world. Maybe love. Maybe sex. I get it."

I remained quiet, waiting for the knockout blow.

"I am well aware how attractive you are. None of this surprises me, really. You have three more years of high school, and you will be able to fuck anyone you want at that shithole of a school. And if I break up with you, my hope of college gets smashed. And ..."

"Wait a second.   My Dad. My Mom, they both promised
you. You will have their support. You have my support
no matter what. Don't put that on the table. That's not
fair."

She looked like she was going to cry again. Or maybe I
was going to cry.

"I know." She muttered. "I know." Then she did cry.   "I
don't know what to do, Julian. I don't want to lose
you."

"What about you, Mel? You are so damned hot. You'll
have tons of guys over at the college. God, even at the
high school, right now, the whole jock crowd fawns over
you and you treat them all like shit. What are you going
to do; or say when they ask you out over at the big
college? My boyfriend is a SOPHOMORE at the high
school, you'll say. He will get his driver's license by the
end of the year! Jesus."

She laughed through the tears.

"Or when we perform? If you perform. If *we* perform. I
have no idea about Retro, now. The band is freaking out.
Anyway, guys at these bars are already hitting up on you
before, during and after the show. That's another
subject altogether and that bothers me too." She found
a Kleenex and blew her nose.

She curled into a ball, now on her side.

I went over and curled next to her; our eyes locked.

She palmed my hair again.   "I love you Julian. That's all I
know. I have no idea how this works. What the hell am I
doing? Are we doing?"

"I have no idea either. But I love you, too."

We kissed lightly. The brush of her lips relieved days and days of pain. Hopefully for both of us.

"You need to get rid of these black frames." She said, taking off my glasses.

We kissed again. Deeply. Our tongues searching for reconciliation.

I could hear the moms talking in the other room. I was harder than a rock and tried to settle down before leaving Melanie's room. She smiled as I left.

Jennifer

Never in my life would I have told Stephanie, but I was sick to death of rehearsing *The Sound of Music* with her. When she wasn't putting in long hours over at the Nest, she was constantly singing around the house. It was driving us crazy. Steph has a nice voice. Beautiful. Hearing, *doe a deer, a female deer* for the six hundredth time, however, made me want to kick her out of the house. Danny was staying at school longer and not because he had to. Even Louise was going to weekday mass more often.

She was sounding good. She had Maria perfected. Now I know why Tim, in the old days, made fun of me when I started with *Fiddler*. Except, even now, I liked *Fiddler*. And I liked *Gypsy*. Never mind my opinion, I thought; I encouraged Steph endlessly. She deserved it. She was wonderful.

Who calls on a Friday afternoon? Karen. She wanted to talk with me. I rolled my eyes. She wanted to take Sam on a *fun* date to Jimmy's to see Retro Sky; they were really trying hard again, she said it three times. I was not sure who she was trying to convince. Could they join us? Sure, what could I say. We were going to be there. In fact, James had asked if we would take him. He and Julian had been hanging out the last few nights. James was curious about their new music. Louise was going to join us. Shelly and Rhonda and even Gene. Steph was coming along too – she asked me if she could bring the actor playing Captain Von Trapp, who I knew to be twenty-six year old and already divorced, sharing custody of a two-year-old. In the middle of my raging rant of screaming *absolutely no way*, she laughed and said, *gottcha*. I called Jimmy's and asked to reserve a table for ten even though they didn't reserve tables. I begged. Just this once.

It was crowded. Turning people away crowded. No introduction, Julian came out first as the band followed. He had on his new glasses, which he had received on rush order. Expensive. John Lennon style with his cropped hair and what little non-shaved face he could manage. Those dark glasses he stole from France, which fit over his new ones in perfect round cylinders. Black leather jacket and white tee-shirt and black jeans. And that French wool cap. Hat on, then hat off. Funky dude, my son. Melanie had on a long dark emerald dress, bold green makeup, especially around her eyes. Big hoop earrings. Channeling someone, no doubt. I'd find out soon enough. They kissed, the two of them; no, more like embraced and then kissed before starting the music.

Stuart played alone, a nice bass riff, for a good minute leading into Julian's acoustic as he did a good impression of Kris Kristofferson via Robbie Robertson doing "Me and Bobby McGee." The crowd sang along towards the end until the entire band joined in, and a pink bar spotlight hit Melanie and she did a pseudo-Janis Joplin - someone else I couldn't identify - finale with Julian. Then Julian switched guitars without skipping a beat and the electricity rose, intensified. Melanie upped her tone, her volume, her blues chords, blowing the ceiling off its pillars with "Piece of my Heart." She was right in Julian's face when she sang. He kept his head low, staying with her on his Fender. *Break it*, she'd draw it out longer and longer. *Another piece of my heart*, *now, baby,* with so much pain, the place went crazy. Not like Janis exactly, more like an older black woman possessing her passions. Hard to tell. Danny was grasping my hand in ecstasy. I rubbed his knuckles, it was too difficult to talk, it was so loud. James and Steph stood and danced with about half the audience. Julian, to my surprise, came in at the end, harmonizing perfectly on a lower register. Their noses almost touching, Julian about two inches taller, sweat dripping off their faces already, spitting the lyrics onto a shared microphone. Standing ovation, already. Sam and Karen kissed. Locked. I had no idea what to think. Rhonda and Shelly both leaned into me and Danny. "We need to talk," they practically said in unison over the noise. Gene pulled his chair closer, yelling into my ear, "what the fuck?" It was the first time he had ever seen them perform.

It quieted down slightly. Julian said, *thank you very much*, in his best nonchalant impersonation and they went into their faster dance numbers, right on cue. All new songs for about twenty minutes. No one could sit still. Jimmy's was full of sweat and beer and cigarette smoke. Stifling. Exhaustion was everywhere. Except with the band. They took a quick break. Drenched in sweat. Mostly to rearrange the keyboard and an amp, then they played non-stop until their three hours was over. Standing ovation, hollers.

The band exited outside into the cold air. Julian and Melanie took up their acoustic guitars and pulled over two bar stools, placing a single mic between them. Julian played a long solo for nearly two or three minutes, then Melanie joined note for note. She adjusted the microphone and looked Julian in the eyes. "Is Love so fragile, and the heart so hollow, shatter with words, impossible to follow, you're saying I'm fragile, I try not to be, I search only, for something I can't see" ... all the way through the second verse ... they then sang together, you could hear a pin drop ... "Lovers forever face to face, my city your mountains. Stay with me stay, I need you to love me, I need you today, give to me your leather, take from me my lace ..." The lights went down to roaring applause. I wiped my eyes. Louise was crying like a baby. Even James looked choked up.

The following weekend was the opening of *The Sound of Music.* Because of Steph's large part she couldn't work as a waitress nor as a hostess like I had been so many years ago. Almost the same gang went to see her perform as who went to Jimmy's to see Julian. We were seated, Danny and I, with Karen and Samantha, at the cramped booth, center row. Awkward and yet I looked at Karen with understanding. She'd always had a thing for Danny. I was proud of him, resisting her. She was a very attractive, sexual woman. Sam still looked at me the same way after our encounter back in memory. A glimmer of hope and desire. And yet, they were holding onto something in their relationship. Our foursome lingered even now, like a shadow or reminder of what I was not sure. Then my memories drifted to another foursome when Tim and I did *Bob, Carol, Ted and Alice* here on this exact stage, theater in the round. The laughter was explosive in this small theater. Maybe the most fun I ever had in my career.

My mind drifting as tables were cleared in dimming light. Men had certainly 'hit' on me over the years. Usually politely. Even though they may have known that I was married. Never as overtly as Karen had with Danny. I was tempted once with a museum director out of Tulsa. A pure gentleman, handsome. A gentle smile. I was on the road, alone. A few drinks. But no. And four or five women over the years made known more than subtle advances. Especially in the League. I felt that being *famous* was sometimes a shield which protected me. I was nervous for Stephanie. I shared that butterfly effect I knew she was going through at this very moment. I was not all that nervous for her when she had performed at the high school. She seemed so 'ready' and not as concerned back then. This seemed more intimate and more vulnerable of a setting.   Professional exposure.

The hills are alive, with the sound of music, her voice boomed in clarity and beauty, as the stage descended with blue light, a mountain set engulfing her beautiful body, her Bavarian dress swirling in delight. She looked incredible. She was every bit the young woman fully embodied, with strength, delight, and purity of purpose. She had the crowd immediately. Stephanie sang with joy and range.   Her bouncy demeanor among the actors and the little kids – although I read in the program that one of the 'children' was being played by a sixteen-year-old – was pure entertainment.   I was glad that they did not give Stephanie's actual age. She looked like she was in her twenties to me. And the 'age song' we called it, was pure comedy for Danny and me as the kids counted off their ages. Ironic, given the situation. I guessed that no one even put it together.

It was a fast-moving play. Terribly entertaining, I now remembered. And horribly demanding on Steph. She was the center in an almost solo performance. She handled it with grace, composure and steadiness. Never a failed line or miscue.   Always a smile or earnest look, always in charge. I was impressed. And more than a little bit stunned when she looked directly at the audience, beckoning us into her world. She looked directly at me and her father in the middle of one of her countless soliloquy songs with effervescent delight.

A standing ovation as she finally appeared among the large cast, taking her bow. A few flowers thrown at her feet; one bouquet tossed up by Melanie as Julian blew her a kiss.   Once again, Louise's crying her eyes out with happiness. I was so happy she was with us in all these family times.

Danny and I hugged in parental pride. Steph came back out and bowed again. Our memories of being in this theater in years past were now erased for this present reality. Our daughter. Our wonderful daughter.

Danny urged me to go backstage, which I did, making my way slowly. The passages, the various doors, were rushing back in familiarity. I found what was most certainly the ladies' main changing room. Entering the chaos of costumes and chatter and makeup being removed, and colors and more chatter. Several giving Steph a quick hug. Stephanie slowly revealing herself as a kid instead of the mature adult she had only recently commanded. Shedding her skin. She looked so vulnerable to me. I hugged her, her choked up laughter and smiles pressed against my shoulder and face. *My vocal chords hurt*, is all she could manage to muster.

Sarah Johnson had been in the hallway with a cameraman from *This is Santa Fe*. Sarah was still, after all these years, covering culture and life in our fair city. She loved it, she often told me when I'd run into her, never got tired of it.   She had now become the most recognizable face in Santa Fe.

"She was wonderful, Jennifer!" Sarah hugged me. "Do you think Stephanie is up to an interview? I'm the paparazzi, you know, springing an attack." She was about as friendly as they came.

"I can ask, if you like, hold on."

"You want to be in it?" Sarah asked me with no chance in hell. She smiled.

I brought Stephanie out into the hallway as we found a relatively quiet area with a poster of the show in the background. Steph had cleaned up, looking all her teen years. They bantered back and forth, giggling, smiling, Steph was in shock and probably didn't even know what she was saying. Her voice seemed strained, and she cleared her throat a few times. Taking sips of water. Then the question came that I should have protected Steph from. I should've seen it coming.

"I hear you have completed a film. In Europe? How was that Stephanie? Tell us about it." Microphone in her face. Innocent enough but I wanted to jump in and drag Steph away.

Steph handled it easily. I was shocked. "Yes, but it's not been released. Details are forthcoming. I'd be happy to speak with you on your show once we get the go ahead. It was a great opportunity, and I learned a lot."

"So, you were in a movie?"

"Yes. Yes, I think I can say that."

"What's the title?"

"Not now, please."

Sarah kept going, which was pissing me off, "Was your mother involved? Rumors are that she's made her comeback."

"Like I said, I can't comment on anything about a movie right now." Steph was handling this marvelously. No training either. Or coaching as to how to answer these kinds of questions.

Then Sarah did a wrap, the usual cheery thing.

"Fuck, Sarah," I confronted her.

"Jennifer, come on. I had to ask you know that."

I grabbed Steph and led her back to her dressing room. I was furious. Then I settled down.

"Mom don't be upset. You know, better than I do, that this was going to happen. Better now with her than some dude from god knows what newspaper."

"Yeah, you're right. I guess the cobwebs are coming off your old mom."

She smiled. "We should do this together. It would be fun."

"I know. Yes, I agree. I'll call Sarah tomorrow. She's feeling like she's getting a scoop. I'll see what's going on at the studio first. Anyway, this is about you and Maria and *Sound of Music.* I wanted it to be about the play. About you."

"She covered it all Mom. It will be a good interview, I think. For the play."

"Good. I hope so."

"Did the show sell out tonight?" She asked me. I laughed hard, hugging her. My showbiz daughter is off and running.

I got through to Phil on his private 'portable phone' on a Saturday. He apologized for not telling me that word was out about *Purgatorio.* Tim and the studio had 'leaked' the film to Anthony Lane of the *New Yorker*, making just about everyone angrier than hell. He said Stephanie and I could do whatever we wanted or not wanted in New Mexico. A more formal promotional schedule in the United States wasn't even discussed yet.

A European schedule was near completion for late May, when Steph would be out of school as well, flexible enough for any or all, or none, of the three main actresses to participate. Tim was taking it on. Phil asked quickly about *The Sound of Music*, happy it went well. He told me that he would call Steph for his percentage. No laugh on that one. *Jesus*, I thought. He was also faxing the Anthony Lane article ahead of going to press:

"Don't be fooled, Purgatorio is worth the wait;" Anthony Lane, The New Yorker, April 7, 2001. <u>About Cinema</u>. This is not a review, given that the film has not yet been released. I've seen it and it will be worth your wait. Here are some observations: Tim Prescott has a filmography of thirty-one films. Sixteen of them are classified as 'Hollywood block-buster,' all of which are action oriented. I've reviewed over half of them. Upon reading those reviews again, the tone of those dated words sounds begrudging. Only one of which is outright negative, and that was a sequel that turned heads with the highest gross. What do I know, I now ask myself? Prescott has now given us his first serious directorial effort since Purple Flowers. Purgatorio is cloaked in turn-of-the century (the last century) European gloom. Existential costuming of Bergman and Fellini and Bunuel, even Kurosawa. Black and white, glorious camera work. Surrealist's delight. Don't be fooled. This movie is pure Prescott. He is the hero once again, as American as apple pie and Superman. I won't say much about the story line here, except to say Prescott saves the day, just as in his action series. As the United States saved

Europe in a decade long struggle and two World Wars, he saves our helpless soul in this one (a true enough Dante-like Purgatory) in little less than a week of storyline, or twenty minutes of movie time towards the end. It's okay if you applaud and cheer. You will need to do so in a restrained manner, however, as you pretend to be French.

What else is worth the wait? The return of Jennifer Braxton. Agree with the mythology or not, she is the Greta Garbo of our time. She arrives from the atmospherics, stuns us, mesmerizes us, and then she is gone. She may never return. We have no idea. I am grateful, in a prayer of thanks, that she is back. You will join me in that prayer after you see this. What is new, however, is that she wrote the screenplay, along with a great comedian – of all ironies, given the darkness of this one – Vincent Calibrasella (more later). Braxton may not win any awards for her acting because when the film ends I was speechless. She is a painter by trade and by artform, and acting, for her, is a hobby. Or makes it look as easy as a hobby. When she acts, she paints (as many observers have already deciphered) and this character – I won't give her away – is painted much like her now famous, iconic self-portrait, we are all so familiar with. See her in this movie from a distance, a back row, or the balcony. Do not sit too close to the screen. It would almost be an insult to discuss simple awards for Jennifer. Like a statue or heavy object above the fireplace. No, I suspect that she wouldn't want any of them anyway. But she, and Vinny, will most certainly win every award that various bodies of pomposity can scrape up for *screenwriting. Purgatorio is beautiful and original in scope, largely due to their pen. Enough said at this time. It's good to see her back. I hope she doesn't disappear again for a decade or two, or even for a year.*

I also dusted-off my sixteen reviews of movies starring Sharon Preston. The most recent review I wrote was only a few weeks ago, discussing her comedic genius in Woody Allen's latest, and her much overlooked body of work in that vein – most notably, and beginning with her very early partnering with the late Jackie Gleason. She has infuriated me, tested me, and the entertainment industry generally. That is only one of the many reasons – which I've written here exhaustively over the years - why I have always ranked her as the most compelling actor of my lifetime. Her character, this time, is Madame Rosette. Feel free to hate her. Call her Sharon or Rosette, it doesn't matter, really. And, again, don't be fooled. She is as much the type A villain as in any of Prescott's action movies. Do not fear, he will set you free from her clutches by the last scene. Cloaked, disguised, as is the entire movie, in French debauchery and hopelessness, she will seduce you then leave you to rot. Enough said. Be prepared, as always. How many awards, this time Sharon? What cause, what purpose will you espouse? Will you even show up? Oh, and would you please return my phone calls? Which brings me back to your husband. Yes, your husband. He co-wrote this gem. I've interviewed Vinny. He's a nice guy. Funny. I need to know how he came about writing this character that possessed you? Questions abound.

All of this is well and good and predictable by you the reader. Until you witness and experience the character Manon. A young girl who rises above these two actresses you are so familiar with. Yes, I say, rises above. A soul drifting and exploding with one close-up after another. Raw, vulnerable, anonymous. She is practically unnamed and certainly unknown.   I will not go into her identity in this segment.   You will find out all about her in good time. Which is a shame because I already know how the industry will tilt this performance into something it is not because of her identity. It is best that you, once again, don't be fooled, and savor the ethereal quality of this character.   If it is at all possible, and it isn't, it would be best if you have no idea who she is when you watch Purgatorio. For now, her name is Stephanie. That is good enough.   She is not listed in any promotional pamphlets or studio release. She is not registered in the Guilds with any additional information other than a birthdate and a hint to her birth city – which I am not offering. You will not find her in any magazines or have seen her on any talk shows. Stephanie is fourteen. Going on thirty.   She looks nine years old in early scenes and brutally tough and mature by the final act. Stephanie is born out on the screen of these giants we know intimately by way of Tim and Jennifer and Sharon, even Vinny. She will be around for a long time, fodder for many critics and reviewers that will follow me. As a side note, I met Stephanie's father once and I will tell you that she is far more like him than her mother – meaning nothing to you now -   but once you pull off her disguise, I will need to write another column, *just about her and about him, and yes, about her mother. Even then, it will be difficult to explain my meaning. It is an enormous compliment to both parents and to Stephanie specifically. This is no judgment on her mother or their family. You will understand soon enough. Be patient. Whether you stand in long Hollywood lines at mega theaters, or ache in the cold movie houses of art films and obscure releases, this one will be worth the wait. Promise.*

I was not ready for this. It's just one of those sections that will be found in the front of the *New Yorker*. A tease piece. I like Anthony. What the hell, though? What's he getting at about Danny? True enough maybe, but why bring him up? And just another action movie of Tim's disguised in black and white? I hate this bullshit. But I decided to call Sarah Johnson. I apologized for the other night. She was gracious. We scheduled an appearance for Steph and me at the local television studio in three days. Half-hour segment. She told me that the live interview she had with Stephanie after the opening of *The Sound of Music* went over big with her audience. Santa Fe and New Mexico were ready even if I was not.

Danny

Crisis in Faith. I knelt on the right transept of the Church on a Friday morning. The Spanish mass was to start in an hour. I liked being near the candles of offertory prayer beneath the Madonna. Silence mingled with the aroma of burning wax with spiced hints of incense.   I was fighting back tears. Then I let them flow. Before my supplication, I gave thanks for so very much. Endless praise for such overwhelming blessing. Jennifer and Stephanie, who would leave in May on a promotional tour throughout Europe. Sharon and Tim would join them off and on. Stephanie, my dear young daughter had finished her three weeks, fifteen shows of *The Sound of Music*. She was marvelous. She'd taken the town by storm; on television and in the papers. We had to get a tutor for her to help until Spring break, which started next week. Steph was going to spend spring break with my friend David in Taos on their horse ranch. His wife, Linda and the entire Cabrera-Valario family extended an invitation to her, all of us, but we couldn't go up there right now. Steph was eager to go. Jennifer, my dear Lord, such a blessing. Our love remained unquestioned. We were leaving tomorrow on the surprise trip I promised.   Instead of my initial thought of New Orleans, I decided to take her to the wine country in Napa Valley, flying into San Francisco at 6:00 am. She still had no idea where we were headed. Julian and the band were leaving this morning on a long road trip. Stu's parents, Shelly, and Alo's uncle were leading a caravan beginning with shows in Albuquerque, to Phoenix, finishing in L.A. Rhonda would meet them in California, arranging gigs in two beach-front bars, as well as studio time to cut a CD, meet with some producers. Rhonda was also trying to find a more permanent agent for Retro Sky. They would be late returning from break.

School is going well. The boys' basketball team got knocked out in quarter finals, but the girls went to finals, only to lose by six points. You know me, Lord, I'm invested in our basketball programs. A prejudice of mine. The teachers know it. Everyone knows it.

So, why the tears, dear Lord? I am so heavy at heart. James is not well lately. He won't go to the doctor, but Jennifer and I notice his wheezing and coughing. Please, God, take care. Take care.

That's not it, though. Jesus, I can't believe any of this anymore. I've tried and tried to be faithful. With more and more stories surfacing of sexual abuse in the Church, the cover-ups and outright lies. Horrifying stuff. Even after your bountiful provision, allowing me to meet His Holiness, even that added to my disillusionment. I am aligned and love the people of our community, the ageless native peoples most of all, and I grow to resent the Church more and more. The seemingly entrenched superstitions, grown over the historical abuses. I cannot stomach it anymore. Christianity in all its professions is swamped in hypocrisies. Afraid of living the gospel itself. Clinging to doctrine and judgment.

I know you, Jesus. I do not give up on that relationship. That faith. But I must walk away from the rest of it. There is a power. A mystery. The earth. The Universal. Even in the energy of matter. Your creation, Jesus. You are behind all that has occurred with me in my life. The change of destiny. The visions. The bending of time. All of it. You did SOMETHING with me and Jennifer. Look at the beginning when we were only fifteen, and now our lives. Endless blessing. All in order that we can see,

KNOW. Now my two children are yours. From Gaia, James has said since their conception. And they, too, are seeing. KNOWING. It frightens me. You have created a new order, Bill taught me. These dreams, these fantastic happenings, unbelievable wonders, are that Garden of Eden repaired by the Cross, or before the fall, or something without sin or conflict or resistance. I still don't understand the metaphors in religion. They swirl in common tradition, ultimately remaining a mystery.

I cry now. Unburdening my soul in this place. I will not return. My communion, my sacrament will be found in the circus at the end of *Purgatorio*. The symbols will continue to be made manifest.

I stood and went to the statue of Joseph carrying baby Jesus. I said goodbye. To both of them. I knelt after dipping my fingers in the cistern, crossing myself for the final time.

The winter morning sunrise was blinding. Older Spanish congregants were moving slowly into mass.

CHAPTER NINETEEN

You are a God and never have I heard anything more divine … the eternal hourglass of existence is turned upside down again and again ... Nietzsche's Eternal Recurrence.

Stephanie

Said my goodbyes to everyone, hugs and kisses: The two cars, a van and a trailer leaving for Albuquerque and beyond; and Mom and Dad departing for an undisclosed location – *San Francisco* printed on the plane tickets in my dad's office, he didn't even think to hide them. Louise rarely drives her car beyond ten miles, but she agreed to get me to Taos. A friend of hers, Nola, came along.   I was beyond excited. Done with the high school play, major movie, local theater and tons of homework, so, when dad's high school friend with a horse-training ranch invited us, I jumped. No one else could go. I spoke with Mr. Cabrera on the phone, he insisted that I call him David, and briefly with his wife Linda. They had two daughters who were fifteen and twelve. They repeatedly insisted that I come. Plenty of room. The girls would love someone to ride with. Their family had seen me in a matinee at Eagle's Nest, and the kids were especially eager for my visit.
Sandra, the oldest, and Tiffany, joined David and Linda in getting me settled in a comfortable guest bedroom, decorated with dozens of horse competition and long track racing photos. We then walked the training grounds. Forty-two horses were boarded, fifteen being trained for show, seven for racing. The remainder were

owned by private parties.   Six additional horses were theirs.

In the afternoon the girls had our horses saddled and the three of us toured the large facility, then the perimeter of their property, departing into public lands on a trail that led northward. The two girls were obviously expert riders; both were competitive in one form of horseback endeavor or another. Their approach was much more sophisticated, traditional, than what I was accustomed to on the reservation. They, did, however, compliment me on my handling of *Max*, a quarter horse of selective breeding on their ranch.

I learned a lot about racing, interval training. Schedules, speed and endurance, diet, and even veterinarian needs. Especially breeding. Sandra quickly became my mentor. A year older than me, she showed me everything about saddles, track distances, how their trainers operated, and even the stylistic differences between the many jockeys on site. She was the brains, where Tiffany was the medalist. Tiffany's expertise was in showjumping, which I was extremely nervous about. I spent one day with Tiffany and her show horse, Legend, and then I bowed out, preferring the track area. Tiffany was fine with it; not bad with some of the long-distance races herself.

I had a fabulous time once the trainers and the jockeys let me do some sprint work.   I had never run any horse that fast. And I was only reaching three-quarter capacity of most of the horses most of the time.   I had to learn an entirely different way to ride, burning on my thighs, and ever alert to each individual horse. It was a rush.

One of the jockeys – Roberto – took me under his wing, as he went through his daily training routine of four or five different horses. Sandra and Tiffany rode, too. Three or four times that week we raced, usually a half mile. I was never close to them, no matter which horse I was on.

I was never so exhausted as the week wound down. David put on many dinners and barbecue - small fiestas at night, which would last past midnight a few times. He played an accordion and Linda played a guitar and the party would become quite festive. The girls asked me several questions about acting and my mom, and Sharon, and about Tim Prescott, who they knew was our friend. I'd tell funny stories, keeping it light. Where they were looking up to me and what I had done on stage, I felt that I was looking up to them, maybe more so.

Jennifer

When I realized that Danny was taking us to San Francisco I was delighted. Not a terribly long flight. A romantic setting with great food. He insisted that the surprise was not just being on the bay. I'd find out soon enough.

He had two things to apologize for, but honestly I didn't mine at all. First was that we flew in coach. No one recognized me and I slept the entire way, that early in the morning. Second, Jimmie and his wife Denee' were driving up from his company headquarters to meet us for dinner. We were on our own after that.

Checking into our suite at the Ritz-Carlton for *only* two nights made me wonder where we were headed from there. This was over the top special. We took a long swim and hot tub. A bubble bath and fucked in the tub, splashing water over the elevated floor. We fell asleep in our lush, warm robes, starving when we awoke.

Jimmie had arranged for us to eat at a modest place, The Old Clam House, urging us to dress casually. *The food is to die for*, he guaranteed.

Jimmie's wife Denee' is an attractive, devil may care, fun-loving sort. She wore jeans, a heavy winter sweater and light jacket. Jimmie was just as easy going. You would never know that they were one of the wealthiest couples on the West Coast. And Jimmie was right – the food was remarkable. Seafood with chef spices and butter. Lots of local, homemade butter. We drank the best wine in the house and stuffed ourselves. It was a celebration of sorts, Jimmie's company stocks shooting through the roof. Which meant a great deal to us, to Danny's dad, even Billy, back home in Santa Fe, had invested for himself and Cindy. Sharon and Vinny had been investing for years. Hi-tech was taking over the world.

Danny's secret was let out of the bag, when Jimmie handed me a packet.

"Open it," Danny urged.

I opened to a pamphlet, five nights at the Four Seasons in Napa Valley. Unlimited driver, or bicycle use, depending on our mood and weather, and amenities and passes to the best orchards and wineries in the region.   All expenses paid for food, alcohol, and everything else the five-star location offered.

"Oh, my God, Jimmie. What's this?" I was staring at the photos.

"Danny wanted to surprise you. A promise he made to you or something."

I looked at Danny.

"I hope you like it, love." Danny kissed me on the cheek.

"I'm jealous!" Denee' said with a big smile. "You'll love it, Jennifer! We've stayed there, it's amazing. You practically have a personal servant. Anything you want. I mean that, too, ANYTHING YOU WANT." I was perplexed by the look on her face.

We had a wonderful time in San Francisco. We went to the ballet, ate well again and again at the most expensive restaurants, saw a few of the sights – Golden Gate Bridge, the Wharf. Then a shuttle took us to Napa Valley. It was very chilly, feeling like winter on the first day. A car from the hotel took us around to three different vineyards, learning about the families who owned them, the uniqueness of each blend and year. Early in the evening we went to a wine tasting, learning the ins and outs and *manners* of the process. We were not very good about spitting out the wine. We were wasted in no time and were in bed early.

The next day we laid around the pool, ordering massages in our suite. It was a naked process, with scents, a fireplace, dim lights, tantra music, lush oils and hot towels. We had unlimited time, if we desired. I asked the masseuse what the tripod and camera were for in the corner of our room. She explained that we could film the sights or even ourselves anywhere in our suite or on the grounds, then watch ourselves or the tape on television. She was allowed to operate the camera for us if we chose. Danny and I looked at each other in curiosity. She showed us how to turn-on the recording machine, set up the desired angle, then rewind, inserting the cable into our television for viewing. Easy enough.

She also informed us that we had access to any sexual stimulant, or *toy*, or instruments of bondage, anything our imagination could fathom. A small guidebook and price ranges were provided. She opened a trunk, leaving it at the foot of our bed. The other masseuse showed us how to order porn videos on our TV if we wanted to check it out. Their matter-of-fact demeanor seemed as though it was all part of the package. Repeating herself, one of them even offered to operate the camera for us if we so desired. Hourly rates were also in the package. We shook our heads *no*. Thank you. Because we didn't have any further questions, they left.

We laughed. We'd never heard of such a thing or this kind of service.

I ordered up room service. Tuna steaks and crab salad. Two bottles of wine. A pack of cigarettes - Danny didn't seem to mind.

"That was an amazing massage." Danny said, changing the subject from the options that had been presented to us.

"Perfect. I really needed it. She found my spots in my neck and shoulders."

The food and items arrived. I lit up a cigarette. Danny did too. He coughed and called down on the phone for their best cigars instead. He wanted whiskey too. He was tired of wine. I agreed. Soon we had more liquor than we knew what to do with. Figuring out what to do with the trunk in front of us.

As we ate, I finally rummaged through the trunk of sex toys. Boxed dildos and vibrators. Butt plugs and vaginal beads, power balls and *combination imaginings*, whatever that was. The price listed for each. Various lubricants of different textures and flavors. A flimsy whip. Scarves and bracelet-like hand cuffs. Leathered items of bondage, we weren't sure how to use.

"Do you think this is available for everyone who stays here?" I asked.

"Doubt it. I have a sneaky suspicion that Jimmie is behind this. He always had a freaky sense of humor. Just seems like him. Our senior year, back in high school, he always told wild sex stories. Stuff I had no idea where they came from. And since he comped us for this entire package. Just figures he'd do something like this. And didn't Denee' strike you as wild, maybe a kinky type?"

"Probably." I said, putting plastic handcuffs on my wrists. Sitting there naked trying to eat. We were laughing harder and harder. Getting entirely drunk again.

Danny was walking around the room naked, slightly hard. A cigar now puffing away, swirling whiskey in his mouth. He was setting up the tripod, looking through the lens at the bed. "There, ready for close ups right in the middle."

"Danny, really?" I looked over at the bed.

"Sure, why not. We can destroy the tape later."

I was game. Even an eagerness surged inside of me. Being *naughty*. "Let me put on some makeup." Then I stopped. "Let me check out one of these porns first. See how they look on video."

I turned on the TV, following the directions. I chose *Women of the Night* and hit *play*. It only took about four minutes of bad plot and worse acting to get to the first scene. Redhead sucking massive dick. Dark haired girlfriend, making out with some guy at the same time. A threesome. Lots of makeup and big hairdos, not much else to go by. Probably a cheap motel room. The dude fucked the dark-haired girlfriend first, while the redhead made out with her. The dark-haired girl did not appear to be having much fun. As she tongued and kissed the redhead, she practically begged the redhead to take over. Then they finally switched positions. The redhead was far more into getting fucked by this enormously endowed, but ridiculously ugly guy. All three of the actors, or performers, or whatever they considered themselves, looked strung out. That was my impression. Danny agreed. The dark-haired girl was useless at that point, merely stroking the redhead's hair with a slow caressing hand. Not much to it.

"Jennifer, we don't have to do this if you don't want to." Danny said, covering himself with a pillow. I swallowed my whiskey with a big smile and went to the bathroom. I put on layers of makeup and my negligee top. No bottoms.

"Turn that thing on." I said to Danny, pointing to the tripod.

"Better leave the lights on, keep the fireplace going." Danny suggested.

"Good idea, you being the great cinematographer that you are."

I sucked on him for about two minutes, and he was soon quivering. I stopped, wanting to see what else we could do. Or what Danny wanted to do. We had not rehearsed; smiling, whispering, as if the camera would not catch us. I improvised, taking out two leather straps and had him tie me to the bed.

I said something like, "Fuck me, big daddy," with a Georgia drawl, the best acting I had done in my entire life. And he did. Danny was attempting to act while he breathlessly pounded into me. "My sweet southern belle, I've wanted you ever since the ball." He emphasized the word *ball*. Terrible, and I nearly laughed, biting my lip. I was nowhere near coming, in fact I finally burst out giggling about ten seconds after Danny came.

I retrieved two robes, refreshed our drinks and lit another cigarette. We watched ourselves on the television. We both laughed again, then settled into the sexiness of it. Slow motion, rewind. Over and over. I was fascinated to see myself suck on Danny's cock. And we lucked-out on the camera angle because it was enough from the side view, I could see him thrust into my spread legs. I enjoyed it; I was admitting. Danny was obviously having fun, not wanting to say so.

Danny was glad I was going with the flow. We made a few comments, like we were critiquing the whole thing, how we could *take two*, make it better.

"I need to slow down," Danny said, observing his own performance on screen.

"Yes, you do. For my sake, you stud."

"Maybe we can design the set better. The camera angle needs only a tiny adjustment. I wish we could hit the *closeup* button. Ah, but we can't. And let's make more noise. Like orgasms. Talk more too." Danny said it seriously. Like he really did want to make it better. He was making this more fun than I thought possible.

We found chairs, sipping our whiskey, and grinned at the funkiness of this whole moment. I turned on the same *Women of the Night* video. Danny stole the controller and fast forwarded it to an entirely different scene. This one was filmed in black and white.   Poolside on a towel – somewhere in southern California I suspected with the hillside background. A beautiful blond, not of the *Night*, but very much in the heat of day, with large 1980's sunglasses and a sun bonnet, disguising her face completely, spread out on a deck couch getting hammered by her pool boy. Her fake boobs bounced with purpose and gusto. He had on an open work shirt, that did not fit well, reading *Long Peter's Pool Service*. He was Peter, we assumed, because he was truly *long*. His bushy mustache with grimacing face highlighted his cheesy one line, *I service your every need*. She responded with her one line, obviously well-rehearsed, *I love when you spray my deck*. The camera angles were overhead and then up close, shifting to the poorly engrained music, heavy beat of bass and synthesizer. I guessed at least three cameras were involved in this elaborate, over-the-top, porn production. We had to admit that the editing was impressive.

He shot his load all over her tits.

Danny and I were clinking our glasses, "Cheers, that was a good one."

Julian

David Hidalgo was becoming my newest hero as our over-extended spring break was winding down. Rhonda managed to get us studio time at Mammoth Records in Burbank. Mammoth's headquarters were in North Carolina but maintained a two-room, single booth, studio in Los Angeles.

We came off our whirlwind road trip through the Southwest, playing four different venues. The energy was high in each one, my favorite being in Flagstaff where we played as an opening act to nearly 500 people. We were establishing ourselves as a good live band that liked to dance. Our 'oldies' were such that audiences liked the recognizability, still grooving on the new stuff we were perfecting. When we got to L.A. we were playing at a dance club in Redondo Beach. The capacity was only 200, which didn't matter. The pay and exposure were the best we had received thus far. Mammoth was giving us a discount rate, or so they said. Twelve songs, all of which were ours. Arrangements were ours. Joey Shelton was our engineer. Joey's a good guy, realizing that we did not have a producer,

basically cutting a demo CD, trusting our gut. He
dabbled in producing, anyway, and offered a great deal
of advice. I worked well with him, as did Bird, who was
stepping up with ideas for our sound. They were
experimenting with slight twists to our percussion.
Melanie and Joey talked endlessly about harmonics,
voice modulation, tracking vocals, voiceovers. I realized
that our vocal combination was easily the strongest
aspect of Retro Sky.

I arrived with Stuart nearly two hours early on our final
scheduled day. Joey and a guy named Steve Berlin were
working with a band called Faith No More. Joey waved
us into the booth, letting us listen and watch. Steve was
a master, he whispered to me. The session broke up
after twenty minutes.   Stuart and I met the members of
the band as they left for the day, as well as Steve Berlin.
Steve is a big guy. Commanding presence. I was
embarrassed when Steve and Joey talked about Los
Lobos, their most recent CD, *This Time*. I was unaware
of the album, and ignorant of Los Lobos. Steve plays
saxophone primarily, and keyboards.   He is also a
producer. We talked about our brief tour, being from
Santa Fe. Steve had relatives in New Mexico where he
visits often. We talked more and he knew of my mom's
gallery, he had been there several times with his wife.
He asked me about James, whom he remembered in
detail. I laughed, telling him that James lived in a
cottage on our property. He was wonderful friend
whom I've known my entire life. That seemed to
change the tone of my being there immediately.

Steven asked Joey to cue up one of our cuts. Joey set-up "Only the Pavement Knows." I joked with Steve that Mike Campbell had played on this one a few months ago, last time we were in L.A. with Sharon – who was like an aunt to me. That caught his attention as well. I had the tape if he wanted to hear that one also. He knew Campbell, is all he said, but I could tell that his mind was processing everything. Then he added that he would like to hear it next, after this version of "Pavement."

"I like it," Steve assessed carefully. "I like the drive. Straight ahead rock and roll. Let me hear the old tape." Joey popped that one in and Mike Campbell's lead was prevalent. Can't miss it. Steve smiled, "Yeah, a bit different flavor. You do a nice job, or whoever took up lead. Mike's hard to duplicate."

"It's me." I said.

"This is a great demo. Nearly ready to go. Can I add some keyboard? Sounds like you got two electric guitars, an acoustic, the rhythm section. Awesome vocal arrangement. Who's the girl?"

"Melanie's in the band. She'll be here soon."

Steve set up what he wanted Joey to do, then we went into the studio.

"Stuart, go ahead and hook up your bass. Won't hurt to have you overdub a double bass line. Will add to the drive." He motioned me to the piano. "Go ahead and play the keys. We'll see how it sounds. I'll play this." As he sat down at the B3.

We went through the song three times. The rest of the band had arrived as I waved to them in the booth.

"Let's do another," Steve said up beyond the glass. Everyone came into the studio and met Steve.

"How 'bout 'Crashing my Beloved's Red Mustang'?" Joey asked through the intercom. Thumbs up from all of us. It was our newest. Melanie and I wrote it when we passed a wreck in the desert. Very fun lyrics, symbolizing the heart, of course.

Joey played the tape. Then Steve asked us to play the song again. Then again. He was still in the studio with us, walking around near each of us individually.

That's when I met David Hidalgo. David was an ominous presence, even from a distance. He was standing in the engineering room, listening to us. I had no idea who he was. Steve waved him in, then introduced us. We talked briefly. David is a thoughtful, reserved professional, who listens very carefully to every word and every lyric. Especially to the minutia of music. David can play almost every instrument extremely well. He smiled at our song, "Crashing." David and Steven spoke to each other at length, out in the hallway. They came back into the studio with a joviality of brotherhood they obviously shared.

"You know James, in Santa Fe, huh?" Hidalgo asked me.

"He's like my grandpa. He and my mom are very close." I answered.

"I know who your mom is too. Pretty cool, I'd say." David added, looming larger than life with his easy manner.

I just nodded, wondering about James's connection here.

David asked me if he could sit in on our session. He wanted to give the accordion a whirl if it was alright with us. Steven was pulling out his bass saxophone. Steven practically ordered me to take the organ. He asked Melanie what she was playing on the song. She answered piano. The simple chord progression. He nodded and asked her to play it again, feel free to play over the original with some improv. Sing it again as well, layering her own backup vocal to her previous lead and to mine. We wanted her to raise her register at the bridge. David was going to sing as well. Giving the song a powerful chorus sound. Before starting, David went to the drums, moving Bird out of his seat, showing Bird a slightly different riff, asking him to use the maraca lightly during the slow section. David deferred to me as lead. We took six or seven takes, listening to each one before adjusting for the next round.

We already had two guitars on the tape, mine and Frankie's, but on the final take, David asked if he could add more acoustics. He played alongside Frankie, just the two of them on that one take.

The finale was much bigger in sound than anything we had recorded thus far. It was easily the best song now, but it ruined the balance of the whole CD. Joey said just as much when we were all in the studio laughing, congratulating ourselves.

David told me, then Joey up in the booth, "Just layer in a bit more into each one. Julian can play in the gaps. Melanie's voice is a good one to create more harmony."
Then back at me, "Oh, and say hi to James for us."
Then he and Steven left.

We stayed up till 1:00am, taking advantage of our last day in the studio. Simple things were added, experimenting with various percussion sounds. Using mild distortion on one song. Enough to change up each lyric or melody, leaving two of them in their raw form. Joey liked it. We were all excited.
We called the resulting CD, RETRO SKY, *Nonstop*. Rhonda was having the original photo of us touched up in an art department owned by the studio, adding a funky back cover for the jewel CD box. David's and Steven's names would be added as guest performers.

Stephanie

Staying up with the girls was a blast. We'd drink pop and eat popcorn, looking at their yearbooks, gossiping about boys. Sandra had a boyfriend of sorts, showing me their homecoming pictures. Only recently had they starting dating, going out in his truck. Tiffany had circled the cute boys in her yearbooks, and x-out the one she didn't like. She had a lot to say about the ones she liked. I did not have much to add. I talked about a few of the older boys who had parts in *Music Man*. But I didn't like any of them *in that way*. None of the male actors I had met at the *Nest* or in France were in my age range. I told them about the boy I had danced with in Paris, which gave them a giggle. I had plenty of boys interested in me at school, I just didn't like any of them. The jocks were terribly obnoxious, cliquey, and not as cute as they thought they were.

"I guess I'm stuck up," I said almost seriously. I was not sure why I was so picky.

"You could have anyone in the whole wide world, Steph!" Tiffany prodded.

"Maybe." I made up my mind that I'd take a closer look when I got back to school.

My last day on the ranch, Roberto had me mount a mile and a half racer, Degas, a thoroughbred who needed a full-out run. Unleashed, so to speak. Roberto would ride beside us on Glamour, his favorite horse. We warmed-up Degas and Glamour in easy tempo, eventually leading to the start, where we took off. I almost panicked feeling Degas' sheer power. He was moving incredibly fast for me. Roberto was side by side till the half-way pole, then he gave me the signal to let him go. I realized that I was holding back because of my lack of experience. I tried loosening my tight grip and said something to Degas and sure enough he cranked into another gear. Nothing like a horse responding in such overdrive. Maybe even two more gears for him. We pulled ahead of Roberto and Glamour for about a quarter of a mile. I was exhilarated making the final two turns. Then Roberto and Glamour caught us into the homestretch. Roberto had a big smile and gave the go ahead to his beloved Glamour. They beat us by I don't know how many lengths. Not even close. Both girls were cheering when I began to slow down. Finally. I was out of breath, standing in my saddle to relieve my burning legs. Degas was like a train, huffing like a machine, cranking down his gears for over a quarter mile. I patted his mane when we finally reached a slow gallop and thanked him for being good to me. A true professional horse. He certainly took me for a ride more than the other way around.

It was the highlight of my visit. Of all the late-night parties and staying up at all hours with the girls. The many horses I got to know and ride. The wonderful *horse people* everywhere. David and Linda were loving and happy to have me. I hardly saw them, honestly. Degas was the highlight. I'd never felt such a rush. Not on stage, not in front of a camera. This was entirely more fun.

Danny

"Wait a second, let me adjust my jacket." I said to Jennifer before she started the VHS recorder. Jennifer had offered to have one of the masseuses come back to our room and act as a cameraman, but I was too self-conscious. We had figured out three scenes, and how to stop the camera after each. We made up a role play where I was an airplane pilot named Alan and she was a stewardess named Fran. We found the best clothes we could to play each scene. The general idea was in place, what we were going to say and what to improvise.

Scene one, in front of a painting of a nature scene in our suite.

"Fran, I'll come to your room later. After I make sure the crew is settled." I said to her.

She looked around not wanting to be seen. "Sounds good. I can't wait. Let's see," Jennifer looked at our room key, "I'm in room 248." Jennifer had on a scarf and lots of makeup. Her skirt was hiked up so we could see her legs. She had unbuttoned her white top so I could see, ever so subtly, her black bra. Her hair wispy with plenty of hairpins.

"I want your landing gear on my runway," she exclaimed, as if she was being secretive.

"I'll make sure and make a smooth landing, not hitting the pavement too hard." I said, trying not to laugh.

"It's okay if you do. Hard landings sometimes give me a thrill." She was saying it with a straight face, playing with my lapel.

"When I dock in your terminal, I'll make sure to give you a signal." I had no idea where that came from.

"Please do, I'll want to make sure and give you everything I got as your favorite stewardess. Make you happy as a new member of your crew. One more for you to rely on whenever you need it." I was struggling with keeping a straight face when she rattled off those lines.

"You always make me happy, Fran." I said, eventually, playing with her scarf.

"Yes, but you've never asked me to dock in this airport before. It will be a new experience to get to know your full piloting skills." She was staying true to our plan, her face glancing away to a far-off bedroom. I was biting my lip.

We cut, as I dashed to turn off the camera. We set up the next scene by the bar. We'd each have a drink in our hand, with a lot of our clothes nearly off.

I hit *play*.

"This is a nice room, Fran." I said. Not sure how to start off.

"It is. I'm glad we can relax. Finish your drink." She finished unbuttoning my shirt as we stood there.

Then Jennifer undid her hair, allowing it to fall.

I set down my glass and cupped her black bra. She leaned into me sucking an ice cube from her drink.

"You know, Alan, I've always wanted you. Ever since I was assigned to your crew, I wanted to show you how I'd give you my everything." She kissed me on the cheek and smiled.

"When I watch you bend over to help passengers on the window seat, I can see that you've prepared yourself for all contingencies." Jennifer smirked at that one. We were both trying hard to stay in character.

I undid her skirt and it slid to the floor. Her matching black panties and Jennifer's hips moving near my crotch. She undid my pants as I caressed her stomach. I was getting hard.

"We will be docking soon," She whispered loud enough for the camera.

"I know. I've wanted this since we took off, thinking about it the entire flight."

"Me too." She took out my dick and knelt. She was pumping her hand, bobbing her head with intensity, making sure the effect would be captured by the lens. It was very difficult for me to break away and turn off the camera.

I set up the tripod by the bed. We arranged it perfectly for a *rear entry*.

We went over some of the things we'd say, wanting to
be loud, orgasmic. Put everything into it.
Our dialogue was quickly forgotten once we 'received
the signal from the tower to engage.'
"Oh yes, Alan, push hard against my … against the …
The engine is locked and loaded." She had forgotten her
lines. First time in her acting career.
"Fran, I can feel you open to perfect penetration. I'm
ready to give you full force." I slid into her.
"Give it to me Alan. Give it to me now!"
I was standing behind her, almost exaggerating my
thrusts. She would turn around and look at me and
right at the camera, practically yelling, *fuck me hard Alan.*
We were extremely loud with our exhales, and ecstasy.
She put her head down into the pillow when I grabbed
her ass and finished hard. She was screaming as loud as
she could, over the top loud, into the pillow, and I was
almost as loud.
Once we settled down and finished, I ran to the camera
and hit *stop*. We burst out laughing so hard, I was
stuttering to say something. She had tears in her eyes
from the laughter.
Sleep eventually came. We had dinner sent up when we
woke up, sometime around midnight. We took a
shower together, carefully soaping each other.
Sensuous but not sexual. Standing long in the hot water.

We put on our robes, made fresh whiskeys for both of us.
Jennifer lit a cigarette at the table near the television. I
lit a cigar. I rewound the tape and we relaxed, watching
the new movie we had made. It was so much fun to

watch ourselves. I forgot that we had put the stereo on as background music. It was muffled on this ever-critical viewing. Very cheesy like in a bad porn movie. Which it was. It lasted about twenty minutes, with two very crude, abrupt cuts between the three scenes. The camera angles were perfect for each, especially the last scene.

I'd say we watched it four or five times, making comments. Laughing. Sometimes giving each other the eye with a wicked grin.

Satiated with sheer sexual fun.

Julian

We got a late start getting back to Santa Fe. Rhonda was busy meeting with people, so we slept-in, watching crummy TV shows in our rooms. Exhausted.

Once on the road, Shelly abruptly had us stop at Copper Motel in Ash Fork. Stuart's parents wanted to drive through, but she said she had to rest. It was 9:00 pm by then.

We barely unloaded anything. Finding a bed, falling asleep. This is the only time Melanie and I slept together. No sex, just cuddling. Sleeping. No one seemed to care. Stuart was in the other bed.

Mel and I had managed to have a few sexual moments, even some romance in Redondo Beach on the pier. We were close, wanting to be with each other, but it was impossible under these group conditions. We had fun at times, although most of the trip was about our music — which we took seriously. Mel was content, if not extremely happy about the outcome of our shows, the recording sessions. Everything. I was as well. Honestly, I was one horny guy, wanting Melanie to myself in the worst way.

We meandered in the bright early morning sunshine over to the Route 66 Museum. Surprisingly, in this dusty desolate place, it was an amazing museum. Old cars and trucks, photos of families moving west during downtrodden times. Road workers living on the hope of progress. A lot of interesting history going back to the 1920's. It was a nice break from the boredom.

We made it back to Santa Fe by 2:00. We had missed three days of school. Each of us had a copy of *Nonstop*. It was far better than we could've ever hoped for. It sounded great. Our gigs went over well, we played hard. It was a successful trip.

We'd keep playing in the area, rehearsing as always. Our direction was now in the hands of Shelly and Rhonda. Time to get back into school. Regular life.

Mel was dropped off at my house. Louise greeted us, taking all our dirty clothes, wanting details. We provided the most we could, eating sandwiches and chips.

I took Mel down to my room. We lay on the bed, as I began kissing her. She responded for a while, then stopped me. She was on her period.

"I want to just lay here and talk, Julian. I want to look into your eyes. I want to relive our time out there. In the studio. I've never felt closer to you. You were amazing. You are amazing."

"So are you," I kissed her again, softly. I looked into her blue eyes. She looked exhausted. "What was your favorite time during all this?" I asked her.

She was thinking. Quietly. She even closed her eyes. "The pier." She finally answered.

I remembered the pier. All we had done was kiss. For what seemed like an hour. Holding each other. The ocean waves. The night lighting. It was the most in love I had ever felt.

"I agree." I said.

"What about our playing. Live, I mean?" She asked me this time.

I had flashes of some amazing times. We had done well. I did not feel like we had a low point as a band. Some songs went over better, depending on the audience.

"Mel, every time we sing Everly Brothers, and now Stevie Nicks, I get choked up. When it's you and me." She smiled and closed her eyes again. She was running the palm of her hand over my cheek. A tear formed in the corner of her eye. "Me too." She whispered.

I closed my eyes.

"I'll be graduating soon, Julian. Ummm. Well. This is weird, but would you take me to prom?"

"Really?   I'm sorry, it never crossed my mind. Of course."

"Just, I went to Homecoming this year with Sammy, that band kid who asked me out. Nice guy. He's sweet, really. And last year I went to prom with a guy you never knew. He moved."

"Who was that?"

"Bobby Peterson."

"Right, I don't know him."

"I've never really been to a dance with someone … someone I cared about or wanted to be with, is all."

"It will be fun."

"Yeah. I'll be with a freshman. People will probably make fun of me. Lots of the senior guys, especially. Most everyone knows about us, though."

"I don't care about them."

"I know, Julian. They'll be jealous more than anything. And I'm not saying that because I'm special or anything. Just that we have something, you know?"

"The band?" I said it sarcastically. She hit me lightly on the shoulder.

"Yeah, the band."

CHAPTER TWENTY

Young love is like a raging fire that can't be tamed. It's addictive and borderline obsessive. Satisfying in every way, yet never getting enough.   Paige P. Horne

Jennifer

The problem with having so much fun, being away from it all, is the returning. Not so much for me, I assured myself, but for my family. I can retreat to my studio. The Gallery is fine. Our regular staff meeting did not indicate anything pressing. A small book maker made an offer on *Kid*. I'd talk with Frankie and his mom about it. I felt like two thousand dollars was a lowball offer, especially since the buyer wanted all rights.   I'd recommend to Frankie that he sell the book for ten thousand and retain the rights. I liked the idea of negotiating.

Of course, I had a ton of messages regarding the promotion of *Purgatorio.*   Normally I'd escape but I wanted to run interference for Steph.   I expected, even anticipated this enormous task. Before making the key calls to Tim and Phil and Sharon, I went into my studio, taking a chair, staring out through my massive picture window. Traces of snow lined the mountain range. I sipped my fourth cup of coffee. I smiled, remembering all the crazy things Danny and I did. We used that tripod and camera off and on for two more days. We bicycled, ate out, went to two more vineyards, swam a lot.

Always returning with giddy ideas for the camera.
Danny found enough comfort in having a masseuse
control the camera on our final try. Her name was
Willow. Willow showed no reservation or shyness. She
had us explain what we were going to do, closeups as
we had directed or wide angles or whatever we thought.
Willow made clear that she could not participate in any
other way than as a cameraman. It was weird to have
another person in the room, a stranger, no doubt.
Danny almost showed-off. I know that I did. We
destroyed all our tapes except that one, taking it home,
hiding it immediately.
Our thank you note to Jimmie and Denee' was tongue in
cheek, saying we couldn't find anything fun to do.
Mostly boring. But thank you, anyway.
Stephanie and I would fly just the two of us to Europe.
Sharon didn't want anything to do with a long-drawn-
out trip. She'd fly in for the premiere in Cabourg. She
didn't want to go to Moscow, either. Otherwise, she
agreed to do the New York talk shows and interviews
and only two similar events in Los Angeles. My
daughter and I would leave for London as school let out
for summer. We'd be gone six weeks.
Press releases would go out in full force next Monday.
Stephanie's bio and identity would not be revealed,
exactly, but the entire world would figure it out
immediately, if they hadn't already. With two
appearances on local TV, she was already making waves
in Santa Fe. My hope was that she finished school in
one piece.

Prom night was rapidly approaching, May 6. Julian asked us if Melanie could use our car. Her mom couldn't lend her car that night, she was driving up to Denver. Julian and Mel planned on going out alone and hoped to use mine. Stuart and Frankie had girlfriends. Bird asked a girl one year older than him, and she said yes. They'd triple date. Stephanie was a freshman, and it was highly unusual for freshmen to attend. Julian would most definitely be the only freshman guy there. Melanie was wanting the night to be special, just for them. There were all kinds of unspoken rules. Danny told me that there were no actual school policies other than no one over 21 years old could attend. One or two couples had a male graduate return to take their younger girlfriend, never a girlfriend return to take a younger boyfriend, that he could remember to the dance. Gay couples were beginning to rumble over the past few years about the unfairness of the whole thing, yet not one had attended. Danny and the counseling office were spreading the word that they'd receive no opposition from administration.

Our front doorbell rang one night during dinner. All of us were startled. We had seldom heard our own doorbell. Danny got up and answered. He was talking in hushed tones.

"It's for you Stephanie." He said as we all sat in wonder. Louise, especially.

"Who is it?" she asked.

"Not saying," he said with a grin.

I could hear from a distance Madonna singing "Rescue Me" via a car stereo. There was excited chatter. I heard a male voice, sounded nervous, even as I ate. Then the door shut, and I could hear the music tail off as the car drove away.

We waited for Stephanie to come back and eat.

Stephanie walked in with a sheepish smile and sat down. Julian asked, "Well, who was it?"

"Cameron Jackson." She was smiling, not saying anything else.

"Who's Cameron Jackson?" Julian asked.

"He's a junior. He plays basketball."

"I know Cameron," Danny said with approval in his voice.

"So, what happened? He asked you to prom, right?" Julian prodded.

"Yeah. Yeah he did."

"AND?"

"I said yes. I hope that's okay Mom and Dad? I didn't know what to say. He was so nice and polite. He knew I liked Madonna. Or used to. Whatever. He had it loud on his car stereo. It will be a group date with two other couples from the team."

"That's wonderful, Steph." I said. I had no idea who Cameron was. She was awfully young to go to prom, but Stephanie was older than her years.

Danny got up and patted her on the head, kissing her on the head as well. He seemed happy for her.

"Tell us about Cameron, dear." Louise asked.

"I don't know him very well. His sister, Janice, is a freshman. I don't know her very well either. Janice worked on the costumes for *Music Man*. I think I've talked with Cameron twice my entire life. Once at my locker when he said that he saw me in *The Sound of*

Music. He was terribly nervous. He was just now, too. He could barely say my name, my full name. Steph-a-nee."

We laughed.

"But he was so sweet. The other time was in the hallway after school. I was going to my locker. He was standing right by my locker and asked me if I knew Tim Prescott. Was it true? I said I did. He was friends of the family. I was a little perturbed by the question. Then he quickly added that the guys wanted to know and made him ask me. He was almost apologetic."

"I'm surprised you don't get more of that." I said. "And you better watch out once news of *Purgatorio* gets out, you will be swamped."

"I suppose. People leave me alone most of the time. After *Music Man* and all that died down. Even after *The Sound of Music* … oh, and he brought up *Sound of Music* again, just now. He said how wonderful I was. He loved me singing at the end. I looked older than I am at school. I think he was trying to compliment me."

Julian asked, "D'you think he's good looking? I mean do you like him?"

"Yeah, yeah. He's cute. He seems so scared to death of me, though, and I'm only a freshman. He's a big junior."

"Come on, Steph." Julian added. "Everyone is scared to death of you. You've been on TV. Twice. Articles in the paper. They know about Tim and Mom. No matter what Cameron asked you at the locker. And Sharon too. Everyone knows. Not to mention. Especially not to mention. You are the principal's daughter! Jesus, Steph. He probably peed his pants ringing the doorbell." Julian was not holding back. "And then Dad answered. He was probably shaking like a leaf."

"He was," Danny interjected, grinning at Julian.

"You are a very pretty girl, too. Don't listen to your brother. He was just nervous, that's all." Louise joined in.

"Thank you, Louise." Steph said reaching over and grabbing her hand. "I'm sure that's it most of all." They both smiled.

I sat there watching all of it unfold. For some reason I thought back to France. How Stephanie talked back to Tim. How belligerent she was. Out of line. It scared me then. It scared everyone. Except Sharon. I wondered what would happen to this poor Cameron if he caught even a glimmer of what Steph could be like. I tried hard to ease the image from my thoughts.

"Tell him you don't like Madonna anymore." Julian said to his sister with a smile.

Stephanie

I knocked on Julian's bedroom door. I could hear music playing, REM's "Imitation of Life." Julian was singing over Michael Stipe's vocals. He probably didn't hear me knocking. I went in, startling Julian.

"Sorry, I knocked." I said. I looked around at all the original posters, concert venue things. Like John Lee Hooker Live in Detroit. Buddy Holly Live in Minneapolis. The Pretenders in London. Of course, Elvis Costello in Yorkshire. Julian had a large bedroom, and every wall was filled with these amazing images.

"No problem. What's up?" He was sitting at his desk, turning in his chair. I flopped down on the beanbag chair. His hair was growing in, almost combable. I liked his new glasses. He was looking rough around the edges, unshaven, ratty stubble. I looked around the room some more. I hadn't been in there in I had no idea how long. Music, music. Sheet music. Classical and jazz magazines. Biographies scattered on shelves, on the floor. I saw one on Leonard Cohen. Another on John Coltrane. He had two guitars propped up near him. I had no idea, at this point, how many instruments Julian had. Especially considering he stored most of his stuff at the studio. Albums and CD's, 45's and even 78's. A music museum of clutter.

"I wanted to ask you about the road trip. I haven't had a chance to catch up with you." I said.

"It was great, Steph. Retro rocked. We sounded good. You know better than I do what a thrill to have an audience cheer. That kind of thing." He was proud, no doubt.

"I bet. You guys are good. I really like "Pavement." Great song. Now that I'm hearing your demo more and more, it's impressive."

"Thanks." Julian looked at me with a big smile.

"Oh, and that new "Crashing" one is even better. I can't sit still listening to it." I said it and he turned away before saying anything.

"Steph, you are amazing. You were off the charts good in that movie. And I loved seeing you over at the Eagle's Nest. You made those songs a lot of fun. I enjoyed it – well, you."

My turn to say, "Thanks." I reached over and touched his hand. He looked at me carefully.

"Look, Julian, I hope you and the band go far. It'll happen."

He didn't respond. Only smiled, again.

"How are you and Mel?" I asked.

He pulled his hand away, looking for something. He had pictures of their trip. He was searching for a specific one to show me, I could tell. It was a picture of them live in Redondo Beach. He was standing with his electric guitar, close to Melanie. They were singing. She had a tambourine. It was a great shot.

"Rhonda took this with her Nikon. Cool, huh?" He said, handing the photo to me.

"Wow, you two look awesome. I have to say, you look so much older, Julian. And Mel looks like she's about twenty-five. There's no way you're fourteen!" I laughed.

He laughed, too. "Older than you, Steph. Don't forget it."

"Are you excited to go to prom?" I asked him.

"I suppose. You know they asked us to play at the dance. Retro Sky, that is. I turned them down. I wanted this to be about me and Mel. It's important to her. This is tough, graduating." His voice trailed off.

"I bet. She'll be fine. You'll be fine." I assured him.

"What about you?" He asked me.

"It'll be fun. Cam, Cameron came up to me in the cafeteria today. I was reading, all engrossed in this *Ladies' Detective Agency* book. You know how I get. Anyway, he's never in the freshman lunch. I have no idea how he skipped his class. He handed me a long

note as he sat down by me.   It's a sweet note. He
wrote all this stuff about me being an actress. About
Mom and Sharon and Tim. About you and Retro Sky.
About Dad. It said how beautiful I was, and he was lucky
to take me to the dance.   He was thanking me for saying
yes."

"Wow." Julian was considering what to say. "Good for
Cam, I guess. He is in a tough spot when you think
about it. You can be intimidating anyway, Steph. I get it,
even without all that stuff. Fame and all that."

"I guess. You know. I've never really had a boyfriend.
That junior high stuff was like who you sat with at lunch
or held hands with at recess. I hate to say, but I've never
really been physical, other than kisses. God, I can only
imagine you and Mel."

He didn't say anything right away. "Yeah, I guess we're
close. Committed in a way.   Feels weird saying that
being so young. I love Mel.   It's obvious probably."

"Yes it is, my dear brother. I'm happy for you. I'm
jealous in a way."

"Don't be."

"Can I ask? You know?"

"No. Don't ask." He smiled. "Let's just say we're close.
We'll keep it at that."

"Okay." I understood.

"Just have fun with Cam.   He seems like a good guy."
Julian was encouraging me.

"I think he is. I need to get him to relax. God, I just sit
there reading, eating a sandwich, and this cute guy is
saying all this stuff. Or too damned scared to say it,

writing it all down. And I have a weird disconnect. *Just talk to me*, I want to say to him."

"You should call him. I mean it. Ask him to come over or something. Break the ice for the guy."

I considered it. I'd never do that, but it seemed like the thing to do.

"Steph, I wanted to ask you about something else."

"Sure."

"I've had dreams of those towers. The Trade Center. Vivid. I had one last night."

I shivered. So had I.

"Me, too." I replied. "They are quick. Like a movie interrupting whatever is happening in my brain. Like you said, *VIVID*."

"What in the world?" He asked me.

"I don't know. James seems very much aware of it all. You know that. I get worried, I think it's tied into James dying. He makes it sound that way."

"I know. Spooky how he talks sometimes. He told us to not worry about it. I guess I don't."

"Yeah, what can we do anyway?"

We sat in silence for several minutes. Julian went to his stereo and put in The New Pornographers latest, *Mass Romantic*.

"You and mom will be going back to Europe. That'll be fun," He said, sitting back down.

"I have to confess; I'm looking forward to it. The whole idea of interviews and openings, film festival stuff. Expenses paid. I'd be freaking if it were just me, but mom will be there. We'll have fun."

"So cool, Steph." He was smiling that wonderful smile he has. Different than his usual smile.

"Yeah."

"Sharon isn't going?" He asked.

"No. I think we'll see her at Cabourg."

"She's amazing. I don't talk about her much to people. You know how she is. So damned beautiful. So, I don't know, scary talented. I can hardly believe she's our aunt, or you know."

"I know. I gotta tell you, Julian, I was having a tough time. You know that. When we started filming."

"I know."

"And when Sharon slapped me. I was like in the place of ferocious anger. It's hard to explain. It's acting, I guess. And we weren't even filming. Tim was terrified, I could tell. Sharon decked me, meeting me right where I was, in character. I know you're not an actor, just so amazing. I've never in my life experienced that. We were like that over and over when we finally began filming. Sharon is one scary woman. She's amazing."

He was quiet. He was doing this even after I said everything. Like his mind was reeling. "I have to say, Steph, Sharon is so beautiful, sometimes, I forget she's famous or my aunt or whatever she is. Sexy, I guess." He finally spoke.

I laughed with a boom. "You mean, she turns you on?!"

He laughed, too. "Yeah, I guess so."

My turn to be silent. At least until I quit laughing. "Julian, no big deal. Join the club. Like every other guy in the world. Just you get to see her up close and personal.

And how many times has she kissed you? That's the way she is."

"No shit." Julian said. He changed the subject. "How was it working with Mom? I mean really. You've never said."

I had him stand up and face me. "Like this. Look in my eyes." He did, nervously. "What do you see?" I asked.

"I don't know. You have nice eyes. A lot in there."

"Well, I know it's uncomfortable. Mom was able to pull all of that out of me once Tim said *action*."

He sat back down, uneasy. "Look Julian. Sharon is over the top great. Mom is harder to describe. It's strange, like our dreams, maybe." I tried to find the words. "Let me put it this way. I imagine that when Stuart and Bird are playing, it becomes engrained inside of you, you automatically respond with your voice or piano. Whatever."

"Yeah, I get that." He was listening closely.

"When Mom and I had scenes, she flows so easily into me. I was Manon in a way that was different than being a prostitute's daughter. Mom was elevating me in an almost religious way. Purity. Like music, maybe, is what I'm guessing."

"Not sure what you mean, but I feel that way sometimes when Mom and I talk. Especially over at the studio. And in the gallery. She's another person when we are surrounded by her art. The creative process. She's different from Sharon in those moments. Not that you can compare them. I hear what you're saying."

I nodded my head. I got up and found a Bob Dylan biography on his shelf, by a guy named Anthony Scaduto.

"Dad gave me that. I was probably only ten. He's like Dad's hero." Julian said.
"Is it good?" I asked.
"I've read it at least twice. Well, you've heard me play my whole life. The Dylan thing is still alive with me.
"Isis," of course. That's just one of many."
"Dad's so cool. I can see why Mom loves him so much. I mean, think about it. Mom could have anyone she wants.   Dad is not into painting or the fame thing. He loves movies, all that. Music. He listens to music almost as much as you do."
"I know. He knows his stuff."
"It's like Mom and you and me, doing everything *out there*." I was motioning like there was an audience.
"I get you."
"Dad's, well, Dad. He's into his golf. His coaching. Teaching. The school. He's so religious, too. Mom seems so into that about him. Must go back to being in high school, I guess."
"I agree. I've thought about it a lot. They still act like high school kids. He's the jock and she's the hippie art chick. I get it."
We laughed.
"Ah, Julian. Thanks. I'm going to go call Cam now. I'll ask him over to hang out. I'll be nice."
"I know that's hard for you, Sis." Julian said, kidding with me, as I left his room.

I used the upstairs phone in the den, finding Cam's number in the phone book. I thought it was his because of the address and where I thought he lived. Wasn't sure. I dialed anyway.

He answered. My heart skipped in an unexpected thrill, a sense of utter shyness. My freshman self-surging in my veins. He said *hello* again.

"Is this Cam?" I asked.

Hesitation in his voice, "Yes. Who is this?"

"Stephanie."

"Oh! Hi. I wasn't sure."

"Hope it's okay that I call you."

"Sure, sure. Absolutely."

"Not the usual thing. I know."

"Stephanie. Well, I'm glad you called. Really glad you did."

"Why's that?" Now I was being unfair. I had regained my balance.

"Just glad. A nice surprise." A slight defensiveness in his tone. Back off I told myself. Be nice.

"I wanted to see if you'd like to come over some time. We can hang out here. Watch TV or we have a pool table."

Excited, "That would be great! When?"

"Anytime. Tonight? Now? Whenever you want."

"Sure, sure. I can drive over now. It's close to dinner, though."

"Eat here. I think we're having hamburgers."

"You sure? Your parents okay with it?"

"Dad might not like having you over here. He gets pissed off when boys try to come over here."

Dead silence.

"Just kidding, Cam. Sure, it's fine. We can eat downstairs. We don't have to hang out with them. Watch a movie, maybe."

"Sounds fun. I'll be over in about a half hour. Okay?"

"Sure."

I ran to my room to clean up. Change into something nice. I called Mom at her office. She was fine with it. She made a sly comment and we laughed. I told Louise, too. She smiled and didn't say a thing. I ran downstairs and told Julian to behave himself. He said, "Way to go, Sis. I knew you could do it. He's going to be scared out of his mind coming over here."

"I'm a bit nervous too." I ran back upstairs again to see what kind of pop we had, snacks, that kind of thing. Louise reminded me we'd be eating when Mom and Dad got home. I told her we'd eat downstairs. She took out some paper plates and plasticware.

"You look very cute. *Darling*, is the word." Louise told me.

"God. I'm not sure *darling* is what I'm after. But thanks." She laughed. I was getting nervous. Really nervous. Where in the world was this coming from? I hardly got this nervous in front of a camera. Or on stage. I was freaking out.

The doorbell rang.

Cameron is tall, probably 6'1", a good four inches taller than me. Brown hair, strong looking. He had on a letter jacket with lots of stuff on it even though he was only a junior. He took off his Santa Fe baseball hat, being a gentleman.

"Thank you for inviting me over, Stephanie." He had rehearsed it.

"Come in. It's cold out, with the wind." I was drawing blanks, unrehearsed entirely.

Louise introduced herself to Cam. She'd call us when the food was ready. We went downstairs.

Cam looked around at everything. Framed ski posters mostly. I had an enormous mural of horses on one wall. It was painted by one of Mom's friends. Julian had a wall taken up with a framed Broadway billing of the Philharmonic. An original. *A Night with Strauss*. Julian had been through his Strauss phase with his piano teacher years ago, I explained. I showed him the rest of the lower floor, bypassing Julian's room. We walked out on the lower level. I showed him where James lived. Who was he? Cam was taking it all in.

"Nice," he said. "No movie posters. I kinda thought there would be."

"Nope." Is all I could reply. I braced myself for questions about Tim and movies. Sharon and Mom. Nothing. He let it go. I was glad.

"Let's play some pool?" He asked.

I turned on the overhead light, set up the rack, "Look out." I added. Then, "you break."

He took off his jacket. He had on a dark blue sweater and jeans. I could tell he played football. He was good at pool, easily winning the first game. We talked about the basketball team. How Dad was a great coach. That *Coach Billy* was a great coach, too. He wanted to play basketball in college. I told him about Dad. The golf, too. He seemed to know all about Dad.

We talked mostly about him, which was fine by me. He even started to brag about himself, reluctantly, relaxing a lot. I asked him if he had previous girlfriends. He told me about Michelle. A cheerleader. She was a junior, too. She broke up with him around Christmas time. She was going out with one of the seniors, Matt someone, I didn't know. It took a while for him to get over Michelle he said.

He finally asked about me. If I ever had a boyfriend. I said no. I liked some guys in junior high. He looked questioningly right at me.

"I can't believe that. I mean, you are like famous. You made a movie in Europe, I read all about it. And acting. I mean, I don't mean to be rude, but you're very good-looking Stephanie. I have a hard time believing that. I thought you'd say *no* to prom because of some guy in New York or somewhere."

I laughed. "Nope. No guy in New York."

We played an almost entire game without talking. Louise called us up. Julian almost ran right into us going up the stairs. They said *hi* to each other and that was that with the guys.

Everyone was polite serving up our plates. Dad was busy on the phone, then finally hung up. He came over and shook Cameron's hand. Dad said something like he could take Cam one on one, and Cam said no way. Something like that. Mom hugged him and told him he looked nice in his sweater. I swear, Cam blushed. Really blushed. Simple as being hugged by my mother. We ate downstairs, eating quickly, we were so hungry. I turned on the TV. He asked if we could watch *The 70's*

Show. He liked Mila Kunis. He even asked me if I had
ever met her. No. I didn't want to talk about any of that,
I thought to myself.

He asked me where we should eat on prom night. I
wasn't picky. I liked everything. I was antsy. Couldn't
sit still.

I ran upstairs to get us fudgesicles. Mom asked me if it
was going okay. Sure, I told her. Julian mocked-kissed
me with his lips, acting like we'd make out. I laughed at
him.

We sat on the couch, eating our fudgsicles. When we
were done, the program switched to the show *24*.
Neither of us were interested. I asked what music he
liked. I put on the *Pretenders* because he liked Chrissie
Hynde.

Cam put his arm around me when I sat down on the
couch. He turned to me and told me how much he liked
me. Then he kissed me. Softly. Holding my back with
his hand. I opened my mouth slightly, like he did. His
tongue barely touched my lips. I felt a warmth run
through me. Then we hugged for almost the entire time
"Back in the Chain Gang" played. My heart was racing.
He felt good. I held him tighter. He kissed me again and
we slid down on the couch, I was almost on my back.
He was more intense. Our tongues more active. My
legs were partially spread, and I could feel his thigh on
my pelvis. My excitement was surging. I could feel his
penis. A brand-new sensation completely. I had to
stop.

I stopped and sat up creating distance.

"Is something wrong?" Cam looked questioningly, like he had done something wrong.

"No. No." I hugged him.

"Okay."

"Just." I looked at him closely. I studied his facial features. The spots of facial hair he had shaved. His nose, which I liked. His dark blue eyes. His mouth. His teeth. He must've had braces perfect. "Just, I have to be honest. I've never done this. Anything like this."

"Oh." He sat up even straighter and looked at me as carefully. He hugged me. "I like you, really, Stephanie, and ..."

"Call me Steph, okay?"

"Right. Steph. I'm not all that experienced. Like I said, I thought you'd be experienced. Like a boyfriend or someone."

"No. Never have." I repeated.

"Michelle was my only girlfriend, ever. Maybe that's why it was hard when she broke up with me. We didn't go that far. Really."

"Like how far?" I asked sheepishly.

"Really?" He was shy to say.

"If you can tell me. You don't have to."

"I went in her pants once. She let me at a party." I didn't say anything. I thought he wasn't a virgin for sure. I was glad for some reason.

I was not sure what to do or say. I liked him. Even though I was entirely sure of myself in so many ways, so smart, accomplished, even spoiled rotten in my life, I was scared and wanted to go slow. I realized that now.

He must've read my mind. "Steph. I liked kissing you."
"Me too." I kissed him. We held each other and kissed until the CD stopped. It was dead quiet. I couldn't even hear anything upstairs. My mouth was wet and my hair a mess.

"We can stop if you want." He said. He was holding my hand. I didn't want to stop, and I was not sure about going any further. I had weird thoughts in my head, comparing my body to what I remembered Michelle's looked like. In her cheerleading outfit. She had bigger breasts. She is slightly taller, darker, longer hair. Gymnastic body. I liked my body. I was strong from horseback riding and skiing. I was sexy. Younger, is all.

"You okay?" He asked. He seemed genuinely concerned. I kissed him and whispered that I was fine.

He was rubbing my left breast on the outside of my long sleeve blouse when I heard more talking upstairs. I got nervous. Probably for no reason.

"We should stop." I said.

"Okay." He agreed – reluctantly I could tell.

He was sexually aroused as he tried to rearrange himself and calm down. I smiled and kissed him lightly on the lips. "That was nice, Cam. Can I ask you something?"

"Sure."

"Do you find me attractive? I mean, I'm only a freshman. Michelle was so beautiful. This is all new to me. Are we boyfriend and girlfriend? I sound so stupid. I know."

"Oh God, Stephanie. You are incredible. My heart is going nuts right now. I cannot believe that I'm with you. Kissing you. I never dreamed you'd say *yes* much less ask me over. To kiss me like you do."

"It's nice."

"Yes it is. Do you want to be my girlfriend? I'd love to take you out. If your parents will let me.   I mean us alone. Not like a group date. Sounds like you've never been on a date. It's weird taking out a freshman. The guys make fun of it. They'd normally crucify me, but to be honest, don't get mad. It's YOU. No One finds it weird. Everyone is jealous as hell that I'm taking you to prom. If we go out, I'd be the luckiest guy in the world."

I laughed. "Cameron. Please don't think of me that way. I'm just a girl that's never been with a boy, really. Yes, all that other stuff about me is true, but I'm just a fourteen-year-old. I can be tough and mean and strong and smart and do almost anything I set my mind to. Like in a movie or in a play. And I'm talented, I know that. But I'm trembling here. I need to be honest with you. With me. I'm scared. This is new to me. It's real, not like a script or something. Don't think of me that way, okay?"

"I'll try.   In a way I can see that. You are shivering almost. When you kiss, when we kiss, it's like you are doing it for the first time."

"Well, it is. Honestly. For real anyway. Not the stupid stuff growing up."

He kissed me and we embraced. I was glad that we had talked. I was not as strong as I thought I was. This was different.

Danny

Our PTA is the best in the world. They had prom planned down to the smallest detail. They had so many volunteers, our teachers and staff hardly had to do a thing. I volunteered to work the photo station. Jennifer agreed to help. It would be fun to take the traditional picture of each couple upon their arrival to the gym. We'd only have to be there from 6 to 8 covering every possible arrival time. Supervision was taken care of, so we could go out for dinner afterwards. Jennifer picked-up Melanie at 4:00, early enough for her to come over and for us to take our own pictures with Julian, and then hand her the keys to Jennifer's Volvo. We gave Melanie our bedroom to put on her dress, clean up. She was beautiful in her new blue tiered dress. Her blond hair highlighted with several braids. Julian had a rented tuxedo, dark blue, conservative for him. He was going to take Melanie to dinner at the only real upscale restaurant in town. We were sure they'd do a great business that night. They were going to go to an after-party at a friend of Stuart's. They'd be home by midnight. Melanie would spend the night. They promised up front that they would not sleep together. I believed them.

As they were leaving, Cameron showed up in a western cut, bolo-tied, tuxedo. Polished cowboy boots. He'd taken Steph out twice since he'd asked her out and they seemed to be an item. She was very relaxed about being with him.

Stephanie came down the stairs with Jennifer. Steph had on a light pink and white floral dress. My daughter was grown up. A big smile on her face. Cameron kissed her on the cheek, handing her a red corsage, and she handed Cameron a white boutonnière. He told Steph that she looked beautiful. She demurred telling him that he looked handsome. We got quick shots of both couples together, then Mel and Julian headed out. Cameron shook my hand, and then Jennifer's, promising to have her back by 11:00 as he had agreed earlier. I asked him about any after-parties with 'the guys.' He told me there was one, but he was going to bring Steph back early instead. Jennifer and I looked at each other and gave the go ahead for midnight. He looked almost as happy as Stephanie. Off they went.

Jennifer hugged me. We were very happy with both couples. Melanie was like our own already. We just shook our head about the age difference, having no idea how that was going to play out. Melanie was more and more on her own, her own mother drifting out of the picture. Talking about moving to Denver. Melanie did not want to go with her. And Cameron was a good kid. Of course, I had done my principal deep dive investigation. No behavior concerns. Cameron was raised in San Diego, moved to Santa Fe in seventh grade. A *B-plus* average. His mom was a doctor, his dad a banker. Second highest scorer on the basketball team. Billy thought he was a great kid. That was enough for me.

The photo station was decorated with a Jamaican theme. Fake palm trees and a fake ocean. Cheesy stuff like it should be. Couples trickled in slowly. Jennifer did the arranging and I snapped two pictures for each. What a blast to see the tuxes and suites, the dresses, the hair styles, the makeup. The chatter. The nervousness written all over most of the couples. Almost all the early arriving couples were the younger ones. Couples who were probably on their first date. Even some last-minute agreements and negotiating to go with each other.

Steph arrived with a group of four couples who had gone to a house for a catered dinner. She whispered to me and Jennifer how delicious it was. A lot of fun. Taking their picture was emotional for me. More than at our house. Steph was so incredibly happy. I don't know if I had seen her look so at ease, laughing, and carrying on with Cam and the group. Jennifer and I thought the same thing. Like our early days together.

Mel and Julian were one of the late arrivals. She was poised, glowing. This was a special moment for her, we all knew, and she was relishing every second. She held Julian's arm with pride. He was leaning into her, their body language groomed with perfection behind a microphone or – whenever they were alone. It was obvious. Julian whispered in Mel's ear as I took the photos. She laughed too hard once, so I snuck in another shot. Mel thanked us again for the use of Jennifer's car and then went into the dance.

We were out of there by 8:10. Jennifer and I drove out to a tiny restaurant that had a nice view of the city at night. We ate hors d'oeurvres of sliced flank steak with the chef's special cream sauce and drank spritzers. My assistant principal was on-call, so I didn't need to worry about anything for the evening. Just in case, though, I had learned to stay sober on nights of big activities.

Neither of us wanted to drink too much anyway. Our reminiscing was over the top fun. We told just about every story we could think of. All the dances we had been to. Our two proms, mostly. Jennifer had a memory like a trap. What everyone had on. The restaurants and houses with parties. The songs we danced to. The sex we had. I just remembered her and how gorgeous she was. By her senior year, she was like a model, nothing like the innocent young girl I had first asked out on a trampoline in her back yard the summer before our junior year. I was the luckiest man in the world. I kissed Jennifer with an enjoyment of her lips like the very first time. She smiled, almost shyly.

CHAPTER TWENTY-ONE

What is that feeling when you're driving away from people, and they recede on the plain till you see their specks disappearing? – it's the too huge world vaulting us, and its good-bye. But we lean forward to the next crazy venture beneath the skies. Jack Kerouac, On the Road

Jennifer

Stephanie and I had our own private jet. Tim would meet up with us on his own. So would Sharon. Stephanie was teary when she said goodbye to Cameron that afternoon. He was in shorts and a tee-shirt, sunglasses on. The world may just as well be coming to an end the way he looked.

I curled up and stared out the window. We were probably over the Midwest by now. Steph was asleep with another novel. I didn't even bother to ask what she was reading. I'd ask when she woke up. I was choked up saying goodbye to Danny. I really wasn't ready to be gone for six weeks. I made a joke about him giving Karen a call, but it wasn't funny, and I regretted saying it. We'd be fine. School was over. He was going to go on a golf trip with friends after he sent his staff home. Phoenix for seven days. I wiped a tear from my eye remembering Melanie embracing Danny on the podium as she received her diploma. She wouldn't let go of him. He wouldn't let go of her, either. Everyone in the audience hushed for that lengthy minute. We talked about her moving in with us until we figured out her school schedule, found an apartment with roommates. Her mom was leaving for Denver. Mel was already working temporarily at a grocery store twenty hours a week. She told the owner she'd be on the road sometime with her band. All he asked for was a few days' notice, if she could. He didn't seem too concerned. Julian was telling the band that Rhonda was handing Retro Sky over to a colleague she heard about, David Williamson in Los Angeles, who agreed to be their *informal* agent. He and Shelly were discussing another, lengthy road trip over the summer. They'd probably head out while we were in Europe.

What disturbed me was that James was not doing well. He was coughing all the time. He left the cottage to stay at the pueblo. I hated to leave for that reason most of all.

We landed in London. A train took us all over the British Isles. We had a car lined up and hotels and restaurants. A studio lady named Franny, who was incredibly efficient, ran us from place to place. The press treated us like gold. Some of the rag magazines said some raunchy stuff about Stephanie getting her acting job because of me. Ridiculous if it weren't true. I laughed, glad that Steph was so good in her part. It made them sound stupid. We did a lot of big auditorium interviews. Tim joined two of them. All of which were on campus sites around the Isles. Film crews and reporters were being taken care of with quotes and handouts and press releases. Stephanie gave one interview by herself in Ireland. The hostess of a national program was gentle with Steph for an hour-long interview. I was grateful for the kid-glove treatment.

On to Germany. On to several Nordic cities. France. Italy. Spain for an overnight. The Baltic countries. Back to France. Stephanie handled it better than I did. I was cranky half the time. She learned quickly that almost every set of questions were the same. That it was okay to give the same answer, repeatedly. She smiled and talked about music and books and television and being a sophomore in school. She liked school. She liked New Mexico. No, New Mexico is not the wild west. They have toilets and running water and everything. People loved her cheery, youthful way. Steph had an innocence they craved from actors. No presumptive arrogance. None of it. That she had a boyfriend became of great interest as the weeks went by. No, she wouldn't tell them his name. It was great working with Sharon. It was fun working with her mom. Tim is a great director. She began sounding as much like a tape recording as I did. She met a lot of people in the business. Also, in the college scene. Stephanie went on tours of various cities with young people. I let her go, staying quiet by myself, or I'd go to a museum or gallery, or just hang out with Franny. Franny liked matinees in any language or sitting for tea or coffee. Walking long miles. Franny showed me around a lot of Europe with no fanfare. Low key. The premiere in Cabourg was one of the best moments of my career. The people who ran the festival were kind, considerate and incredibly appreciative. To have Tim and Sharon and me and Steph there was a big feather in their cap. Every event was sold out. *Purgatorio* won best picture. The jury adhered to rules that stated that an individual film could only receive a maximum of three awards. They were trying to spread the wealth. Sharon received best actress and she gave a wonderful, light talk. She wasn't political or controversial. She bragged about her friendship with me and Steph, how wonderful Tim was. Stephanie received best new actor. She was so excited and elated. All of us were. We were staying on the beach and enjoyed the ocean, the cool air. It was beautiful. Steph talked me and Sharon into renting bikes and we spent a whole day riding along pavement near the ocean waves. She wore her inscribed medal around her neck the whole time. I had a very poignant interview with a French writer. He was a young man, straight out of university. We talked about my art and acting, nothing unusual there. But he took the conversation to my being a mother. The process of parenting Steph and her twin brother. He wanted to know what Danny and I had instilled in her beyond acting. Steph was rapidly finding a fan base with young people across the continent, her photos appearing everywhere, and people were curious about our family lives. He was not prying at all. He was simply curious about Steph. I told stories about us horseback riding and skiing. Reading books. Steph read voraciously. I tried to keep up with her. Her dad and she would go on hikes, they were very close. Danny was easy going with her even though he was a principal. The journalist asked about Danny being a *headmaster,* finding it difficult to believe that he wasn't strict with her. We laughed about that. I talked about Julian, for the first time with any journalist, and his band Retro Sky. He took careful notes on Julian and asked about their songs and their CD *Nonstop*. Right away I knew that word would spread. I should start dropping the hint the remainder of my interviews, especially when we got to Moscow. It dawned on me that I shouldn't protect my family so jealously. This was a good time to brag about them.

I mentioned that idea to Stephanie after we said our goodbyes to Sharon. I asked Sharon to please come to Moscow for the premiere. She told me she already told everyone she wasn't going. Besides, Steph was stealing the spotlight. She kissed us both with tremendous love and joy. She was incredibly proud of Steph.

Sharon and I did talk, alone, about her award. She was pissed that I didn't receive it. I think she was genuinely angry. I told her, again, how great she was. She'd have none of it.

I was evaluating how I was being received. Most of my accolades were for the script. I was answering questions about writing with Vince. Everyone wrote, however, that I had returned as an actress. Magnificently. No questions about that. Then most articles failed to address the actual performance. I did not get one poor review. It was the tone that bothered me. The whole mystery of my life and career. Steph seemed to enhance the mystery. I was being treated as an icon rather than as a performer. No one in their right mind would vote for me to win an award. Jennifer had already achieved all that. Sharon had won awards. Sharon was an actress. I was, well, something altogether different. One article, the only one I saw, that said anything like this anyway, hinted that I deserved a French Legion of Honor. I had only a few films to my name, but with *Purgatorio,* I had risen to Mount Olympus. America would never fully appreciate me. It didn't matter how many awards I was given. Stuff like that. I was blowing this out of proportion in my head, but the overall tone irked me.

Moscow. The Russian Federation was a *lurking* kind of government. Everyone at the film festival whispered about it. Paranoia permeated our conversations. We enjoyed the new metro, the enormous freeways, the construction thrusting the Russian capital into the new century. Steph was alert, taking note of all aspects of her generation in this city with a dark past. Everyone was dutiful, matter of fact charming in a stiff kind of way. Our film was accepted as a European product, and yet it screamed the United States in the studio listings, the producer's names.   The cast and crew and the director were of course American. Stephanie and I were alone under the microscope. Our hotel was brand new. Even then, it felt hundreds of years old.   Steph and I whispered as if we were bugged.   We probably were. A Russian film, HOBbIN BEK, *A New Century*, won the Festival Prize.   Surprise, surprise, we thought. The movie was clunky and stiff propaganda. I won Best Actress and Stephanie won Supporting Actress.   I gave a gracious, short speech. Stephanie said a bit more, excited as she was, looking forward to being back in Russia someday. Even a simple sentiment as that was blown into an act of ambassadorship.   Both of us liked the engraved bronze statuettes of a bear given to us as our prizes.

We gave two interviews in Moscow. Both were in the large crowd format, an interpreter acting as politically sensitive as he could. Stephanie chatted away about culture, Retro Sky and music, how the arts would unify her generation across national boundaries.   Inside myself, I understood her exuberance, knowing full well that everything she said would be twisted. Probably by the press on both sides of the long forgotten cold war. I don't think I was as able to foresee things as my daughter did. She was honestly excited about what was happening in Russia, especially the young people she had met. She had hope. I wanted to get the hell out of there.

Our premiere in Chicago was scheduled for the July 4th weekend. Steph and I opted to go home for three days, freshen-up, get new clothes. Besides, she was missing Cameron, and I was missing Danny. Julian, too. Absolutely. However, priorities with our beaus took first consideration, I'd tease Steph.

Julian

Melanie was sound asleep. Her blond hair beneath my nose, making me itch. Her naked body sprawled out over me, her breasts buried into my ribcage and stomach. Her legs straddled over my thigh. I needed to move her; my leg was falling asleep, numb. My hand caressed her butt. Elton John was singing "Where to Now St. Peter?" on the local radio station. I thought I'd love to play any song off *Tumbleweed Connection*. His piano was extraordinary. I made a mental note, still unwilling to move her.

Mel's mom had moved out only two days ago, headed to Denver. It was not a nice scene. Cold, matter of fact. For a guy up there, Melanie had never met. A better job. Whatever. Melanie had their apartment to herself until the end of June when the lease ran out. At least her mom paid for that. The place was even more sparce now. Mel's bed and a small three-drawer dresser. A couch. A card table and two folding chairs. Some food in the refrigerator. A box of cereal and a small jar of peanut butter.

She did have a ton of clothes, mostly in the closet. The winter things in boxes now. She was going to move in with us until the fall when she found some roommates near campus.

It may not matter. Rhonda, and probably Phil in L.A., had placed our fate in the hands of a guy named Donald Williamson. We hadn't met but we talked numerous times on the phone. I liked him and he seemed to believe in Retro Sky. He wanted me to think about changing the name to just Retro. I couldn't decide, I vacillated. He was getting us a tour together through the South. Four weeks of summer grind, starting in July. The heat of summer. Humidity and sweat. Radio stations were receiving our CD en masse and ahead of time. Several local TV stations, too. We'd have a detailed schedule any day now. Being underage was a problem, but Shelly and Donald would be with us at least.

I was getting phone calls from the press; spill-over from interviews Stephanie and Mom had given over in Europe. They wanted to know about me and Retro Sky. I probably spoke with four or five reporters in a very short period of days.

One day prior to our leaving, Melanie took an early shower and got dressed, geared up for our rehearsal. She had a lot on her mind, a lot to sing. We were using my mom's car until she got back from Europe. Dad was fine with it. Mom would probably freak out if she knew Melanie was driving her brand new 2000 Volvo. It was plush with all the goodies attached. The stereo system especially.

We went to the studio to rehearse like always. Stuart was late again, all gaga about his new girlfriend. I'd never seen him so happy. Frankie arrived with his new Gibson. He spoke more about that than his girlfriend. I loved his new guitar. He had accepted the offer on *Kid*, even though my mom tried to talk him out of it. Mom practically begged him and his mom to wait, but Mom was in a hurry to get going to Europe and left it to them. Frankie's mom needed the money, or whatever was left over after buying a brand new Les Paul, so they sold the rights to *Kid* anyway.

I sat at the piano playing "Burn Down the Mission" by myself. Everyone just listened. Melanie hummed a bit, chimed in some backup vocals.

"You should do that," Mel said. "Just you. Especially in these small towns. In the south, that would be cool."

"Thanks, I wanted to, but wasn't sure what you'd think." Then she asked me about us singing Lenny Kravitz's "Fly Away." We played it on our stereo a couple of times. The band quickly figuring out the instrumentation. I wanted the bass for this one, moving Stuart over to acoustic. I also wondered about the singing arrangement, letting Melanie take the lead. She wanted me to chime in with the final verse, *I want to fly away, yeah yeah yeah*. We would trade off on *I want to get away*, each taking a turn. It sounded great. We worked on it a good three hours.

Everyone was antsy, ready to go on the road, see what it would be like. This song only added to the nerves. Summer was here and Santa Fe was boring, inching through June. School was out and already forgotten. We had an enormous song list; we could play for hours if needed.

Bird's uncle was not doing well, however, and was near death, the way Bird told it. His uncle had already told him goodbye; *get out there and play some music.* Alo had some extended family on the reservation, he told us. He just shrugged his shoulders, acting like it was inevitable. No emotion. Bothered the hell out of me. I told him he could come live with us. He shook his head *no*. He'd be fine, he repeated. *Just wanna play the drums, man.* That's all.

Melanie asked the group about the possible name change. Everyone was unanimous that we liked the word *Sky*. Alo was particularly adamant, and he never spoke up about anything. Retro Sky we would remain. I'd let Mr. Williamson know.

No way I can sing like Steve Winwood. I come close on the keyboards, so when Frankie wanted to do "Sea of Joy," try his Clapton thing with Blind Faith, we gave it all late afternoon, into the night. It was ambitious. Melanie asked if she could sing it, which sounded way better than me. She could find that ache, that distant range. Besides when she sang, *oh, is it just a thorn between my eyes, waiting for our boats to set sail, sea of joy, sea of joy,* her authenticity was incredible. Frankie was struggling with coming anywhere near Clapton. Part of the problem is that Eric played it on a Tele Strat and my Fender fit the part much better. I never lend my instruments, but Frankie was getting progressively better. By late in the afternoon, Frankie sounded incredible on my guitar, at least for that song, and we went with it. What really made us sound at least close to the original was Bird's take on Ginger Baker's drums. Incredible.

Stephanie was the talk of the town. Talk of the country. By the time she and Mom got home, shows like *Entertainment Tonight* and *Good Morning America* were running clips of *Purgatorio* and interviews she had done in what appeared to be London. Sharon, Mom and Tim, were getting their share of airtime, but nothing like Steph. Dad was nervous. He had just returned from Phoenix for a golf trip. Phoenix had two billboards of *Purgatorio* on the way to the airport and Steph was the only actress in the enormous photo advertisement. His daughter in that black and white, larger than life picture, wearing a peasant dress and chopped hair, bold and wonderful, peering over the names of famous people listed and involved in the movie. One of them being his wife. He was happy, but nervous. Maybe in shock. He knew what was in store. The phone was so crazy, Dad unplugged it.   He got word to Mom somehow that he'd pick them up at the airport and zap, no more phone. Those three days were hectic. Our plans for a road trip came through. First stop, Amarillo, through northern Texas, into Oklahoma City and points beyond, down to New Orleans, finishing in Nashville. We quickly brushed up on our *Sun Records* catalogue. I dared not attempt Elvis Presley, but already had Jerry Lee Lewis solid. Carl Perkins was a better fit, that rockabilly sound was so damned fun, finding three songs we could pull off. "Gone Gone Gone," being my favorite. Johnny Cash was hard for me to get vocally. We got "Folsom Prison Blues" quickly in a yee haw fun way. I felt all my fourteen years of age singing about being in prison. Shooting a man in Reno just to watch him die. Wasn't going to cut it. We made it fun and not pretentious. Melanie chose two Rosanne Cash songs, "I Don't Know Why You Don't Want Me" and "Runaway Train." Those two songs alone would play well. Our sense of being dual fronts for the band had found a balance. She had the strength of someone like Stevie Nicks and I felt like Lindsay Buckingham, or Tom Petty next to her. Whoever ranged in my mind as a comparison, it didn't matter. We were good together. As Melanie sang Rosanne, it dawned on me that she not only sounded like Rosanne, but she was built like Rosanne. If not for her blond hair, who'd know the difference? We were good to go. Steph and Mom barely told us about their European trip, so much was going on. Steph had Cameron over and he *forgot* to go home, falling asleep on the couch downstairs. That was the story anyway. Melanie fell asleep in the den on the floor in a blanket with a pillow under her head. I joined her instead of moving her somewhere. Like my bed. Awkward. She was rapidly becoming part of the family. Question was, under the same roof? The guys all spent the night before we left. Just like brothers now. Mom and Steph said goodbye for Chicago on a quick turnaround. Mom took me on a quick walk outside before they left. She hugged me and told me she was proud of me. She missed me; sorry she was gone so much. I looked forward to being with her later down the road. Dad was going to Chicago, too, but on a later commercial flight. He wanted to be around to send off Retro Sky. The whole family would then fly from Chicago to Oklahoma City, joining us on our tour once the premiere was over. Whirlwind of whirlwinds.

Stephanie

Jet lag, I was learning, is a strange animal. An irritable inability to sleep even though that is exactly what I needed. All I could think of was seeing Cameron. Would I feel the same after being gone so long? Would he feel the same about me? All the while my heart was racing towards Chicago. Another plane. Time blurring. The press would be there in droves. Sharon and Vinny, and Tim would be there. Ashley Judd and Robin Wright. Reviews of *Purgatorio* were trickling out, mostly through European publications or foreign bureaus. All of them favorable except maybe the darkness of the tone and theme being questioned. Now the film would be unleashed officially.

Cam and I made-out downstairs on the couch for hours. I let him take off my bra. He even sucked my nipples, which was a thrill. I was so excited to be with him. For whatever reason, however, I put a firm halt to any progression beyond that. He was frustrated, pent up, but I was resolved. No way. I like you, Cam, but I am in no hurry. You will just have to deal with it.

He did. He was even cracking jokes about his little friend in his pants becoming his angry big friend, wanting to be let loose. We laughed as I changed the subject. I told him stories of Europe. Moscow mostly, because that part of the trip left the biggest impression on me. His demeanor was partially star struck fan, having difficulty picturing me at press conferences, in large lecture halls giving interviews with Mom. In front of cameras. Being with Tim and Sharon. All the guys that were probably hitting on me. Not one, really, I assured him. One or two guys flirted, asking me for my autograph. That was it. Just talking about autographs threw him for a loop.

And here I was, going to be gone again for weeks. Joining the Retro Sky tour as a family. Yes, Sharon and her family might join us too, at least in one city or another. Tim might, too. It was most definitely a big deal for Julian, and we all wanted to support him. We'd fly back from Nashville in a few weeks. Be brave Cameron, be brave. I smiled, putting my bra back on. Cameron handled all this well. He was kind, careful with me. He did not want to lose what we had in these brief moments. He referred to our dates, and prom, how special it all was. Repeatedly, he called me his girlfriend, looking forward to when I'd be back. Fun stuff he wanted to do with me. Go to the swimming pool, out to dinner, to movies. His anticipation in seeing *Purgatorio* was evident. Should he wait until I returned? I said, *no*, go ahead and see it with his family. Or his buddies. I'd probably be nervous sitting next to him anyway. But I'd still see it again with him if he wanted.

All four of us drove over to the pueblo that afternoon before we took off. We found James in a chair on the porch of an old lady friend of his. She was probably ninety years old, drifting back inside. Mom and Dad looked at each other as if they recognized her from somewhere. James smoked his pipe even though he'd convulse with coughs. His complexion was white, skin onion thin, but he cheered up seeing us. We embraced him, filling him in on everything. He was excited for my brother's road trip and my movie coming out. I loved the look in his eye.

"All I think about is your visions these days." He said to all four of us. "All those visions. Over and over. Recurring."

We stood there silently. "I am only sorry I won't be here for yours," he was saying to me and Julian. How do you respond when someone tells you that they are dying? We hugged him. All four of us. Those towers looming out there somewhere.

Mom stayed behind with James for nearly forty minutes while we walked around, then sat in the car. She came back, wiping tears. He was the most important person in her life, she said. None of us took offense. We understood.

When we climbed out of the limousine, the barrage of flashing lights and deafening fans hit me like a tsunami. Tim and Shelly had already gone inside the Old Chicago Theater. Then Sharon and Vince. Our arrival and entry were all carefully orchestrated. Dad insisted on going in a side door this time. He hated this kind of thing and took a cab, which I found to be ridiculous, but Mom fully understood. Mom and I had on new dresses. Our hair and makeup and jewelry coordinated by public relations people. This was nothing like our Europe tour. Honestly,

I handled it all very well. I answered questions thoughtfully. Nothing I had not been asked before a hundred times in Europe. Mom scurried inside, separating herself from me by several feet – due mostly to how I had a tougher time moving along, breaking away from the throng of cameras.

Mom had tried to warn me about how this would feel, watching the movie under these circumstances. Full sound, musical soundtrack, sound effects, polished editing - the finished product. Mom on one side of me, Dad on the other. Sharon had kissed me when I sat down. Tim stood up and leaned in giving me another kiss. We were about ten rows back. The place was packed. I watched, glued to who I thought I was, someone I had already forgotten. The lens of *The Sound of Music*, or Santa Fe, or being Cameron's girlfriend, blurred that girl up there on the screen. Mom was glorious, that much I embraced. I squeezed her hand so hard, she had to help me let loose. There is a lengthy scene when the camera descends, panning in from on high, like from heaven, as Sister Marianne is outside in the remains of a garden, finding a few potatoes, some carrots. She is praying *Hail Mary, full of grace, the Lord is with Thee, blessed art thou among Women, and Blessed is the fruit of thy womb, Jesus* - as the camera shifts to ground level, looking up into Mom's face. There is no image like this in any movie I have ever seen. Tim's direction, the cinematography, the lighting, all of which created a miracle on celluloid. No wonder Mom was viewed, primarily in Europe, as an ephemeral Greta Garbo, lurking in the nether world. And the camera continued like this, even when Sharon stormed and looked deep into the audience from that place of superiority, Mom countered with grace, even larger than life. Larger than the story itself. I was absolutely stunned that I was sitting next to her. That person up there on the screen was my mother. And I had no idea how she did it. And those scenes with both Jennifer and Sharon – paragons of this art form, and with all three of us, absolutely made me tremble. I withdrew into my inner place, inside of me so very deep, sitting there frozen in my padded theater chair, wondering where I had found this strength and performance. I was good. I allowed myself to accept this judgment.

The last twenty or thirty minutes of the film were stunning. When the circus arrives, like an apparition appearing amidst the rubble. Tim is his larger-than-life self, taking over in mastery of the universe. Those brief scenes with Ashley and Robin are so moving, transitorily beautiful. Even Vinny in that pseudo comedic role, made the audience laugh. Maybe the only time we had received any relief during the movie. Sharon ultimately scared the hell out of me. I could not remember shooting these final scenes. She was a terror, hell's fury let loose. When we fought, physically battled, the emotional wretchedness made me rub my face out of a scared memory. The brutality of it all. Mom put her arm around me. Dad had a tear streaming down his face. I had never quite experienced these scenes like at that moment. They were far more real, exacting – nothing like I remembered at the time. Painful.

And my resilience and response. Matching Sharon in equal ability. I rose to overcome this woman whom I now rejected. These circumstances of evil. Finding equal resolution to turn away from Marianne and the Church.

My image running away, drifting and fading out, ended it all. The circus out there somewhere, presumably taking me in. The crowd erupted in standing ovation. I sat there unable to stand. Dad lifted my being, holding me tight.

Danny

I was glad that we didn't stay long at the after-party. Stephanie was exhausted, probably numb. Or maybe I was projecting my own fatigue. Inundated. Sharon and Vince didn't even attend. Tim was distracted and Jennifer whispered in my ear that we needed to get out of there. For Steph's sake. They had let too many of the press attend this thing and it rapidly became an extended fiasco of publicity ops, like wolves pouncing on fresh prey. Sharon had invited us back to their place, but we wanted to get back to the hotel and catch our plane for Oklahoma City early the next afternoon.

Steph slept in a creaky bed in our aged motel room on the outskirts of an Oklahoma skyline. We agreed to stay with the band wherever they stayed on their journey. She said a few quick words to Julian and everyone and slid away. We begged off their performance, promising to go that following day. Julian had no problem with that, he was excited, saying everything was going great. They were being well received thus far.

We went out to a Mexican food place before the show, which was awful, but Jennifer and I said nothing. The guys were ravenously hungry, barely saying anything the entire time. Melanie had dyed her hair with streaks of black, going with purples and greens pulled from her wardrobe for that night. Julian was wearing those circular, ancient, dark glasses all the time. Stephanie was alert, moving over near Bird, chatting with him during dinner. She was laughing. The two of them were laughing. It was good to see her relaxed and rested, in jeans and a light blouse, like she was free.

The concert hall was called *Lucky Dance Hall*. It had a capacity of three hundred. The place was packed. I watched this scroungy group I knew so well play an eclectic set of old-fashioned fifties dance music, hard core electric, soft acoustics, even one or two long psychodelia jams. Julian was in rare form. He could shift from Elvis Costello to Marty Robbins and then to Keith Richards, desperately clinging to Little Richard. Melanie sang with fun, with pathos, with misery, with blues. She captured every emotion. Jennifer and I danced, but stuck close to the side tables, drinking whiskey. Decompressing. Steph danced one or two dances, but stuck close to Shelly. I think Shelly had bought her a bloody Mary. We didn't care.

"Those two look like a couple, don't you think?" Jennifer shouted to me through the noise. She was talking about Julian and Melanie.

"I'd say so. They don't hide it very well." I sipped my whiskey, wondering if they were sleeping separately on this trip. I hoped so.

"She's so good. Julian is sounding amazing."

I shook my head.

"I forgot they played "I Can Tell." Sounds great." Her voice rising above the band.

I agreed wholeheartedly. The crowd was revved up, too. Julian had an excellent voice. He knew how to rock. He played with passion. I could not see or hear a weakness in the group. What was evident, was that Melanie was superior in a way that I could not quite describe. It wasn't her range or ability to sing any genre. Something about her demeanor. Bird and Julian carried the music. Melanie cracked the ceiling.

The band finished three fast-paced dance songs. One of which was their own. Then Julian brought the crowd to relative quiet. He apologized, saying that the band wanted to give this a try. First time ever live. *It's a long one*, he warned.

Julian started off with a very familiar riff, powerfully slow on his Fender. He looked at the band and nodded. Frankie joined with his Gibson. Melanie pulled her acoustic close to her body and hit her stride. Stuart and Bird came in on cue. Everyone was moving their heads in an instant groove. It was edgy and pure.

Be on my side, I'll be on your side, baby, there is no reason for you to hide, it's so hard for me being here all alone, when you could be taking me for a ride, Julian hitting perfect notes with the lyric. Then they jammed. Hard. All of them sang *down by the river I shot my baby*

… dead … shot her dead … Melanie took over, *you take my hand, I'll take yours, together we may get away, this much madness is too much sorrow, it's impossible to make it today …* the ache in her voice, looking directly at Julian. The crowd was stone silent listening intently, watching the dynamic between the two of them. Stuart's basslines kept up with Julian's drive. They picked up louder, jamming harder. Julian fuzzed out the amp for a verse. Frankie and Julian facing off trading lead on their guitars. It was intense. Loud. They played the song a good seven minutes. Julian's face was dripping wet. *Dead …* he droned into the microphone … *shot her dead …* then ripped hard into his strings, Frankie frantically keeping pace. The pot smoke rose in the small dark arena, overcoming the stale beer aroma. I put my arm around Jennifer. She buried her head in my chest. The moment was transcendent as the giant speakers vibrated with each of Julian's power strides into chord changes. Then Melanie and Julian sang together … *you take my hand, I'll take your hand, together we can get away … right on cue … she can drag me over the rainbow, send me away …*

Then the band brought it down and dragged out the ending, Bird hitting his snare in solo softness. It was over. The crowd roared. Julian wiped his face with a towel. The band was taking sips from their cups and chatting. Melanie took off her acoustic and sat at the electric keyboard. Julian sat at the piano with a lone white light on him. He channeled Elton John; the keys rattled like back in the day of his recitals. Mel was stirring her back up vocal into her drawn out vibes.

Julian sang the lyrics with passion. *So, where to now Saint Peter?, show me which road I'm on ... beyond the rifle range*, strewn out into the rafters ... *I may not be a Christian, but I've done all one man can* ... Once the applause calmed down, Julian turned to the band and counted down, they tore into their new songs. Dancing wild now, the crowd let loose with Retro Sky. By 11:30, the entire place was exhausted. The cloud of smoke, empty plastic cups, sweat under everyone's arm pits. The lights went up once Julian said goodnight and they exited, playing the Everly Brothers as their usual encore. We stayed up late at a coffee place on the edge of town. The band was tired but pleased. Shelly and Donald sitting at a table by themselves, right next to us, going over a notebook and map. It was the first time I met Donald. He was a serious guy. No nonsense. He liked the band and felt optimistic. He seemed to get along with the guys. Julian and he would laugh about something they did on stage. He told me that all their performances thus far on this road trip had been like that. Over the top good. Well received. They were getting invitations to come back – *anytime*. Julian and Melanie were doing a radio interview tomorrow at 10:00 then we could hit the road. A night in Shreveport then Baton Rouge, then two nights in New Orleans. Retro Sky would be playing at Robbie Robertson's friend Al's place, The Spiced Crawdaddy, right in the tourist district. A two-day break, then northbound to Montgomery, over to Jacksonville and Tampa Bay, back up to Nashville for three nights. Then home. Jennifer and Stephanie had our own rental car. We had fun listening to the radio and the interview as we left town earlier than everyone, driving slow through Eastern Oklahoma. Melanie and Julian on an FM channel, talking about their love for old music, thus the name Retro. "Sky" was also how they felt about their limit of what they would perform. The radio program played "Pavement," as the DJ praised the sound. Julian carried the interview, Melanie laughing, sounding sweet as can be. They took a few calls from the audience. One of the callers saying he was in love with Melanie, is she dating anyone? She laughed. The DJ turning it into a question about the band's lives in New Mexico. Melanie talked about how beautiful it all was. The native culture being a great inspiration. Julian avoided talking about his age or being in high school. He was good at keeping the conversation about music and how he and Melanie worked hard on their sound. He sounded older through that tiny box speaker in our rental car. That was it. The DJ played another song off their CD wishing them good luck.

Sharon spoke with Jennifer on the phone in Baton Rouge. She said she'd like to make a quick trip to Nashville to see the band. She'd come alone, in and out. Stephanie was on the phone for an hour with Cameron. The call was collect, which meant that the Jackson family was going to get stuck with a hefty phone bill. She was missing him.

Sleeping in motels, eating at road stops, surviving the terrible heat and humidity, taking-in the South in general, was testing our spoiled ways of comfort. Jennifer was ready to break with the norm and we stayed a night at the Ponchartrain Hotel on Saint Charles in New Orleans. Jennifer and I sat in the Howlin' Wolf Bar just to relive one of early high school dates when we saw him live in downtown Denver. Stephanie had her own room, thanking us repeatedly. We didn't go see the band that night, or even listen to music. Stephanie stayed in her room, calling Cam again. I made sure the front desk put the phone call on our bill.   She watched TV and read books. We did not go to every Retro Sky concert.   Usually, the first night of a two- or three-night schedule in each city. Otherwise, we took in the town. Finding nice restaurants or a bar to lounge around in. Or we'd stay-in, find a pool or hot tub.   I read two Stephen King novels in short order.

Jennifer and I stayed out until 3:00 am one night, just walking the streets, listening to jazz here and there. Eating and drinking.   Wandering, taking it all in. Laughing a lot. Being in love in a southern city of great history.

Purgatorio was showing in theaters everywhere we went. We would pick up magazines and newspapers with reviews.   All of them were favorable, and all of them warned the potential viewing audience of the grim nature of the movie. Stephanie was getting praise as a newcomer. Only one writer picked on her for being Jennifer's daughter.   And that was not too harsh given the blunt truth of it all.   The usual hubbub about Sharon giving another Academy Award performance. Jennifer was getting those accolades, too, but she was, again, mentioned more often as a lock for screenwriting. The cover of the August *Rolling Stone* was a stark black and white photo of Sharon and Jennifer and Steph. Probably a stock picture from the studio. Neither Jennifer nor Steph had any idea of posing for that one. The inside article was ten pages, giving a big background on Santa Fe, Rio Blanco Gallery, Eagles Nest Dinner Theater, even Santa Fe High School. It showed Steph on stage in both *Music Man* and *The Sound of Music*. Jann Wenner, the journalist, had done his homework, but he never mentioned me as her father or as principal. I was glad for that. Jennifer was also glad that she and Sharon were only mentioned with the usual chatter about them. Nothing new. The article was mostly a favorable profile of Stephanie.

By the time we got to Nashville, everyone was ready to get home. Julian and I talked for hours about the music. He had played every song they knew on one night or another. Their new songs were going over well. He liked them and so did the audience. Julian and the band were feeling tight. No glitches. He and Melanie were falling in love, I could tell. He spoke about her with reverence and adoration. He respected her talent. She brought out the best in him.

The front desk had a message from Louise. My heart skipped. I immediately thought of James. When I called, she sadly relayed to me that Alo's uncle 'Red' had died the day before. The family planned on a simple burial without waiting for Alo to return. In fact, Red had left a message to relay to Alo, telling him to stay in Nashville. It was where he was intended to be right now.

I found Bird alone in his room watching TV. I sat on the bed and told him about his uncle, reaching over and grabbing his hand in sympathy. Bird asked me to turn off the TV. A tear came to his eye.

"I expected this," he said.

"Do you want me to get you a flight home? I can go with you." I volunteered.

"No. We talked about this before I left. He thought he'd leave while I was on this trip. It makes me sad but in a way I'm glad he's not in all that pain anymore."

"What can I do? Do you want to cancel your last show? Finding another drummer might be hard."

He smiled. "No way. Old Red would want me to play for him. It's all he ever wanted anyway. Thanks, though. I'll be alright."

I hugged him and went and told the rest of the band as I found them scattered about. They immediately headed over to Bird's room to be with their friend.

CHAPTER TWENTY-TWO

I hereby embrace all contracts I made unconsciously and consciously before I knew the depth of my own Spirit; the silent ones, the ones I inherited, passed down and accepted as my own from generation to generation.
Bryonie Weise

Julian

Nashville is a music town like no other. There are more studios and record producers here than even in Los Angeles. And it's not only country or bluegrass. It's everything. Donald had something going in the works, behind the scenes, but we weren't sure. Lots of people were asking about us, our demos, the songs.

Shelly assured me something would break soon as she asked me to come into her room, which had a larger table than the other rooms. Donald stood up and formally shook my hand. He had a big file in front of him. Melanie came in, looked around and smiled, sitting next to me. Mom and Dad were next to arrive and sat on the edge of the bed. Bird came in, too, which surprised me a bit, taking the last chair. We all expressed our condolences to Alo again, even though a day had passed with profuse sympathy. We had finished performing for the tour and we were all gearing down. Donald then went on and on about how successful the tour had gone. He congratulated Shelly for being a wonderful road manager. Besides, radio stations played our songs more than he expected, which led to better ticket sales.
Then he cut to the chase. Shelly and Rhonda had handed over managing the band to him. A record label had contacted him and had sent a representative to two of our shows. They liked the CD, all the songs. Then he got silent. Something ominous took over, a mixture of good news, bad news, kind of approach. I was nervous now.
"FFR Recording Company has given me two offers for you to consider. One thing I have to say upfront is that Melanie is eighteen, and Alo will be eighteen in a week. They have the right to decide things on their own." All eyes looked at them, acknowledging their independence. "Stuart and Frankie will need their parents involved if it gets to that. Julian, you have Danny and Jennifer here. I think I'll go on, if that's understood." We were all chomping at the bit.

"FFR Recording is big on Melanie. I want to say that up front. I am representing the band Retro Sky, but I am acting as a go-between for her, if she likes." Melanie's face looked perplexed. She was staring right at me with angst. My heart was sinking. Some internal fear was rearing inside of me. The cliché of cliché's made manifest – in some terrible way. Like I knew this was going to happen.

"Option One. The band changes their name to "Melanie and the Retro." Like riding the Retro line. A play on words. This contract," as he lifted one of the files, "is for ten grand. It's a one-time album offer. CD remix and re-engineered with your songs. Melanie must sing on all the songs, either as lead or with Julian. You get to retain rights to your songs. The label will package and promote the CD. You will get a small percentage of sales."

I put my head in my hands, not even looking at Donald or Melanie. I wanted to cry. This sucked. Melanie tried to hold my hand.

She spoke up, "I don't like it. Retro Sky is the thing here. Julian put this together. No way."

"Okay, okay, hold on." Donald said. "This is worse, then. I just need to let you know what the second option is." I held my breath when he said the word, *worse*. "Melanie, this contract is for five years, fifty thousand dollars up front. Just for you. An exclusive recording contract. They'd like you to sign ASAP. Three albums minimum. Percentages are favorable. Trouble is they want you to stay in Nashville. Now. They have a studio apartment, paid, for one year. Living expenses stipend, not much, for one year."

"Oh, fuck." I muttered under my breath. I looked up at Melanie. Her mouth was slightly open. She was frozen. The room was cold. Mom and Dad were rubbing my back. This was not good.

"This is where Alo comes in." No one said anything. Alo perked up to listen. "Melanie, they want to form a studio band, probably a road band too if you go with the second option. Alo is eighteen and they like his abilities, his talent. They'd like to sign him as well. That is, if you go along with this."

"Jesus." She muttered. "I hate this."

"I know," Donald said. "I'm the messenger here. Alo, they'd negotiate with you. Probably a standard studio musician contract, matching the five years of Melanie's offer. Much less money. You may even have to live with Melanie until you got your feet on the ground."

I got up and paced the room. I wanted to leave.

Mom spoke up. "Don, this is terrible. You know that. I mean, the first option is not even an option. And the second, well, that's tough. It's up to Melanie, obviously. Just, you were supposed to represent Retro Sky. And Danny's father is an attorney." Jennifer looked at Melanie, "Probably a good idea to have him look at this contract."

Then Don spoke up, a bit louder, "I know. I know I'm representing the band. I am. But I don't have a legal agreement with them and I'm acting as a conduit for all of you. I don't have any offers right now for Retro Sky as a band. At least, other than this one. They're head over heels with Melanie, and I have the obligation to let all of you know. It would be worse if I did this with Melanie alone. You'd resent me even more." He was talking to Melanie, "And if you want a lawyer, that's fine. Should probably act quickly."

"That's bullshit," my dad chimed in.

Melanie grabbed me and stood up. "Let's go outside, Julian."

The sunlight was blinding. She hugged me with concern and shock. I was stunned too. The two of us walked away, out of the hotel, and into the city. Getting further from it all.

We walked.

"What the fuck," she said looking at me through her questioning eyes.

I didn't respond, just holding her.

Finally, I said what needed to be said. "Melanie, we know you gotta take this thing. Christ, I can't stand it. We have a good thing, you and me. And I love you. But you have to go."

"No, no I don't."

"This is an amazing opportunity. A dream comes true. I know, I know, this is what happens with bands. They break up. You are an amazing singer, musician. You deserve this. And the money. Jesus. Melanie, you gotta grab it."

"No. I can't."

"Look, you're not into the whole college thing anyway. You'll go crazy in Santa Fe. I'll be in third period history class and shit like that. While Retro plays at Jimmy's on Friday nights, you'll be thinking about Nashville and what might've been. I can't live with that either."

She was quiet, leaning her body into me. I felt her warmth and love. I didn't want her to go.

"And Bird. He's not going to want to go back to Santa Fe. He deserves to be here, too." I added.

"Yeah, I hear that. He needs to stay here somehow." She was sniffling.

"Maybe we should call your mom. Talk to her about it."

"No, I don't think so. I will call her eventually. But this is my decision."

When we made our way back to Shelly's room, the meeting had broken up. Donald would be in his room, Mom told us. Shelly looked pained. Upset. Everything had unraveled on her. And there, next to my dad, stood Sharon. She had been to our final performance last night and we had barely said *hi*. She was talking with Dad in heated tones.

Sharon then hugged me, then embraced Melanie in a tight grip.

"Great show last night," she said to us.

"Thanks," I managed to say.

"This sucks," Sharon spit out. "Listen, Mel, it's a great opportunity for you. What do you think, if you don't mind me asking?"

Melanie looked at the very famous actress. They had met, talked a few times, but here she was larger than life.

"I don't want to do it."

"Why not?" Mom interrupted. "Incredible offer, Mel."

"I know. Just. Well, I don't want to leave Julian. I don't want to leave the band. It's not right."

Mom and Sharon, even Dad, now were surrounding me with concern. They wanted to hear from me.

"She should go. I know I'm only going to be fifteen, but I love Mel. I will miss her. I don't want her to do this. It's my band. And yes, it's not right. But she's amazing, she should go."

Mom and Dad agreed with me, gently. They were trying to help Melanie shift her thoughts towards a career taking precedence over our relationship. Give her the freedom to go if she wanted.

Then Sharon became firm. "I've seen this before. Lots of times. You know, when Mic Fleetwood offered Lindsay Buckingham the open spot as guitarist in his band, he told Lindsay that he didn't want *the girl*. We all know that the girl was Stevie Nicks. Lindsay turned him down unless he took her too. Easy to see how that turned out. We should call their bluff. They're moving way too fast, like you must decide today. Something doesn't sound right. *Take it or leave it*. They're even using Alo as leverage. Tell Donald to *fuck off*. Tell him it's the whole band or nothing. Let me get involved, Mel. I'd like to tell him what he can do. He's representing the band, not just you. But only if that's how you really feel."

Mom and Dad were smiling. Almost giggling. Sharon was finding her mojo. They nodded their heads in agreement. Worth a try if Melanie was up to it.

"You'd do that?" Melanie asked.

"Hell yes. These fuckers think they can dictate shit. It pisses me off. Look at you. Look at Julian. Even Alo, now, in his room wondering if he's going to stay here in

Nashville from now on. Poor guy. He's excited. He's scared. He's wondering what Mel's going to do. None of this is right, I agree with both of you on that one."

"Okay. Can Julian be here when we talk to him?"

"Sure. Let's have the whole meeting over again. Call Alo. I'll call Donald in his room. Get his ass back up here."

We reconvened. Donald looked a bit more sheepish. He and Sharon were politely introducing themselves. Sharon was in her rare form that would scare anyone. Donald tried to talk to Melanie alone, and Sharon would have none of it. "Donald Williamson, let me say a word before we go on. You took over this agent role from Rhonda, and Shelly here, right?"

"Yes. Glad to do it. They're a good band."

"And did Phil have anything to do with it?" Sharon grilled him.

He looked at Mom specifically. He was flushed. "Yes, I guess he did. He gave me a call when Rhonda asked me to take over."

"And Shelly, here, she talked with you?" Sharon was acting like a lawyer, like Mom had in *Rio.* I saw it in her eyes. Mom and Dad were fighting back a smile. Shelly kept out of it. She had seen Sharon act this way before. I just watched and marveled, almost lusting after Sharon all over again. Melanie sat down on the bed like she was watching a good movie.

"Yes, Shelly and I have worked closely during all of this." He pleaded to Shelly with his eyes to step in. She sat down, too.

"Sit down, Don." Sharon commanded. He sat down next to me.

"So, when you talked to Shelly, who in the world did you think you would be representing? Just fucking curious, Don."

"You don't have to get upset. I was representing Retro. I knew that. I am aware of that. I'm just relaying what FFR has offered. That's all."

"And you then set off a time bomb with these kids. Jesus Christ, man. What is wrong with you?"

"What do you mean, Sharon? I did what any agent would do."

Alo walked in. He found a place to sit on the other bed.

"And you are so stupid you couldn't foresee what would be the fallout?"

"Yes, of course I could see the implications." He was murmuring his answer slowly.

"And FFR? Have you even checked them out? This town is full of fly by night operations. I've never heard of them."

"Yes, they're new on the scene. I know that. They seem okay to me."

"And, this is the key point, Donald. You couldn't see that you were in effect destroying Retro Sky? How in the hell is that representing their interests?" Sharon was looking at everyone in the room like they were the jury.

"I guess, so, now that you say it that way. I thought Melanie would be happy. Alo, too. You're excited, aren't you, Alo?" He looked over at Alo for salvation. Alo sat like a statue, timid to respond with Sharon's larger than life presence dominating the room.

"Of course, he's excited, Don. Now tell me. Take a good look at Julian."

Don barely turned and looked me in the face.

"What do you see, Don?" She was badgering him now.

"A kid. I mean, no offense, but Julian, you are only in high school. You will get an offer some day. You are good. Great, really. I look forward to representing you."

"No fucking way, Donald Williamson. You answered wrong. This is the leader of the band, Retro Sky. He *is* the band, ass hole."

He was quiet, fidgety.

"Donald, I know your agency out in L.A. It's a good agency. For Phil to recommend you, you must have some sense of what you're doing. I just don't see it. Look around here, Don. You got Jennifer and me. Phil is our long-time agent. We have how many awards between us in this godforsaken show business? Take a guess." She was pissed off beyond turning back.

Donald just sat there. "I don't know. A lot. I get it." He managed to say.

"Do you know Phil?" she asked.

"I've met him." He replied.

"Would you say that he's good at what he does? His reputation?"

"Of course. He's the best in the film industry." He had his head down.

"And Tim. You know Tim, don't you?"

He shook his head *yes*.

"How do you think Tim will react when he hears about this bullshit?"

"I don't know. I was just doing my job letting everyone know."

"Oh my god, man. You are pathetic. That's not your goddamn job. A secretary can do that much."

"I should leave. I will call them, tell them Melanie, the band, said *no* to their offers. Maybe a new agent would be in order."

"You can't run now, asshole. You want to work ever again in this business?"

"Well, sure. What do you mean?" He looked scared.

"You are going to go over to their office and play some hardball. Right now. Do I have to do your job? Do I need to go with you? Or, why in the hell haven't you worked the people in L.A.? It's your backyard. You have one week, Donald. Get it done. This band kicks ass. Melanie kicks ass. Julian. Alo over there. And don't worry Alo, you'll be playing drums your whole life because Donny here is going to do his fucking job for the band, not just you."

He shook his head meekly. "But Sharon, they're in high school. I mean, that restricts a lot of options."

"Don't give me any buts. Julian's sister just came off making a multi-million-dollar movie and she had more balls than you do. And she's not even fifteen yet. You can get this done. If not, find a job doing something else."

Don was about to leave when Shelly spoke up. "Did you ever check out Chrystal Records in L.A? We spoke about that often. I gave you Peter Fontana's name."

"No, I thought they were too big of an agency. Besides the road trip was ending in Nashville. That's where I started." Sharon was nearly going to pounce on him and tear him to shreds. He left the room quickly.

Mom shut the door. We all waited with shit eating grins. Then we burst out laughing. Melanie got up and hugged Sharon. Sharon was still fuming.

"I don't know what just happened. I probably threw that one away." Melanie said to Sharon.

"Nonsense. He's a lightweight. Sorry, Shelly, but you guys deserve someone like Phil to get things done. A hard ass. Phil pisses me off all the time, but I know that he will do exactly what he says." Sharon was taking a deep breath.

"It's all right." Shelly said. "Tim felt like they put someone on this from the bottom of the totem pole. Doing the hard road, travelling. Taking on a young band. Unknown quantity." Then she changed the subject. "You okay Mel?"

"Guess so. I mean, let's see what happens. Guess we're going back to Santa Fe tomorrow." She came over and hugged me. We kissed.

"How 'bout you Alo?" Shelly asked.

"I'm okay. I really thought I wouldn't be going back to New Mexico with you. I was looking forward to it to be honest. It's all Unc wanted." He looked discouraged.

"It'll happen. Anyway, you should go back and pay your respects to your uncle." My dad added.

"Oh God, Sharon. I still can't believe it. It was like we were on the set. I wanted to break out laughing. You are good. I mean really good." Mom said, hugging her again.

"Now I just hope that it works. I don't want these kids strung out like that. Those assholes." Sharon was lighting a cigarette.

"Well, the riptide will be felt." My Dad added.

"Better be." Sharon took a drink from the sink. Using her hand. She was thirsty. "I'm all in, now, Julian. Hope you are okay with it. I'm in the fight." She said wiping her mouth with her free hand. Anxiously, then, taking another drag off the Marlboro.

I got up and hugged her. I felt the warmth of her soul, her body. Her love for me. I'm sure she felt my love too. I just wish I could get over this weird infatuation. Watching her do her thing only me made me more – well, infatuated. I was extremely happy to have her fighting for us.

Stephanie

I don't know what happened exactly. What I do know is that Mr. Williamson was not on the plane with us back to New Mexico. Everyone seemed pissed off at him or whatever was going on. Julian was terribly irritable. He and Melanie isolated themselves and she was seemingly trying to make him feel better. She would be living with us until she got settled at college, taking over one of our guest rooms.

We said goodbye to Sharon, filling Tim's plane. She congratulated me again with a big hug and kiss. The idea of getting home was exciting after living on the go. Besides, I missed Cam and he was going to meet me when we got back to the house.

Parents and girlfriends were there to pick up Stu and Frank. An aunt picked up Alo. We'd see him soon for a memorial or ceremony. And there was Cameron. We rushed to my room and kissed and held each other for a long time. He felt so good. A part of me wanted to take off all my clothes and cuddle up to him in my bed. Another part of me was still entirely not ready.

"I saw Purgatorio," he whispered.

We separated and I looked at him. He was looking at me carefully. "Yeah?" I asked.

"I really don't know what to say, Steph. I mean, you were so incredible. I saw it with my parents, and they were speechless. It's an intense movie. You're so tough. I didn't know that about you. I don't think I would know that was you unless, well, you know."

"Thanks. I'm glad it's over. I need a break. I've been acting for a good long stretch. Strange to say, but I'm looking forward to getting back into school and being normal."

"Steph, I saw it again with my friends too. Everyone is talking about it. So many people want to meet you. You know what I mean. Like, again, or ask you about the movie. Sharon was so amazing. And your mom. I want to go ask her for an autograph, and I'm so intimidated by her all over again after seeing it. Not exactly like Sharon. In a different way."

"I know. I get it. Please, let's not have a big get-together with anyone yet. I need some time. And you probably shouldn't ask my mom for her autograph. She'd give it to you, but she likes that we're relaxing around here."

"I don't think I can be normal. Look, Steph, you did *Music Man,* then the movie then over at the theater. Bang, bang, bang. And you made it all look easy. Almost not real. If I weren't sitting here with you right now, I wouldn't think it's humanly possible. I mean, I'm really, kissing you, like now, is so not normal. Being alone in your room as *Alone*. And we really are kissing. It doesn't make sense. I'm happy as can be, though. You know what I mean, don't you?"

"Like I've said. I need you to see me as Stephanie. That's all."

"But that was you in that movie. That was you doing all of that. I am so in awe. To be honest, I'm a little bit scared. Nervous."

I just hugged him. There was nothing I could do or say at that point.

"Will you see the movie with me, Steph?"

"Honestly, no. I don't want to. We will someday. I promise. I just want to go out to dinner with you. Or to a bookstore or the park. Take a walk downtown. I know you don't horseback ride, but it would be fun if we could go out to the reservation, or up to Taos. Ride for a day or two."

"I'd try. I'm up for anything, Steph."

"We only have a few days till school starts. You'll be a senior." I stood silent, pressed against his chest. "You know, I'll be fifteen soon." I added.

"Really. When?"

"The eleventh."

"That's a weekday, I think. Maybe I can take you out the weekend before?"

"I'd like that."

Jennifer

Danny headed to school the minute we got settled at home. School started in a few days, and he needed to be there a good ten days ago. He didn't seem concerned; everything was organized and set-up before he went on these various adventures.

I was worried about Julian. His pride had been hurt. His ego. All indications were that he and Mel were fine. She was in good spirits re-locating in our guest bedroom. She and Louise were laughing. I overheard her saying that she wanted to help Louise clean and cook and do chores. I smiled. In a lot of ways, it was my perception that she needed a home right now more than a big payoff in Nashville. If she and Julian would just be careful and not get pregnant, then all the better. I'd make sure Danny had a conversation. Again. Reminded him of all the options. I wanted to talk with Melanie in a motherly way, and just might do that.

I went over to the Gallery to check up on things. All was well. Business was fine. I had a message that I should check on James right away. He was still living out at the pueblo. I drove over to find him bedridden. My heart ached, wanting to move him to the hospital or hospice care or wherever he wanted. He was insistent that he wanted to die right where he was. I was numb, not sure what to do. He asked me about the trip, the kids, wanting details. I told him everything. He smiled, then took me by the hand, as he spoke, "Julian is fine. He and

Melanie will be okay. It'll be soon for those two and the rest of them. And give Stephanie a hug. She needs to rest for several seasons. Many moons."

I held his hand firmly when he continued, "We had an informal memorial for Red before Bird got back. Have him drop over. I need to talk with him. He and I need to do our own private ceremony. We can do it right here from my bed. I have something for him, too. Oh, and tell him he will be a drummer. I KNOW this. He must be patient. I'll tell him that too when he comes over."

I lay down on the bed next to him. We didn't talk. I held my good and dear friend. He whispered in my ear, "All the paperwork is in order. You're the executor." I was aware of all this. We had a local attorney involved as well. "Most everything goes to the reservation. I'd like Danny to administer much of it as he sees fit. The community will appreciate all that he can do."

We lay there quiet, and he went on, "I've left your family a nice collection of artworks. It's not for the Gallery. You do what you like, Jennifer. I have a ten-acre lot on the edge of town. I'd like the kids to have it for their college." He didn't have to do that. He was much like their grandfather in this regard.

He was on the verge of sleep, coughing hard kept him awake. "The vision."

"Yes. I'm listening."

"It will be here in days. I will be gone by then."

My embrace was warmer, firmer. His heartbeat beneath my hand. My palm absorbing each rush of life and blood with his frailty.

"The baptism will be confirmed. Julian and Stephanie will be as you and Danny are. It's only a beginning for them. A great deal of responsibility will be put on their shoulders. They will only have you and Danny." He struggled to get those words out of a raspy voice. "And Sharon ..."

I could only trust. He was nearly gone, finally finding sleep.

Melanie and Julian were at the kitchen table when I got home. Melanie jumped up and offered to make me tea or a drink. I smiled and stared at her. I went and hugged her tightly, looking her in the eye.

"Mel, I know that was hard in Nashville. I couldn't have walked away from an offer like that. I hope you have no regrets." She was about to speak but I didn't let her. "I'm glad you are here, let's go on the porch." I patted Julian on the back, grinning at his inquisitive stare. We sat in lounge chairs outside. "How you handling your mom leaving?" I asked pointedly.

"It's tough. I knew it was coming. The guy in Denver sounds like a jerk. Oh well. I'm grateful you have been so understanding. Supportive. Taking care of me." She looked radiant in the sunlight.

"Mel, I want to talk with you about something."

"Okay," she looked pensive.

"You're eighteen, you know all this, but I want you to know you can talk with me about anything. Julian's my son and that makes it awkward. Frankly, I need to ask."

"Okay. We're careful, if that's what you're getting at."

"It is what I'm getting at.   Are you on the pill?"
She froze. "Yes. But come to think of it, I don't have insurance anymore.   I have a prescription through September, then my coverage will run out."
"We'll take care of it. When did you have a physical?"
"Maybe two years ago."
"And the dentist?"
"I can't remember. My teeth are good though."
"Let's get you appointments to both; will you do that?"
She shook her head, *okay.*
"How are you with clothes?"
"Fine. Too many." She grinned.
"You need anything?"
"Maybe. I'm low on makeup."
"Get what you need. I'll give you my credit card. And you can keep using my car.   Just talk to me about it.   If you want to drop me off at work, or whatever, we will figure it out."
"Wow. Really? Thank you."
"Absolutely. When does school start? Do you have your classes yet?"
"In two weeks. Yes, I have fifteen hours. Mostly intro stuff. I will need books."
"Sure. Like I said, get what you need." I emphasized, then asked, "Are you - Retro, going to play at Jimmy's still?"
"Every other Friday. Shelly is looking for some more dates."
"Is Julian okay? That was hard on him. His ego, you know."

"I think so. He's smiling again. Laughing. I feel terrible that it happened at all. He's amazing with me. The whole thing sucked."

"You deserve it Mel. The contract, I mean. You are that good. Hang in there. Thank you, too. It means a lot to Julian; he just might not say it."

"He tells me. He's sweet." She smiled at me. "I want to help around here. I can't pay much rent. Maybe do chores or something."

"Hey, we all chip in. We rotate dishes. Helping cook. Pick up after yourself. Maybe help Louise with laundry. She's not good going up and down the stairs anymore. I'm not always around."

"Yeah, I'd like that."

We stood and hugged. She looked me in the eye. "Can I call you Jennifer? I mean, I never know what to call you."

I smiled. "You better. And you better come talk to me about anything. Anytime. You've been on your own too long, young lady. It's okay to be a part of us around here. We want you here. Danny wants you here. Steph is excited. I know you're an adult but consider yourself adopted."

She laughed. "You know, Jennifer." She paused to hear those words spoken. "I think of being in Nashville right now. In my own apartment. With money. Getting a new band. The road to stardom. Or not. Who knows? It would be exciting. I have second thoughts already. But I have to say, I've never been happier. I really do love your son. This will be weird here. Strange with all that is ahead. Unusual. But I am much happier here. I already know it. I'm tired of Santa Fe, but I know this is the best way for me."

As we went back inside I rubbed her back. She's a strong girl. I KNOW this is the best way for her too.

The next day at my office, I got a call from Pete Fontana with Chrystal Records.

"Hi, Jennifer. I'm glad I reached you. This is Pete Fontana, I know we haven't met, but I met your kids when they came out here with Sharon. Probably months ago."

"Yes, yes. You helped Julian make a demo. He visited your studio. Isn't that when Mike Campbell sat in?"

"Yes. So much fun. I think Julian had a friend with him."

"Stuart."

"Yeah, I remember. They were excited. Pretty good it turns out."

"Retro Sky just returned from a road trip. They played a lot of bars and venues, ending up in Nashville."

"I have to say, I've heard all about it. My phone has been ringing off the hook. Whatever happened out there caused a ruckus."

"I bet. Sharon can do that." I said.

"No shit. Sorry."

"That's okay."

"Oh, I loved *Purgatorio*. Amazing movie. You were amazing. And your daughter, she stole the show. No offense."

"None taken." I smiled.

"I don't really want to go into how shit has hit the fan out here. With Phil and Tim especially. Some guy named Don. Jesus, what a putz. Sorry, again."

"No problem."

"Phil gave me your number. He wants this fiasco, whatever it was in Nashville, to go away. Not sure how to do that, but first step was calling you, Jennifer."

"I'm glad you did. Thank you. I appreciate it."

"Anyway, I've heard the recent CD Retro Sky made. It's good. I like it. Even without the screaming out here, I found their sound interesting. Julian is great. I haven't met this Melanie, but she's outstanding. I can see how this scenario unfolded. Stupid, though. FFR is a shit storm. I'm glad that fell through, no matter what happens."

"Me too."

"Jennifer, I have to be honest with you. I'm getting pressure. Friendly pressure, as you know."

"Uh, huh."

"But I don't mind on this one. The band is good enough that I want to see them. I am going to Albuquerque with my partner Jonas. He really wants to visit your Gallery, so we will take the drive up there."

"You're welcome anytime. Just let me know and I will give you a tour."

"I appreciate it. I'm curious, too, but he's into your art. He thinks you're the best in the world. We have a small work of yours in our bedroom. *Star* something."

I remembered, interjecting, "I did a series about fifteen years ago called *Constellations*. I sold them to a gallery out there."

"They were expensive. At the time we were working from the ground level on our production company and barely afforded one piece."

"I appreciate it. Thank you."

"I swear, it was the best investment we ever made. Its appraised value is through the roof now."

"Hope you like it in your bedroom every day and every night." I was smiling.

"Of course, that, too." I think he was smiling too.

"Anyway, I'd like to hear the band. Maybe in your living room or something."

"Better yet. They play at a local bar, a place called Jimmy's. Friday nights. Let me know in advance, so I can make sure they're playing there."

"Perfect." He was talking to someone. Sounded like his secretary. "Sorry about that. You know, I'd like to make this a romantic getaway. Can you recommend something out there?"

"I know the best place in the world. It's called The Manor, now. New ownership, but we've stayed there. It's an old Victorian home, bed and breakfast. Very romantic. Beautiful gardens, views. You two will love it."

"I'm not familiar with New Mexico. Will they be cool with the gay thing?"

"You kidding? This is art world central, very gay friendly."

"Thanks. I will let you know our plans ASAP."

"Thank you, Pete."

"Oh, wait. Your daughter. She met Madonna when she was out here. We had a party or something."

"I remember, she talked about it for days."

"Anyway, I spoke with Madonna a day or two ago and she raved about Stephanie's performance in *Purgatorio*. Madonna seemed like the fan for a change. Happy she got to meet Stephanie."
I laughed. "I'll tell her. She'll go crazy."
"Okay I gotta run. We'll talk soon."

Danny

School kicked off in great success. Once again I had to thank my staff, the teachers, especially my secretary Cheryl, for their hard work.   The building was in spic and span shape. Our student body had grown by twelve percent, and we were prepared. I had hired some great teachers, all of whom were eager and well qualified. The only negative was that I put Mr. Bonham, the science teacher I was having so much trouble with, on a Level Two process - which meant that I could dismiss him at Christmas break if he didn't get his act together. Our preliminary meeting for the new school year between the two of us and the union representative did not go well. Bonham's contention was that he was singled out unfairly. What he meant by that, he could not clarify, nor could he account for the mounting documented evidence of his insubordination. The union representative was there to make sure that due process was followed. I was not optimistic that this would work-out favorably.
Julian was back in great spirits, rehearsing with the band. He was excited that Pete Fontana was coming in town to hear Retro Sky. He had gotten along well with him back

when he met him in California. Melanie was lighthearted about everything. She was fitting right in at the house.

All of us went to visit James, but he was sleeping, drifting in and out of consciousness. He'd been like that for three days. We all said our goodbyes. He seemed to acknowledge us, gripping our hands. Fluttering his eyes. A lot of tears that day. Stephanie was terribly shook up.

Jimmy's Bar was another full house gig. Pete and his partner Jonas had the front table. Our entourage accumulated and packed ourselves in. My attention was on Steph and Cameron. They were being more and more affectionate. He was almost like a puppy following her around, wanting to make sure she was happy. Jennifer told me that she had a long talk with Stephanie, and I left it at that. Some of the details I was not prepared for yet. Birth control and my daughter – full denial of reality on my part - maybe when she's thirty years old was my opinion.

Julian was almost hilarious how he carried on with the band. They were comfortable in Jimmy's. It was like their home base these days. They knew most of the crowd. The crowd had heard their entire repertoire and kept coming back, so Julian pulled out the stops knowing they were being scouted.   Julian showed off, playing a Hendrix like rendition of "Hey Joe." Melanie countered with the two Rosanne Cash numbers, back-to-back. Julian jumped on the piano, playing a quick medley of Elton John. The crowd ate it up. Retro Sky played three hours jumping from various eras of sound, slow and fast, highlighting every one of their own compositions in between the more recognizable songs. A lot of fun. As sensitive as Julian was about what happened in Nashville, he gave the encore to Melanie. The lone spotlight. She strummed her acoustic, said a few words to the crowd, thanking them. She still had black streaks in her blond hair. A lot of native jewelry that Jennifer had given her. "Here's to my lover," she whispered into the microphone.

When she sang the Bee Gees, "How can you mend a broken heart?" the crowd was nearly wiping their eyes. Her voice was clean, hitting every octave. Her head bent downward almost the entire time. She quit playing her guitar and held the microphone in a kind of clutch, singing a cappella. "Please help me mend my broken heart and let me live again."

Standing ovation. The band came back out and took a bow. It was late. Melanie and Julian kissed on the lips, holding each other tight. They looked good together, I had to admit. They sounded even better. The crowd would not relent. They wanted one more. Julian said something to the guys, and they took their places.

Bird, Stuart and Frankie started jamming. Frankie was truly at home on his new guitar. He sounded wonderful out front. Melanie sat at the piano and Julian was at the electric keyboard. They joined in once Julian gave her a look, a cue. Allman Brothers' "Midnight Rider." Everyone recognized it immediately. Julian was doing his full force Greg Allman sound. It sounded incredible, driving forward in a more keyboard-driven cover. Melanie and he must have practiced because they were trading licks at a ferocious pace. She took the vocals for a verse, then they sang the remainder together.

The jam went on a good ten minutes, solos thrown in from everyone. Impressive, clean sound. All of them blew me away. Julian told me he'd play it for me someday because I kept hounding him about one of my favorite bands of all time.

I looked at Pete Fontana and he was writing something down, showing it to his partner. Jonas shook his head in agreement, whatever it said. It was terribly loud at that point. Jamming as it was meant to be done.

Pete and Jonas were flying out that following evening. Jennifer was going to show them around the gallery. Afterwards Pete wanted to meet with the band over at their studio at 3:00.

I took Melanie and Julian over to the studio at 1:00. The guys were already there, ready to rehearse one new song, and Julian wanted to polish Spoon's "Everything Hits at Once" for Pete to hear before they took off. *I go to sleep and think you're next to me* - Julian singing, perfecting the synthesizer of the original. I left them alone, finding Jennifer with Pete and Jonas. They were eyeing a painting of Samantha's, which was one that I always liked, but found to be exorbitant. We made our way into the studio after talking in Jennifer's office. The guys were happy with the bed and breakfast, they had a great time. They raved about Santa Fe, wishing that they could stay longer.

"Here's a contract I would like to have reviewed, by either of you, or the families, preferably by an attorney. I want you to feel comfortable about it all." Pete pulled out a manilla envelope and handed it to me. "It's very standard, basic, entry level contract. Retro Sky would agree to two studio albums within two years. There are some requirements in terms of promotions, touring. All of it would be in the Western United States. I had that portion modified, given that the kids will be in school. With extended weekends, holiday breaks, that kind of thing, it won't be a problem. We guarantee packaging, marketing, setting up the appearances. It's all spelled out. All of Julian's songs, and Melanie's, or whoever is taking writing credit, need to have that spelled-out and decided upon as far as who is listed first for copyright purposes."

Jennifer and I were elated but had not heard anything about money yet. Pete could read my mind. "We're only giving twenty thousand up-front. There are additional incremental payoffs as each of the two albums is completed and various touring dates are fulfilled. I think you will find royalties to be generous."

"Sounds fair enough." Jennifer said.

"The contract also spells out that the agreement will be terminated at the end of two years if sales don't reach certain levels, obligations are not met, that kind of thing. Again, it's all spelled-out."

"Understood." I shook my head.

"Jennifer," Pete looked right at her, "I need you to know that your influence, Sharon's and Tim's certainly caught my attention. I felt taken off guard. But, honestly, I like these guys – and Melanie, too. They're good. It's a risk taking them on, but the talent is oozing all over the place. Julian is one hell of a musician. Right now, I place him there among many of the best because he can play so many instruments – proficiently - and so many genres. He knows how to write, not just cover music."

"Thank you," I was about to go on, but Pete wasn't finished.

"I can see why things got sticky in Nashville," he continued. "Melanie is special. Her voice is so mature, captivating. She's gorgeous, a natural draw. She's easy going with the crowds. Well, they all are, and for their age, I'm more than surprised. This is my challenge. We have a duo in Julian and Melanie. The band is fine, but everyone is going to end up putting the boyfriend-girlfriend together as the main thrust in the band. And she will be the major attraction. It's just the way I foresee it. Julian is far more talented than Sony Bono but look at how Cher eclipsed the whole act. Those two are going to have to work on it and be very conscious of how they are dealing with it."

Then Jonas spoke up. "This is Pete's business, but we were saying how Nashville will not be the only time this kind of thing happens. I guess, we're aware that in this industry – well, Jennifer, you get it – we're expressing our concern up front for those two."

"I appreciate it," I said. Jennifer was shaking her head in agreement. "I can't thank you enough. These guys are going to be ecstatic."

ENCORE

Stephanie Tomasetti

School was well underway. A routine was falling in place. Cam took me out twice. Once, we went to the park downtown and walked around, eating at a deli, hanging out at a bookstore. He bought me *The Adventures of Kavalier and Clay,* which he had recently read and thought I'd like to give it a try. It was different than most of the books I read but was happy that he was trying to find something in common for us. Our second date was to see *Purgatorio.* I finally gave in to see it with him. It was an early matinee, only four other people in the theater. I watched, trying to detach myself from the whole experience. I told him before the movie started that it was okay for him to ask me questions while the movie played. He was begging me; he was so curious. I was glad that hardly anyone was in the theater. Football was underway, and I was excited to see him score a touchdown at our first home game. We could talk about his life, his achievements. He was one of the big men on campus and I never even knew it. Slowly, very slowly, I was getting to know his friends. His jock crowd. They were terribly polite with me. Same with the girls that they hung out with. It made me sick. Finally, I told Cam that they should all relax. I'm a sophomore and they were all seniors. I'm just trying to fit-in like everyone else. He got it.

Julian and I were getting excited about our fifteenth birthday coming up. Mom and Dad always told us that we were born almost two weeks premature. James told us once that it was because of the full moon and mother earth saying it was time. Being fifteen sounded cool. A big step up from fourteen. The four of us – Julian, Melanie, Cam and me - were going to double-date for dinner and then go our own way that prior Saturday. Melanie and I were rapidly becoming friends, almost sisters in the house, but she was gone a lot. College was a full-time endeavor for her, and she took it seriously. Retro was still rehearsing regularly, planning a trip to Arizona on an upcoming extended weekend. Their actual album recording wasn't going to be until October. Anyway, Mom and Dad would have a small celebration for us on our actual birthday, a low-key event with a few friends.

Things changed on that Monday the 10th. We got word that James had finally died. Our *Beloved Keokuk.* He had been in a coma for days. No one knew for sure how his body kept on going for so long. He wasn't eating, barely breathing. I cried and was terribly sad, but for some reason I had already entered a phase of grieving that would last a long time. Louise told me that she still felt that way about her husband George passing. James, next to Mom and Dad and Julian, was the most important person in my life. Maybe even more than Sharon. He was my priest or *seer.* He knew me. It's like from my birth, our births as twins, he had knowledge about each of us that maybe even Mom and Dad didn't have.

Mom was devastated. I had never seen her so quiet and withdrawn. Dad took over all the planning for a memorial, even though he didn't look so good either. It would be extremely large given that James was known and loved far and wide.

The following day, a Tuesday, rolled around and Julian, and I knew it was our day. Happy Birthdays said at breakfast. Louise shrieked from the other room, calling for all of us. All five of us rushed in. Dad was already nearly out the door and pivoted back inside. Mom, terribly disheveled as it was, grabbed her coffee and quickly followed us. Louise had the television on the *Today Show*. We were all perplexed as Katie Couric frantically filled in the scattering details of a highjacked commercial airplane crashing into one of the twin towers at the World Trade Center.

Julian and I looked into each other's eyes and KNEW.

Life would never be the same.

Paul Turelli was born and raised in Colorado.
He was a middle school teacher, coach and principal
throughout his career. He holds Master of Arts in both

History and Education. Currently retired, Paul teaches part time at the University of Denver.
He lives with his wife Rachel in the town of Parker.

WEBSITE: paulturelli.com

Send correspondence to: pwt627@yahoo.com